CAVE OF DESIRE, CAVE OF DOOM

Birdie Jacobs tried to avert his eyes from the naked, golden body of Jody Robb as they huddled in the cave. Outside the storm still raged—the night cold, dark and threatening.

"You followed me all the way to this place," she whispered softly.

"Don't take it wrong," the handsome black Sergeant answered. "I would have done the same for any woman in your situation."

"And would you be sitting in a cave nude with just any woman?" Her blue eyes mocked him.

His hands shot out and caught her bare shoulders with bruising force. He pulled her to him, her long blonde hair cascading over his face.

Outside, a chilling sound arose, like the shriek of some evil spirit. A bobcat was perched on the ledge just beyond the mouth of the cave, screaming fiercely.

Birdie looked into Jody's eyes, their faces only inches apart.

"He's not howling at us. Someone has followed us here—and I have no more bullets."

"If we are to die," Jody murmured, "please, please hold me close—nothing else matters now."

As he held her tightly in his powerful arms the forbidden nature of their desire was forgotten, and they were swept into abandoned love-making—even as the spectre of sudden, violent death drew closer . . . .

THE
BUFFALO
PEOPLE

Lee Davis Willoughby

A DELL/BRYANS BOOK

Published by
Dell Publishing Co., Inc.
1 Dag Hammarskjold Plaza
New York, New York 10017

Dell ® TM 681510, Dell Publishing Co., Inc.

ISBN: 0-440-00776-3

Printed in the United States of America

First printing—June 1981

THE
BUFFALO
PEOPLE

1

THE MEN OF LARSON's company of the Ninth Regiment of the Frontier Army lounged about the wagons drawn up in a circle opposite the rushing waters of the Milk River. They had the uneasy look of men caught loafing on the job. When one of them made a wry comment about why the wagon train was stalled there, two others laughed nervously, then spit and looked away from each other.

The soldiers eyed the tent, the only one set up in the center of the encirclement.

"Hain't Capt'n Larson's fault," was the general concensus. "It's his'n!"

"Damn nigger-lover!"

"How can he help it?" Sergeant Harrison demanded. "Most of the regiment has done turned midnight black with his brunette soldiers."

Somebody laughed. "Harrison, your nose is brunette from sticking it where Weaver's brownest!"

8 *Lee Davis Willoughby*

At that moment, the man under discussion came out of the tent, freshly shaven and sporting a uniform free of sweat and grime. Major Lothar Weaver looked about him as if he were camped by the Hudson River of West Point and not the Mill River of Ute Indian lands and waved Master Sergeant Noel Harrison over to his side. A few of the loungers sauntered along after Harrison.

"It's ten minutes past the hour, Sergeant," Weaver said, "by the clock. Post a look-out. Captain Larson is an hour overdue."

Somebody snickered and someone else muttered, "Time's always by that damn clock of his when Larson's not around."

"And Larson wouldn't be overdue if Weaver had sent us regulars with him 'stead of buffalo soldiers." Use of the term brought instant silence. It might be all right for the Indians to compare the curly-haired black soldiers to the American bison, but it was against all regimental policy. Major Weaver was a West Point by-the-book soldier and court-martialed men for such offenses. The short, stout officer, so fat he had to be helped onto horse, was not a beloved commander. He seemed well aware of that fact, even flaunted it. It embarrassed him that his official stationery had to bear the legend: "Ninth Regiment Cavalry, United States Colored Troops." It rankled him that the men regarded him as only a *temporary* commander and looked to Captain Larson whenever the major gave an order.

Captain Nils Larson was more soldier than officer, a hard-nosed veteran of the Civil War who had seen more profit in remaining in the Union Army with his battlefield rank than returning to the dying farmlands of New England. By clever scheming he had been able to keep his company all white, until it was reassigned to the Ninth and sent up from Fort Robinson on this assignment. Larson made sure that "his" men blamed Weaver for that. Nils Larson hadn't fought to free the slaves; he had gone to war because he liked nothing better than a good fight.

The mission Weaver had selected him for that morning irked him; everything about Lothar Weaver irked him.

"Why take nothing but nigger soldiers?" Larson had asked, when the major called him in to give him his orders.

"Captain, unless word has spread up from Texas or out from Oklahoma, the Utes are unaware of the black men in our ranks. It might just scare them into submission without resorting to violence."

"You think they've never seen a nigger before?"

Weaver sighed. "How could they, Larson? In three years we haven't had any blacks this far west."

A kind of slow dawning of intelligence spread over Larson's narrow face. He was not a good officer and he led a hard and thankless life. Next to his fellow officers, he hated Indians the most. Now he wiped the sweat out of his eyes with his coat sleeve and asked, "Why no violence?"

Weaver sighed again, this time with irritation. "Larson, our orders are to get this wagon train from San Francisco escorted safely through Mormon land to Fort Rawlins. By treaty, as federal troops, we have no right to even *be* on this side of the Milk River. Need I say more about caution and no violence?"

Nils Larson thought he needed to say a hell of a lot more. It was his company, yet he had been told little or nothing about this assignment. With the transcontinental railroad completed four months ago, he

thought these people travelling back by wagon train
sheer fools, and the Army out of its mind for giving
them the protection of a hundred soldiers. "Then
why *are* we on Ute land?" he asked.

It was in the make-up and training of Lothar Weaver to delegate authority whenever possible, except
when it came to Captain Larson. The major wished
more than anything in the world that they were not
on Ute land. He had been an intelligence officer under General Grant during the closing days of the
war between the states. Now that Grant was in the
White House, Lothar saw success of this mission as
a transfer ticket back home. Only he knew that twenty
of the thirty-three wagons the Ninth was escorting
belonged to the Government, that their drivers were
actually soldiers in civilian clothes, and that beneath
the flooring planks of the twenty prairie schooners
lay twenty million in gold. Gold the Union had
stopped from coming out of California during the war
years. Gold the Grant administration now wanted
safely back east without the French or British hearing
of it. Gold that the Government especially did not
want Brigham Young to learn was crossing his territory. Transporting it by rail would have been far too
obvious for all concerned.

But Weaver told Larson none of this. What he did
say was: "You amaze me, Captain. We are practically
the only law west of the Mississippi and white lives
seem to be at stake. You heard what the rider said.
The Utes are refusing to obey the laws laid down
by the authorized Indian agent. They will not send
their children to school. They will not plow up their
grazing land to farm for themselves. They will not
attend church services. We are the closest force available to aid this agent and make the heathen Indians

see that they must obey the law. You will make them see that, Captain Larson."

Larson had seen it much plainer than the Major might have wished. Weaver never addressed him by his rank unless he was up to some con. The captain personally selected the soldiers who would ride with him, while spreading the word that they were Weaver's choice.

The twenty-five black soldiers had ridden out after Larson in two ragged files, each line following a rut that meandered across the meadowland and into the red-rock foothills and pine forests. There had been a good bit of laughing and some talk. They didn't have much idea of what they were going to do when they got to the Indian agency compound; it seemed like a white man's joke to them. The Indians were being forced to go to school, something the black soldiers had never been allowed as slaves. It was hard for them to understand.

It was even harder when Larson stopped them a mile short of the agency compound and gave them their final orders. But, if nothing else, the "buffalo soldiers" had learned to follow a command to the letter.

"That's 'em comin' now!"

Only three of the returning party were a-horse, and these three were not any of those who had ridden out. Only six of the original group returned, afoot, walking as if the devil were on their tails.

Captain Larson plodded along, hunched forward like a man ploughing. By nature, he was a fighting man, but this fight had been unbelievable. He had planned something that would be quick and daring and unforgettable to the Utes. He had wanted to save the whites at the agency compound while at the same time staining the reputation of the black troops. All the way back from the compound he kept trying to decide what he should tell the major. As it turned out, it was Inez Robb, the agency schoolteacher, who got in the first word.

"Massacre!" she announced through clenched teeth as she scrambled out of the saddle. She was like a gangling crane come to roost, all legs, flapping arms and a long, seemingly disjointed neck that swiveled and jerked.

Lothar Weaver blanched, but not because of what the woman had said. She was the epitome of everything he had hated about his school years. She towered half a head above him, her flinty gray eyes narrowed into slits of accusation, making her thin face seem even thinner. She stood poised like every schoolmarm he had ever loathed—sufferingly straight of back, the black hair with wisps of gray twisted into a bun, tight to the point of making him wonder if it didn't give her a headache. His nostrils detected the faint aroma of lavender escaping from the hidden cachets sewn into her stiff black taffeta skirts; her pointing finger affected him like a whipping rod.

"And I shall be answered," she thundered, "for the actions of this arrogant young fool."

"Major," Larson pleaded, all manner of tiredness apparent in his voice. "I've been subjected to her for miles. May I report to you in private?"

For the first time since he'd known him, Weaver felt a twinge of sympathy for the man, but the faces of the five other returning soldiers told him of the lies he could expect from Larson. Still, out there in the open was not the best place to conduct an inquiry. He nodded sternly and turned to lead the way to his tent. "Just a moment, Major." A young man in the trio of riders jumped down and blocked Weaver's retreat. "Your first obligation should be to these two women after what they've been subjected to, thanks to this idiot and his nigger soldiers."

"Sir," Weaver said, with icy calm, "you had best have facts to back up any accusation against the men under my command." He was looking up into steel-gray eyes two heads above him, but he didn't flinch as he had with Miss Robb. Men, no matter their size, Lothar Weaver felt capable of staring down. But Maxwell Bundy didn't stare down easily and didn't know what it meant to back off. "Then I pity the men you command, Major. I pity everybody in this wagon train, and you and me, because we're as good as dead because of what happened back at the agency."

"Damn lie!" Larson tried to protest, but there was something about Max Bundy that made Weaver listen.

"Sir, just what did happen?" he said quietly. "Who are you?"

Bundy calmed down. He sensed that this would not be another screaming session like the ones involving the captain and Miss Robb. "I'm Maxwell Bundy. My father—he's dead now—started horses with the Utes back in Forty-eight. My brothers and I still run his ranch, down on the Cache de la Poudre. I've been up here a week, putting together a horse deal. I was in the village when we heard the gunfire—"

Weaver cut him short with sudden irritation. "Get to the facts, sir!"

"I'm trying to tell you I got to the compound about the same time as Okala's men and saw what the niggers were doing."

"Interesting," Weaver said, colder than ever. "I can't help wondering why you were there in the first place, Mister Bundy. After all, there's no longer any reason to sell horses to the Confederacy, and Major Quantrill and his raiders have long since been dispersed."

Maxwell Bundy's ruggedly handsome features turned to stone. Lothar Weaver smiled triumphantly. His intelligence-oriented mind had not failed him; his methodical brain had latched onto the man's name and the location of the ranch, both of which were known to the Army. A man who traded guns to the Indians for horses was of interest, but not at the moment.

Maxwell Bundy kept his lantern jaw clenched. For the past week Horace Henderson, the Indian agent, had been throwing the same accusation at him and denying him the right to negotiate with Okala without the agent being present. Max knew the Utes, had known them since he was a boy, and knew what they would and would not take in trade for their horses. He was glad that he had defied Henderson and was with Okala when the first gunshots were heard. That might save his neck—if the braves recognized him in time. But, for the moment, he had no desire to help save this arrogant fat man.

Bundy's silence made Weaver feel righteously superior. "I gather you have nothing further to add then, sir?"

"How can he, Major? But I have."

It was said so quietly, in a voice still filled with shock, that Weaver was forced to turn and stare up at the third rider and saw that it was a young woman. Until then he had thought it was a child, cowered by fright.

Jody Robb was beyond the point of simple fright. Her mind still reeled from the sights and sounds of the last hours. She knew that she could never erase them as long as she lived, but she did not want to relive them. That was her fear now.

With a nervous little motion of her hand, she indicated for Max Bundy to help her down from the horse. She questioned whether her trembling legs would support her, but her icy-blue gaze never left Major Weaver's face. If he had an ounce of humanity in his soul, he would listen to reason. She pushed the concealing pokebonnet off her head and the sun glittered on golden curls.

"They will come after us for revenge," she said softly. "Nonsense," Weaver scoffed. "Miss—whoever you are—how long have you been dealing with the Indians?"

"She is my niece, sir," Inez Robb said sharply. "Miss JoAnn Robb. And our time with the Utes is immaterial to the truth of her statement. It has been Mister Bundy's greatest concern all the way from the agency. He may not be a very Godly man, but he does seem to know these heathens." Weaver looked at her. She was the other side of the Indian-lover's coin: Bundy would side with them for profit, women like Inez Robb for the souls they might save to win their way into heaven. He looked from woman to woman and imagined he could smell their missionary zeal. Except for height and facial features, they were peas in a pod; the poke bonnets and drab-colored Mother Hubbard dresses reeked of Puritan starchiness. Looking at them, he knew why the Indians had refused to go to school or to attend church services.

But another glance told him that the smaller, younger woman was no mere zealot. Her sweet face was troubled. Why, Weaver thought, she's lovely. Without the bonnet, her small head was a mass of tight golden curls that refused to be pulled back into a bun. A widow's peak above a delicate nose gave the impression of a heart-shaped face, in perfect larger proportion to the cupid's-bow mouth. Her small chin had just the suggestion of a dimple. If there was a flaw in that delicate beauty it was that the nose turned up slightly.

Weaver liked to consider himself a good judge of people. Now he saw truth staring at him from those clear blue eyes and could no longer ignore it. He still would have preferred to conduct this inquiry in the privacy of his tent, but that option was fading fast. A crowd was beginning to gather, people from the wagons came to see what was going on, and the last thing the major wanted was a panic on his hands.

"Miss Robb," he said gently, thinking that if he kept his voice low she would follow suit. "Why do you use the word revenge?"

JoAnn Robb felt the nausea churning again in her stomach. For eighteen years she had known nothing but the secluded, simple life of one boarding school after the other. As Inez Robb's ward, she had followed the woman from one teaching position to another. She had, at first, resented being brought as her aunt's "assistant" to such a remote and alien world. During her first week at the agency compound, she had been deathly ill because of the Indians' sickish-sweet smell. Her illness was compounded by the fact that she was the product of an all-female world; the braves terrified her, while she was a great curiosity to them.

Unlike most straw-gold blondes, her skin tone was not dead-white alabaster, but the warm shade of cream rising in a standing milk bucket. The braves and children all sought to touch her, to stroke the golden skin and curls. Their touch made her skin crawl.

But Miss Inez and Horace Henderson, the Indian agent, did not cotton to malingerers. Henderson wanted the school established immediately, and roughly ordered Jody to get out of bed and accept her responsibilities or be dismissed.

"Major," she said now, not liking to recall any of these images. "I had to . . . to make friends with the village children. I was with two of Chief Okala's children at the compound this morning when the raid took place. I . . . we . . . could not believe what we were seeing." Her voice broke; it seemed for a moment as if she could not go on, but then she turned and stared at Captain Larson.

"The agency compound is set apart from the Ute villages. There were mostly women and children at the trading post. The two Henderson boys were learning how to shoot a bow and arrow from an Indian boy about their age. No more than a dozen braves were in the compound. Suddenly, this man"—she pointed at Larson—"and his soldiers came riding in, yelling like banshees and firing as though it were an armed camp—"

"We were shooting into the air!" Larson protested. Weaver waved him angrily to silence.

Jody closed her eyes and went on. "The noise brought the braves in the nearest village on the run. They went for the soldiers' horses, to block their escape. The soldiers fired, then flung down their rifles and attacked the Indians with their bare hands. The compound was suddenly filled with men clubbing each other with rifle barrels, swinging hatchets, and yelling. There were no shots now. A Black soldier dragged Okala's children from my arms and—"

She couldn't go on; it was impossible to describe the sickening sound of a revolver butt crushing bone and flesh and the horrible silence that had followed. An arm had circled her and started to drag her toward the woods. She had screamed and screamed until, through a haze of tears, she had recognized Max Bundy. As if from afar, she had heard Miss Inez screaming, a small, oddly clear sound.

By now the Indians were on the rampage. Anything black or white became their target. The sullen hatred that had been growing for Horace Henderson and those who helped him run the agency like a feudal realm was unleashed. They stormed the trading post, the school and the Hendersons' log cabin. Henderson had emptied the chambers of two six-shooters except for a single shell. That one he wisely saved for himself.

The soldiers who could fled. Max Bundy, who knew the territory, guided Jody and Miss Inez away through the woods. Jody couldn't remember when she had replaced one of the fleeing soldiers on the three available horses. She had felt sick, unable to think about anything except that she had not been able to save the children.

"Why didn't the Indians pursue?" Major Weaver asked of no one in particular.

Max Bundy eyed Jody anxiously before answering. Only one thing had kept him haggling over horses with Okala for a week—Jody Robb. In his twenty-two years he had never met a woman like her. His women had all been fast and flashy and easily forgotten. He possessed a muscular handsomeness and boyish charm the ladies could not resist. Jody Robb was the first woman he had known for over a week who had not let him count the number of petticoats she wore, and he was determined to save her from the debacle he knew must come.

"Would you?" he asked Weaver now. "Would you pursue before you had all your men together? Okala has a thousand braves housed in three different villages. He must gather them together and make them look upon the bodies of his slain children. Then he will come and count your forces against his own."

"I think he is already counting," one of the mule drivers said, and pointed. Everyone turned to look. The hills ringing the meadowland had begun to sprout mounted Indian braves like an instant forest. They were as silent as the trees behind them, but their number grew with each passing second. Major Weaver forced his voice to remain calm. "Hanson, take these two women to the other women in the train. Larson—to my tent. Foggarty, tell Billie Joe to saddle up and prepare to ride to Fort Rawlins. Sergeant Harrison, everyone else to their posts and stand at the ready."

The only person not given an order was Max Bundy. He stood to one side, grinning. He knew Okala and the ways of the Utes well. A docile, nomadic people, slow to anger, they were methodical and unrelenting in warfare once aroused. There would be no immediate attack; Okala would keep his braves on the mountainsides for hours, even days, wearing the wagon train people down until their nerves were raw. Only then would he send the never-ending assault waves against them. In the meantime, Max had to figure a way of getting Jody and Miss Inez safely away.

2

PRIVATE BILLIE JOE HAWKINS didn't exactly lie, he just neglected to inform the patrol commander of exactly how the Ute uprising had come about.

"Thirty-three wagons full of people, Captain, surrounded by hostiles and fighting for their lives. I'll be getting on to Fort Rawlins with the news."

When Billie Joe had departed, Captain Ferris Ferguson blew through his lips and ordered his men to break camp.

He and his thirty-five Negro cavalrymen were, by design, law officers. Their patrol extended from Fort Lyon, on the Arkansas River, to Fort Laramie, on the North Platte River. Mere patrolling of the vast region in their charge was a well-nigh impossible task; it was hundreds of miles of plains and mountains, of incredibly rough and broken terrain, where temperatures ranged from above one hundred degrees in summer to well below freezing in winter.

Their problem, normally, was not the Indians. The end of the Civil War had brought to the West an abundance of white riffraff, ever ready with gun, knife, rope and branding iron to ply any trade which afforded an easy and illegal dollar. Lurking in the background was the shadowy and elusive "agent," with his trade goods, whiskey, guns and ammunition to reward those who stole cattle and horses for him.

Captain Ferguson was a man of sense, the first white officer of the patrol units who had managed to grasp just how effective the Army's black soldiers could be, in spite of the difficulty of the tasks assigned them. Ferguson had long since hardened his troops to their most difficult problem. They could wipe out rustlers, jail pistol-happy Saturday night cowboys, disband stealthy "agent" operations, but they could not wipe out the poison of racial prejudices in the citizens of the frontier they were there to protect.

And, although it was a hundred miles out of his territory, this was also a call for protection. There was only one thing left to do. Before departure, Ferguson confided fully in his sergeant.

It gave Sergeant Birdwell "Birdie" Jacobs a strange feeling, that September evening in 1869, to hear of the Indian attack; to look down from where the patrol was camped and see the Bundy ranch peaceful in the still-hot September air and see children playing in the ranch yard who had probably never even seen an Indian.

They had seen blacks; a third of the –B– cowhands were black and treated little better than slaves. The thought brought back the bitterness Birdie had felt when these, his own people, had stood dumb and silent before the soldiers. Captain Ferguson believed the ranch was a cover for a large and lucrative agent operation. But in three days of surveillance nothing unusual had transpired to confirm his suspicion.

Twenty-year-old Birdie Jacobs hated leaving a task undone before starting a new one. That had been his training since birth on the Jacobs' plantation in Alabama. But this was the Army, where many tasks were never completed.

"Mount 'em up and ride 'em out!" Ferguson called.

Far below, Clayton Bundy followed their departure through a captain's spyglass, a grin creasing his craggy face with deep ruts. He was unaware that his youngest brother was one of the people they were riding to rescue. His only concern was the hundred head of Montana cattle that had been kept hidden in the foothills for three days. They would bring far more than the rifle a head he had bargained for—a lot more, because the rifles had been stolen, too.

Ferguson's patrol straggled up the canyons of the Laramie Mountains, down the valley and up again into the Medicine Bow Mountains. The cold, bright night came swiftly. They stopped for a cold supper and pressed on. The icy wind of the Colorado Rockies was a far cry from the balmy breezes of the South the black men had been born in. But they knew better than to complain to Captain Ferguson; it would only be repeated to Sergeant Jacobs who would have no sympathy for them. They hunched down into their collars and rode silently toward their unknown destination.

They were well aware that Birdie knew where they were going. Birdie always knew everything and told them nothing. They resented that; they resented much about Sergeant Jacobs. He was too quiet, too sensitive, too secretive. He was vastly different from them.

His six-foot-two height and taut, muscular frame

proclaimed his Ashanti heritage. But, except for its milk-chocolate color, his face was hardly African. They suspected that he bore mulatto blood, but he was not friendly enough with any of them to discuss his background. The high Celtic cheekbones, square jaw, thin sensuous lips and straight, aristocratic nose was a far cry from their round moon faces, squashed flaring nostrils and full lips. Only from the eyes up was he African, with a high broad forehead, curly jet-black hair and bushy eyebrows. His lashes were long on evenly spaced eyes that were piercingly black, dark pools, so deep no one who looked into their depths could fathom what had transpired in his short twenty years.

But there was one other thing about Birdie Jacobs, and it was what they resented most. From somewhere, somehow, he had been given something they had not been allowed to acquire by law: the ability to read and write and do figures.

It was also what Ferris Ferguson always wondered about. Jacobs' five-year-old service record didn't afford a clue. It was as if his life had only begun the day he became a private. His file was packed with letters of commendation, reports of his unfailing courage and initiative, letters which had quickly raised him to the highest rank permitted a Negro: the non-commissioned officer rank of sergeant, a rank he already held when he was assigned to Captain Ferguson and his newly formed patrol.

They had been together now for fourteen months, fourteen months in which Ferguson had grown quite used to Birdie's quiet ways.

He was so quiet now, riding the point, that Ferguson wondered what he was thinking about. When the captain rode up beside him, he found his sergeant staring down at a badly cracked tintype of a woman while tears rolled slowly down his cheeks. His bowed shoulders and his silent crying made Ferguson feel closer to him rather than embarrassed.

"Your mother?"

"Yes." Birdie nodded. "She's in Alabama." He did not look up when he spoke. "The past few hours, Captain, I've been remembering her. I've been feeling different lately. Now I wonder if it isn't going to be too late."

"Too late?" Ferguson tried to understand. "You mean, you might get killed?"

"No, no. Not that. Too late to find her and bring her West. No boy ever had a finer ma, Captain. I want you to know that."

He went suddenly silent, his hand pushing the tintype back inside his tunic. He was quickly closing off his past again, before any more questions could be asked. He smiled and wiped the tears away with the back of his hand. "I should be worrying about them, shouldn't I?"

Ferguson knew immediately whom he was talking about. It was his concern, too. He held out a small flask fastened to a loop of rawhide.

"It's brandy," he said, knowing that Birdie drank very little. "Brandy's the next best thing to a fire on a night like this."

Birdie said politely, "If you say so, sir."

"It's even more warming than the bed of a woman." Ferguson took out a handkerchief and blew his nose hard.

Birdie knew the reason and silently took a sip from the flask. He recalled the joy in Ferris Ferguson's eyes the day his wife had arrived at Fort Lyon from St. Louis. But surrounded mainly by Negroes, Helen

Ferguson had stayed only two weeks and hastily departed. Ferris had not seen his wife in a year, nor did he wish to confide the fact that she was demanding either his retirement from the Army or a divorce.

It was a subject he should never have raised with Birdie in the first place; it was one of the things he respected most about his sergeant. The other soldiers in the patrol would pay whatever the traffic would bear for a prostitute for the night. Birdie was chaste; he had never known a woman. Ferguson was also chaste, as long as he was properly married. Birdie took a good deal of abuse from the other black soldiers because he was still a virgin. He had been kept that way by his father, who planned on turning him into a "stud man" after the war.

The war. How it had changed so many things for so many people. It had taken Birdie's father away from him. It had burned Meadowdale to the ground. It had separated him from his mother by two thousand miles.

But mainly it had cost him his father. That was a hurt bottled up so deep inside of him that Birdie dared not think about it even after five years. Slavery? He hardly knew what the word meant until he found himself in a prisoner-of-war camp in Arkansas.

He was the son of Colonel Emerson Jacobs, the owner of Meadowdale plantation, and a slave mother. Emerson Jacobs had many children by his slaves and none by his wife, who was barren. He was sixty years old the day Lincoln took the oath of office as President. He wasn't sure who was right and who was wrong on the slavery issue. His people were family—well-housed, clothed, fed and schooled, even though the latter was against the law. But because of his wealth, land and European education, Jacobs was automatically made a Confederate Colonel.

Because Birdie had always been one of his favorite, most promising offspring, he went to war as the colonel's "kit boy."

"War is for fools," Emerson Jacobs told Birdie, the day they made him a general. "And I am the biggest fool of all for being here at age sixty-four."

The next day he was dead, and Birdie was a prisoner of war at fifteen. Birdie was bitter. His love and respect for his father had been monumental. Emerson had counseled him for months about the lost cause they were fighting for. Birdie now wanted it over as quickly as possible. To the amazement of the Union officers who captured him, he was a walking encyclopedia of facts and figures and troop displacements that would shorten the war by months.

To keep anyone from learning about his role, he was quickly moved to Arkansas and given the opportunity to join the Union Army as a private for service in the West, with all mention of his background history carefully deleted from his file.

The end of the war had been bittersweet at most. Able once again to communicate with his mother, what he learned from her was demoralizing. Carpetbaggers had taken all but five acres of the plantation for back taxes. But Laurie, his mother, was not about to leave there as long as senile old Harriet Jacobs, the colonel's widow, lived. Loyalty to the master and mistress was one thing the war could not burn away, or cast before the wind. Heritage was another.

Birdwell Jacobs had countless step-brothers and step-sisters, but his mother had known only one man in her life—his father. He would be like her in that respect, knowing only one woman in his life, even if it took him forever to find her.

"How do you find the situation, Sergeant?" Ferguson asked suddenly, deciding it was time to return to the matter at hand.

Birdie was silent a moment. Though he knew Captain Ferguson respected his opinion, he had never before had him ask for it so directly. His head came up. When he replied, it was as if he were answering Emerson Jacobs.

"Difficult, sir," Birdie said. "For reasons known only to Billie Joe, he took three days to reach us. We'll make that same march, God willing, by dawn tomorrow. But, after four days, what will we find? What will find us? Billie Joe said they were a hundred cut down by nearly a third. Our thirty-five is going to seem like a drop in the bucket, even if we get there in time."

Ferguson was almost sorry he had asked the question. Birdie was sometimes almost too matter-of-fact.

The Indians made no move to attack that first day. They sat motionless on the mountainside while what was left of the Ninth Regiment prepared to defend the wagon train. Weaver knew that Okala knew their strength and allowed fires to be built. It smelled like rain; slate-colored clouds with trailing veils of white rose over the western hills. There was a distant rumble of thunder, but no rain came. Fires burned at the front of each wagon. The smell of pork and bacon frying filled the encampment. Soldiers sat together grumbling because they would not get to sleep that night.

"I bet the Indians get to take turns going home to their squaws," Sergeant Harrison said.

"That won't make for sleep," another soldier remarked.

"Harrison wouldn't be thinkin' of sleep either, if he could get into that wagon with that hot little number from San Francisco," said Ladlo Hanson.

Harrison laughed. "I thought of that, first day we joined the train. But her uppity drivers act like they'd shoot the first man come near 'em."

Hanson winked at the other black soldiers. "Besides, it seems like Black Mary would be more to your likin', Harrison."

"What you talkin', nigger? Ain't a man among us big enough to fill her cavity!"

Hanson let his eyes roll in mock surprise. "Why, Bo Harrison, you admittin' you ain't got that big stud-pole you been braggin' about?"

"Hush such outlandish talk!" a stern female voice commanded from the next fire.

This was followed by deep, booming laughter. "They don't bother me none, Miss Robb. Mary Fields is safe in the hands of her Lord. He closes her ears to the talk of foolish little men."

Miss Inez Robb sniffed indignantly. She was thinking more of the offense to her own ears than those of the big black woman. She had pouted most of the afternoon about being dumped in with blacks, but after a quick inspection of the white families in the dozen other wagons, she decided that Black Mary's company was the lesser of several evils.

"Utterly disgusting," she had informed her niece. "The misfits of the world carping and complaining about their lot in life—the Indians have the best land, the Chinese got the railroad jobs and the South was ruined because the North took away the slaves. Now their lives are in the hands of the stupid blacks. Tommyrot! Poor white trash that never had anything and never will because they have no backbone."

"I'm suddenly very tired," Jody said, not wanting to admit that she really didn't want to hear Miss Inez go on and on.

"Then why don't you lie down in that nice clump of grass under this wagon?"

"Nonsense," a flutelike voice said from inside the wagon. "I have a bed here that she can use."

This was one of the evils Miss Inez had hoped to avoid. She might be prim and a puritan, but she had also traveled enough to know a harlot when she saw one. In her eyes, Carrie Holmes was just too beautiful, too large in the bust, too slender in the waist and too expensively gowned to be anything else but a harlot.

"My niece cannot—"

"Cannot thank you enough." Jody cut her aunt short, scrambling up onto the tailgate.

It gave Miss Inez something new to fume about until Black Mary had supper ready. They ate in silence, because Carrie Holmes joined them, announcing that Jody was still sleeping. Miss Inez felt she had nothing in common with a twenty-five-year-old black woman and, therefore, saw no reason to communicate.

It amused Carrie rather than angered her. She had gone out of her way to have as little as possible to do with anyone on the wagon train these past ten days. She wanted no one to know what was concealed beneath the heavy canvas that took up three-fourths of her wagon. But her compassion for Jody and what the white girl must have gone through overcame her caution. Still, she ate quickly and returned to the wagon, to be there when the girl awoke.

Miss Inez breathed a sigh of relief. "That was certainly an excellent meal, Miss Fields," she said.

Again came that booming laughter. "I do much better in the Mission kitchen with proper fixings. Can't carry much on a horse. Most of these things are Miss Carrie's."

Miss Inez instantly decided to ignore that fact and picked up on another. "A horse?"

Black Mary rose and began to clean up. She was a towering six-foot, three-hundred-pound woman, but from the way she moved in the tentlike dress, it was obvious that the giant of a woman didn't have an ounce of flab. Squashed atop her watermelon-sized head was a knitted stocking cap which was never removed. Her face was as craggy as one of the Rocky Mountain peaks, but her soft brown eyes twinkled with the enjoyment of life. She was perhaps the only person in the wagon train who didn't fear having to count upon the soldiers for protection; she was an army unto herself.

"Yep, a horse. I was doing real good, coming down out of Montana, 'til I ran into this bunch. That ole Major wouldn't hear of me going on alone. Probably would have been in Denver by now."

"Montana?" Miss Robb said on a note of confusion. "But . . . you mentioned a mission."

Mary Fields chuckled. "Yep, Saint Peter's Mission, outside of Cascade. Finest school for Indian girls in the West."

It was said with so much pride that it aroused Miss Inez's curiosity.

"It sounds Catholic."

"Ain't no other, and run by the finest woman in this world. Now, I might be a little partial, seeing

as how I worked for Mother Amadeus's family back
in Ohio before she became an Ursuline nun."

"Oh, I see. Then you came west with her?"

"Not quite." Mary sat back down on a log and
rested her elbows on her knees. "She came out long
ago to establish the school. When she got sick, I
hurried on out here to nurse her 'til she got back on
her feet. Mission seemed to need me, so I stayed."

"I don't mean to pry, Miss Fields, but why have
you left?"

Black Mary's eyes twinkled. "We got ourselves a
Bishop in Helena, Miss Robb, who don't cotton much
to Black Mary and her rough ways. Nuns ain't ever
paid me none, but Mother Amadeus got together a
little poke. Black Mary's gonna buy a wagon, team
and supplies in Denver. Back home I'll keep that
wagon rollin' the seventeen miles 'tween Cascade and
the Mission. That ole fart can't say nothin' then, not if
I charge the Mission for their supplies, now can he?"

Miss Inez thought not, if Black Mary survived to
carry out her dream.

"Well, you look most rested."

Jody yawned, sat up and stretched. She almost
hated to leave the comfort of the feather-bed mattress
covered with cool silk sheets. She lifted a corner and
rubbed it gently against her cheek.

"At Miss Esterling's school," she said, giggling,
"some of the girls insisted that their parents supply
their 'private' rooms with silk sheets. Now I can understand why and I no longer envy them."

Carrie smiled but made no comment.

"My sheets were rough-spun cotton," Jody went on;
it was a simple statement of fact, not a bid for sympathy. "Since my aunt was a resident teacher there,

Miss Esterling thought free schooling was all she should have to bestow on me."

Carrie laughed then. "It sounds very much like my schooling, but in reverse. There was plenty of money, but I was *forced* to have a private room because I was the only black girl."

"That must have been very lonesome."

It was said with such sincerity that Carrie was touched.

"Not really. Mammy Pleasant made sure that I got home most weekends and every holiday. How about you?"

Jody swung her legs over the side of the narrow bed and frowned. She had never been one to discuss her private life, but an honest question deserved an honest answer.

"Not quite the same. Grandmother Robb left my aunt a small legacy, so she was usually off to Europe or Asia to further her education. I would get stuck in a summer boarding school."

"That's a lot of schooling."

Jody flinched. She had thought the same thing year after year. Before she could think better of it, she blurted out: "That's my problem. I've been taught too much, and it's all bottled up inside with no way out!" She blushed then. "I'm sorry. I'm not usually this personal with anyone."

"Nor I," Carrie said. "I was never admitted into the b.s. sessions at school. I would store everything up inside and share it with Mammy Pleasant." She leaned forward and pointed. "There are brushes in that chest if you would like to do your hair."

"B.S.?" Jody asked, reaching toward the chest.

Carrie laughed gaily. "Bull shit, my dear. Each of those Nob Hill brats had to make out like her family had more than anybody else's. Little did they know that Mammy Pleasant held i.o.u.'s against most of their fathers."

Jody frowned as she pulled the brush through her tangled curls. "Excuse me for asking, Miss Holmes, but why do you call your mother 'Mammy?'"

A veil dropped over Carrie's emerald green eyes, and then she shrugged indifferently.

"It's no secret in San Francisco, so why should it be a secret from you? She's not my mother. I was left on her doorstep when I was five years old. That was during the gold rush days, when Mammy was the richest and most respected Negro in the Bay area. Her husband had died the year before, leaving her fifty thousand dollars which she loaned out at a high interest. She had just opened a boarding house, and her fine cooking was attracting all the leading businessmen in town to her place. They tried to help her find the man or woman who had dropped little Carrie Holmes off with a note pinned to her dress, but turned up nothing. Mammy thought I was a good luck charm and decided to keep me. And I wish you would call me Carrie." Jody smiled. "And I prefer Jody to JoAnn. Mammy Pleasant sounds just marvelous."

A glow of pride warmed Carrie's face, making her look even lovelier. The charcoal tone of her unblemished skin was tinged with a rosy blush. Like an Ethiopian queen of old, she lifted her head regally and smiled.

"Marvelous? That's an understatement, Jody. Her neighbors can't understand how she became so rich and are sure it was magic, that she's a sorceress. That's laughable. I've learned something about my background, thanks to her money. I know my people were West Indian blacks, and like them I believe in certain elements of voodoo. But Mammy Pleasant? She is as direct as the day is long and believes only in cold hard facts. That's what makes her more than just marvelous. There was one time though, when—" Carrie stopped short, suddenly remembering that the girl she was talking to was, after all, a stranger. Like Jody, she was a private person who did not share her feelings easily.

"Oh, don't stop, please!" Jody said. "You can't just leave me dangling in mid-air."

Carrie hesitated, then whispered, "Jody, what are our chances of living beyond tomorrow morning?"

Jody gulped. Okala's image came to mind. She recalled the day she had gone to meet his youngest children. He had stood stiffly under his blanket, his small dark eyes flickering here and there over her petite frame.

The Indian had asked in English as good as Jody's, "Why do you wish to give my children an education?"

"I want them to know all the world around them and not just the world within this valley."

He had stood silent, weighing her words carefully. At last he said, "I give them to your charge and protection."

The words now echoed with horrible clarity in her mind. She had failed him.

"We have no chance," she told Carrie.

Carrie sank down beside her on the bed. "I thought not, but I dared not discuss it at dinner with Black Mary or your aunt. They are strong women, each in her own way, although your aunt thinks I'm a whore."

"Carrie!" Jody gasped. "I'm sure she thinks no such thing."

Carrie chuckled. "Voodoo is born within you, Jody,

and her mind is an open book to me. But, it doesn't matter, because I have known no man—Mammy Pleasant is very strict in that way." She hesitated and, acting on impulse, Jody took her hand. An electric current seemed to pass between them. They stared at each other, each moved in a strange way, each knowing that, for that moment, they were as close as sisters. "What I started to tell you about Mammy Pleasant was, well, she could almost be accused of starting the Civil War!" Carrie said. "I was fifteen when she took me on a trip to Canada, and I've been sworn to secrecy ever since. If we die tomorrow, then the story dies. If we live, then I'll be thankful that someday the story may be told."

She was silent a long moment, holding Jody's hands tightly. "The man scared the hell out of me!" she said suddenly. "In the candlelight, he looked like a maniac—wild-eyed, with a long gray beard. He ranted on about needing a thousand weapons, bowie knives, he said, fastened to six-foot poles, to set up a free Negro state in the mountains of Maryland and Virginia. But little Mammy Pleasant—she was skinnier than a pencil then—faced right up to him as if he wasn't a servant right out of hell." She stopped and her eyes met Jody's. "I'd best tell you right here that Mammy's husband was an abolitionist. He worked with a man named William Lloyd Garrison. Pappy Pleasant, when he died, told Mammy to use his money to help free the slaves. She thought this wild man's scheme might work, so she gave him a bank draft for thirty thousand dollars and a note she scribbled. Years later, she told me that the note read: *'The axe is laid at the foot of the tree. When the first blow is struck, there will be more money to help.* M.P.*'"

Jody shook her head. "I'm sorry, Carrie, but I don't understand."

"That man was John Brown, Jody, the man who staged the raid at Harper's Ferry, Virginia. Without that, the Civil War might never have started." This event was still such recent history it was not even a footnote in Jody's memory of the causes leading up to the war. She had been only ten when Fort Sumter had been fired upon, and Miss Esterling had been careful to keep the "brutalities" of life away from her girls, while Miss Inez was prone to keep life itself away from Jody.

"I thought I knew everything," Jody sighed. "And I really know nothing. Thirty thousand is a great deal of money. Was it all she had?"

"Not at the time, but . . ." Carrie hesitated, then seemed to come to some kind of decision and went on. "We live in a rather grand house, which the idiots call 'the House of Mystery.' A mystery, Jody, because when the man Mammy Pleasant bought it from came to collect the final payment, he fell from an upstairs porch and later died of his injuries. Now, those who owe her money have started the rumor that she pushed him with 'black magic' and are refusing to pay their debts. That's why I'm off to Denver."

"I don't understand," Jody admitted again.

Carrie patted her hand. "I might as well share one more secret with you. Come and look."

Carrit rose and began to roll up the heavy canvas that concealed and protected her cargo. She smiled seeing Jody blink in amazement; the wagon area was jammed with some of the handsomest furniture Jody had ever seen.

"Isn't it magnificent?" Carrie said. "It once belonged to a relative of the Czar of Russia, who lived in Sitka, Alaska."

"It's like nothing I've ever seen before," Jody said. "What's to become of it?"

"Hopefully, a buyer will be waiting in Denver. Back when they were taking gold out of Sutter's Mill, Mammy had a boarder who fell in love with it. He said then that he would like to have it copied for him someday. Well, why not buy the original to get Mammy out of debt? He can certainly afford it."

"Carrie?" Jody frowned. "Do you think you can trust him?"

Carrie threw back her head and laughed. "Jody, my dear, I know what you're thinking, and he's not some evil white man waiting to take advantage of this poor innocent black gal. Barney Ford is not only blacker than the ace of spades, but a millionaire. He'll pee in his pants when he sees what I've brought, but Carrie Holmes will hold out for the price Mammy Pleasant's asking. You'll see."

Jody believed her; she had never met anyone like Carrie before. She was what Miss Inez had been fired for trying to be: a liberated spirit capable of surviving in a man's world. She said as much. "I wish Miss Inez could hear what you're about. She is forever getting herself into hot water, preaching that women are just as capable as men."

"Except where you are concerned," Carrie said, then bit her lip, thinking she had said too much.

Jody knew the remark wasn't meant to hurt, but it did. "I haven't been a very good piece of clay for her to mold, Carrie. I was like you, in a way, abandoned on somebody's doorstep, except she knew she was going to get stuck with me as her ward for life.

My mother died giving birth to me and my father died of heartbreak over her death. My uncle Joe was just sixteen, too young to take me, and my uncle Hiram was just starting his first term as a senator from Rhode Island. I had nurses and governesses until I was six and went to live in the school where my aunt was teaching."

"And she's done her best to ignore you ever since?" This time Carrie didn't try to hide her opinion of Miss Inez.

"She didn't ask for me to be born," Jody said.

Carrie was instantly aware, by the way she said it, that Jody had used this argument many times before. She opened her mouth to say something else, but never got the chance. Major Weaver had assured them the Indians would not attack at night. The flaming arrow struck at the top of Carrie's wagon and a little stab of orange mushroomed out, followed by a black coil of smoke. Instinctively, Carrie screamed, "Fire!" She and Jody were on their feet instantly, pounding at the flames devouring the canvas.

An owl hooted three times and the tall meadowland grass disgorged a solid mass of rifle fire that made a single stunning impact on the ear. The volley tore through the wagon's canvas covering like hail through paper.

"Out!" Carrie shouted. "To hell with the damned furniture! Out!"

As Jody jumped from the tailgate, something slammed into her chest, knocking her sideways and down. A horse screamed and went charging off. Scrambling to her feet, Jody turned to see what had knocked her down just as Carrie jumped from the wagon.

A large shadow hulk leaped up and caught Carrie

in its arms. Jody screamed, "Let her go!" but the voice was lost in the growing turmoil. The air around her was filled with the dull endless crash of muskets and a weird high shrieking. Jody turned to follow Carrie and the shadow, but they had vanished.

Instead of Carrie, she saw the Indians rising from the tall grass, ghastly in the light of the burning wagon, streaked with vermilion, black and white. From the first group to rise an orderly discharge barely passed over her head. A hand jerked her down behind a barrel.

"Get down, lady, and help me reload these rifles!"

She grasped the rifle the soldier shoved at her, having no idea what to do with it.

Miss Inez came running up, spotted her niece wearing only the chemise she'd slept in and shrieked inanely, "JoAnn! Go get yourself properly dressed before you embarrass me to death!"

"Shut up, you old prune!" the soldier screamed. "I could care less if she was naked! I've got one chance to show her how to reload my rifles—or we're dead!"

Carrie Holmes thought she was as good as dead the minute the Indian began to drag her away. She kicked and scratched, but he was too strong for her and forced her down into the tall grass. She knew the worst when he cuffed her head from side to side and began to tear away her clothing. Why, she wondered, oddly detached, were black men credited with being such sexual animals when it was the red men who were always doing the raping?

She had never before in her life been so close to death and was strangely calm. The stinging blows to her jaw had not stunned her; in fact, her mind was as clear as a bell. She could even hear the footfalls of the other Indians rushing by them where they lay in the grass. In that moment of clarity she found herself wondering why this brave was trying to seduce her when the others were screaming out their lungs in the attack. He didn't tarry, but plunged into her with a single quick thrust. The pain was like death but she held the scream echoing in her brain, knowing instinctively that uttering it aloud would give him pleasure. She came near to fainting and reached up to push him away. Her hands grasped cloth, woolen cloth! Her attacker was a soldier, not an Indian.

The realization was momentarily staggering. The uncountable numbers against the wagon train and here was one of the soldiers thinking only of satisfying his own needs.

She tensed, ready to attack him with words, and the tension in her caused him to curse and pin her harder to the ground. He was too far gone to turn back now.

From far off, like a harp playing in her ears, Carrie recalled Mammy Pleasant's voice:

"Honey, men are going to pant after you like you be a bitch in heat. When it happens, honey, you just relax—"

Relax, Carrie counseled herself; relax and let the bastard have his way. Remember what Mammy Pleasant said: "It ain't going to make you no different than you were five minutes before, except sore and feelin' like you been stuffed by a pig." *So stuff me, you pig*, Carrie thought grimly. *I ain't going to fight you no more.* You ain't Indian, you a black boy. Black boys do their thing and then roll away with a grunt,

Mammy says. *Grunt quick, you bastard. Grunt and roll away.* I thought I was dead, but I ain't going to die just because you stuck me.

He did grunt and he went suddenly limp, but he didn't roll away. For a moment, Carrie thought maybe Mammy Pleasant was just too old to remember exactly how it had been. She rolled her head to the side and tried to dislodge him, but he was a dead weight.

Then she saw why. A six-foot lance jutted out of his back. Carrie froze. She did not want an Ute brave to discover that she was there alive, beneath the dead soldier. She lay still, listening to the sounds of battle all around. She could feel her attacker shrivel and release from her and nearly gagged.

She felt her insides retract. She thought, wondering at herself, *That's my first man ever,* before she rolled him away. She stayed on her hands and knees for some distance, crawling toward the circled wagons, and then she was up and running.

Jody was passing a newly loaded rifle to the soldier, not realizing that he no longer had need of it, when she saw Carrie come running. With a fierce yell, an Indian tried to cut her off. Without thinking, Jody put the rifle over the dead soldier's body and pulled the trigger on the first image that filled the sights. The butt bucked against her cheek. Carrie jumped the wagon tongue and fell down beside Jody, as Jody watched the Indian she had fired at buckle at the hips and fall face-down.

The two women looked at each other silently. Jody felt her stomach tighten into a hard knot; they didn't need to discuss what had happened to Carrie.

* * *

There was no sense, at first, in any of it. The Indians departed as quickly as they had come. For the next half hour the exhausted soldiers lay where they had dropped, shooting toward the hills whenever they saw a rifle flash.

The soldiers had been less than effective. Only for Captain Larson would they give their all, and Major Weaver had confined the captain to the tent until he could determine what court-martial charges to bring against him.

In the confusion of the battle, no one noticed that eight of the white wagoneers had not fought at all, but had used the time to hitch up their teams and prepare for a quick departure. When they saw that Major Weaver was busy taking the toll of dead and wounded, they raised their whips and began a rapid-fire assault in the air over the teams to move the wagons out of the circle. The iron-rimmed wheels screeched but the noise was lost amid the shouts, the moans and cries in the aftermath of battle. Too late the wagons were spotted—jerking, getting started, moving out.

"My God!" cried Major Weaver. "What do they think they are doing?"

He ran after them, shouting orders to turn back. All he got for his effort was the tip of a rawhide whip biting into his cheek and opening up a four-inch gash.

A figure darted out of the tent after the last wagon.

"Stop that man!" Weaver shouted.

Not a single black or white soldier moved; there seemed to be nobody to stop Captain Nils Larson from making his escape.

Harley Pearson had a wife and six children to protect. He had thought the departure of the wagons a stupid move and had refused to go along with the scheme. A farmer from Tennessee, he had little faith in the ability of black soldiers, but he laid the blame for their present troubles on the white officer who had lead the agency attack. But Harley had used up his last round of shells.

As Larson darted past the Pearson wagon, Harley grasped his empty rifle by the barrel and swung. Larson's big body swayed with the impact. He reared back and, as Harley prepared to strike again, crashed to the ground. Except for Major Weaver, who came running up, everyone else's attention had been drawn elsewhere.

The war cries from the hills meant only one thing: the Indians had not been able to resist the temptation to chase the eight departing wagons. A number of Okala's braves, envisioning easy scalps ready for the taking, streaked down out of the timber line. A brassy bugle call sounded, sending the soldiers automatically racing for their tethered horses. Major Weaver spun around.

"Rescind that order!" he shouted. "Get over here and start pulling these wagons into a smaller circle!"

The soldiers stopped as though stunned. Private Carl Smythe stammered, "Bu-but, Sir. Those folks are white—just like us. They're going to need help."

"And so will the people they deserted if we leave this gap for Okala's ponies to come riding through. Move!"

No one was sure which white soldier said it: "I'll kill that bastard for this!"

Weaver didn't even turn his head. He was well aware that men said things they later regretted under stress of battle. If he had looked around, he might

have acted differently at another time. Behind him,
Nils Larson glared up from the ground with murder
in his eyes. Ironically, if the eight wagons stayed put,
the entire wagon train would have been destroyed in
the next hour. The Indian attack had been intended
to force them to waste ammunition. All through it,
two hundred rifle-carrying braves had sat their horses
under the trees, awaiting Okala's signal. But when,
at last, Weaver began to rally his men and get the
circle closed up, the Indians made no attempt to attack again. They were too busy with the intoxicating
business of chasing the fleeing wagons, killing the
horses, then falling upon their helpless victims.

3

FOR THE NEXT two days Okala played with them. At dawn he would attack from the east, so the defenders would have to squint into the sun. At sunset he would attack from the west. He was waiting for them to run out of food and water and ammunition.

No soldier stayed in the same place for each attack. It was impossible to give intelligent orders or get them carried out. The resentment against Major Weaver grew with each attack.

With no reinforcements in sight, his men all saw it as revenge on Weaver's part to send Private Carl Smythe out for help on the fastest horse available. Captain Larson saw the reasoning behind the major's move, but said nothing. He knew he would now be charged with desertion under fire, and that could only mean the firing squad. He could only pray that Billie Joe had not gotten through and that the same fate would befall Smythe.

He got his second wish within the hour; Smythe's horse came back at a gallop. The nude body of the young white soldier was lashed to the horse's belly, the scalp deftly removed.

Weaver stumbled into the tent carrying an Indian spear in one hand and a revolver in the other.

"Do you know what we now face?" He jammed the butt of the spear into the ground.

"Your problem," Larson sneered.

"No, ours. Counting the walking wounded, we are down to fifty people. I can't afford to keep a guard on you day and night. You'll have to fight, too."

"With that damn spear?"

"Perhaps," the major said, tossing Larson the revolver. "I've told the men to start collecting them. When the ammunition is gone, that's all we'll have left."

Larson played with the six-shooter. "What does this do to my court-martial?"

"Nothing can change that, Larson."

A whoop from the west end of the encampment announced the dusk attack. Weaver spun around out of the tent. The men who had been guarding Larson were already running to take up their positions. Larson belted the revolver and took up the spear. He was out of the tent in one leap. Bracing himself, he hurled the spear forward, catching Weaver in the small of the back. The major screamed only once, just before the spear broke the skin of his belly. Larson lifted him, spear and all, and shoved him out of sight behind the tent.

"Hell," he muttered. "No sense wasting a shell on a bastard like you."

Larson turned now to take command; his men, he knew, would not betray him to higher authority.

A giant shadow stepped quickly back behind the supply wagon. Black Mary had seen it all. She had come along with the major to fetch the last box of ammunition. But it would be her word against the white captain's and she knew how that would come out.

The major, the spear sticking out of him, was still alive and trying to crawl around the tent. The odd thing was that he wasn't bleeding. Black Mary let Larson get across the wagon circle before she went to Weaver. He half turned to her. When his mouth opened, the blood began to pour out, soaking his tunic. "Wagons—" he gasped. "Gold—Colonel Hastings —Important. . . ."

His murder was secondary to passing on information about his mission. Now Black Mary was really troubled; she was not about to report the major's dying words to Captain Larson. It began to seem as if the fighting would never stop that evening. The firing kept up until an hour after dark, when except for sporadic outbursts here and there, it died. Larson's voice reached the men, sounding surprisingly loud. "Gather up their lances and hatchets, boys. We'll need them come dawn."

They found the lance in Major Weaver; they automatically assumed an Indian had killed him.

Dawn began to etch the eastern horizon. The attack to come would be the last they could withstand. Harrison had seen movement in the hills and had warned the men. He would let Captain Larson sleep until the moment of attack . . . .

Birdie Jacobs brought his horse to a stop just behind Captain Ferguson's. They were on a slight rise. Below them, in the wide meadowland, they could see the circle of wagons. It was eerily silent. A quarter mile down the valley lay strewn the burned-out hulls of eight wagons, dead horses, and the mutilated bodies of men, women and children.

"Indians—I can smell them," Ferguson whispered. "I can't see them, but they must be all around us."

All Birdie could smell was the sweat on his horse and himself. All he could think of was how were they going to get into that make-shift fortress before the Indians spotted them, and was it really worth trying.

Motioning his men to stay alert, Ferguson led them down out of the timber and onto open ground. Every rifle was at the ready, but only nature seemed astir. Blue jays squawked and fluttered off, cool spots of royal blue against the gray dawn. Squirrels, chattering, raced to escape the horses' hooves. A bellicose porcupine raised his back, but kept his quills in check.

The men rode in single file, making their own path through the tall grass. When they came to the river, the horses dipped their heads and drank. Nobody stopped them; the beasts had been pressed to the limit of endurance. When the horses were finished, the soldiers looked up, startled, to see angry faces peering at them from between the wagons.

There was no greeting and no wagon was moved aside to admit them. They had to dismount and walk their horses over a wagon tongue. Within the circled wagons, a terrible sight greeted them. The fifty-odd dead had been stacked like firewood. Twenty wounded lay in a long row, waiting to die from their wounds or the next Indian attack, whichever came first. But it was the still-living who gave the patrol their greatest shock; these were eyeing the thirty-six travel-stained soldiers with silent resentment and dismay.

"Ludicrous!" Captain Larson bellowed, when Captain Ferguson reported to him. "You and your damn niggers won't be of any big use. I need thirty times your number. I'm amazed Okala let you come across that meadow with your scalps."

Ferguson held his tongue and nodded to Birdie. From the look in Larson's eyes he could tell that the man was walking a thin line.

"Begging your pardon, Captain," Birdie said. "I guess the Indians think we're just a small advance company, and they don't want to reveal their positions."

Larson's eyes snapped dangerously. "When I need a nigger's opinion I've got enough of my own to ask."

"Silence, sir!" Ferguson was appalled. "I want to speak to Major Weaver—at once!"

"Do that." Larson chuckled. "You'll find him over in that heap." He indicated the pile of dead. "In the meantime, Captain, we're out of water, so your men will share. We are down to nothing but some dried corn, so your men will share. If we have two dozen shells remaining, it is a miracle, so your men will share. Then they can share dying with us."

Ferguson stood stock still. He had seen the faces of the survivors when they had ridden into the encampment; they were too exhausted to withstand another attack. A quick death would be easier. He had to take command quickly, or it would be a disaster. It was pointless to think that Okala would give him much time to regroup the forces. He just prayed that Larson wasn't up on the rules regulating chain of command.

"Those on guard," Ferguson shouted, "retreat and rest while you can. Sergeant Jacobs, replace them with our troops."

"What in thunderation do you think you are doing?" Larson demanded.

"Doing?" Ferguson said innocently, as if the man should know full well. "Major or no major, this command would automatically come under my control due to the circumstances. If we share dying, sir, you shall do so under my command." But Larson could not afford to give up easily. "Circumstances? I know of no circumstances that give you the right to take command. What is your date of rank?"

"Immaterial," Ferguson snapped. "You are within my district of Territorial Law Enforcement. Until your wagon train is back on the trail, sir, I will expect your full cooperation."

Larson stopped smoking, though his pipe was still held fast in his teeth. He said nothing, but nodding for Corporal Kerman Fletcher to follow him, silently withdrew into his tent. Inside, the Corporal stood at rigid attention. Larson waited until he knew they could not be overheard, then he said, "Fletcher, who got you your first stripe?"

"You, sir." The Corporal gulped.

"And your second?"

"You again, sir!"

Larson grinned mirthlessly. Kerman Fletcher had seen that look too many times before; to gain standing within the company, he had done every rotten, illegal, dirty thing the captain had ordered.

"Then sew on your thin stripe," Larson said casually. "You will inform Harrison that you are replacing him. I want to know every order this son-of-a bitch captain gives to our niggers."

Fletcher started to protest. "But—"

"But what, Fletcher? Jesus Christ, man. We are the last two whites in this company and this captain

has already showed he's a nigger lover. Do you understand me, *Sergeant* Fletcher?"

Most of the men did not understand Ferguson's
taking over the command. What they did understand
soon enough was that Sergeant Jacobs was no Sergeant Harrison.

"Hard-nosed nigger, ain't he?" was the general
opinion.

"Yup; so hard-nosed he was the first to empty out
his canteen and share his food," one of Birdie's patrol
pointed out. This was ignored. "Appears almost white
ta me. He got some behind-the-barn stuff goin' wid
your capt'n?"

"Shore do," Private Hector Rodgers said. "Respect.
We ain't got no problem wid our officer, 'cause all
his orders come through *our* sergeant." By the end
of the day the black soldiers of the Ninth became
even more aware of Birdie Jacobs. Every time a soldier stood up where he could be seen, a rain of
bullets showered into the camp. Though many of the
corpses were now three days old, Birdie got the men
to place them around the encampment to draw the
Indians' fire.

When dusk fell, Okala again didn't attack. It was
a mystery to all but Birdie. Even though it turned
bitter cold, he kept his own men on patrol, and
crept from man to man, whispering words of encour-
agement and cracking jokes.

Larson's men were envious. This new outfit had a
camaraderie they had never experienced; Larson's
new "actint" sergeant could learn nothing from them.

"We just boiled some fresh coffee, Sergeant."

Birdie spun around. "That's a waste of water. Too
much of it will boil away."

Then he felt silly. The three women were only trying to help. But there was more to it than that; Black Mary was trying to decide on the man to put her confidence in.

"Well, as long as it's already wasted," she said simply, "enjoy it, sergeant. I'm Mary Fields, and this is Miss Carrie Holmes and Miss Jody Robb. Anything you need us for, we're ready."

Birdie stared. He had never met three such different women. Black Mary was a little frightening, but the contrasting beauty of the other two tied his tongue with shyness. How he wished the wagon train troops had been as eager to offer help, instead of leaving almost everything to his men.

Black Mary chuckled. She saw the admiring look in Birdie's eyes. She liked a man who could appreciate a woman's beauty and still remain a gentleman.

"We picked up the rifles and revolvers of those who got killed. We've got them stacked by Miss Holmes's wagon, if you want to look at them."

Birdie followed the three women silently. Black Mary did all the talking, but his eyes flickered from Carrie to Jody and back. For a moment he too wondered about Carrie's "profession." He never once thought anything of the kind about Jody. She was such a perfect younger version of Colonel Jacobs' wife that it made him a little homesick.

In the past days Jody had learned more about weapons than she would have thought possible. Now she explained to Birdie, "We've sorted them according to kind, the same with the ammunition. It seems a horrible jumble—all types of guns and rifles." Birdie smiled. "That's our lot on the frontier, Miss Robb. We're expected to use up all the material left over from the war. You learn to pray every time you fire your gun that the shell will discharge."

"We've discovered that the hard way, Sergeant," Jody said. "I've told my aunt that when we get out of here, she must write her brother. That's Senator Robb. It just isn't fair."

Birdie liked her attitude; her tone said she was positive that they would get out of there. He found himself saying, "One voice ain't going to do much good, miss. Back east, they don't worry too much about our problems out here."

"Then it's time they did. If my uncle can pull strings to get his sister a teaching position with the Indians, then it's time he also saw to her protection." Two of the women who heard Jody had different reactions. Black Mary decided to keep her secret a little longer. She could see that the handsome young buck had taken a liking to the white girl, and what Black Mary had to tell might come better from her. Jody would be the vessel to carry the truth about Major Weaver's death.

Inez Robb, sitting propped against a wagon wheel, smiled grimly as she listened to Jody and the sergeant, thinking that Hiram Robb would probably rejoice at the news of their death at the hands of the Indians. The Senator considered his sister an "embarrassment" to the family, meaning himself and his younger brother Joseph. Senator Robb was too close to the White House and President Grant to want the world to know that Miss Robb had been fired from her teaching position in New England because of the liberal European views she tried to implant in her young ladies' heads.

He had not pulled strings; he had demanded that the Bureau of Indian Affairs find a position for her. He didn't care how many weird ideas she expounded two thousand miles away from Washington.

But Miss Inez was not the only skeleton in the closet he was trying to keep from rattling. For eighteen years he had dreaded the day when JoAnn might accidently learn that she was the illegitimate child his brother Joseph had fathered at sixteen. Hiram was serving his first term in the Senate then. Vice President Millard Fillmore had become President after the death of Zachary Taylor. The control of the Whig Party was at stake and the young senator had much to gain. He could not afford a scandal. Joseph was packed off to school in England, the young mother paid off and her name promptly forgotten, and the child handed over to a wet nurse.

As Hiram's power grew, so did Joseph's position in the diplomatic corps, until at thirty-four he became the youngest ambassador to the Court of St. James. Neither brother wished to acknowledge Jody; she was silently swept under the same rug as Miss Inez.

No, Miss Inez thought, *I won't be writing any such foolish letter—not that I expect to be alive to post it if I did.*

It was driving Birdie crazy. He kept looking longingly toward the river which he could hear gurgling over its rock bed. He knew it would be instant death to try to reach it, but he knew too that if some of the wounded got water it would not only save their lives, but make some of them strong enough to help fight off the next attack. He felt he owed it to the women and children in the train; they were being so strong, not uttering a single word of complaint. Miss Jody, for instance—he had seen her give her ration of water to the Carswell children who were too young to really know what was going on. Birdie could not

help but admire the quiet manner in which the girl
was handling the situation.

Jody was not so quiet inside at the moment. Black
Mary had confided her secret and now Jody was wondering how best to pass on the burden. She had not
even met Major Ferguson and was shy about approaching him with such an accusation. At the same
time, she did not feel she knew the sergeant well
enough to ask him to carry the tale to his commander.
She had just about made up her mind, however, to
confide in Birdie when she saw him creep between
two wagons and start toward the river, a dozen can-
teens slung over each shoulder.

Jody didn't even take time to think. She picked up
her skirts and ran to the tent, bursting in on Captain
Ferguson without warning.

"It's Sergeant Birdwell!" she gasped. "He's going
to the river for water!"

"For water?" Ferguson echoed blankly, and pushed
by her.

Jody was instantly aware of the man lying upon
the cot. Captain Larson lay stripped to trousers and
socks, casually puffing on his pipe. He saw no reason to acknowledge Jody's presence.

Jody saw it differently and was outraged. He wasn't
making a move to alert his men to help Sergeant
Birdwell. That settled it. Major Ferguson was going
to hear Black Mary's tale.

But the time was not right when Jody came to
stand beside Ferris Ferguson. His face was tense and
filled with concern as he watched Birdie sneaking
through the tall meadow grass toward the river.

Then it came echoing out of the woods, a high,
barbaric sound repeated over and over.

"What is it?" Jody whispered.

"A call for his death."

A barrage of bullets began to kick up the grass about him, but Birdie dodged them expertly and fired back with his revolver.

"Isn't there anything we can do to help him?" Jody asked.

Ferguson sighed. "We would be wasting ammunition on an enemy we can't see, miss."

A derisive chuckle behind them made them turn. Larson stood at the tent flap, smiling contemptuously. "And who wants to waste ammunition on a stupid nigger?"

Ferguson's face reddened with anger, but it was Jody's anger which erupted first.

"Perhaps you think a spear would be better, sir? Like the one you used to kill Major Weaver?"

Larson kept smiling, but his eyes were wary.

"What did you say, miss?" Captain Ferguson snapped.

"That he murdered Major Weaver with an Indian spear!" Jody said flatly.

Larson covered his ears with his hands. "I won't listen to this!" he cried. "I won't! These people all hate me. They'd tell any lie about me!"

"Silence!" Ferguson shouted. "Miss—"

"I'm only repeating," Jody explained calmly, "what an eyewitness told me. But, first, what about Sergeant—"

The rest of her question died on her lips. A sound erupted from within the encampment that turned her blood cold. It was a high, piercing and demonic cry.

Captain Ferguson stood gaping at the giant black woman who stood fearlessly out in the open in the center of the circle of wagons. The sounds coming out of her throat were electrifying. Black Mary had removed her stocking cap and her hair, standing out on all sides like a long-bristled brush, made her head look enormous. With her long arms stretching high above her six-foot frame, she seemed double that height. There wasn't a sound in the encampment when Black Mary finished her eerie chanting, and the Indians had stopped firing. Down by the riverside, Birdie heard the woman and sat stunned. A long-unused memory bank snapped open. Tears welled up in his eyes; he had not thought of Old Proud John in a decade. At least, he had always seemed old to Birdie. Colonel Jacobs had insisted that he take schooling from the proud African as he did from Miss Effie. But Old Proud John taught Birdie in Ashanti, so the ancient tongue would be burned into his young soul. The old man's teaching had not failed him; Birdie was only fairly sure who had uttered that cry, but he had no trouble with the translation:

"*Warrior, your village worries for you!*"

He stood erect, fearless now himself, and put his head back. His normally soft, sensitive voice boomed out like a cannon. "*Village, the enemy is all about!*"

"*Then confuse them, my son. Roar like the lion and we will answer like apes,*" was the response.

"*I shall walk like the panther, O wise voice, and you watch me like the buzzard.*"

"*Begin your walk, O son of our village, and we shall chant you safely home.*"

Carrie Holmes scrambled down out of her wagon. The cadence of the calls was pure voodoo and most of the ancient words she had understood. Now, in a high, lingering soprano, she began to echo Black Mary's deep baritone.

Birdie had begun walking back slowly, and the calls back and forth created a diversion. The woods hiding Okala's braves were silent. The other black soldiers leaned on their rifles and stared, understanding slowly dawning on their faces. Those who could still recall the ancient teaching of a father or grandfather joined the calling so there was not a single moment when the air was not filled with the eerie, discordant sounds. With each step Birdie took they grew, building up to a feverish sing-song pitch until finally the sergeant stepped between two of the wagons. Then, as if all of their memories had been reawakened, the callers burst into a joyous welcome-home chant that grew to ear-splitting shrillness. Even the wounded were up on their feet.

They would have water, though the amount was small. It had been a victory over the Utes. Confusion of the enemy had always been the strong suit of the Ashanti. Most of the blacks there were not Ashanti, but they recalled enough of their days of slavery to accept one who had Ashanti blood as their acknowledged leader.

Even the blacks who had served with Sergeant Birdwell the longest stood a little in awe of him after his return from the river. There was nothing physically different about him, but in their eyes he had taken on a different aura.

And as though Black Mary were the village chief, Birdie approached her with quiet reverence. The cap was back on her head and she was just another big black woman.

"Don't let their confusion grow cold," she told Birdie softly, then she turned and began walking slowly toward Jody and Captain Ferguson.

Birdie understood. She was a woman; she had fulfilled her role and was stepping back again for a man to carry on. She would be there to support him, but he answered now to the whole tribe if he failed. The matriarchal power of the Ashanti followed a rigid code. Birdie wanted to learn more about Black Mary's heritage, but this was not the moment for him to ask.

Captain Larson knew this was not his moment, either. He had looked upon this weird scene, his worried eyes moving feverishly from black face to black face, and then to the faces of the surviving white settlers.

Nowhere could he find a face that might help him counter the charge leveled by JoAnn Robb. Couldn't any of them see that Major Weaver had been a threat to all of them? That he, Nils Larson, was their salvation?

But he was faced with two enemies—Jody and the eyewitness. He withdrew to the tent to dress and prepare for battle. He would vanquish his enemies and take back his command. He was convinced in his own mind that he was the only one Okala feared.

Ferris Ferguson was looking at Jody and really seeing her for the first time. Her blue eyes were radiant as she looked from Birdie to Black Mary. Pride glowed so strongly in her face that he regretted not being the object of it. She was a woman who could make any man want to be above average, he felt. But . . . who was she?

"Miss," he said. "I—I'm afraid I don't know your name."

Jody looked at him and blushed, aware suddenly of the captain's lean handsomeness. *Holy Minerva!* she thought. *He's beautiful!*

"I'm JoAnn Robb," she introduced herself. "Miss Inez Robb is my aunt."

"My pleasure, Miss Robb. Now, you were speaking to me about?"

She put a finger to her lips and motioned for him to walk away from the tent. "Actually, Mary Fields should be telling you this," and Jody described what Black Mary had seen.

Ferguson called Black Mary over. After speaking with both of the women, the captain knew he had a problem on his hands that would have to be handled with great care. The arrest of Captain Larson could immediately undo all the good Birdie and Black Mary had just brought about. The feeling now was that enough time had been bought for Billie Joe to return in time with fresh troops.

And Major Weaver's death statement was a mystery Ferguson had to solve. Until then, he advised Jody and Black Mary to steer clear of Captain Larson and asked them to keep what they knew to themselves a little longer.

4

WHEN JODY GOT BACK to Carrie's wagon, Sergeant Birdwell was just leaving. Jody climbed the tailgate, ignoring Miss Inez's desire to talk to her, and went to the bed where Carrie sat bent over a cup of black coffee. Her posture was an eloquent expression of despair. Jody sat down beside her and put her arm around her shoulders.

"Are you all right?" she whispered.

Carrie looked up. "I had to tell him," she said dully.

"Whatever for?" Jody asked. "The man is dead."

"He came to me for help," Carrie said with gentle dignity. "It was only fair to tell him the truth." Jody was shocked. "But how could you bring yourself to discuss such a thing with a man?"

"He *is* a black man, Jody," Carrie said. "Somehow we blacks are able to discuss such things without em-

barrassment. Besides, he's quite gentle and understanding."

"I still don't see why you had to tell him."

Carrie raised her head slowly. "I couldn't do what
he asked of me because I've been bleeding ever
since—"

"Bleeding!" Jody gasped. "Where? Why?"

If her condition hadn't been so serious, Carrie
might have laughed. Jody had grown up very quickly
in the last few days, but about some matters she was
still as naive as a child.

A spasm of pain gripped Carrie and she nearly
fainted. She had gone too long without help and was
reluctant to ask for it even now. But the stain spreading over her dress was too obvious for either of them
to ignore. Jody fought back a wave of panic. "Shall
I get my aunt?"

"No!" Carrie said sharply, then fell back weakly
against the pillows. "You . . . only you. I'll explain
the problem to you."

One problem was immediately obvious to Jody
when she had Carrie's skirt removed. Carrie needed
cleaning up, but she had refused to waste water that
way. The bleeding was internal. Carrie had not worried about it at first because it had stopped, but then
it had begun again with greater intensity. Jody tore
up a petticoat and dampened a section for a com-
press Carrie could hold tightly between her legs. She
tried to talk of other things to distract Carrie.

"This help the sergeant needs, is it something I
could do?"

"Not unless you've got some black blood hiding in
you."

"I see," Jody said thoughtfully. "Does it have something to do with those strange sounds all of you were making?"

"Strange to you, but hopefully not to the Indians. They are just as primitive in their way as my ancestors were in theirs. For them, life is not controlled by man, but by many gods and spirits. The Indians know the white man has only one God, but they're not sure about we buffalo people. Sergeant Birdwell wants them to learn."

"You like him, don't you?" Jody smiled at her. "That was a brave thing he did, going for water that way."

"Damn fool stunt that could have gotten him killed!" Carrie said, but her answering smile was tender. Suddenly she cried out, seized by another spasm of pain, and this time she fainted. Jody debated for only a second her next course of action. Bounding out of the wagon she came face to face with her aunt.

"JoAnn," Miss Inez said sternly, "I wish to speak with you."

"Not now, Aunt Inez. There's something I must do first."

"Young lady, I will not tolerate one more minute of your insolent attitude. I demand to know what is going on around here!"

Jody looked around; the encampment was a beehive of activity, but nowhere did she see the person she so desperately sought.

"Aunt Inez," she said in a rush, "Miss Carrie is very ill. I must find Black Mary. If Carrie calls out, do what you can for her, please."

The pious look that spread over Inez Robb's face told Jody that the woman was not about to lift a finger for a woman she believed to be a whore. She hurried away, seeking help for Carrie from more compassionate quarters.

Amazingly, in such a small area, she did not see Black Mary. She did see Sergeant Birdwell disengage himself from a group of white wagon drivers being lectured by Captain Ferguson.

Birdie stalked toward her, his mind seething with such anger that he didn't even notice her. Jody had to step in front of him to attract his attention.

"Sergeant Birdwell?" she said timidly.

"What is it?" he barked.

Jody swallowed nervously, not because of his tone, but because she was embarrassed about the subject.

"It's Carrie Holmes, Sergeant. She—" Jody curled her toes hard within her shoes and steeled herself. "She's bleeding bad and I can't find Black Mary anywhere!"

Birdie stared at her blankly for a moment. He, too, had been surprised by Carrie's frankness. He had nearly run away in his embarrassment and had not understood the true seriousness of her condition. It was one more burden being placed on his shoulders, one he could back away from a second time.

"Do you know how to care for her?" he asked Jody.

She stared at him; it would have been so much easier to lie and save embarrassment.

"No," she whispered, blushing. "Until she explained certain things to me, I didn't even know how—I mean . . . that's why I came for help," she finished awkwardly.

Birdie looked at her, but now his gaze was gentle. She had done what she could and then been smart enough to go look for more expert help. More and more she reminded him of a younger version of the Colonel's Miss Effie.

"I'll go to her," he said. "You go tell Captain Ferguson that I need Mary Fields. Our plan will just have to wait."

Ferris Ferguson wasn't having any luck getting anything out of the group of wagon drivers surrounding him. Once he had heard Black Mary's story, he had checked out all the drivers and had spotted them as Army men, not mule-skinners. They were well aware of what they carried in each of their wagons, but had been sworn to secrecy, and had grown even more close-mouthed since the death of Major Weaver. No man among them knew how much any of the others knew, and each thought himself privy to the whole truth. They didn't want to share that knowledge with Captain Ferguson any more than they had wanted to share it with Captain Larson, never mind what Major Weaver's dying words may have been.

Jody, shoving through the group to give Ferguson Birdie's message, overheard just enough of the foolish debate to grasp the situation.

"That's been our folly!" she said, pushing through at last to where Ferguson stood glaring at them.

"Miss Robb!" The captain stared at her. "I am afraid this is not—"

Jody stopped him. "I'm sorry, Captain. I'm looking for Mary Fields. Sergeant Birdwell needs her."

Ferguson hesitated. He had gained very little from these men who had refused even to admit that they were soldiers, even under the threat of court-martial. Instead of answering Jody's question, he asked one of his own.

"What do you mean, Miss Robb, by 'folly'?"

"I didn't mean to speak out of turn." Jody blushed. "But I never did understand why these men stayed so close to their own wagons during the Indian attacks. I didn't understand until just now. Of course, they were protecting the gold they're carrying."

The looks and gasps, the glances from man to man, were near comical. No one admitting anything, everyone knowing everything. Captain Ferguson had to struggle to keep from laughing.

"Well," he said, "the truth will out."

"What truth?" someone demanded.

"Why," Jody said, before Ferguson could stop her, "Major Weaver was murdered!"

Instead of the outcry Ferguson had expected, her words were met with sickly silence. Ferguson did not want the moment to pass.

"All right!" he shouted. "Now the whole truth is out. But that does not change the picture Sergeant Birdwell was trying to paint for you—we still have the Indians to face."

He was met with cold, indifferent silence.

"What does Sergeant Birdwell want us to do?" Jody asked softly.

"I'm really not sure," Ferguson said, scratching his head. "Something about gods and spirits. What would the Indians know about African gods?"

"What do we know about Indian gods?" Jody pointed out. "I may be wrong, but I think I can guess what he has in mind."

Jody stepped over to the cold campfire around which they were gathered. She dipped her hand into the charcoal residue left by the pine logs and then began to smear the stuff over her face. "Sergeant Birdwell and his men are black by birth," she said. "They need us just as black to blend in with the night. You heard them chanting before, you saw the Indians' reaction. We have failed fighting them our way. What

do we have to lose fighting them Sergeant Birdwell's
way? Forget the gold! It isn't yours in the first place.
Tonight, think about your own lives." In the end, the
majority agreed with her, but two men slipped away
from the group to discuss the matter with Captain
Larson.

From Okala's vantage point it was an unbelievable
sight. It was as though he were looking down upon
one of his own villages. In the center of the wagon
circle burned a gigantic bonfire, but of greater amazement were the near-nude black figures dancing about
the flames, their voices raised in prayerful chants.
The gods of the buffalo people must be very powerful, Okala thought, to allow one of them to gather
water without fear of being killed and now to let
the majority sit about and sing the tune for the medicine men to dance to without fearing a massacre.

A portion of Okala's brain said that this was the
time to launch the final attack, but another portion
asked whether Manitou was a greater god than those
who were now being worshipped in the meadowland
below.

Had the chief owned one of the white man's spy-
glasses, he would have been able to see that the
rather unceremonious dancing and horrible singing
was being performed by whites smeared with charcoal,
among them a loudly dissenting Miss Inez Robb. And
that the cross-legged observers sitting around the
campfire were propped-up dead and wounded assigned to keep them propped up.

But he could not see this and he, like his braves,
was fascinated by what he thought he was witnessing.

"Don't turn around, Okala, or your tribe loses
a chief."

But Okala did turn. If he was about to die, he wished to look upon the man who would bring it about. But even more important, according to his code, was the desire to salute the brave warrior who had out-smarted him.

The man was tall and looked even taller naked. That was the first measure Okala took of him; for a man to possess such length of manhood must surely make him a great chief. Behind this chief were other naked warriors.

Okala smiled a little as he looked at Birdie and shook his spear in welcome. Birdie felt a little foolish. No man or woman had ever seen him totally naked since childhood. He knew what Okala was grinning about and it embarrassed him. He gave no sign of it, however. Raising his voice, he addressed the Ute braves. "Who will become chief if Okala dies?"

Okala stirred and his smile faded. "Many will die with me."

"There is no need for anyone else to die, Okala. The man who started this killing also murdered our chief. He will be tried and put before a firing squad."

Okala was unimpressed. "What about our law? We must have the man first."

Birdie was silent. After a moment, he nodded. "That is a matter which requires the approval of my chief, Captain Ferguson." Now it was Okala's turn to withdraw into silence a moment. When he did reply, his voice was stern. "Let it be done before your wagons go from our land forevermore."

Birdie and his soldiers departed almost as silently as they had come. Far down the mountain, they stopped at the spot where Black Mary was guarding their uniforms.

She shook her head sadly when she heard the news. "Ain't no white gonna turn another white over to the Indians, no matter how much of a bad one he is."

Carrie, under Black Mary's orders, remained in bed. When Jody left the dancing and bonfire for a few seconds to look in on her, she found her sleeping peacefully. Her nightgown and sheets showed no sign of fresh bleeding.

"That's good." Jody sighed with relief.

There was a light tapping on the tailgate, and one of the wagon drivers peered in cautiously.

"Miss," he whispered. "The Captain wants you. It's important."

Jody tucked the blanket back around Carrie and scampered down from the wagon. She followed the silent man. As she moved between two wagons, she heard a sound behind her and turned her head to see a black-bearded, heavy-shouldered man lunging at her. As she opened her mouth to scream, his massive fist drove into her jaw. The first man caught her before her unconscious body could touch the ground.

Captain Nils Larson stepped from the shadows and grinned. "Bellinger," he told the man holding Jody quietly, "bring up the horses. Hollis, lash her across one of the pack mules."

"They're pretty well weighed down with gold, Capt'n."

"She won't burden the beast too long. Besides, we'll have to walk them for a mile or two anyway."

"What about the dame you said saw you kill the Major?"

Larson chuckled. "She went up the mountain with those other stupid niggers. You think Okala is going to let any of them come back alive? No more than he's going to let anybody here in this camp live to tell about the gold. Come on! Move out."

Henry Bellinger's greed for gold was one thing; now it suddenly dawned on his slow-working mind that Larson's plot to steal it included murder. Up to now, he had gone along with him without question. As Nils Larson had told them, Birdwell's plan gave them the perfect opportunity. The man guarding the horses and other livestock never questioned the approach of Captain Larson. Henry saw the soldier slump to the ground and thought the captain had knocked him out. He did not see Larson quickly hide his knife beneath his belt.

The frantic activity at the bonfire masked the sound when they pried up the floor planks on Henry's wagon. They left it to Larson to determine exactly how much gold to steal—enough to make them each very rich men, but not so much it would impede their escape.

But Henry had not counted upon Larson seeking revenge against Jody Robb, and he knew nothing about the conversation that had taken place between Larson and Hollis while he was off fetching Jody.

"Henry ain't the best one in the world to keep quiet about things," Peter Hollis grumbled.

Larson patted the knife in his belt. "There are ways of shutting his mouth . . . when the time is right."

5

"How long—?"

Ferguson's face was grim.

"I don't know. Nobody saw them leave," Birdie admitted. "But the guard seems to have been dead about an hour."

Ferguson closed his eyes. Without opening them he said, almost apologetically, "I don't know if I could have turned Larson over to Okala anyway."

Birdie left him then, suddenly realizing that the captain might like to be alone with the decision he still had to make. He went to Carrie Holmes' wagon where Inez Robb sat in her tattered black dress, her hair mussed, a venomous kind of terror on her charcoal-smeared face. She looked up at his approach.

"A lot of good you did," she said. "You know he took her, don't you? We'll find her lying out there somewhere come dawn. He's not going to let her live. Well, that's what she gets for messing into affairs that didn't concern her. But maybe she'll be better off. It isn't half of what the Indians will do to us—"

Birdie broke in savagely, "They will do nothing!" It was as if she never heard him. "They won't be satisfied with just killing us. That man! He should have been locked up from the first! My poor Jody!"

Turning away, Birdie saw Carrie Holmes standing by the wagon tailgate, watching him. Her lovely face looked thin and drawn. A wave of pity washed over Birdie and he walked up to her, taking her arm without a word. She didn't protest, but went with him quietly, even though she was dressed only in a flannel nightgown. He searched for a place where they could have some privacy.

"Let's go up here," he said, climbing up on a wagon seat. He helped her up beside him and she sat leaning against his broad shoulder.

It was the nearest she had ever been to him. He could feel the slim, round hardness of her body through the nightgown. Her curly hair had a faint attractive smell of its own, like spice over the body scent.

She waited for him to speak; she still could not believe that Jody was gone.

"What would you do, if you were me?" he asked suddenly.

"Nothing." It seemed an awful thing to say, as if she were killing Jody with the words. "There is nothing any of us can do for her, is there?"

She felt him grow stiff and when he spoke again, his voice was tight.

"It does seem hopeless. You know, I think she is the finest girl I ever met."

It wasn't what he had set out to say, but he meant it. Carrie was suddenly as stiff as he was.

These were not the words she wanted to hear from him. She felt guilty, being jealous of a girl who was probably dead. On impulse, she leaned towards him and they kissed, briefly.

He pulled back quickly, and as Carrie looked at him, held out his hand. She took it and they held hands for a moment. Then he said, "I think I know how to save the rest of us."

"How, Birdie?" It was the first time she had called him that.

"I'll go back to Okala. I'll never see you again!"

They sat silent for a moment, still holding hands, and then Birdie sighed. "It's the only way."

But Ferris Ferguson was of the same opinion as Carrie. "You'll do nothing but sign your own death warrant, Birdie."

"Sir, if that were true, we wouldn't have come back alive the first time. Okala has got to respect me for coming back. I would advise, sir, that the wagons be ready to roll at dawn. If there are no Indians in sight, get as far out of Ute territory as possible. Go without me, if you have to, but go."

Major Weaver would have put him on report at once for insubordination. Captain Ferguson listened with a heavy heart and saw the wisdom of his young sergeant's demand. He blamed himself for letting Larson get away with the girl and the gold. He held out little hope of ever seeing Jody Robb again. No woman had ever affected him so quickly before, not even his wife. He was sorry that he had not had the chance to make his feelings known.

She had been marvelous, persuading the white soldiers and wagoneers to smear their faces black and cavort around the bonfire like savages. She had even made up some gibberish for them to chant, not that words mattered. She had been the ringmaster of their strange little circus, even inducing Ferguson to don black face and dance about like a carefree child.

And the men had sung her praises along with Birdie's. They were going to be safe; they were going to be able to leave there with their scalps, thanks to little Miss Robb and the sergeant. Jody's abduction had stunned them all. The last anyone could recall was seeing her enter Carrie's wagon, and Carrie, who had been asleep, could add nothing more.

Tears had dimmed Ferris's eyes as bits and pieces of the story came to light. He had not cried since he was a boy and he choked the tears back. They left a hard pain in his chest. Now that pain was to have a companion.

He let Birdie go with a nod. As with Jody, it was too late to put his feelings for the man into words.

As word of Birdie's mission spread, a remarkable thing happened. One by one, Ferguson's black soldiers came to him to volunteer to ride after Birdie and give him some protection. Only a week before they had all bitterly resented the man; now he was a valuable leader they could not afford to lose.

Ferguson denied each and every request, including one from Black Mary, but with such gratitude that his men's respect for him grew as well. When he issued the order to assemble the wagon train, there wasn't a single belly-ache or complaint.

New drivers had to be found to replace those who had been slain and the two deserters. Everyone vied to replace Carrie Holmes' dead driver-bodyguards until Black Mary announced that she would handle the wagon alone.

And Mary minced no words with Inez Robb. "When we roll out at dawn, I want you back there seein' ta Miss Carrie. That, or you walk!"

There was nothing to do but wait . . . .

Birdie found no Indians where he had found them before. He rode along, not trying to hide or be quiet. He rode through the burned-out agency compound; it still smelled of death and he shuddered. The first Ute village he reached seemed deserted, until he was noiselessly surrounded by braves.

He made them see and understand at once that he was unarmed and wanted to see Okala. He was put into a tent under heavy guard; they seemed to be in no rush to inform the chief. The passing minutes turned into an hour. Birdie began to lose heart. Perhaps it was a foolhardy mission after all. Before, he had taken Okala by surprise; the chief had prudently seen no reason to hurry along his own death. But this time Okala would have the upper hand, and Birdie suspected he was purposely playing on his nerves.

The Indians would not let him see what was going on outside the tent, and he could only wonder at the sounds he heard. Here, the Mill River flowed rapidly, cascading over the rocks. Mingled with the sound of rushing water was the clink of a tomahawk being sharpened, the raised voice of a laughing brave, the hoot of an owl.

Suddenly, there were many men's voices, then silence. Several seconds passed before a hand pulled back the flap on the teepee and old Okala stepped inside. He bent his head with dignity. He was wrapped in a buffalo robe and he scarcely seemed to crease it as he squatted down, his dark-skinned face wrin-

kled into a frown. Out of respect, Birdie remained
standing at attention.

"I have not brought the man you seek, Chief
Okala. He has killed again, and possibly a third time,
leaving the wagon train with two other men and gold
which they had stolen. These things came about while
I was with you."

Others of the tribal council had begun to filter
into the tent as Birdie spoke. For a moment, no one
said anything, but they all looked at Okala. "Then
we no longer have a bargain." The chief's voice was
cold.

Birdie's heart sank. "That is so," he admitted. "But
I come now with a different proposition."

Okala was silent, his face impassive. "I will stay
as a hostage until your braves can ride down the
man we all seek."

"Why my braves?" the chief demanded. Birdie was
ready for that. "Okala is said to be a man of great
wisdom. Would he allow the buffalo soldiers to ride
out after the man? He would not, for he would fear
that we would keep riding into the dawn."

For a moment, the council gaped at Birdie. Then
they began to babble excitedly. Okala sat silent in
their midst, his eyes on the black man. He admired
his courage for coming alone; he admired him for
coming at all. It was something he wished he could
instill in his younger braves; they were growing lax.
They coveted the rifle over the bow and arrow; they
had tasted too much of the white man's whiskey.
School would not have been a bad thing for his people. His children had thought a great deal of their
gentle young teacher. He had admired her himself,
because she had not wished to learn the ways wanton
young braves behaved. He longed for the old days

when a single word from him would have stilled the noisy council and made his wishes as chief known.

Crops would have been good for his people. But who could eat the cotton plants the government had sent them? And this God they demanded that the Indians worship? He was not peaceful and loving and caring. He was cruel and hard and full of anger. Why did the white man demand that he be worshipped on just a single day, when they worshipped their gods each and every moment of every day? Religious? He had become chief because he was the most god-fearing, pious man of the tribe.

By now all in the council were shouting and the braves outside the tent had added their voices to the clamor. It seemed to Birdie that nobody but himself was looking at Okala. He saw the old man sitting there, his face pained, his eyes worried. He saw him measure the shouts of the council, blow out his breath and lift his head.

"Be still!" he roared. "You begin to sound like the voices of women. I would hear from this one who has lately been murdered."

"A soldier guarding the livestock, so they could steal horses and mules to make their escape. They also stole the young teacher who taught your children. We think he will kill her, too, if he hasn't already."

"Why?"

"It was she who exposed him as the murderer of Major Weaver, and a silent voice can no longer accuse."

Okala's response was bitter.

"I will tell you all one thing. It is the innocent who are always made to suffer. My youngest children and now this young woman. We will ride. The black

one will ride with us. He calls himself our hostage.
I call him Umadan—Black Bear With Teeth. So declares Okala!"

Jody's head was bursting. She opened her eyes to
an upside-down world. Every bone in her body ached
from being bent over the back of the mule. She tried
to clear her head and focus on the scene near at
hand. It was so weird she thought she must be dreaming.

A man—she thought she recognized Captain Larson—stood in long underwear, donning the rough
clothing of a mule skinner. Another man, his back
to her, was dressing a third man, lying on the ground,
in the captain's uniform.

She was so light-headed she couldn't be sure that
it wasn't a dream. Then the man with his back to
her turned and her mind froze with recognition. She
could see his fist coming at her again.

"Now for her," Larson snarled.

Jody closed her eyes tightly. No one had to tell
her that the man on the ground was dead, or what
Larson's words meant. Surprisingly, she felt calm;
death had been so much a part of her life of late,
that somehow she did not fear her own.

Peter Hollis hesitated. "It seems like a waste," he
said. "She's a good-looking cunt."

Larson scoffed. "Anything would look good to you,
after all the sheep you've had to settle for."

"How'd you know I was raised on a sheep ranch?"
Hollis demanded.

Larson laughed. "Not only do you stink of mutton,
but all you've ever talked about is the sheep ranch
you plan to buy with your share of the gold."

"Well?"

"Well, what?"

"Her!" Hollis pointed.

There was a long silence during which Jody died a hundred times.

At last, Larson shrugged. "If you want that scrawny piece, you take those two mules and her. I'll take these two and the extra horse. But we part company here, understood?"

Hollis thought it over. His desire was to head back west, to the Idaho mountains and sheep country. Women were scarce there and he could be a big man with gold and a woman of his own. But it meant back-tracking through Ute country.

He was beginning to wonder how far he could trust Nils Larson. The speed with which the captain had knifed Henry Bellinger to death had stunned Hollis. What was to keep Larson from killing him in his sleep and taking all of the gold?

"Sounds okay to me," he said slowly. "Which way do you aim to head?"

"Due east."

"South for me."

Larson shrugged and, without another word, mounted his horse and turned the animal toward the east, thankful to be rid of the man and Jody. Actually, he wasn't sure he had the stomach for another murder. Major Weaver's death had filled him with an intoxicating feeling of exhilaration. The soldier on guard had been an obstacle that had to be eliminated. The murder of Henry Bellinger had been almost anticlimactic, unnecessary. He had felt nothing when he stabbed him.

Jody now meant nothing to him. His main purpose had been to escape the firing squad, or Okala's scalping knife. That he could do it with gold was an added blessing, and with the gold he could build a new life, safe from Army justice. Let the girl live. Life with the boorish Peter Hollis would be a fate worse than death.

Larson stuck pretty much to a due-east course. Hollis headed south for an hour, retied Jody into a sitting position, then headed toward the rising sun, keeping the dust cloud Larson raised ahead of him.

He was being very cautious, and very foolish. They were on a steady climb up into the mountains.

"It's not Captain Larson," Birdie said, his voice heavy with disappointment. "It's a man called Bellinger."

"Then only part of your assumption is correct," Okala said quietly. "The man has killed again, but the girl lives."

"How can you be so sure?"

"What did you find?" Okala called.

Three braves who had been scampering over the ground came running back to him.

"They are no longer one party," they reported. "One mule, going south, carries more weight."

"Take Umadan south with you," Okala ordered. "We will go east after the other. We must hurry before the coming storm takes away their sign."

But within an hour, they were all back together again. They were gaining ground, but the parallel course the others were traveling puzzled them.

A blue-white knotted rope of lightning burned down out of the clouds, followed instantly by a barrage of thunder that seemed to shake the earth. It rolled, as if banging from cloud to cloud, and boomed along the peaks, rumbling away at last into silence.

Jody felt the electricity in the mule's mane; it seemed

to tingle through her nerves. The air had a weird, bright cast. The heavy clouds swallowed more and more of the mountains. Another dazzling blue-white blaze showed the mountainside in bold relief. In the flaring light, Jody saw Hollis's frightened face.

With a deafening roar came a torrent of rain, a cloudburst. It was like a solid wall of water. With her hands lashed to the pack-rack, Jody couldn't wipe the blinding rain from her eyes and face; it was easier to ride with her eyes closed.

She became aware of how nervous the mule was. The animal was smart enough to know that they should get out of the storm, out of the reach of the mighty forces of nature. But Jody was thankful that they kept moving on. She tried not to think of what Peter Hollis might demand of her once they stopped.

The rain fell steadily. The fury of the storm did not diminish. In the higher crags the massive downpour was creating rills and streams and roaring rivers. Still Hollis pressed on. He thought that deep within the canyon the storm's punishment would be less severe. He didn't heed the strange hollow roar that was sweeping down upon them.

Those with greater knowledge and experience of nature's power had more respect for it. Nils Larson, no less than a mile north of the canyon Peter and Jody were entering, had kept a sharp eye on the storm since the clouds had begun to gather. He was afraid the lightning would spook the horses and mules and had searched for and found a cave large enough to hide them in. His desire for a hiding place was based on more than the coming storm. Being on higher terrain, he had been aware of pursuit for some time. He rightly judged it to be a party of some twenty riders, but wrongly judged who they might be. He was dead-set

on the notion that Captain Ferguson had sent the
cavalry after him. Well, the storm would wash out his
tracks and he could sit comfortably inside the cave
until his pursuers gave up.

Okala deduced correctly where the two parties
would be and how far they would be able to travel
during the coming storm. To pinpoint them more
accurately, he sent two scouts northeast, and Birdie
and two braves toward the canyon mouth. Then he
took the rest of his braves deep into the forest to wait.

Captain Ferris Ferguson didn't like the way the
wagons were strung out or the way some of the wagoneers were using the dry washes to make better time.
He watched the sheet of blackness come down over
the mountains like a falling curtain. He had seen hundreds of such storms: storms that stampeded cattle,
lightning bolts that split giant pines and rolled moun-
tainous rocks down, storms that caused dangerous flash
floods.

In his opinion, the wagon train was more vulnerable
to the storm at the moment than to the Indians. There
had been no hot pursuit as they rolled away from the
encampment and forded the Milk River. He knew that
they were being watched and tracked; the fact that
there was no attack gave him heart that Birdie's plan
was working. But working or not, the storm was the
greater danger. To the utter dismay of most, he ordered the wagons up onto a flat-top mesa and the
horses and mules shackled to keep them from bolting
when the lightning flashed.

The rain was so heavy, Peter Hollis could barely
make out his horse's head. Only the tautness of the
drag line told him he still had the mules following.

All of the beasts were terror-stricken and he had to keep lashing the horse to get it to move. He was not intelligent enough to know that they were more frightened of his terror than by anything else.

Suddenly, the gasping horse would not move another inch. Hollis wiped the rain from his eyes. In front of them a huge windfall blocked their path; there was no way around. The forest and rocky canyon walls rose steeply on either side, the great trees shrieking and bending under the weight of the storm.

The hollow roar was deafening now. Hollis looked up, squinting against the rain, to see a fifty-foot wall of gray-black water filling the canyon. The scream that rose in his throat was never uttered.

The wall of water washed over them. Hollis was torn from his horse and pounded against the canyon walls. The gold on the mules kept them weighted down and they were carried along by the flood waters. Jody, who had been riding with her eyes closed, was not sure what had happened. But within seconds her lungs were straining and cold fear gripped her. The pack-rack was torn loose from the mule, but Jody was still lashed to it. She struggled to wiggle her wrists free of the rawhide. The soaked leather finally began to give and Jody fought for the surface even before she was actually free. It was a horrible struggle, as if some huge hand were gripping her legs, trying to drag her back to the canyon floor. She gasped and spluttered on reaching the surface, then bobbed under again.

Surfacing once more, she saw a jagged tree stump hurtling toward her. Her fingers caught at the dirt-crusted roots. The stump veered and the current jammed her into the root maze. The stump rocketed along in the flood tide. Jody dragged herself forward, the roots raking her body. Her clothes caught on them and she had to reach back and tear them free. Her strength waning, she clawed her way to the top of the stump.

It crashed with a violent jolt against the trees on the canyon side. The wind-driven pine branches lashed at her. Jody reached out to find the strongest branch and held on fast.

There were silver flashes in front of her eyes and her head was ringing. She lurched to the center of the tree, scrambling up into its branches. Her heart was thundering and her breathing was harsh and uneven. But, for the moment, she seemed to be out of the water.

The rain slashed at her, but the floodwaters didn't seem to be rising. The deep canyon was now a river of raging white water. A hundred feet separated her from the top of the canyon. If she dared to jump from treetop to treetop, she could make it.

After jumping to the next tree and nearly falling back into the flood, she grew timid. Her head was throbbing so it was hard for her to keep her eyes open. The rain beat against the back of her head and sluiced icy water down her back. But try again she must. Here the trees were thicker, the larger branches almost intertwining, and her confidence grew when she was able to scramble from tree to tree. When her goal was almost within reach, a branch tore loose just above her and knocked her out of the tree to the ground. She didn't feel either the shock of the landing or the pain of it. She twisted as she landed, clawing at the rain-soaked earth to keep from slipping back down into the flood.

That was her only conscious thought. She dragged herself upward, working her way to a rocky outcropping that thrust out of the mountainside like supplicating arms. Once there, she collapsed, breathless.

Suddenly, without warning, she began to laugh. She tilted back her head and laughed until tears ran and her sides ached. She had won out against Nature, and now Nature was easing her fear and tension.

Birdie would not let the two scouts stop looking even during the height of the storm. He had prayed for Jody. It had seemed futile to pray after they had spotted the carcasses of the horse and mules being washed along in the flood, but it was the only thing he could think to do.

He had almost given up hope, thrashing through the soggy underbrush, when he heard the laughter. For a moment, he was like stone. Then he raced for a rise while the Indians with him went directly toward the sound of the laughter. When Birdie looked down from the rise, he saw Jody sitting on the rock, laughing, while the braves approached her cautiously.

All Birdie could thing of was how dirty she looked. Her face was almost black with mud; her hair was matted mud and pine needles; her bodice was torn and her skirt looked as if she had been lost in a briar patch. Still, she was the most beautiful sight he had ever seen.

"Jody, Jody! It's all right!"

She raised her face and looked up at him. Suddenly, her laughter died and she put her face down into her hands and began to sob.

Tears sprang to Birdie's eyes. He couldn't speak, he could only nod at the braves to bring her up to him. Jody didn't protest but let the Indians support her on either side and guide her slowly to the top of the canyon.

"I go for horses," one of the braves said softly.

But Birdie shook his head. "I'll carry her."

He swept her up into his arms as though she were a weightless thing. She wrapped her arms about his thick neck and nestled her head against his shoulder. It was the safest place she had been all day and she wasn't about to let go of him. She had never been this close to a man before; she had never felt a man's arms about her like this. She liked it. It was warming, soothing, comforting. And she was so very, very tired.

She was not even aware that a brave held her until Birdie could climb into his saddle and take her back again. She seemed so small to him, just like a little girl. His heart ached over the terror and torment she must have gone through. He could only assume that the man who had had her, whichever of the two it had been, was dead. For this he was grateful, because his thoughts had been running toward murder.

But now his heart was filled with peace and love. She was safe, she was alive, she was in his arms.

Oddly, he thought of Carrie Holmes' lips on his. She was of his people; he should have felt flattered that she was showing him such attention. She was fantastically beautiful, he had to admit, but he had felt nothing—nothing like what he was feeling now. Jody asleep against his chest made him glow and feel strange all over. He didn't want her to move, ever.

But Birdwell Jacobs had been raised to be a rational man. He knew that the love that was growing in his heart could never be. For him to be fathered by a white father had been a measure of the time and culture into which he had been born. That time was now buried forever more. He had lived in the white world of Colonel Jacobs as long as Colonel Jacobs had lived. Now his world was the black world of Carrie Holmes and Black Mary and the other buffalo soldiers.

As much as he wanted to touch Jody's sleeping lips

with his, he did not. Reluctantly, he handed her down
into the waiting arms of Okala.

It all seemed like another dream to Jody. The
warmth of the roaring fire . . . the Indian blankets
wrapped about her . . . the low voices of men speaking quietly . . . the clop of horses' hoofs . . . the coyote
serenade as the storm passed . . . the sense of warmth
and sweet lingering scent of Birdie's manliness . . .
and the drifting away into deep slumber.

Once, during her dreamlike sleep, she thought she
heard Birdie and Okala talking.

"Can we be sure?" Birdie asked.

"Manitou works in strange ways to punish men of
evil," Okala responded. "My scouts are certain the man
and his beasts were inside the cave."

Birdie shuddered. "It seems a horrible death, buried
alive by a mountain of rock and mud, closed in a cave
where you thought you were safe."

"You are a strange man, Umadan. You can feel compassion even for an enemy. It is not true of all the
buffalo soldiers."

"Perhaps it's because I am half white," Birdie admitted openly, perhaps for the first time in his life.

"A heavy burden," Okala said. "You are not a whole
part of any one world, and now I increase that burden
by giving you an Ute name."

"Which increases my compassion, Okala. The white
side of me had land taken away because it owned
slaves. The black side of me was given that land—at
least forty acres and a mule. Now, because you have
land, they want to take it away and give everyone
one-hundred-sixty acres and build a railroad to bring
people here quickly to develop it. I don't blame the
black side of me for wanting to be free. I don't blame

the white side of me for wanting something to show for that freedom. But must man always make someone else suffer?"

Okala chuckled. "I should have named you 'one with great thoughts' rather than 'black bear with teeth,' my wise son. But don't despair. In this case, it would seem that red, black or white men are the same. For thousands of years, in white man's way of measuring time, the people of my nation have fought the people of other Indian nations over land, women, horses and buffalo. We were at times strong and at other times weak. When weak, our tribes were enslaved, but no man can enslave a heritage. A people's history cannot be taken away from them."

"Ours has," Birdie said sullenly.

"If you speak as a white man," Okala said, "that is possible. History for the white man is from setting sun to setting sun, from meal to meal, from birth to birth. If you speak as a black, then you speak foolishness. My people do not have a written language, but I could spend days relating the deeds of my ancestors."

He sighed regretfully. "But this is not the time for such matters. My men have built a travois to carry the teacher. It is time to take her back to the wagon train."

"That is a great distance."

"Not so. My scouts have brought me reports. They made good progress before the storm broke. They are but a few hours ride."

Birdie grinned. "You could have stopped them."

"Of course, but should not Okala have compassion as well? Alive they can tell the story that this fight was not the Indian's fault."

But Okala's hope was never fully realized.

Young Malcolm Hoogh sat inside his sister's wagon

arranging words in his head. The sickly, thin penniless young man had begged his brother-in-law for a place in his wagon as far as the Colorado Territory. A hopeless misfit on the staff of the *San Francisco Chronicle*, he envisioned a better future for himself in booming Denver.

Malcolm's problem was that he dreamed dreams that seemed to find their way into his newspaper accounts. His stories got him into trouble with the publisher because they got the publisher into trouble with the reading public.

But the words Malcolm Hoogh now juggled in his head were destined to find their way into print and be believed as gospel. In ten years, when another uprising would take place on the Milk River, some would proclaim Malcolm Hoogh a prophet for his previous appraisal of the blood-thirsty Utes.

JODY AWOKE to see swaying shadows on a sun-lit canvas above her. She heard Black Mary calling to the horses, heard the slow, regular creak of wagon wheels. She saw that she was in Carrie's bed. Other than that, she might have been waking from a night of dreaming. She rose and peeped out the back of the wagon.

An exquisite scene surprised and enthralled her. She saw a level space, green with long grass, bright with fall wildflowers, bordered by graceful pines reaching up to towering crags, rose and gold in the sunlight.

Eager to get out where she could enjoy an unrestricted view, Jody looked around at her clothes. She had, she saw, been cleaned up and dressed in one of Carrie's nightgowns. How could all of that have taken place without her waking? At last she spied some things laid out on the top of a trunk that she assumed were meant for her. Hurriedly, she dressed.

Among the items was a pair of moccasins. She studied them dubiously for a moment, then finally slipped them on. To her delight, they were warm and tight and made her feet feel as light as air. She grabbed a length of hair ribbon Carrie had left out for her and jumped down from the moving wagon.

The tangy morning air, fragrant with pine and spruce, made her stop a moment and breathe deeply. With a giggle, she took the ribbon and fashioned it into a band about her head like the Indians wore. Now she did look like a little girl, full of life and color and joy. With the borrowed blue flannel shirt and corduroy skirt, the transformation from prim and proper school teacher was complete. She ran lightly to the front of the wagon and climbed up on to the driver's seat.

"God bless us!" Mary Fields grinned broadly. "You sure are a pretty sight."

Impulsively, Jody threw her arms about the woman and hugged her. "I have a feeling I have you to thank for putting me to bed."

"Now, child, Miss Carrie helped. She wanted to put out one of her fancy dresses, but I thought this would be better for traveling."

Jody laughed happily. She stuck out her feet and wiggled them around. "And wherever did you find these moccasins? They're just marvelous!"

Black Mary beamed with pleasure. "The Indian Girls at the mission made a couple dozen for me to sell in Denver. I'm pleased you like them."

It was the kind of thing Jody needed at the moment; it wasn't the time to question her about what had happened the day before.

Unfortunately, not everybody was as tactful and understanding as Mary Fields. Miss Inez came striding back along the line of wagons, saw Jody and scowled angrily.

"Well, young lady, don't you think you might have let me know that you were awake?"

"Yes, ma'am, but I just woke up."

"Get down!" Miss Inez snapped. "I'm not about to run alongside a wagon shouting up at you. Herded along like sheep, we are. Well? Come down. I want to know what those men did to you."

"Yes, ma'am." Jody was appalled. "I mean, no, ma'am, they did nothing to me."

"JoAnn Robb, get down here! Haven't you given me enough trouble?"

Black Mary raised her eyes toward heaven, then focused them on the rear end of the horses, which was exactly what she thought of Inez Robb. The woman had all but refused to help her and Carrie tend to Jody and had scoffed at Black Mary's contention that the girl appeared to be untouched. She had set her mind on the fact that her niece had suffered the worst and nothing was going to change it.

"Must you go on making a fool of yourself?" she said now, as Jody reluctantly joined her. "For God's sake, can't you take my feelings into consideration? Don't you think I worried myself sick over what might be happening to you?"

They did not hear Carrie come up behind them.

"Good morning," she said cheerily to Jody, ignoring Miss Inez. "How was your second time sleeping between silk sheets?"

"If you don't mind!" Miss Inez snapped. "We were having a private conversation!"

"So I heard," Carrie replied coolly. She looked lovely; there was nothing about her to suggest the pain and misery she had recently gone through. "I suppose it's good of you to worry about your niece. The trouble is, my idea of worry just doesn't jibe with yours."

"And I don't recall asking for your opinion!"

"Stop it!" Jody said suddenly. "Right now I don't want to hear or talk about what happened to me." With that, she broke into a shuffling run.

Miss Inez sniffed and turned back toward the oncoming wagons. There was no use wasting her breath, she decided, the way Jody was always siding with the Negroes. She would straighten the girl out once they were back in civilization.

Carrie smiled to herself, then frowned. Up ahead she could see Birdie riding the right point of the train. She automatically assumed that he was the one Jody was running to see. She had experienced a strange feeling of surprise and resentment when she saw the peculiar interest Birdie showed in Jody when he brought her back. He had been the one to lift her off the travois and carry her gently to Carrie's wagon. He hadn't shown that much concern over Carrie; he hadn't brought his bedroll over and slept beside the wagon when she had been so ill.

"Now you stop it," Carrie told herself. "Of course he would be concerned about Jody, being the one who found her."

And Jody, of course, would be grateful to her rescuer, nothing more.

Actually, even Okala had been concerned about the girl. Hadn't the Indians stayed around until Birdie could report on her condition? That was why Carrie had been all but ignored. Birdie hadn't been neglecting her, he had just been very busy. Once they were alone again, things would be different between them. Besides, Carrie thought, smiling to herself, there was another man who was concerned about Jody's welfare. She looked out to the front of the train where Ferris Ferguson was acting as wagonmaster. There was a man whose heart Jody had already captured.

Carrie didn't suspect that there was still one more.

The rider came in fast from the right flank and let out a whoop that stopped Jody short.

"Lord God, are you a beautiful sight!"

Jody shielded her eyes against the sun and then smiled in recognition. "Maxwell Bundy, are you trying to scare me to death?"

As he leaped from the saddle, his eyes roved over her. "That's the last thing I'd want to do. Good Lord, look at you! Who would know you were the same girl that nigger and the Indians brought in here last night?"

"His name is Sergeant Jacobs," she said. "Are you forgetting he saved my life—all of our lives?"

"Boy, are you quick to forget!" he said. "Seems to me I saved your life in the first place."

Jody blushed. "I was thinking about that, too."

"Were you?"

Suddenly, she put out her hand to touch his. He turned his hand over and grasped hers firmly.

"I was scared sick when I heard Larson took off with you."

She laughed nervously. "I didn't feel very good, either."

He did not answer, but he began to increase the pressure on her hand. It frightened her, and she looked into his face; it seemed hard and cruel.

"You're hurting me!"

He let go. "I'm sorry. I didn't mean to do that. I just don't know my own strength." He smiled apologetically.

Jody nodded absently. She was trying to recall what

Max had done to help during the Indian siege and
didn't even remember seeing him, but then she had
been too busy to pay attention to anything but what
she was doing herself.

"I hear Captain Larson is dead." He looked at her
questioningly.

For a moment, her mind went blank. She was being
forced to remember something she was not quite
ready to remember.

"I—I'm not sure."

It wasn't what Max Bundy wanted to hear. He
wanted Larson dead and all suspicions about himself
dead with him.

"That nigger—pardon me, Sergeant Jacobs—wasn't
sure, either. I didn't get a chance to ask Okala. This
Captain Ferguson kept him pretty much to himself,
making peace promises he won't be able to keep
probably. I don't mind an Indian-lover, but that man
is all nigger-lover."

"Max!" Jody gasped. "How can you say such things?"

"With authority," he said. "He knew I knew Okala,
but he sent his sergeant to parley instead."

"Birdie seems to have handled it very well," she said
coldly.

"Birdie?" He glared at her. "My, my, ain't we
chummy."

She wasn't afraid of him, but she was afraid of his
attitude and tried to appease him.

"Max, almost everyone calls him Birdie."

He scowled darkly. "You would say that. All you've
been associating with lately are niggers. Well, that'll
change when we get to the ranch tomorrow."

"The ranch?"

"That's one battle I won with Ferguson. It's the

closest place to give you and Miss Inez a chance to rest up before you go on to Denver."

Jody suddenly wanted to be very rude to him; he was trying to make decisions for her again, just as he had done at the agency compound. He made her feel corralled, like a horse. But all she said was: "I didn't know that you and Captain Ferguson were battling."

"Mainly over you," he lied smoothly. "I wanted to go to Okala for help, and he turned me down. I wanted to form a search party—no dice. I would have gone out alone, but he put a double guard on the horses."

He had carried the lie too far. She was thankful to see the rider approaching; it kept her from having to lie in return and thank him for his concern.

"You left the right flank unguarded, Bundy," Birdie said as he rode up. "The extra livestock have stopped to graze. Keep them moving."

"Look," Max started to protest. "I didn't ask for this—"

"Did any of us?" Birdie cut him short.

With a muttered curse, Max flung himself into the saddle and turned back to round up the stalled horses and mules. Jody started to turn, too.

"Don't go away."

She hesitated; here was the one man she did want to thank and she was suddenly tongue-tied.

"Turn around."

She obeyed.

Birdie was smiling now. "You look a lot better than you did last night."

She met his eyes and blushed. He seemed so enormous, towering above her in the saddle. Had it all been a dream, or had she really leaned against that broad chest and rested her head on that shoulder?

"I feel like a new woman," she said, a little foolishly.

"And look it. I'm glad they didn't put you into one of Carrie Holmes' fancy dresses."

Despite herself, Jody giggled. "How do you know I wouldn't have liked wearing one of them?"

There was so much of Miss Effie in the statement that Birdie sobered. "I guess you would at that, miss. Every woman likes to sometimes, I suppose. Well, I've got to get back."

"Birdie . . ."

He held his horse back. "Yes, miss?"

"I—I just don't know how to thank you."

Birdie had to harden his heart. Yesterday had been a dream; today was reality. Dawn, and Captain Ferguson, had returned him to the life of a soldier and its responsibilities. His concern had to be for the whole wagon train and not just one individual.

"I was doing what the Army pays me to do, miss." Then he added, trying to soften the statement, "But I would have done it without pay."

For a few seconds more, Birdie gazed at her, then he turned to ride back to the point.

Jody watched him ride back and take up his position by the first wagon, alive only to the splendid picture he made on horseback. His coldness was forgotten; she remembered only his soft confession.

Ferris Ferguson made an unintentional blunder that evening. Because of Army policy, he was used to eating alone on bivouac. But the opportunity seemed right to him to share a bit in the limelight of Jody's rescue.

As a married man, however, he felt obligated to include Miss Inez in the dinner invitation. Miss Robb,

who had taken pity on the recently widowed Alice
MacAllister and her children, thought they should be
included in the captain's invitation. That meant that
Alice's brother Malcolm Hoogh had to be included,
too. Since the "white family wagons" had been sharing a common cook fire, Alice MacAllister took it
upon herself to turn it into a potluck supper. Maxwell Bundy automatically invited himself.

It caused an uncomfortable three-way split in the
camp: the blacks, the whites, and the white wagon-
eer-soldiers who considered themselves too good to
eat with one group and were considered not good
enough to eat with the other. It was hard to believe
that twenty-four hours before they had all been ready
to fight and die, side by side.

The evening bored and embarrassed Jody. She was
ashamed that no one seemed to be aware of the
insult they were giving. To hear her group talk, they
had done it all alone. Malcolm Hoogh was all ears.
She thought she would scream if her aunt mentioned
her "honor" one more time, as though discussing it
openly made it gospel. The look on Alice MacAllister's face made her want to vomit. Granted, the
woman was a widow of only three days, but she
was playing her part to the hilt.

Ferris Ferguson was oblivious to it all. He saw and
heard nothing but Jody, cared about nothing except
that she was there.

"You look tired," he told her anxiously. "May I
escort you back to your wagon?"

"We'll do that," Max Bundy said, indicating himself and Miss Inez.

"I'm not ready to go," Miss Inez said bluntly, before Jody could protest and to everyone's surprise.
But no one ever wanted to listen to Miss Inez talk

about her travels, and tonight she had found a good listener in Malcolm Hoogh. She was not about to miss such an opportunity.

"Thank you, Captain," Jody said. "But, frankly, I'm not sure where I'm to sleep tonight."

"All arranged," he told her. "I prevailed upon Miss Carrie to let you have another night of good, sound sleep."

"But that hardly seems fair."

Even as Jody protested, Ferguson guided her away from the glow of the campfire. Max Bundy didn't argue; he had gained valuable information by keeping quiet.

Jody and the captain walked silently back toward the far campfire. There had been no need to circle up the wagons. They were still within Ute territory, and had no fear of Indian attack.

Suddenly, Jody stopped short, looking up at the stars through the dark pines. They seemed so close, so large.

Ferguson misread her reason for stopping. He drew her swiftly into his arms and covered her mouth with his. His kiss was gentle but demanding. It came as such a shock to Jody that at first she made no effort to resist him. His arms were as strong as Birdie's; his scent as masculine and as enticing. It was her first kiss ever and it was exciting. But instinct made her pull away at last and turn toward the safety of the light of the campfire.

She did not recognize Ferguson's voice; it was low and husky and breathless. "I admire you greatly."

She kept walking.

"I want you as a woman. I want you like no woman I've known before."

Jody turned to face him then.

"Is that why you had me rescued?"

He saw then that she was trembling.

"Isn't that reason enough?" His heart began to pound with anticipation.

She walked over to him slowly, deliberately. "By your reasoning, Captain, the prize by rights belongs to Sergeant Birdwell Jacobs."

Ferris staggered back as if she had slapped him. The affront left him speechless. Before he could recover, Jody turned and scrambled up into Carrie's wagon.

"I'm already in bed," Carrie said sourly out of the darkness.

"I'm sorry. The captain said—"

"And now I know why he talked me into it. Hot bastard was after you—and him a married man!"

"Carrie, I didn't—"

"I heard! I got ears! Your cherry rightfully belongs to Sergeant Birdwell Jacobs."

"That's not what I said."

"Don't lie! I don't care! I don't care that you made us all feel like slaves again tonight! It's my bed! That's why I'm sleeping in it! Do what you want with that black stud of yours!"

Jody scrambled down out of the wagon, her mind reeling. She was not surprised that the blacks had sensed the evening's insult, or by Carrie's mistaken jealousy. But she was surprised by one thing Carrie had said: Ferris Ferguson married? It made her feel cheap and used.

She picked up a bedroll and began walking. Suddenly, she just wanted to get away from them all.

7

CARRIE HEARD HIM stealing into the wagon and she smiled wickedly. She was determined to hold her silence and give Birdwell Jacobs the shock of his life. She could picture him as the soft thud of boots hit the planking. Metal scraped on metal as the belt was unbuckled and then there was a soft shush of cotton being drawn across skin. The heavy trousers fell with a whoosh and the legs stepped out of them.

What he wore under the trousers, Carrie couldn't guess, but he seemed to be in no hurry to remove it.

His slowness, his confident approach to the whole matter underscored her conviction that he was there by invitation, a cunning invitation extended by JoAnn Robb and then cleverly masked by allowing Ferris Ferguson to walk her home from the whites' party. But the joke would be on her, Carrie thought grimly. She would let Birdie's anticipation build to a smoldering peak, allow him to crawl between the cool silk sheets, and then she would—Carrie sniffed. Something was wrong with the scenario. Bay rum? Birdie didn't use such stuff. She almost giggled as the man began to slip in beside her.

She would continue the charade. She would give Captain Ferguson—for now she had decided that was who it was—an even greater shock than she had planned for Birdie. She waited, expecting Ferguson to assault her like a soldier, and was prepared to roll away and start screaming her lungs out the moment the man touched her. Help would come in the form of Black Mary, who was asleep under the wagon.

But the man was as slowly deliberate in his approach to her as he had been in the removal of his clothing. She could tell that he lay on his side facing her, could smell the tobacco on his breath. She couldn't recall ever seeing Captain Ferguson smoking.

She waited, wondering if she should scream or not.

Fingers touched her breast like a butterfly landing. Her breath came out with a shudder and the hand stilled. A strange flame ignited in her loins. The fingers again began to explore her breast with gentle probing; the saucy nipple stiffened with passion. Then the rosy peak was eased between warm, moist lips; a tongue flirted over the hardening surface.

Carrie had not been expecting this. She realized that this was the moment to pull away and scream, but a part of her being refused to end the charade. She trembled; he rolled closer. She melted against him, and their mouths met. Instead of being aggressive, he was gentle in building up her desire. Without pressure, he parted her lips and tasted the sweetness of her mouth. Trickles of enjoyment spread through her. He smelled clean and mannish, not rancid like that other ape. He had even shaved for Jody.

Carrie realized that at that moment she was jealous of Jody. Ferguson thought he was in bed with her; he wasn't there for the pleasure of Carrie Holmes.

His tongue and hands grew bolder, and a new thought came to her.

Perhaps it would be old-fashioned for her to scream. If she allowed "that" to happen again, and Ferguson was pleased, then she would be the victor over Jody. She would have stolen Ferguson away from her, just as Jody was trying to steal Birdie.

But it was a fearful thought. What if it caused her to start bleeding again?

Even as she thought this, the man was making his entrance. Surprisingly, it was not painful as before. He gasped out his appreciation. A jarring voluptuous thrill began. His thrusts, the intensity of his pleasure, began to make her dizzy with want. There was a surprising new depth to her sensations; she felt on the edge of something strange and wonderful . . . .

Suddenly, just as she was being transported to an erotic peak, he whispered into her ear:

"Carrie, baby, you really are great!"

She came back to earth, to the bed. He knew! she thought wildly.

"Did you think I was fooled?" He chuckled. "I saw Jody go storming off into the woods with a bedroll. I figured better you than nothing at all."

It was not thrilling now; her plan was turning against her. She was indeed playing second fiddle to Jody. But it was too late to scream; she couldn't pretend rape now. She bit her lip, tears forming in her eyes. To resist could cause more problems; let him finish.

She felt the outpouring of his desire, and he sank down on her, quaking, still stroking . . . .

When he quieted and rolled aside, she scampered out of the bed and began feeling around in the dark for her nightgown and wrapper.

"Nice of you to be prepared," he whispered. "Who were you expecting?"

Carrie shuddered, clutching the wrapper tightly around her. Swiftly, in a series of sudden little remembrances, her nerves exploded. She had made the most horrible mistake of all. Anger built inside her.

"It's time for you to dress and leave, Mister Bundy."

"Tired? Or still expecting someone else?"

"Please," she begged, "you don't understand at all."

He sat up and swung his legs over the side of the bed. "Now the crap comes about not telling anyone, I suppose. Your reputation. Shit, it's my reputation I'm thinking about. My brother Clayton would skin me alive if he knew I'd strapped on a negress. So, when we get to the ranch, your mouth is shut and my mouth is shut, or it won't happen between us again."

She wiped the tears from her eyes, ashamed of them now. She felt a wave of contempt for him, for *all* men. They were so sure of themselves, so confident that women were just there for their taking.

"It won't ever happen between us again," she said.

His only answer was a scornful laugh as he rose and began to dress. She moved as far away from him as possible.

"Remember," he warned. "Not a word to anybody, especially not Jody. The last thing I want is for my future wife to learn I've been screwing black cunt."

Carrie didn't answer. She wanted him gone. She was not what he thought she was. But no amount of words, she was sure, would ever convince him of that. But his words had shocked her in a different way; she had not been aware that he coveted Jody as a wife. Instinctively, she saw it as a mismatch. He was the type of man who would cheat on any woman he married.

But she could not warn Jody about him. Nor was it his own warning that would keep her silent. No, it was her pride that would not let her admit that she had stooped to such dishonor.

The next day, throughout the whole train, the atmosphere was tense. Mary Fields sat on her high perch considering all that was on her mind. What chiefly troubled her were the things she had overheard the night before that she wished she had never heard. She didn't think either Carrie or Jody was right in their quarrel. And her heart had sickened on hearing the bed squeak over her head.

Black Mary wasn't sure when she had been born but guessed her age to be somewhere between forty and fifty. She had never known a man and was Catholic enough to believe a woman shouldn't know a man without the blessing of God. She just didn't understand why Carrie would pull such a stunt, and with a bigot like Maxwell Bundy. But, until her opinion was sought, she would say nothing.

Because Jody and Carrie both steered clear of him, Birdie Jacobs puzzled over what he had done wrong. Maxwell Bundy feigned illness and rode in Alice Mac-Allister's wagon. Carrie Holmes had been his first black woman and with the dawn had come the reaction to what he had done. He felt dirty and afraid, almost as if anyone looking at him could tell the disgusting thing he had done. Not the disgusting thing that he had done to Carrie, but the disgusting thing he had done to himself by lying with her. All the blame, in his mind, was Carrie's for enticing him into her bed. That would be his story if she ever opened her mouth. Anyone looking at her could see what she was. How could he be blamed for giving in to temptation?

And how, Captain Ferguson was wondering, could he make amends for his moment of ungentlemanly weakness? He had behaved like an ass with Jody, and that wasn't like him. He wanted to approach Jody with an apology, and it wasn't like him to keep stalling.

But, he reasoned, the time was not right. He had to be a free man first. He had to be free of the burden of the wagon train and the gold first. And he had to free his heart of the fear that the apology might not be accepted.

He spun his horse around and galloped back to the point, coming to a decision.

"Sergeant Jacobs, we will split the train here. I'll take the main force and wagons on to the fort. You take ten men and the Denver contingent on to the Bundy ranch. Once you get them to Denver, report back to Fort Lyon. You'll have no obligation to protect Miss Robb after that."

The last remark was uncalled for and stunned Birdie. Was this the reason for Jody's coolness towards him? He had seen her and the captain arguing the night before. Could it have been him? Women and white officers were a puzzle to him; friendly as pups one minute and biting your hand the next.

He saluted smartly and rode back down the train to determine whom he would be escorting. When it was learned that he would have only the MacAllister and Holmes wagons, his force was cut to five. To Birdie's amazement, Ferguson gave him five soldiers who were not of his regular patrol. Ferguson thought he was being clever: to keep Weaver's unmilitary-like soldiers in line, Birdie would have to play sergeant the whole way and he would have no time for Jody Robb.

The arrangement was most agreeable to Miss Inez. She could go on riding with Alice MacAllister and not have to delve into what had prompted Jody's black mood that day.

Since they would be able to travel at twice the speed without the heavily laden gold wagons, walking was dispensed with. Everyone had to climb aboard a wagon or get on a horse. Max Bundy was forced out of his "sick-bed" and back to his horse to make room for the MacAllister children. It also meant that Jody and Carrie were forced to ride together whether they liked it or not.

It was a silent, uncomfortable three-hour ride. Not until Max Bundy let out a whoop and galloped on ahead did any of the women aboard Carrie's wagon speak.

"Right pretty place," Black Mary remarked.

Jody looked up. Her tension had eased somewhat during the past hour because Carrie had gone inside the wagon to lie down.

Up ahead, Jody saw green slopes leading down to newly whitewashed barns and shed. Wide corrals stretched high-barred fences down to great fields of purple-blossomed alfalfa. The bottom of a dammed up hollow shone bright with deep blue water upon which thousands of migratory fowl splashed and squawked. The quarters for the bachelor cowboys stood on a long bench of ground above the lake. Back in a pine grove were the shanties, housing for the black and Mexican cowhands and their families.

All that was left of the original Bundy homesite was

the fireplace wall, but around it, over the years, had sprung up a massive structure with wrap-around porches and gothic trim. It was an ugly structure that seemed alien to the land, but it had been Katrin Bundy's dream house. It was all she had out of her unfortunate marriage to Lemanuel Bundy. The young "picture bride" from Minnesota had been saddled from the first day of her arrival with the nursing care of the bedridden Horace Bundy, her father-in-law, and the care and feeding of Lemanuel's younger brothers, Clayton and Maxwell.

For ten years, Katrin was little more than a slave to the four men. Her only solace was a new wing added to the house each winter. Childless, her spare moments, which were few, were spent furnishing the rooms and hand-sewing curtains and drapes.

Horace Bundy had been born on a poor excuse for a farm in Georgia, although he boasted otherwise. Before the riding accident that crippled him, he had dreamed of bringing slaves to the ranch. When the Civil War broke out, he knew that dream would never be fulfilled, and he just closed his eyes and died.

Katrin was probably the only one who grieved for him. Although a tyrant, he had appreciated her many little kindnesses. Lemanuel was too busy running the ranch to hardly know she was alive; Clayton was too busy fighting with his wife Lottie Louise and his four badly spoiled children, and Maxwell was too busy chasing every skirt in the territory. Horace had had no more use for his sons and grandchildren than they had for him.

To quiet Lottie Louise's strident demands after Horace died, it was decided that she and Clayton and their children would move into the main ranch house.

That night Katrin went to sleep for the last time, too.

A Mexican woman was brought in to do the cleaning and cooking. Katrin was not missed at all, though the house never really became Lottie Louise's.

As the wagons approached, the ranchyard quickly filled with shouting children, barking dogs and glad-handing cowhands. Everyone seemed to be glad to see Max except his brother Clayton.

"Why the damn Army and these people?" he demanded, not caring who heard him.

Maxwell tried to explain, at the same time making himself look as good as possible, but the deeper into his story he got, the deeper Clayton scowled.

"Stow it!" he barked finally. "I've been counting on those horses. Get rid of these people so we can talk."

Clayton Bundy was weathered far beyond his thirty years. His stomach burned constantly from an ulcer he didn't know he had, and the pain was reflected in his acid disposition.

"Come on, Clay," his brother said. "We're tired and we haven't had a decent meal in a week."

"That's hardly my concern," Clayton said sourly. "This is not a stage stop!"

"What in hell is all the caterwaulling about?"

Lemanuel Bundy strode out onto the porch, Lottie Louise bouncing along in his wake. They were a comical contrast. Lemanuel was over six feet, but his erect carriage, the sparse flesh on a thin frame and the massive mane of white hair made him seem taller yet. He surveyed the ranchyard scene out of piercing light gray eyes. His pronounced Roman nose looked as if it were sniffing something unpleasant.

Normally, it was: cow manure, nieces and nephews who had never been properly potty-trained, and the stench that emanated from the corpulent person of Lottie Louise—a stench she was unaware of because she had grown accustomed to it as everyone else on the ranch had grown accustomed to her lazy, slovenly ways. She wore the same dress day in and day out until not even the Mexican housekeeper would take it as a gift. She was the first to the table and the last to leave, spending the in-between hours munching on bon bons from Denver and taking long naps.

Nor could Lottie be faulted; she had not always been a four-foot ball of fat weighing nearly two hundred pounds. In 1859, when Clayton had brought her home from Baton Rouge as his bride, she had been a petite southern belle. She had been led to believe that she was marrying into a very rich family. The ranch was a devastating shock to her and her carping began almost at once.

Clayton, Lemanuel and Maxwell tended to spoil and baby her from the first. Horace thought she was a horse's ass. Katrin said nothing; Lottie Louise was just one more person to look after.

But after the birth of Lottie's second child, Horace made Clayton build a house of his own and get a Mexican woman to see to his wife's needs. Katrin was blamed for putting the girl out of the main house and the two women never spoke again.

Now, Lottie Louise was the mistress of the –B– and acted the part to the hilt.

"Why, little brother," she cooed at Max. "Whatever have ya'all been doing? You look simply disgraceful."

Max nearly burst out laughing. Lottie Louise looked as if she had just gotten up from one of her naps, her hair sticking out every which way from under a white cap. The remnants of a dozen meals were evident on the bodice of her gown. But Max was respectful enough to answer his oldest brother first:

"It's a long story, Lemanuel, but these people need food and rest before they go on to Denver."

"Impossible!" Clayton declared.

Lemanuel raised a bony hand for silence. He saw nothing in the request to rile Clayton, but then his brother riled so easily lately. He wasn't sure just what he was going to do about Clayton and Lottie Louise, but that wasn't something he should be considering at the moment.

"I'd like to hear Max's story," he said quietly.

"Soldiers!" Clay hissed vehemently.

Lem Bundy looked blank. All he saw were six black, tired, trail-dusted men.

Except for the uniforms, they could have been some of the nine blacks he employed as cowhands. He didn't fear the Army because he knew nothing about his brother Clayton's illegal agent operation.

"I think I had better wait for Max's story," he said now. "Sergeant, you'll find room for you and your men in the bunkhouse down by the lake. Miss Lottie Louise, tell Carmen to prepare rooms for the ladies."

His sister-in-law gasped in utter dismay. "I'll not be having niggers in my house, Brother Lem!"

There was an embarrassed silence.

Carrie stepped down from her wagon. To sort out her troubled thoughts, she had spent the past hour primping, dressing carefully for the arrival at the ranch. If there was to be a confrontation with Maxwell Bundy, she wanted to look every inch the lady Mammy Pleasant had raised her to be. Her gown of beige crepe was high-necked and long-sleeved, molded discreetly to her high bosom and slim waist. The fabric cascaded into a long train from the high bustle. As she walked with dignified grace, Carrie allowed her straw picture hat to slide back down on her shoulders. She stopped and posed, her hand on her unopened parasol. She appraised Lem Bundy as Mammy Pleasant might have appraised a banker. Carrie liked what she saw; here was a gentleman, and a gentleman would accept what she had to say graciously.

She was aware that everyone was looking at her and that was the way she wanted it.

"Thank you, sir, but no," she said in her voice in flutelike tones. "My wagon will suffice for Miss Mary Fields and myself."

"Damn whore," Max Bundy said under his breath, loud enough to make it a warning to Carrie. She didn't flicker an eyelash. But Jody had heard him, too. "Max! How dare you say such a thing?"

She looked to Birdie for help, but he refused to meet her gaze. Mary Fields fumed, but knew any word from her wouldn't help much.

"I'm sorry, sir. I can't stand by and let your brother insult Miss Holmes that way. I'll stay with her and Miss Fields, if they'll have me!"

"JoAnn!" Miss Inez gasped. "I forbid you to do anything of the kind. I—"

Without warning, Black Mary now took matters into her own hands. She clucked the team into motion, calling down to Carrie. "I think the lakeside would be nice, Miss Carrie. I'll have a fire going by the time you walk down."

Miss Inez scrambled down from the MacAllister wagon. She stormed up to Lem with fire in her eyes.

"Sir, if you are a gentleman, you will put a stop to this nightmare. These Negroes have been all but running our lives. They practice voodoo, and I am sure now that they have my niece under some kind of spell!"

Lem looked to Max for an introduction.

"Lem, this is Miss Inez Robb. She was the school teacher at the Indian agency."

"Well, Miss Robb," Lem said smoothly, "may I escort you into the house? It's much cooler there, and I have a feeling I have a lot to hear about. A few more minutes can't do your niece much harm, now can it?"

Miss Inez gave in. It was so comforting to be around a reasonable human being once again. She would just put everything into this man's capable hands.

"My gawd!" Lottie Louise said now. "That woman's got children!" She was gaping at the Widow Mac-Allister's brood.

Lem laughed. "A few more hellions added to your own won't make that much difference, Miss Lottie Louise. Now, how many extra will we be for dinner?"

Pouting, Lottie began counting with a pudgy finger.

Max rudely pointed out the bunkhouse to Birdie and then quickly pulled his brother Clayton aside.

"Look, Clay, I had no choice but to bring them here. That Captain Ferguson ordered it while he took the gold on to Rawlins."

"The *what*?"

"About thirty wagon loads of gold," Max said stupidly.

"Max, you were born with your brain in the wrong end. Here we are messing around with penny ante stuff, and you stumble on a find like that and just about forget to mention it!"

"I didn't think, Clay."

"As usual," his brother sneered. "Get your ass up the mountain and find Jeeter. Tell him what you know and then have him ride hard for Hole-in-the-Wall. They might be able to catch up with that wagon train before it gets to the fort. Jesus! I wonder how much gold thirty wagons can carry?"

"I heard tell it was about twenty million."

Clay held his brother with a hard gaze. "Boy, don't you ever again call somebody a whore when you got nothing but shit for brains."

Jody walked down to the lake and sat down on a flat rock. She knew she was in serious trouble with her aunt. She had never really defied Inez before; it had been a question of survival. Though it had not been discussed, Jody assumed that they would be returning East, now. It was too bad; she had rather enjoyed her short journey into a new and exciting world.

Something tapped on the rock. Jody looked up and saw Carrie leaning on her parasol. "May I join you?"

Jody shrugged. "If you wish."

"I wish very much," Carrie said, kicking back her train and sitting down on her bustle as if it were a pillow. "I want to thank you for coming to my defense."

"I thought Max's comment was uncalled for."

"Perhaps he had reason."

"What reason?" Jody said, surprised.

Now it was Carrie's turn to shrug her shoulders. "Did you know he plans to make you his wife?"

"His wife?" Jody's face was filled with astonishment. "Why ever would he discuss such a thing with you?"

Carrie sighed. She was determined to tell Jody everything, no matter how embarrassing it would be.

"I'll come to that, Jody. It may take me a little

time to find the right words to describe what my feelings were last night and what they were a few moments ago. What Max Bundy said didn't hurt me. I've seen his type before in San Francisco, and believe me, he's not the right man for you."

Jody was bewildered, and suddenly, furious. What right did Carrie Holmes have to pass judgment on every man who came into Jody's life?

"Why not?" she said icily. "Is Max married, or black?"

Carrie winced. "I deserved that," she said slowly. "I deserve a lot more than that. Last night I thought Birdie would come to you, thinking you were in my bed. We don't need to go into why I did, but . . . Anyway, Birdie didn't show up, but another man did. I thought it was Captain Ferguson, it was too dark to know different, and I aimed to hurt you by stealing him away."

"Carrie!" Jody stared at her. "You knew I had no interest in him!"

Carrie smiled. "You will learn, Jody, that a woman isn't rational when she's jealous. I was going to let the man undress and try to seduce me, then scream for help to embarrass him and you."

"I didn't hear any scream."

Carrie leaned forward suddenly, all her ladylike dignity gone.

"There wasn't any. I let him. It was gentle and different, and I began to enjoy—"

"Carrie," Jody whispered. "You don't have to go on. I think I know. It was Max Bundy, wasn't it?"

Carrie was on her feet now. In a gesture that was both absurd and touching, she dropped to her knees and clutched Jody's hand.

"But I must go on! You see, Max saw you go

into the woods carrying a bedroll. He knew I was the one in the wagon. He knew I was in that bed. He . . . he said that I was better than nothing at all. That's when he told me he didn't want his future wife, you, to know he had gone to bed with a black woman."

Carrie scrambled to her feet. Now that it had all been said, she feared Jody's reaction.

"I don't understand now, Carrie. Did you let him, well, go ahead because he said he wanted to marry me?"

"Good God, no! I didn't know that until after I—" Carrie stopped suddenly. Nothing sounded right.

"Don't let Max know I told you," she finally said, lamely.

"Of course I won't," Jody said. "But there's somebody else who must not know."

"You mean Birdie?" Carrie said. "In time he would have to know, Jody. I couldn't become his woman under false pretenses. He knows I'm not a virgin because of the rape. He would have to know that I am not pure either."

"You said it yourself, Carrie. In time. This is not the time. When we are away from here will be soon enough."

When we are away from here, Jody thought. It sounded so simple on the face of it. When she was away from there she would also be away from their world, which was how it should be. Carrie and Birdie were of the same world; she was not. She wasn't even of Max's world and didn't want to be. Only . . .

Birdie just had to come into view and the wild sweet madness stirred in her. He could look at her casually, his thoughts on something else, and she could think only of his tenderness, his warmth, his caring. It was like that. But it couldn't be. When she was away from him she would just have to forget.

"Evening, ladies. Wagon Tom Smithson is the name, and blacksmithin' is my game. The Bundys ain't needin', so I cowhand for my feedin', and feedin' is why I'm here. Carmen sent me down with some vittles from the kitchen."

Wagon Tom was no ordinary man, anyone could see that at a glance. But it was not his singsong patter or his hulking barrel chest that set him apart; Wagon Tom was as black as a starless night and he made Mary Fields look like a dwarf by comparison. His log-sized arms were laden now with a load it would normally require two men to carry.

"Now, ladies, you am starin' at Wagon Tom. Ain't you seen a pure black African 'fore?"

"Well, I—" Mary Fields began.

He tilted his massive bullet-shaped head back and roared. "An' dey call you Black Mary. Why, woman, I'se so black I gotta smile on a moonless night so folk can see where I standin'."

"How did you know my name?" she asked.

"How'd I know?" he said with mock surprise. "I ain't color blind. You am a mite black, as she am a mite chocolate and she am a right high yellow. Jes' like dat MacAllister boy done said."

This brought a giggle from Carrie. "Jody isn't one of us."

Wagon Tom rolled his saucer eyes. "Now, why'd that boy say she sang and danced like she was right from de Congo?"

The three women looked at each other and burst out laughing.

"Oh, that Tim MacAllister!" Jody shook her head. "He thought the whole thing was a game."

Wagon Tom grinned, showing two oddly spaced gold teeth. "You shore am a *Jeanne d' Arc* to him."

The French pronunciation was perfect and Jody blinked. Wagon Tom was quick to see her reaction, as he was quick to see many things.

"I be Haitian first, Miss Robb. Brought to Texas when I was speakin' nothin' but French." Then his huge body shook with laughter. "Now I speak pure cowboy."

"Taught by the devil that resides in you," Black Mary teased. "Can I give you a hand with those vittles?"

"Careful there, woman. This be dinner for ten and not just for you."

Black Mary cuffed him playfully on the chin and helped him unload. "Ten?"

"I be going for the soldiers now."

"But that's six and we're three."

"And I be one. Would you be denying Wagon Tom the pleasure of supping with real females for a change? Especially when they're as pretty as you three?"

"Get along with you, big mouth," Mary said. "I old enough to be your mother and these two—"

"These two be sunrise and sunset," Wagon Tom said. "And sunrise is wanted at the table in the main house." He paused, then grinned. "I didn't know till that Miss Robb up at the house said so, that ya'all are a bunch of cannibals."

Jody couldn't help but laugh. "Then I guess that means I eat here."

Wagon Tom hunched his neck down into his broad

shoulders. "Lucky fer me dat Mister Lem ain't got a pot big enough ta boil me in."

"Oh, you fool!" Black Mary chuckled. "Go fetch the soldiers and I'll lay this stuff out."

Wagon Tom started off at a trot and then stopped. He had forgotten to give Jody Robb two other messages. He started to turn back, then decided they could wait until he got back with the soldiers.

Miss Inez felt like a new woman. It seemed as if tons of dirt and grime had been washed out of her hair and off her skin, and she had luxuriated for almost an hour in the tin tub.

To the amazement of all, Lem Bundy had changed Carmen's room assignments, and Miss Inez was given Katrin's old room which had not been occupied since her death, and told to avail herself of any of the clothing stored in the chests and clothespresses, with the apology that they might be old-fashioned.

To the frugal Miss Robb they were hardly old-fashioned. Each garment had been carefully wrapped in tissue paper, and many looked as if they had never been worn.

Inez Robb felt like a princess, able to pick and choose at will. Still, she chose simply: a gingham print of dainty yellow flowers on a field of white. But in the full-length mirror the image was not right. From the neck up she was as stern and forbidding as ever; from the neck down she was as slim and trim as a girl.

For a brief moment she encountered her own eyes in the mirror. Cold and harsh. Without thinking, she raised her hands and undid the bun that held her hair in place. When she was a girl, her hair had hung loosely about her shoulders, because that had been her father's wish. She was twenty when he died unexpectedly. She had stood beside his bier, too stunned as yet to grieve.

"Inez," her brother Hiram had hissed at her. "Are you insane? Go pin up your hair before the mourners arrive. Do you want them to think you don't care?"

And Inez had obeyed. Hiram was now the head of the family. Her hair had not been down since, except when she washed it.

A tug from beyond the grave seemed to release her. Her fingers flew to the pins, loosening them and letting her dark, gray-streaked hair fall down her back. Her breath came out of her with a shudder of relief. She stood quite still, her long hands hanging limply at her sides, the palms turned childishly forward. She was still quite an attractive woman.

Alice MacAllister was considering the future, not the past. Her two youngest daughters lay ill with a fever in the huge four-poster bed, but that was not her main concern.

By careful questioning, she had learned that Lemanuel Bundy was a widower and childless. She was a widow with four children. He was in his fifties; she was about to turn forty. He was a settled, successful rancher; she was unsettled and homeless.

Love was immaterial. She had married Sean MacAllister to escape the Irish slums of Boston. She had followed his wild quest to California in search of gold. All he had given her, in twenty years of marriage, had been four widely spaced children—widely spaced because she sometimes did not see him for two or three years at a time. She had been mother and father to them for so long that they were hardly aware as yet that Sean had been killed by the Utes.

But all that would change. She would snag Lem Bundy for a husband or know the reason why.

Jody literally bubbled with happiness. It was for her a remarkable evening. Taught that it was unladylike to laugh aloud, she hardly stopped laughing.

After everyone had eaten, banjos appeared from nowhere and one of the soldiers brought out a Jew's-harp. The music brought the cowboys over from the bunkhouse and the married families from their shanties in the pines.

The children present delighted at Black Mary's rich alto voice. They laughed until they cried at the antics and stories of Wagon Tom. This encouraged others to join the story-telling.

One broad-chested heavy-thighed cowboy who had swapped life as a sailor for a horse and the plains sang an old sea chantey rewritten to fit his new life-style:

> *O, bury me not on the lone prairee*
> *Where the wild coyotes will howl over*
> *me . . . .*

Then they began dancing, wild and carefree and exuberant. It didn't matter that the ratio was three men for every woman; Wagon Tom borrowed an apron from one of the cowboy's wives and didn't miss a single dance.

Jody protested that she didn't know how to dance, but they soon made sure that she learned. Black Mary was amazingly light on her feet and tired out more than one soldier and cowhand. Birdie hung back shyly until Carrie pulled him into the circle of dancers, then she proceeded to monopolize him. Jody didn't mind; she was having too much fun to feel anything but happiness.

The music stopped abruptly. Max Bundy strode into the camp and confronted Wagon Tom.

"I guess you don't give messages too good, boy."

The big man hung his head sheepishly. "I plumb fergot, Mister Max."

Max looked around. Except for Jody, he was surrounded by black faces, which was what he pretty much expected. The white cowboys on the -B- didn't mix too well with the blacks, and the Mexicans clung together in their own tight little group.

He looked back at Wagon Tom. "Rocky White didn't show up for work again. You got such a lousy memory, you can just go ride night patrol for him." Max turned now to Jody. "The messages were for you. Come with me."

Her impulse was to refuse such an authoritarian demand, but she did not want an argument to spoil the evening for everyone else. She turned and marched smartly toward the trees that masked the main house. But once out of earshot, she stopped and waited for Max to catch up with her.

"Well, what are the messages?"

"It's a little late for one of them," Max said. "You're aunt wanted you to know she'd found a dress you could wear to dinner. But you decided to insult us and stay here with the niggers."

"I don't care to go into who insulted who," she said calmly. "What are the other messages?"

"There is only one more. The MacAllister kids are all coming down sick with the fever. Miss Lottie Louise ain't good with sick people of any age. Miss

Inez says you were always good with the kids at the school."

Jody saw it as a scheme to get her away from Carrie and the others. "What about Alice MacAllister?"

"Frankly, she's too busy making mooneyes at my brother Lem to worry about them."

"Then why should I?" Jody demanded.

"What's gotten into you?" he said, looking at her in surprise. "You've changed and I don't think I like it."

"Nothing has gotten into me, Max, and who hasn't been changed by all that has happened? But for your information, I wasn't about to go up to the house after the way you treated Carrie Holmes!"

She saw his mouth tighten; saw the flicker of fear in his eyes. He leaned toward her.

"What kind of lies has she been telling you?"

She realized he'd misunderstood her and, not wanting to give away how much she did know, said quickly, keeping her voice light:

"Well, Mister Maxwell Bundy, is it a lie that you have designs on making me your wife?"

"Is that *all* she told you?" He eyed her suspiciously.

"Nice girls don't tell the secrets they share."

"Nice girls don't associate with niggers! I'm going to get you away from them if it takes killing every last one of them!"

"Max!" Jody was horrified. "How could you even think such a thing? You can't mean—"

"I hate the black bastards," he growled. "You don't know them like I do. Give them the chance they'll rape you. That's all those animals ever think about."

Jody shook her head. "Don't some white men think the same way?"

She knows, he thought with a feeling of panic. Now he would have to kill every last one of them. But for now he'd bluff it out. He leaned back and laughed aloud.

"That's what *they* want you to think. But white gentlemen save themselves for their wives-to-be, like I've saved myself for you, Jody."

Jody bowed her head. She could never forgive such a brazen lie.

"It's not the proper time," she said, "but you should know straight out—I could never marry you."

It didn't shock him; he thought he knew the reason why. To argue with her would only bring the truth out into the open, and that he didn't want. No, he'd keep his temper and handle the matter another way.

"I've got to get back to the house," he said calmly, surprising her. "I won't try to talk you into coming with me." He leaned forward and kissed her once, lightly, then went on through the trees toward the main house.

Jody stood quite still, her blue eyes thoughtful. Then, very softly, she began to laugh.

"He's up to no good," she said aloud.

Behind her, someone clapped softly, mockingly three times. "That, my dear, is a shrewd appraisal of Mister Maxwell Bundy."

Jody spun about. Less than a stone's throw away, a thin, angular man sat leaning against a tree, his feet propped up on a fallen log. A badly weathered hat had been pushed to the back of his head, revealing straw-blond hair. Nestled in his lap was a clay whisky jug.

"Have you been spying on us?" Jody demanded.

"As the empty half of this jug might testify, I have been here for some time and, therefore, you and Maxie-boy were the intruders."

"You might at least have made your presence known."

"Why, dear lass? I was far too comfortable and, besides, I found your conversation to be most informative!"

"Oh, you are a bounder!"

That made him laugh. "That is kind compared to what I am usually called." Then his laughter converted into a convulsive fit of coughing that doubled him over.

Jody forgot her annoyance and ran to him.

"Are you all right? Is there anything I can do?"

He shook his head and at last the coughing stopped and he straightened up again. "The only help you could give me is a new pair of lungs. Mine seem to have stayed too long in the stinking air of Birmingham."

"I know you," Jody said suddenly. "You were in the ranchyard when we arrived today. I remember because you looked so amused by it all." Then another thought struck her. "I bet you're the disappearing cowboy, Rocky White."

"Good God, the woman is a barrister and right on all accounts. I was amused. Everything Maxie-boy does amuses me, he's such an insufferable ass. And I stand guilty before the bar for being a laggard. But why not? The entertainment below was far more rewarding."

"Then why didn't you come and join in?"

"And ruin it, as Max has done? Look, my dear, the fire dies, the banjos no longer strum, the feet no

longer dance, the songs are stilled and the children
are in bed. The Bundy plague has struck like a swarm
of locusts."

Jody sat down on the log. This, too, was no ordinary man. His accent was that of an educated Englishman, his voice unexpectedly deep. She glanced
down at his hands; they were clean, smooth, long-
fingered; hardly typical of a hard-working cowhand.
What in the world was he doing here?

Bowing his head slightly, he said, "But I am remiss
in my duties. I am aware, thanks to several overheard
conversations, that you are Miss JoAnn Robb, sometimes called Jody. And you, barrister, have surmised
that I go by the rather colorful title of Rocky White.
We are now properly introduced."

Jody giggled. "It does seem an odd name for you."

He looked at her hard for a moment and then his
glance softened. "How does Throckton Brough-White
the Third strike you?"

"As very pompous." She laughed.

"Exactly, but quite proper back home in England.
As a remittance man, I thought it best to reduce it
to Rocky White."

"Remittance man?"

He grinned and for the first time his thin face showed
some animation. "My dear Miss Robb, you are obviously ignorant of the more subtle code of the law
of the West. A man's past is past tense, not to be
questioned in the present. But there is an older law
which states that when you hold the secret of another,
you must share with him a secret equal to it, so both
of you will keep silent."

"And what secret do you think you know about
me?"

"Not you so much, my dear, as Maxie-boy. You were wise to decline his rather altar-boyish marriage proposal. He fears you, my dear. I can only assume that he has been straying out of bounds with that very attractive Negress and naturally wants to keep it hidden under the old bushel, so to speak."

Jody was surprised that he was able to put two and two together so easily. She found that disturbing—not because of herself but because of Carrie. Would Rocky White remain a gentleman and keep his assumptions a secret?

"And what is your secret?" she asked gravely.

Rocky White laughed. "I say, for not calling me a cad and pretending you don't have any idea what I am talking about, I shall gladly share with you what Lemanuel Bundy knows. A remittance man, Miss Robb, is a kind of leech, one of that bizarre lot of Englishmen who have been sent away from home and family for a variety of reasons. Once upon a time, we were shipped off to India and the army, but good Queen Vicky learned that too much of the amoral could be indulged in in that exotic land and decided that the punishment was far too rewarding for the crime."

He paused. "Crime? Perhaps too harsh a word except in the family circle. And the family circle is the sole judge and jury for our banishment. We do not ask to be born the ne'er-do-well offspring of titled fathers. We are remiss in playing too hard, studying too little and producing progeny that were too far removed to ever be considered acceptable, even by marriage. So, we are banished to the plains and mountains of the colonies with regular remittance payments to keep us away until we either disappear or straighten up for an honorable return home."

"The punishment certainly doesn't seem to fit the crime."

"Ah, had you been my barrister I might indeed have become the tenth Earl of Dunwatty."

Jody's eyes widened. "Are you serious?"

He laughed. "There is one minor problem, my dear. I must first outlive the ninth Earl, my father. Since he is but forty-eight and in excellent health, the chance is quite remote. I am doomed to the life of a cowboy."

"If you don't get fired for disappearing too often."

He chuckled. "There are two sides to the remittance man coin, Miss Robb. Not only am I paid to stay away, but Lem Bundy is paid to keep me away. If I do not wish to work, there is little he can do about it. But, now, the fire is very low and the camp almost asleep. Your company has been charming, but I think it's time for you to get back before someone decides to worry about you, and time for me to reacquaint myself with this jug."

Jody walked away, thinking how cruel Rocky White's family was. It never occurred to her that she was little more than a remittance child herself.

The wagon was empty when Jody got back, but a bedroll had been prepared for her on the floor. She felt a pang of jealousy, knowing that Carrie and Birdie must be together, but she refused to think about it. The day had been too long and filled with too much. Stretching out on the bedroll, she was soon asleep.

She didn't hear Carrie come in a few minutes later and throw herself into bed, mad as a hornet. She was frustrated and angry with herself and Birdie. They had walked all around the lake. They had not held hands; they had not kissed; they had hardly even talked. What talk there had been had revolved around Birdie—his Army life, his desire to find his mother and bring her west, his plans for his future.

Those plans didn't mesh with Carrie's plans. She had no desire to be an Army wife. She had no desire to live with an illiterate mother-in-law. She had her own plans for Birdie's future, and those plans meant San Francisco.

When Max Bundy got back to the main house after leaving Jody, he found his brother Lem and Miss Inez on the porch, talking softly. He paused, listening. Miss Inez was telling him about her travels in Europe. She stopped abruptly when Max started up the steps.

"Go on," he said. "I liked what you were saying. I mean, it's like you—cultured and refined."

"And where is my cultured and refined niece?" she asked tartly.

"Now don't get riled, Miss Robb. But I realized something in talking to Jody just now. She's been through a lot with these people and she's become friends with them. I hated to ruin their last evening together."

Lem Bundy raised his eyebrows, aware that Max was up to something.

"Hardly the last evening, Mister Bundy. We must venture on to Denver with them," Inez pointed out.

"Well now," Max said. "I've been giving that a lot of thought. It seems to me you're out of a teaching job."

"Only temporarily, Maxwell. I intend to remedy that situation the moment I return to New England."

"But why return?"

"My dear young man, I am an unmarried woman who must earn her own living."

"My point, exactly. We are forty some miles from the nearest school and my niece and nephew are prime for a bit of education, not to mention Josh Henry and Lonnie Stillwell's kids. That makes a total of twelve right there. What do you say, Lem? Can't we afford a couple of school marms for those kids?"

Lem pursed his lips. He knew Max was thinking about himself, not Miss Robb. "It's something to sleep on," he said dryly.

"Come on, Lem. Don't make this one of your stall jobs. They're leaving in the morning, remember?"

"Which gives me plenty of time to sleep on it. Miss Robb, may I escort you to the door of your room?"

Miss Inez nodded, rose and took his arm. It was something for her to sleep on, too. Neither man, she noticed, had bothered to ask if she would even be interested in such a proposition. She blamed Max for that. In her opinion, it should have been discussed privately by the brothers first. Then Lem, being the oldest, could have approached her properly.

Her heart had gone out to the man that evening. Miss Lottie Louise had behaved worse than a pig at the dinner table, cramming her mouth full and then carping about the sick MacAllister children. Miss Inez had been mortified that Jody had not seen fit to come back to the house to help with the children. She hadn't known, of course, that Wagon Tom never delivered the message.

Clayton and Maxwell Bundy hadn't helped matters, either. They sat pouting, hunched over their plates, silently shoveling food into their mouths.

Alice MacAllister had made up for their lack of conversation. She was, in fact, all of the conversation. She flirted so openly with Lem Bundy that Miss Inez was embarrassed for her and her admiration for her host grew. He was gracious, polite, and handled Alice as if unaware of the spectacle she was making of herself. But he was quite firm when, after dinner, he suggested to Alice that it was time for her to look in on her sick daughters. For the rest of the evening, Lemanuel Bundy concentrated his full attention on Miss Inez.

Now, standing in front of the door to Katrin's old room, Miss Inez suddenly realized that the man wished to kiss her. No man had ever wanted to kiss her before, except her father. She had never desired a man to kiss her before. But now she wanted it more than anything else in the world.

A high-pitched wailing erupted from the MacAllister room, freezing them in place. Miss Inez felt extremely silly, because she had begun to pucker her lips and lean forward. She almost lost her balance.

A mountain of flannel nightgown sailed into the hall. Miss Lottie Louise looked as if she had just seen a ghost.

"Lemanuel, oh, Brother Lemanuel," she cried. "They got the measles!"

"Good God!" Lem Bundy went as pale as his sister-in-law.

He had been a young man, Maxwell only two, when an epidemic of measles had spread from plantation to plantation, farm to farm in south Georgia. Thousands succumbed and the fever killed before it broke. Because slaves were chattel, the death toll forced many into bankruptcy, among them Horace Bundy. But his worst loss was his first wife, a baby son and three daughters.

The word measles brought dread to any Bundy, and what they knew of the disease was still housed in superstition.

"Open the windows! Get wet sheets to wrap them in. Go get everyone to carry out that furniture and burn it!"

"No!" Miss Inez shouted. "That's all wrong, Mister Bundy. Measles are not the plague, sir. I have handled many cases in the schools where I have taught and I should know. Keep that room closed and dark. Extra bedding is needed to keep them warm and break the fever. Above all, no one already exposed must leave this house."

"But we'll need help to keep it from spreading!" Bundy protested.

"No," Inez Robb said softly. "They would only help to spread it more. We must quarantine the house. The children will likely all catch it. But if watched carefully, they will be alright. I myself have had the measles, but what about the other adults?"

"My brothers and I have been through this before."

"I feel faint!" Miss Lottie Louise cried.

"Then go to bed," Inez Robb said sternly, knowing the woman would be of no help anyway.

"What about getting your niece to help?" Lem asked, looking anxious.

Miss Inez shook her head reluctantly. "I am afraid she has never had the measles. It would be wrong to expose her to it for help and possibly end up with another patient on our hands. We shall just have to handle this together, Mister Bundy."

"I am your willing servant, Miss Robb."

8

THE DEATH of Miss Lottie Louise shook everyone. She had been the mistress of the ranch, after all, no matter how poorly she had done her job, and she was still young. Hearts went out to Clayton Bundy in his grief.

Only Maxwell Bundy knew that his brother's grief was not for his wife. Jester Longbough was dead, too. Fear had kept his son Harvey holed-up in the Wyoming mountains for ten days, ten days during which Clay thought he had been double-crossed, ten days during which Miss Lottie Louise's fever continued to climb and her children took sick.

Miss Inez tried to explain to Lem that the measles were not the sole cause of Lottie's death. Her heart, weakened by all the weight she carried, had not been strong enough to handle the stress of fever, too. Lem really grieved. Clay took her death stoically. It was a relationship that had ceased to have meaning for him. His wife did not really belong to him anymore. She was Lem's sister-in-law; she was the mistress of Lem's house.

Then Harvey rode in looking like the wrath of God. "Paw's dead."

"How?" Clay demanded.

"Troops showed up from the fort just as we were attacking the wagon train. We got fourteen dead, Clay, besides Paw."

Clay, glaring at his brother Max, thought savagely that it was just like him to forget that the wagon train had sent for reinforcements. It would take Clay at least a year to bring a gang like Jeeters' together again. He just couldn't afford to wait that long.

He turned back to twenty-year-old Harvey Longbough. "Start recruiting. You'll just have to act like your paw."

The way he said it made young Harvey feel proud. "Yes, sir! How many men should I get?"

"As many as you can trust and who will trust you. Meaning no disrespect for the dead, but your paw was as conservative as my brother Lem and as foolish as my brother Max. I want young men who wear no other man's brand. I want men who don't have wives and children."

"What about the women we already got at the Hole?"

"Let 'em become whores!"

Max sheepishly approached Clay after Harvey rode off again.

"Everybody figured the Indians killed Billy Joe. We gave up any hope having the troops come to help us."

Clay's face was black with suppressed rage. "You might have at least told me that much. Now I've got to depend on Harvey, who's just a kid. I want you to go up there in a few days and see how he's doing."

"Clay," Max protested, "I can't do that. I've got plans. I'm going to get married."

Clay sucked in his breath. He seemed to collapse into himself and his eyes narrowed, but he started to grin.

"Who do you think will marry you?"

Max grinned back. "That niece of Miss Inez's, JoAnn Robb. I ain't been able to see her because of this measles thing, but I want the wedding to be right soon."

"Well, it won't be."

Max flinched from his brother's cold stare, then he stared back defiantly. "Why won't it?"

"Stupid. Women want to know everything their men are doing. We are free of Miss Lottie Louise, Max. We don't have to sneak ten head into the herd here and twenty head there. If we're careful, we can start replacing Lem's cowhands with our own. We can't afford to have a nosy woman around and that's final."

Maxwell Bundy didn't have many convictions, but one of them was his brother Clay always was right—though he was also annoyed with Clay for comparing Jody with Miss Lottie Louise.

Still, he was glad that he hadn't mentioned anything about the school. That might keep the women around long enough for Clay to cool down and change his mind.

He had no idea how determined Clay was that his little brother wouldn't foul him up again.

The death of Miss Lottie Louise made up Lem's mind about the school. He would need a woman about the place now and not just to see to the children. In the past ten days, his admiration for Miss Inez had mounted. She had been in a situation she could understand and handled it expertly, stepping in after Lottie died as if she had always been there running the house. Lem Bundy wanted to keep it that way, but he had serious reservations about the niece.

His way of running the ranch included a loyal spy system. Confined to the house as errand boy and nurse, he had relied heavily upon this system. He was not pleased with the reports he received about Miss Jody Robb. He had seen the wisdom of keeping the soldiers and the rest of the Denver-bound party at the ranch to see if any of them had been infected by the MacAllister children. None had, and now Lem decided it was time for them to go.

Coming down the stairs, the first person he saw was Clay returning from his talk with Max.

"What's wrong?" Lem asked, seeing the dark look on Clem's face.

"I just got word that Jeeter Longbough is dead."

Lem sighed. "Then it's over. You don't know how glad that makes me, Clay. I lay awake nights worrying about our association with him."

His brother stared at him. "You knew about it?"

Lem nodded. "Look, Clay, what we did in the past we did for a cause. Horses and beef for the Confederacy and Quantrill's Raiders was our part of the war effort, and I'll admit we couldn't have done it without Jeeter and his boys. Buying a few head of Jeeter's rustled cattle now, well, I overlooked because I thought we owed it to him. But the war's been over a long time, and now, thank God, Jeeter is beyond any obligation of ours. We've got to start thinking about the real prosperity of this ranch and the future of your children. I don't look to Max to have any so the ranch will be theirs some day."

It was a staggering prospect for Clay Bundy; he had never thought that far ahead.

"You're sure Max isn't going to get married and raise a family?"

"Yes," Lem said simply, "I am."

"I'm not. He's got his eye on that Jody Robb."

"The fool!" Lem shook his head. "Can't he see what she is? Clay, that woman is the worst sort of abolitionist. She's been poking around the colored quarters telling them they're still little better than slaves. She's got Wagon Tom thinking we should set up a smithy shop for him."

"Oh, my God!" Clay said. But his worry was slightly different from Lem's; he wanted to keep the black cowboys ignorant about the work they did. No matter what Lem said, he was not about to give up his rustled steers, and the blacks, at least until he could replace them, were important to his schemes. "We've got to get rid of her, Lem."

"Yes, but that may be difficult." He hesitated, then decided it would be best to tell Clay now what he had in mind. "I've asked Miss Inez to stay and set up a school for the kids."

"You've what?" Clay shouted. "Then that means her nosy niece will stick around and we'll have nothing but trouble."

"I don't think so," Lem said quietly. "I've learned a lot about Miss Inez these past days. The niece has always been a stone about the woman's neck. And she doesn't like the girl's messing with the blacks any more than we do. We can work it so Miss Inez sends her away and not us."

"How will you do that?" Clay didn't even like the

idea of Miss Inez staying around, but he had to admit she didn't let his young hellions get away with a thing.

"Leave it to me," Lem said. "After tonight, Miss JoAnn Robb will cause us no more trouble. . . ."

Max Bundy had overheard most of this conversation. Now he leaned back against the porch wall and laughed to himself. They thought he was dumb, but they had given him an idea. If Jody were to get pregnant, his child, there would be nothing they could do. They would have to let him marry her then.

The delay had seemed foolish to Carrie, and with each passing day, more so. She had begun to feel impatient about completing her business for Mammy Pleasant. Her impatience increased as her interest in Birdie waned. He and the other blacks here had all been born slaves, something she had never been. It was part of them as much as her being used to having money was part of her.

She had come to hate the nightly singing and dancing. The screaming play of the children set her nerves on edge. She had refused every invitation to visit the shanties, because their occupant's clothing was enough squalor for her to view.

This was not her world; this world was dull and drab and she was used to color and brightness. She felt listless and alien. She did not realize it, but she was suffering from a good old-fashioned case of homesickness.

The days had not been dull and drab for Jody. At first, she felt guilty that she couldn't help with the sick, but she understood why she must keep away. Her days and evenings were filled with activity and new adventures. The nightly singing and dancing was an education, and she would join the children at play. She had never played as a child. She felt obligated to accept the timidly extended invitations and did not see the shanties as squalid. Though much too small, they were clean and tidy. She thought the families deserved better and said so.

It was not her world either, but she was made to feel welcome. There was none of the fear she had experienced with the Indians. She even became friendly with the Mexican women and children. Jody didn't realize it, but she was rapidly maturing into a lovely, understanding young woman. She wasn't homesick because there was no home to be homesick for.

Sergeant Birdwell Jacobs had mixed emotions about the delay. A poll of his five soldiers showed that none of them had ever been exposed to measles, so he cautiously decided to wait. He could justify the delay in another way: it allowed him to get a good firsthand look at the –B– ranch operation. The black cowhands had no reason to suspect his questions, because he kept them simple and didn't probe too deeply with any one of them. He steered clear of the white cowboys, and found the Mexicans to be very close-mouthed.

But from bits and pieces he picked up, an outline began forming in his mind. Seventeen cowhands— nine black, four Mexican and four white. There were two married men in each group; none of them the sort of men he could picture rustling cattle or stealing horses. The married whites were immigrants. They, like the married blacks and Mexicans, seemed to admire and respect Lemanuel Bundy, but not his brothers.

Five of the unmarried blacks, in Birdie's opinion, seemed too dumb to know what was going on. That

left Wagon Tom and Ladlo Thompson, and he immediately eliminated Wagon Tom. He also eliminated
Rocky White. That left four men Birdie considered
to be died-in-the-wool Clay Bundy men. It would be
easy now for the patrol to keep track of their activities
off the ranch, and Birdie was anxious to get back to
Fort Lyon and put his plan into action.

That was the soldier's side of his life. Personally,
he was once again being torn by conflicting feelings
toward Jody. How many times, he wondered, could a
woman keep changing before a man's eyes? He
watched her with the children; he watched her with
black wives and Mexican wives; he watched her with
Black Mary and Carrie. He watched her with Wagon
Tom, and once he watched her strolling beside the
lake with Rock White.

She had more changes than a kaleidoscope—playful, serious, attentive, studious, capricious, daring,
enticing—but she was still oddly aloof toward him.

Carrie Holmes? Birdie wasn't even aware that her
interest in him was fading because his interest in her
had vanished long ago. She was just part of his
charge, someone he was obligated to get safely to
Denver.

But Jody was like a slow cancer eating into his soul.
It was there and he could do nothing about it, but
secretly watch her and let the cancer spread and
consume him.

At dinner, Miss Inez announced formally that she
accepted Lem's proposition to stay and teach the
white children, and volunteered to go fetch Jody.

Alice MacAllister sat stunned, blinking across the
table at her brother like a startled owl. The announce-
ment meant little to Malcolm Hoog. For ten days he

had been the forgotten guest. No one had thought to call upon him for nursing duties and that had been fine with him. In Lem's study he found enough paper, ink and quills to satisfy his needs. Now he was anxious to place his efforts in the hands of a publisher.

"Does this mean that we can depart soon?" he asked of no one in particular.

"I found no evidence of spots today on your nephew or nieces, Mister Hoog," Miss Inez said. "Except for some weakness, they are ready to travel at any time."

"But—I—" Alice stammered.

"Must take into consideration that this is a house of mourning," Miss Inez finished for her politely. "The less strain we put upon it, the better."

Lem winked at Clay, who looked away. Maybe, he was thinking, the woman is too smart to have around.

Alice quietly excused herself, motioning for Malcolm to follow. She had lost and Miss Inez had won. She must go and the schoolteacher would stay. She began to wonder what the men in Denver would be like . . . and why anyone would want to stay in this lonely place to teach school to a handful of children.

Jody, a short time later, was asking herself the same question. She was sitting in the parlor, surrounded by the Bundy brothers and Miss Inez.

"You shall handle the four younger children," Miss Inez said to her. "My more advanced experience will be applied to the older lot."

Jody nodded, trying to keep the misery out of her face. Aunt Inez is being kind, she thought; there is hardly enough work for one teacher.

Miss Inez put out her hand. "What's the matter, my dear? Aren't you pleased?"

"I—I am." Jody said. "But, forgive me, it's really you they want. I'm just extra baggage."

"Now, Miss Robb," Lem protested, "why ever would you think that?"

"Because twelve children is only a fraction of the number taught by the average teacher," Jody said simply.

Lem smiled innocently. "Well, that seems to be the total number of children available."

Jody took the bait as Lem had hoped she would.

"What about the black and Mexican children?" she said coldly.

"I say, I didn't give them a thought. How many would they be?"

Jody said calmly, "All together I would say about sixteen."

"As many as that? Well, what do you say, Miss Inez?"

Inez Robb's hazel eyes flashed fire. "What concern are they to us, JoAnn?" she demanded.

"They should be of concern to someone," Jody said quietly.

"Don't be a ninny," Miss Inez snapped. "They are uneducable—it would be a waste of our time and Mr. Bundy's good money."

"That's not true!" Jody said hotly. "They are just as intelligent as Clayton Bundy's four children."

Lem had to hide a smile, knowing she was probably right.

"JoAnn!" Miss Inez gasped, "how can you say such things? We will teach those whom we are commissioned to teach and that will be that!"

"No." Jody shook her head. "I couldn't do that. I

couldn't stand to look at those children and know that they were being denied something that should be their right."

Miss Inez's heart hardened. Jody was not taking her happiness into consideration; she would not be denied this chance. She kept her voice calm.

"I wish you would look at it from my standpoint, JoAnn. I didn't want to come out here and teach savages. I fought against it. But, well, you know Hiram."

"I know he'll do everything he can to get us another teaching position," Jody said.

"I don't think so," Inez said coolly and paused. What she was about to say was cruel and she felt a stab of pity for Jody, but she had to think of herself for a change. She had been saddled with the girl for too long. "He sent us west, JoAnn, to get rid of us and the embarrassment we caused him."

"Aunt Inez, what happened at the school was a tempest in a teapot! You didn't have to let Uncle Hiram browbeat you that way."

Miss Inez realized that she had no choice but to come right to the point. "JoAnn, please don't hate me for what I must now say. I see your mother coming out in you, JoAnn. It is something I have feared for years. It is something your Uncle Hiram has always tried to run away from."

"My mother?" Jody was completely bewildered. "But—but you told me you never knew her."

"We never met, that's true, but I did know her by reputation. Please don't force me to go into the sordid details."

How dare Miss Inez hint at any such thing? Jody blushed scarlet. How dare she?

"If the gentlemen will excuse us?" Miss Inez said.

"I think it is time my niece learned the truth about herself."

No one moved—for different reasons: Maxwell out of shock, Clayton out of fascination, Lemanuel because he already knew what Miss Inez had to say. It was this that would keep Maxwell from marrying the girl.

"Gentlemen? Please," Miss Inez said.

"No!" Jody said angrily. "Let them stay. I'm not ashamed to hear the truth, if it is the truth." She glared at her aunt.

"Miss Robb," Lem Bundy said quietly, "do not put your dear aunt through the torment of having to reveal the circumstances of your unfortunate birth."

Jody stiffened and her blood ran cold.

"It would seem," she said coldly, "that it did not torment her to discuss the matter with you, a total stranger."

Lemanuel Bundy felt very pleased with himself. So far, he had pulled the strings like a master puppeteer. The girl had shown her strong support for the blacks as he had expected. The aunt had shown her strong opposition to them, as he had known she would. Now, if only Maxwell would react as expected . . . .

"Maxwell," he said sadly, "since you have expressed the desire to marry this young lady, I think you should leave the room."

"No!" Max roared, jumping to his feet. "If you know something about her, out with it!"

Miss Inez was appalled. It was the first she knew about Max Bundy's intentions. In that case . . .

"Marriage is out of the question for JoAnn," she said quickly. "To anyone. She is illegitimate."

Jody bolted out of her chair as if she had been shot. She had never expected this! Never! For a moment she stood staring at her aunt. Then, she turned and walked slowly from the room, moving like someone in a trance.

Max Bundy was bewildered. "So what? What difference does it make if she can't read or write?"

Miss Inez's eyes popped. She began to giggle and Lem roared with laughter.

"Not illiterate, you dunce; illegitimate," Clay told him. "It means she was born a bastard."

"And to a most unsavory mother," Lem added.

"That's enough!" Miss Inez said, coming to her senses. "I don't want all of the Robb family skeletons dragged out of the closet, Mister Bundy."

Lem sobered. He had won, so why pursue the matter? "You're right, of course, fair lady." He spun about. "And where do you think you're going, Maxwell?"

"Out! Just out!" Max shouted and stomped from the room. A moment later, they heard the screen door slam.

Miss Inez heaved a sigh. "Whatever shall I do now?"

"Do?" Lem said. "Why, my dear woman, do as your heart commands. You have sacrificed yourself upon the family altar for eighteen years. Isn't that long enough? It is unforgivable of your family to have saddled you with such a burden, to have stolen the bloom of your youth."

Clayton winced at such balderdash coming from his brother, but Miss Inez gloried in it.

"What would you advise, Mr. Bundy?"

"Send her back east and out of your life forever."

"I—I—"

"Dear woman, a house can be ruled by only one female voice. How can I make you that voice with this cloud hanging between us?"

Clayton realized he'd been tricked. Lem had his hooks out for this woman for a wife, not a school teacher. He opened his mouth to object, then quickly closed it. Quietly, he excused himself and went out through the kitchen. For once he was glad he'd kept quiet. This woman was no Katrin, nor even a Miss Lottie Louise. She was a love-starved spinster. She would keep Lem so busy attending to her they could drive a thousand head of cattle under his bedroom window and he would never hear a thing. Yes, Clay mused, she just might be a blessing in disguise.

Max found Jody on the porch. For a moment he couldn't decide whether to speak to her or push right by her.

"Did you hear?" he finally asked.

He sounded so unhappy she turned her face a little toward him.

"I heard laughter."

"They were laughing at me, not you."

"Because you wanted to marry a girl who is illegitimate?"

"God, I didn't know what it meant, Jody. I still don't, for sure." He touched her arm. "Let's walk. Let's go out where it's quiet and people don't use such damn big words."

Her eyes turned toward him, large and haunted. "I know what the big words mean."

"Good. Keep them to yourself. I don't want to hear anything for a while."

He led her down the porch steps, his arm tightening round her elbow when she stumbled in the darkness. He guided her the long way out of the ranchyard, behind the corral and the barns. There he let her go and leaned against a barn wall. In the moonlight, he studied her anew. His gaze swept over her heart-shaped face, the full, sensuous lips. What was different about her from when he had first seen her? How had what was said tonight changed anything? He wanted her just as much as he always did when he was near her, or thought about her. Her breasts were still softly rounded, her waist slim, her—

Suddenly, he drew her into his arms and swung her in front of him. His free hand pressed her back, forcing her against him. She felt his face feeling for hers, his chin scraped across her shoulder in the opening of her dress, moved over her cheek, and his mouth fastened upon hers, hard and demanding. For an instant, taken by surprise, she lay inert against his chest. Then, under the pressure of his arms, common sense returned. Whatever she might be, Max Bundy was not the man she wanted.

"No," she protested, twisting her head away.

"I don't care what they say. I want you, I want to marry you."

"No," she repeated, pushing him away.

"Jody, if you had my kid in your belly, we could make them let me marry you."

She stood there trembling. "Do you know what you're saying? Do you really think that would change their minds? No! That child would be illegitimate too!"

That didn't matter to Max; he wanted her now so desperately that nothing mattered.

He grabbed her wrists and pulled her into a hard embrace. His hands pressed into the small of her back as he kissed her, his breath coming out in a long moan, and began to force her back. Struggling in his arms, she was aware only of her fear and of the man causing it.

"Let her go!" The command came out of the barn shadows. A tall figure stepped forward and stopped. When Max made no move to obey, the figure thrust out a long arm and grasped him by the back of the neck. It lifted Max off his feet and tossed him to the ground.

Oddly, Max did not scream or shout or try to fight back. Except for his harsh breathing, he didn't make a sound. At last he scrambled to his feet and began to run, not toward the house, but toward the corral.

For an instant, Jody's reeling senses followed his noisy progress through the underbrush. Abruptly, the sound ceased, and Jody, her mind clearing at last, knew where he had gone.

"They keep rifles in the tack room next to the corral," she said.

Birdie didn't answer, but started to march her along the side of the long barn. They heard Max shout, then heard him running on the other side of the barn.

"You get on back to the camp," Birdie whispered. "I'll draw him off."

He moved away, crashing through the underbrush up the hill toward the woods. Jody thought she heard Max reverse direction. Reaching the end of the barn, she scrambled over a fence into the lower pasture. A rifle roared somewhere close behind her. Panic swept over her. Without thinking, she started to run toward the camp.

"What in hell's going on?" she heard Clayton shout from somewhere near the house.

"She's running away!" Max called back. "Get some of the boys."

"I thought I heard somebody going up into the timber."

"Then I'll go for the boys and you go after her."

Jody didn't believe him. He meant to kill her if he couldn't have her. She ran frantically, sobbing, yanking at her skirt. For a while she could hear him coming after her, then she was across the pasture and running for her life toward the grove.

She did not stop until she was almost at the lake, and she only stopped then because she could not run another step without pausing for breath. She veered away from the camp, knowing he would go there, and sprawled full-length, drawing in air in great, sobbing gasps.

She was still there when she heard the cowboys coming from the bunkhouse. Her first thought was to go to them for protection, but she changed her mind and crouched down in the concealing brush.

Several of the cowboys were carrying torches. In the smoky light she recognized Max at the head of the group; there was not a black cowboy among them. To her surprise, Rocky White walked next to Max. For a moment it gave her hope; he would protect her, if the others found her.

"Hard to believe," she heard Rocky say. They were only yards away.

"Not for me," Max said. "I saw her half-naked with the black bastard behind the barn."

Jody's heart sank, hearing the lie, and a new fear was born. She could see Rocky White's face by the light of the torch he held, and she knew from his expression that he would not help her.

Not until long after they had gone, until she could see the torchlights on the other side of the lake, did she stumble to her feet. She dared not go back to the wagon and Carrie now. She had to choose a place where Birdie would think to look for her, if they didn't find Birdie first and kill him.

The shanties were dark when she reached them. She moved as quietly as she could around to the nearest one. She was halfway to the door when a dark barrier rose up in front of her, blocking her path.

"Who that?" a voice rumbled unsteadily. In her panic, she did not recognize it at first and turned to run. "That you, Miss Jody?"

"Wagon Tom?" she whispered.

"Praise be! I prayed you'd come this way." He reached out to guide her further into the darkness and down onto a wooden bench. "See Birdie?"

She shivered and tears gathered in her eyes. "He— he took off for the woods to lead them away from me."

"Then Mistah Max, he speakin' some truth?"

"No! It was Max who was trying—was about to—"

"That be enough, little gal. Wagon Tom sees it all."

"They'll kill him!"

Wagon Tom chuckled. "Dey ain't sure who dey lookin' for, Miz Jody. Three soldiers missin' outta da bunkhouse when Mistah Max come."

She shuddered. "He knows it's Birdie, Wagon Tom, or else he wouldn't be telling the lie."

"No matter. You jes' sit and leave it all to Birdie and Wagon Tom."

Suddenly, she was alone in the darkness. Exhausted, she lay down on her side on the bench, too tired to try to think anymore . . . .

Abruptly, her deep sleep was broken. Strong arms lifted her and she opened her eyes to see Birdie's handsome face, sick with fear, looking into hers. Behind him stood Wagon Tom.

"I'll go warn Black Mary," Wagon Tom whispered and vanished again.

As Jody raised her head to what Tom meant about a warning, Birdie kissed her, covering her face with light, brushing kisses—kisses filled with such tenderness that the pain inside her chest was almost unbearable.

"I shouldn't let you kiss me" she murmured, though she didn't want him to ever stop.

"Why?" he said suddenly, fiercely. "Have I turned black again?"

Her trembling fingers reached up and touched his mouth.

"It's not you, Birdie," she said gently. "It's what I learned about myself tonight. I—I'm illegitimate. A bastard."

"So?"

"So, that makes me unclean, unworthy of any man."

"Who filled your head with such rubbish?"

"Oh, Birdie! I've seen it. The cleaning girl at school was illegitimate. She married a man without telling him and their child was born deformed. I—I don't know anything about my mother or father and the law says—"

"Damn the law! It's crazy thinking. Hell, I could be considered illegitimate."

"Not exactly. You know who your mother and father were. You don't have to be afraid to bring children into the world. I—I would."

"But you can't just crawl under a rock and hide. You have a life to live."

"Well, I can't live it here," she said bitterly.

"You don't have to," Birdie said. "We're seeing to that. We leave for Denver at dawn, but the Bundys

will think you left sometime during the night. We're
going to make Max's story look like the truth. I've
sent one of the soldiers on ahead with an extra horse.
Wagon Tom is ready to swear that he saw you leave
with him."

"And where will I actually be?"

"Hidden with Miss Carrie's fine furniture."

"But whatever shall I do in Denver all alone?"

"You just let your true friends worry about that."

She felt warm and comfortable and at peace. Suddenly, she began to giggle.

"Are you aware that you're still holding me?"

"Very much so," he said. "I may just carry you all
the way to Denver."

"No," she said weakly. "Please put me down. Remember what I told you. We—we can only be
friends."

And Birdwell Jacobs, setting her down, suddenly
wondered if she would have this crazy notion if she
were black. The majority of the slave population born
in America could be considered illegitimate. This
didn't stop them from living, loving, and progressing.

He looked down at her tenderly. He'd make her
see it his way sooner or later.

9

LEM BUNDY was delighted to see the wagons pull out, and he pretended to believe the story that Jody had gone off with one of the soldiers. In time, his spy system would ferret out the truth. In time, Miss Inez would overcome her grief, which was not too genuine in his opinion. In time, Max would get over the sulks, which were genuine.

But Max was not about to forget that a black had outsmarted him and stolen his girl. If it took him a lifetime, he would get her back and kill the black bastard. But for the moment, Birdie had nothing to fear; Wagon Tom had convinced everybody about the existence of the other soldier.

"Eighty-seven." The man chuckled. "Only eighty-seven Negros and one Mulatto in the whole area when they were trying to make it a territory. It was an odd time for this mulatto: I had been cheated by a white confidence man in Chicago, by white claim-jumpers at Mountain City, by a white lawyer who swindled me out of my placer claim at Breckenridge. I wasn't going to be cheated again."

The present was an odd time for Jody. Barney Ford resembled a southern planter, with his walrus mustache and goatee, but carried himself with an air of dignity that reminded her of her uncle Hiram. Carrie Holmes hadn't prepared her for anybody like him at all.

He had taken over their lives the moment they arrived in Denver. The ladies were accommodated at Ford's Hotel and the soldiers bunked at the Broadwell House on Larimer Street. Carrie's wagon was stored in the stable behind the Ford until Barney could find time to inspect the furniture. His son Louis was sent off with the MacAllisters to a small house Barney had available to rent, and Malcolm Hoog was introduced to William N. Byers, the publisher of the *Rocky Mountain News*. The last amused Barney, who knew Byers choked at the very mention of the name of Barney Ford.

Jody, Carrie and Mary Field were carted off to the People's Restaurant for lunch with Barney and his wife, Miss Julia. Only Carrie was dressed right for the establishment. There was nothing common about the commodious saloon, restaurant and barber shop which Barney had built on the former site of his open-air barber shop and lean-to, from which Miss Julia had served meals to the early residents of Denver.

In twenty years of marriage to Barney L. Ford, Julia Lyoni had brushed shoulders with the high and the low. In her gentle way, she overcame Jody and Black Mary's embarrassment and escorted them all to a private dining room. Like any gracious hostess, she allowed her husband to do most of the talking at the lunch table.

"Eighty-seven," Ford repeated, "until after the war. Then Aunt Clara Brown, who had been saving the money as a washerwoman to buy manumission for her husband and children, changed things fast. She brought not just her husband and children to Colorado, but thirty-four nieces and nephews, uncles and aunts and in-laws, too. We then had almost more browns than blacks."

It took a moment for the pun to register, but then everyone laughed. Barney's lunch guests began to relax and enjoy the excellent meal.

The former runaway slave was not an expert politician. He avoided, for the moment, any discussion of Jody's circumstances, concentrating first on Carrie and Black Mary.

"I am amazed at you two," he said. "Here you are, two supposedly intelligent women, riding along together for hundreds of miles, blind to each other's needs. Now, I don't mind turning a profit, but it seems to me that A plus B equals C minus B."

"Whatever are you talking about?" Carrie demanded.

Julia laughed lightly, seeing the puzzled expressions on their faces. "Barney believes in the algebraic system for working things out. What he is saying is that Mary Fields, A, needs a wagon, B, and that Carrie Holmes, C, needs to get rid of her wagon, so instead of his buying from one just to sell to the other, they should equal out each other's needs."

Carrie and Black Mary stared at each other and Jody laughed.

"How that would have pleased Diophantus."

"Aha!" Barney chortled. "Do you hear that, Julia? I am being likened to the father of algebra. But, my dear Miss Robb, my human algebraic factors would hardly be recognized by Al-Khowwairzmi or Omar Khayyam. And, speaking of human factors, names are such for me, especially among my own race. As a slave in Carolina, I dared not use the surname of my white father. In the plantation records I was 'one buck nigger, age ten, name Barney'. All I was ever called was 'Hey, boy' so I really didn't need either name. But when I was working with the Underground to get runaways to Canada, they said I needed a surname. Would you believe, by the way, that one of the runaways listed himself as John Heyboy?"

Miss Julia cleared her throat, a long-standing signal to her husband that he was rambling away from the subject.

"Not so, Miss Julia," he said. "My point is the name Robb. But first, let me give you credit for our surname, my dear, although at the time you did not know we would be sharing it." He winked at Jody. "She was so pretty I was in awe of her, too shy to let her know about my law of positives and reluctant to disclose that its discoverer was destined for greatness. Circumstances at the time compelled me to take work as a cook temporarily. She was not impressed by my prospects."

"Get on with it, *Mister* Barney Ford." Julia blushed.

"Now, now, mother, as doubtless the only man in history to acquire his name in such a fashion, I afford you the honor of telling the tale."

"Oh, Barney!" She giggled. "It sounds so foolish now."

"As foolish as John Heyboy?" he asked.

"All right." She gave in. "I was an Indiana farm

girl, fascinated by the railroad and the locomotives. Locomotives had individual names then, not numbers. My favorite was a powerful steam engine called 'Lancelot Ford.' That was my choice, although Barney drew the line at Lancelot except for the initial."

Barney had had a reason for letting his wife tell the story. It left his mind free to puzzle on the human factor that was JoAnn Robb. Her face had grown troubled at his interest in her name. Another part of his mind was thinking about Sergeant Birdwell Jacobs. Barney had quickly recognized that the young soldier had more than just a passing interest in this beautiful young woman.

Barney, like Birdie, had been fathered by a white plantation owner. But Barney owed nothing to his white father or his white half-brother; he owed everything to his black mother, who had whipped ambition into him and showed him the importance of learning, and was proud of the black race. He felt all black men should now feel as he felt; that there should be no further mixing of the two races.

Julia Ford knew it was time to bring the luncheon to a conclusion.

"We all have a busy afternoon ahead of us. Miss Holmes, the stable boy at the house is prepared to unload the furniture, with your supervision, of course. Miss Fields, our cook, will give you a listing of the trades people we deal with and you can arrange for the supplies you want to purchase. Mister Ford, haven't you some business to see to?"

Barney grinned broadly. There was one law he could always be sure of: Julia could read him like a book.

"And you and I," Julia turned to Jody, "have business of our own."

"Business?"

"A slight matter of more proper attire, my dear."

Jody blushed. "But I'm afraid I have no money to buy clothes."

"Mister Barney Ford says ' 'Tis nobleness to serve; help them who cannot help again.' "

"Why, that's Emerson!"

Miss Julia smiled and took Jody gently but insistently by the arm.

They had hardly begun their shopping before Julia had drawn from Jody a good part of her life's history —with the exception of Inez Robb's recent revelations. "I see why the name Robb rang a bell with my husband," Julia said. "Senator Hiram Robb is not one of Barney's favorite people in Washington. Barney loves Colorado, but he will fight to keep it out of the Union as long as the vote is denied to our people. Senator Robb would just like to keep it out of the Union altogether."

"My uncle has very strong opinions on some matters."

Julia's eyes crinkled with laughter. The lines around her eyes were the only sign of age on her almond-colored face. "So does Mister Barney Ford. He tried to walk away from here once. He sold the restaurant and leased the property for two hundred-fifty dollars a month. That was enough for us to live like kings in Chicago. But shame and guilt were all that followed us. He went to Washington to try again to get the vote for our people here, and lost again. So we came back home to fight."

"But how can a black man have a voice without having the vote?" Jody wondered.

"In a way that the white man understands. During the war, when they devised the income-tax law, my husband had the fourteenth highest income in Denver. Few realize it, but he is now going into the banking business. Once the whites realize he has the power of money, they will come to understand his voting power."

Just then, a scarecrow of a man came strutting down Lawrence Street, ringing a huge bell and chanting:

> *Lost child! Lost child! Done gone away from home and nobody know where he gone.*
> *Anybody find this child, take him down to Wolfe Londoners, get five dollars.*
> *Here you is! Here you is!*

Jody laughed. "Perhaps I should go down and claim that five dollars on myself."

"You're not as much of a lost child as Lije Wentworth there, Miss Robb. He's unable to read or write, but everyone loves him, especially the children. Many of them get lost so Old Lije can find them. But, speaking about the vote, the whites hold him up as an example, saying, 'You want an addle-pated nigger like old Lije voting on important national questions?' Actually, we have more white illiterates than black in Denver, but those in power want the literacy test for voting applied only to the blacks. Barney tried to establish an evening class to teach people to read and write. But most of them are farm folk from plantations, and Barney's self-taught book learning and algebraic theory was a little too 'uppity' for them. The plan soon fizzled."

"Perhaps we will have to wait for your children to grow up and pass the literacy test," Jody said.

Julia laughed and shook her head. "Miss Robb

Owen Goldrick organized the first school in Denver ten years ago and, two years later, established two school districts as the superintendant of schools—one white and one black. You tell me which one of them has never had a building or a teacher?"

"Then perhaps your husband's money should go into that instead of into banking."

Julia didn't answer and Jody felt she had probably said too much. She made a mental note of the name Owen Goldrick. Strictly speaking, she was not a qualified teacher, but she had to try to support herself somehow. Then she felt a twinge of guilt; she would be applying for a job that employed the old rules of segregation.

Jody had met the Ford children. Ten-year-old Louis and seven-year-old Sarah had the straight hair and almond skin of their mother. Both could have passed for white more easily than many of the sunbrowned children she saw in the Denver streets. One-year-old Frances Ford, the image of her father, was too young for school, but Jody thought Barney could probably have used his money to get a decent education for the other two.

It was something she would have liked to ask about but hesitated, too.

She did learn one reason why Barney Ford had the money he did. Julia was a careful and thrifty shopper. Only garments that would be worn next to the skin were purchased new at the dry goods stores on Lawrence Street. The rest of the afternoon was spent shopping in the Wazee secondhand stores. Here were the remnants of men's dreams gone sour. Gold had purchased finery as long as the Cripple Creek gold had lasted; then the things were sold for pennies.

But Jody made her purchases according to two

standards; first, it was not her money she was spending, and second, she could not overcome a lifetime habit of selecting clothes for durability and suitability rather than fashion or appearance. Her choices were as drab and practical as those she had lost in the attack on the Indian agency.

Surprisingly, Julia Ford did not advise her differently. The selections were really quite pleasing to her. She would see at dinner how they affected her husband.

Birdie Jacobs sat his horse, tall and stern, with the five soldiers under his command mounted behind him. There were several things he wanted to say to the three ladies sitting in the Ford carriage on their way to the Fords for dinner, a million things to one of them.

Carrie Holmes was as beautiful and stylish as ever, but could never be more than just a friend. Mary Fields, whom Carrie had persuaded to remove her stocking cap and place around her shoulders a borrowed white lace shawl, would always have his admiration and respect.

And Jody? He steeled his heart with military toughness. Part of Barney Ford's business that afternoon had been to talk to Birdie like a father and an elder statesman of their race. His words had impressed Birdie, even though they nearly broke his heart. He had been touched by love and for the first time had desired a woman. But that woman was white.

Now, even with her hair pulled back into a bun, her dress plain, she was still beautiful to him. But Barney Ford was right: they came from two different worlds that could never unite.

So now Birdie said, with military brevity, "Ladies,

Captain Ferguson has returned to Fort Lyon and requires my overdue reports. Until we meet again, my best to each of you."

The salute was smart, the turning of the horse precise. The Ford carriage began to roll almost at once. Jody dared not look back to watch Birdie's departure. Her hands, clenched in her lap, were cold. She was cold all over though it was a balmy September evening. The future now was gray, uncertain. A feeling of desertion grew. Birdie's good-bye had been no good-bye at all.

Her companions' thoughts would not have helped her mood. Black Mary had seen what Barney had seen and was glad that separation would keep it from developing. Carrie's emotions were mixed; her common sense had overcome her initial jealousy, but still, she did not want Jody to have Birdie.

The furniture from San Francisco had been moved into the house. It was waxed and polished. Jody hardly heard the discussion of its fantastic history; her mind was far away, wondering if she would ever see Birdie again.

Nor could Jody share in Black Mary's excitement; she had completed her purchases that afternoon and was now anxious to return to the mission.

There was nothing more, either, to delay Carrie's departure by stage to Cheyenne.

"A few more months, Miss Holmes," Barney boasted, "and you could have made the trip by rail. David Moffat is building the line and I'm working on plans for a new hotel, down by what will be the depot. The railroad will make Denver grow like never before. Too bad you all have to leave."

Leave . . .

The word jarred Jody back to the present. The

journey was over; there was nothing now to keep them together. Soon they would all be gone, all but her. Wordlessly she sat through the dinner.

Barney Ford was almost as quiet, thinking all of the factors were wrong—she was too young, too inexperienced, too white, too vulnerable, too much alone in the world. But a quotation kept repeating itself in his brain:

> "Slaves who once conceive the glowing thoughts
> Of freedom, in the hope itself possess
> All that the contest calls for."

The contest called for education, no matter how small the beginning. He had known for some time that he would not be content with black teachers, whose knowledge would be limited from the outset. Not even Julia knew that he had been turned down by the several white teachers he approached, regardless of the generous salary he offered.

But JoAnn Robb seemed the wrong answer to his personal equation. Was it possible he did not have his facts right, his "human factors" in the right order?

For the first time in twenty years he was willing to go against his own system and fill in what was missing later.

"Miss Robb," he said, without preamble, "I am willing to pay ten dollars a month, furnish room and board, and supply a schoolroom and necessary supplies."

Then he prepared his heart for another turn-down. No white woman would dare risk the wrath of her peers to teach black children.

Jody was stunned. "I—I am afraid, Mister Ford, that"—she paused, and Barney Ford's heart sank and

Julia's face began to crumble—"that I am already in debt to your wife for almost a full month's salary. Is—is there any way I could pay that off in installments?"

Barney leaned back with a sigh, but he was wise enough to control the sudden burst of generosity he felt and stuck with the adage that a gift given too generously was a gift barely noticed.

"Shall we say a dollar a month, Miss Robb?"

Julia opened her mouth to protest but Barney shook his head. Jody Robb had just supplied him with some of his missing information: she was honest to a fault.

10

BARNEY FORD now proceeded to bring the possible out of the impossible. On an unused piece of land he owned, volunteers laid the foundation for a four-room schoolhouse in a single day, working like demons in the suddenly cold weather. The men of the black community cut down timber for firewood, built wooden desks and benches, double-bricked the walls for warmth, and either begged, borrowed or stole a sheet of slate to be mounted behind the teacher's desk. For *Mister* Barney Ford was not a man who promised lightly, and one and all were hypnotized by this particular promise.

But not everyone in the mile-high city was impressed.

"Just leave the rest of the books on those back desks," Jody said without turning. "But if they are anything like these, they won't be used for years."

A book snapped shut loudly. "Not a difficult deduction, I would say."

Jody turned at the sound of the thick brogue. The man was startling to behold: his black broadcloth suit fit his tall, sparse frame as if he had stood stiffly erect while every stick was taken. The boiled shirt and starched collar appeared to be a shelf for his long, pointed chin to rest on. He hardly needed more height, but gained some from the stovepipe hat perched squarely upon his gray hair that flowed down into muttonchop whiskers. Although his thin face was stern, an Irish imp played in his clear blue eyes. He gently placed the book he held back on the stack and casually dusted off his gloved hands.

Jody had seen his type many times before: the missionary home from the heathen land to collect funds for a return to God's work.

"Well, well," he said, striding forward and sweeping off the hat. "You are not exactly the heroine I was led to expect by the description in the *Rocky Mountain News*, Miss Robb. I am, by the way, Owen J. Goldrick."

Jody blushed. "Mister Goldrick, those articles Malcolm Hoog has been writing for that, that *scandal sheet* are fables. The distortions are unbelievable. Why, Captain Ferguson did not perform any of the heroics attributed to him. It was Sergeant Birdwell Jacobs!"

Goldrick grinned at her. "A black man, I assume?"

"Does his color really matter, sir? This man Hoog, who cowered through it all in his sister's wagon, by the way, has made himself an expert on things he knows nothing about!"

"I have it on very good authority, Miss Robb, that the eastern papers are already putting Malcolm

Hoog's articles into pulp form: the blood and violence of the savages against a buxom blond heroine and her staunch Army hero!"

"As an educator, sir, it should disgust you to see history twisted that way. The editor and publisher of the *News* should be condemned for printing such lies."

The Irish imp could no longer be contained. Owen Goldrick's laughter filled the room; the bass rumble seemed strange coming from such a thin man.

"You called it a scandal sheet, a moment ago," he said. "I must admit you have some justification. I must also tell you that I am the editor you wish to call to task."

"No! But—but you are the superintendent of schools!"

"That, my dear young lady, is a point of history which does disturb me. Without revealing all of my ego, I can candidly say that I am the most educated man in Denver and, in my opinion, probably the best dressed. But the winds of fortune brought to our fair city a certain type of woman who felt I was unqualified as a teacher and administrator because of my frequent recourse to a flask of Taos Lightning I carry in my hip pocket. So I wound up writing and editing for the *News*, and the ladies for the past two years have been satisfied, since as everyone knows, whisky and newspaper writing seem to possess an affinity for one another." He winked at her. "And I am here to gain another story for that scandal sheet."

"But there is no story here."

"No story?" he said dryly. "Across town, Miss Robb, is a wizened old hag who is fortunate to bring into her schoolroom three dozen students out of a possible hundred or so. Barney Ford informs me that you will have sixty-seven marching through these doors Monday next. That is news of one sort. What you will teach them and how you will handle so many interest me even more."

JoAnn Robb's face was a battleground of emotions—confusion, doubt, misery.

"I'm really not sure, Mister Goldrick," she confessed at last. "Mister Ford moves so fast. Four schoolrooms, enough children to fill them, but only one teacher—me. And the books! God love him for having acquired them so quickly from his friends in Chicago, but, but they—"

"Are typical Barney Ford," Otis Goldrick supplied. "He is the only man in the territory who outdoes me in quoting the classics, although I also quote them in Latin and Greek. Well, those talents won't be required for a while."

Owen Goldrick looked about the room, sniffing like a circus horse attracted to greasepaint. This was his real world—books and the heady thought of vacant young minds to be filled.

"Treasures, a roomfull of treasures, and yet there are some in this community who would like to see you fail. Odd that it was very near the same for me as a youth. I was born and educated in the north of Ireland, but not without difficulty. A crotchety old schoolmaster tutored me secretly at night because education was supposed to be only for the landed gentry. He was not doing it out of pity or because I was somehow exceptional. The old bullwhacker was sweet on my widowed mother, and it was an excellent excuse for him to court her nightly without having to spend a penny. While my nose was pressed into the books, he was free to pursue his real desire.

"Upon emigrating to America, I found employment

as a tutor in Pennsylvania. The rather spoiled young man was James Donald Cameron. Although I prepared him well for Princeton, I thought he would do little more than live off his family wealth. He amazed me by becoming a railroad president and is presently a United States Senator."

"It would seem that you did very well by him, Mister Goldrick," Jody said.

"One jewel does not make a crown, my dear. I thought to do more of the same by coming west to tutor the children of a well-to-do family in the Herfano country in southern Colorado. Impossible children and a very lonely life, and so I found myself in Denver and now stand in envy of you."

"Of me?" Jody stared at him in surprise.

"You are about to embark upon a true pioneering adventure. As an ardent student of history, would I be too forward if I offered myself as your research professor?"

"Research? Research into what, sir?"

Goldrick grinned. "The very reason I call it a pioneering adventure, Miss Robb. A race, any race, can hardly be considered educated without a large spoonful of its own history. What do you know of the history of the blacks in this country to pass along?"

Jody frowned. "I know nothing, but there really can't be very much, can there?"

Goldrick's eyes glistened with pure delight. The teacher was still a pupil to be taught. He picked up a book from one of the stack.

"Miss Robb, dusty old tomes like this do not tell us all there is to know. Storytellers and keepers of legends were with us long before the written word. That is why the Indians fascinate me so. Down in Herfano country, the old men still tell the tale of a huge black man who came striding down out of the mountains, laughing in the sun. The bright feathers in his headdress fluttered in the gentle spring breeze; on his wrists and ankles were more feathers, red and yellow and green and blue. Strings of turquoise and coral swung across his bare chest; bells around his ankles tinkled as he walked. In his wake came a noisy crowd of three hundred ragged Indians, rattling sacred gourds to announce his coming to the next village so the people would have time to prepare food, clothes and lodging."

"You paint a dazzling picture, Mister Goldrick, but that is Indian history," Jody pointed out.

"That picture was painted to capture your interest," he said. "The man was actually Estevanico, the Black Moor, and the first European to set foot on the dusty deserts and rugged mountains of this great Southwest. He came as the slave of a Spanish officer to the shores of Florida in 1527. For eight years they explored together the land around the Gulf of Mexico, across the Rio Grande and on to Mexico City. The land to the north intrigued the Mexican viceroy, Don Antonio de Mendoza, but the Spanish officers wanted to return home. Estevanico was kept here to guide a party of padres. The Indians adored this first black man they had ever seen. To the disgust of the padres, they treated him like a king at every village they visited. Thinking he would get lost and that they would be free of him, the padres sent him on ahead to search for the rich pueblos called the Seven Cities of Cibola."

By this time, Jody had sat down and was listening to him eagerly.

"The padres turned back to Mexico City to spread the myth of gold and silver and jewels. Estevanico moved on from dusty pueblo to dusty pueblo until 1539. Then it is legend again. It is said that he was killed at Hawikuh and his body cut into small pieces, so each village chieftain could consume a part of his courage, his intelligence and his luck.

"The rest is written history. The next year, a large expedition led by Francisco Vasquez de Coronado retraced Estevanico's steps. It did not find the cities of gold, but Coronado was given credit for discovering that area."

Jody sat for a long moment spellbound, then she reached out and took his hand.

"Have you more such tales?" she asked.

"I have the means of acquiring them."

"Then you will be my researcher!"

Owen Goldrick filled an emptiness in Jody's life. He was witty and gay and intelligent. He was an enjoyable dinner companion at the People's Restaurant and an invaluable assistant in preparing the study guides for the school.

But the association was almost as damaging as it was helpful. Many a Denver belle, impressed by Owen's elegant attire and his polished manners, resented Jody, thinking she had set her cap for the town's most impressive bachelor.

"Mulatto?" Jody was amazed. "Where did they get such an idea?"

Owen knew, but thought it best not to reveal that he knew. He had been overruled by publisher Bill Byers on Malcolm Hoog's works. Byers had sold rights to Hoog's material to Beadle and Adams in New York, and Western buffs in the East were gobbling up the action.

"Pay no attention to the gossip," Owen advised. "A woman like you has nothing to fear from it."

Malcolm Hoog was prolific; he was penning the dime novels at an average of one a week, and they were finding their way back to Denver on the average of one a month. It didn't take long for them to reach Barney's barber shop. He collected a stack of what he called balderdash and took it home to discuss the matter with Miss Julia.

"Burn them!" was her advice.

Young Louis Ford overheard her and thought that would be a horrible waste since he hadn't had an opportunity to read them.

"What are you hiding behind that book, Louis?"

The boy tried to sneak the pulp magazine out from behind the book and sit on it before Jody could reach his desk. It was hard to get away with anything in reading class; only Louis and two other children were able to read before the school opened.

It was the one hour in the day when Jody felt confident. The two young black women Barney had brought in from Chicago were most helpful in teaching the children the alphabet and simple arithmetic, but their own education didn't go much beyond that.

"I'll take what you're trying to sit on, Louis Ford!"

Sheepishly, he rose and handed her the magazine.

Jody didn't know whether to laugh or cry at the lurid sketch of the heroine on the cover and the flamboyant title. The girl pictured had tight golden curls. Her attire was Sunday-school prim—and her skin was the color of chocolate. Jody read the cover copy again, just to make sure she understood: *Mulatto Jo's Adventure Sagas . . . A weekly on-going tale of the True west . . . This week the Brave and Bold Mulatto Jo meets: The Roué of Roaring River.*

Jody looked down at Louis Ford who reddened and hung his head. "How many more of these do you have, Louis?"

The handsome ten-year-old gulped. "Only this one at school, Miss Robb. My father told me to burn them all," he confessed. "Gee, Miss Robb, I don't think they sound anything like you at all."

Jody sailed out of the room and stood trembling in the narrow hall. It was obvious where the gossip had originated. Without thinking, she leafed through the badly printed pages and stopped at Chapter III.

Thwack! Thwack! Thwack! she read.

Unfortunately for Cripple Creek Sam, his eyesight was not up to his courage. His shots came nowhere near the attacking varmints. A hail of hot lead poured in upon him. With a painful wail, the old prospector grabbed his belly, badly wounded.

"It's up to you, gal," he cried, thrusting the smoking rifle back. Bold and Brave and Daring, the figure in black marched forward to grasp the rifle.

"Mulatto Jo!" a varmint gasped from behind a tree.

"What's she doing here on the Roaring River?"

"I've come to rescue the captured children," she announced with savage purpose.

Cripple Creek Sam gasped.

Would the mysterious fighter for law and justice reveal her true identity just to save the children? No, he couldn't let her fall into the hands of The Roué of Roaring River.

No man must learn that she was the children's

teacher. No man must learn that she was white by day and mulatto by night.

Not even Captain Harry Ferry, her true love, knew the real secret of Miss Joan Sobb . . .

Quietly, Jody asked Irene Patton to dismiss the class and donned a shawl and bonnet. It was extravagant, but she hailed the first hansom cab she spotted. When she reached the newspaper office it was closing time. She told the driver to wait and sat in the cab, waiting for all the reporters and typesetters to leave. Then she paid the driver and got down.

She peered into the office. Inside she could see Malcolm Hoog, his back to her, busily writing. She had wanted to confront William Byers, but Malcolm Hoog would do for a start.

She entered the office quietly, walked slowly toward his desk. She was about there when he looked up.

"Hello, Miss Robb." He looked surprised but not at all embarrassed.

Jody stood there, staring down at the magazines on his desk: *Mulatto Jo Saves the Wagon Train. Mulatto Jo Captured by the Utes. Mulatto Jo Saves Denver from Fire.*

"Hello, 'Miss Sobb'!" she said angrily. "Isn't that what you meant to say?"

"What do you mean?"

"Aren't you modeling your heroine after me?" she demanded.

"Why, hell no! Whatever gave you that idea?"

"Gossip and the few pages I read of this trash." She drew the magazine she'd confiscated from Louis from under her shawl and threw it down on the desk.

"Oh!" He beamed at her. "I thought that was one of my best. Did you like the way I kept her from revealing her true identity?"

Jody glared at him. "I didn't allow myself to read that far. Is Mister Byers in?"

"He's in Washington."

"Then I'd like to see Mr. Goldrick, please."

"He's been on a two-day binge."

Jody clenched her fists in frustration. "Then I will find a lawyer and determine the law of—"

Malcolm Hoog began to chuckle. "Brighter minds than yours have already looked into it, Miss Robb. As a woman you have no recourse under the law."

"Then you *are* patterning this heroine after me!"

He smiled and shrugged his shoulders. "You should be happy that I am making your life so famous."

"Thank you, Mister Hoog," she said, shaking with anger. "But I can do very nicely without the notoriety."

Barney Ford was busy as usual, but granted her a few minutes of his time.

"I'll tan his hide for not minding!" he raged when she told him about Louis.

"I'm glad I found out. Now, I want to know if Malcolm Hoog is right and the law won't help me."

"Of course he's right. That's why I was trying to keep it from you."

He saw her stiffen, her whole body suddenly rigid. "What is it you're fighting for, Mister Ford?"

He was surprised by that. "For justice and equal rights for the black man, but—"

"But not for the black woman?"

"They gain their rights through their husbands."

Jody stood. "Thank you, Mister Ford. Tomorrow I shall send the girls, including your daughter Sarah, home from school."

"Why in thunderation would you do a fool thing like that?"

"Why? Simple algebraic logic, Mister Ford. What do they need with an education if they will have no rights until, and unless, they wed and bed?"

He scowled. "Woman, you are beginning to try my patience! You are learning all the wrong things in association with Owen Goldrick."

"On the contrary," she said sweetly, "I suddenly realize that I am not learning enough."

To Barney Ford that sounded like a threat. "What do you mean by that?"

"I really don't know, but perhaps it's time for me to discuss it with another woman rather than with a man."

It was proving to be a day in which Jody could not escape either the unwanted fame thrust upon her or men.

The visitor stood the moment she entered the lobby of the Ford Hotel, resplendent in a dress uniform of blue and gold. She wasn't sure how to greet him, or whether to greet him at all. She hadn't spoken to Ferris Ferguson since the night he had walked her back to Carrie's wagon. But there was really no way she could avoid him now.

"Captain—"

"It's Major now. Thanks to you and Malcolm Hoog, the Army has looked kindly upon me."

"How nice," she said coldly.

He reddened, knowing what she was thinking. "Oh, I made sure a letter of commendation went into Birdie's file."

"How very thoughtful." She could barely hide her disgust.

"It was no more than he deserved," he said pompously. He was uneasy; this wasn't going at all the way he had expected. Taking a deep breath, he said, "Miss Robb . . . Jody . . . I have heard back from my wife."

Jody blinked in surprise. It was the first time he had ever mentioned his wife to her.

"How nice for you," she said, not knowing what else to say.

"How nice for us! She's agreed to grant me a divorce."

Jody stood stupified. How in the world did one deal with such an arrogant assumption? Hysterically, she wondered if "Captain Harry Ferry" had divorced his wife to make "Mulatto Jo" his true love.

"Are you aware of the mockery Malcolm Hoog has been making of us?" she demanded.

He looked surprised. "Mockery? I find his tongue-in-cheek humor delightful. He is spoofing history in the making, and millions of Americans back east are taking him seriously."

"He is making me the laughing stock of Denver and I don't find that funny."

"You are taking him too seriously," he said. He reached for her hand, but she jerked it out of his grasp.

"Am I?"

"Yes, darling. A year from now, when we're married, you'll look back on it all and laugh."

Jody stared at him blankly. Just a year ago there had been no men in her life. The variety she had met since was dizzying. Wagon Tom had made her laugh; with Birdie, she had felt warm and safe. Owen

Goldrick was a stimulating companion while Barney Ford treated her with fatherly concern, though she knew he was using her for his own ends, just as Malcolm Hoog was using her for his.

Maxwell Bundy she feared, because she still feared the mystery of sexual contact with any man. But Ferris Ferguson? How did she feel about him? Hate? No, that was too strong an emotion for him. What she felt was something quite different: she simply could not abide being taken for granted.

She raised her chin and looked him straight in the eye. "I suggest, Major, that you come back in a year then and see if I'm laughing."

She turned and sailed up the stairs. The desk clerk tried to get her attention, but she ignored him. She didn't want to give Ferris Ferguson the chance to recover.

Her room was dark when she unlocked the door. The fall days were getting shorter. She felt her way to the bureau, groping for a lucifer to light the Betty lamp with.

She raised the lighted lamp and turned. A triumphant giggle erupted from the bed. Jody swung back to the bureau and shakily put down the lamp.

Maxwell Bundy lay sprawled on the bed, nude.

"Surprise!" he chortled. "I figured it was you the more I read of them magazines. Damn, hell, it sure is you!"

Jody's mind was in a frenzy. She had never before seen a naked man. She was horrified and yet intrigued, furiously mad and yet curious. Her mind calmed down to focus on a single thought.

"How did you get into my room?"

Max snickered. "Gave the desk clerk five bucks and

some information. Told him I'd been on the wagon train with the real Mulatto Jo, and he gave me the room number right quick."

Jody thought she was going to be sick. "Get out," she whispered.

"Oh, no! I've waited too long for this. I aim to gobble like a wild turkey tonight, then it's back to the ranch for us."

Jody slowly turned, measuring him from head to foot, steeling herself as she looked at what she had never looked at before. She smiled sweetly, taking him off-guard.

"Then say hello to my aunt, when you get back," she said and flung herself at the door. She was out of the room, slamming the door behind her, before Max Bundy could react.

He reared up on his elbows. No woman had ever turned him down before.

"Damn! What's wrong with her?" Frustration and anger grew. He leaped from the bed and began to pull on his clothes.

Jody stumbled downstairs, expecting at any moment to hear Max pounding after her, blind to everything around her.

"Miz Jody! Am I glad ta see you. You see Mistah Max?"

Startled, she stumbled on the last step. Wagon Tom's strong arms caught her as she started to fall.

"Oh, Tom!" she moaned. "Tom! Take me out of here!"

The room clerk watched it all avidly. He was being paid a dollar a week to report on Jody's activities to Malcolm Hoog. This night alone should match the five dollars he already had from the cowboy.

"Fire!" The cry jerked the clerk out of his reverie.

Already a block away from the hotel, Wagon Tom and
Jody never heard it . . .

Barney was aware of a lump in his throat. Ed Chase
and his partner were shoveling sand on the roof of
their gambling house to keep the sparks from getting
hold and heaving it onto the roof of Barney's hotel to
contain the blaze. This was one time when the color
of a man's skin made no difference.

The town marshal had been trying to organize a
bucket brigade to carry water from Cherry Creek, but
found the fire blocked the way. Despite everyone's desperate efforts, the fire swept along the street, and
Barney watched his hotel go up in flames along with
the gambling house. The firefighters continued to
shovel sand but with little effect, and by sunrise virtu-
ally the entire block had been destroyed.

Exhausted, Barney pieced the story together from
what the desk clerk told him. He had known for some
time that Jody meant certain trouble for him, but he
had not expected it to come in this form and now acted
without thinking.

Irene Patton opened the door of the house and stared
in disbelief. Barney Ford's rage had mounted as he
walked to the Five Points district. His clothing and
face were streaked black with smoke, and his expression was grim.

"Where is she?" he demanded. "She's not at the
school."

Irene motioned for him to enter. The twenty-year-
old black woman had come from Chicago fearing this
man and this vast land. She no longer feared the man.

"She's in the kitchen. You'd better calm yourself
before you speak to her, Mister Ford."

There was something in her voice that stopped him short. It was, he realized suddenly, a beautiful voice, with a great deal of courage in it at the moment. He brought his gaze up slowly to her face. It was thin and dark, the nose flat, the mouth wide, the eyes large and almond-shaped—an attractive face, Barney thought. He had paid no attention to the teachers since their arrival and now wondered which one this was.

"Do you feel capable of taking over the school?" he asked abruptly. "The circumstances which have been brought to my attention make it impossible for her to stay!" Barney's voice was shaking with anger.

Irene Patton studied him with soft brown eyes.

"It sounds to me as though you've tried her on somebody else's word, and now you're ready to sell her downriver."

"Which one are you?" he demanded then.

"Irene Patton."

He liked the way she stood up to him; he bet her equations were very good.

"Now look, Miss Patton, this is not your concern. It was my mistake for hiring a white woman with questionable background."

"Who be questioning it?" Wagon Tom filled the kitchen door frame, glowering at Barney, who stared in dismay.

Before Barney could answer, Jody pushed Wagon Tom on through the doorway and stepped around him.

"I would like to ask the same question, sir."

Barney could not help feeling concerned as he looked at her. She was pale and drawn, and her eyes were red and swollen-looking.

"That's something I think we should discuss alone," he said stiffly.

Jody couldn't help smiling. "This may sound odd to

you, Mister Ford, but these people are my friends. I have nothing to hide from them."

"All right," he said in exasperation. "My hotel has burned down thanks to a fire started in your room. Another boarder saw the man you were entertaining dash from the room and saw the flames. You, from what I gather, had already left with this black buck. I can guess at the reason for your departure."

"What you mean?" Wagon Tom took a step forward, but Jody was pulling at his sleeve.

"No Tom," she said. "I want to hear everything that Mister Ford has assumed."

Nothing could have been harder for Barney. He was not a man given to slander and gossip. He had believed what his desk clerk had told him. Reluctantly, he related the facts as he knew them.

Jody shook her head. "I'm sorry about your hotel," she said quietly. "Of course, you have my resignation."

"Aren't you going to fight these lies?" Irene protested.

Jody smiled. "What good would it do? Men, all men, regardless of their color, have a way of sticking together. They want to believe what Malcolm Hoog has written about me. They even add a few touches of their own. And Mister Ford does have to think about his reputation."

Anger reddened Barney's cheeks. "You're making me sound like—"

"Whatever you say," Jody said calmly. "But I doubt very much that you know about the bribe that allowed Max Bundy to gain access to my room, much to my own surprise."

Barney leaned forward, a glimmer of understanding in his eyes.

"Who is this Bundy?" he asked. "Whom did he bribe?"

Wagon Tom stepped forward then. "He got a black soul, like you all got dirty gray ones," he said, and stomped out of the little cottage.

Barney glowered after him, his Adam's apple rising and falling in his throat. But Jody was standing before him, her hands gripping his wrists.

"No," she said, "I will not be the cause of a fight. Tom is the most honorable man I know."

Slowly the dark anger ebbed from Barney's face. Her words stung his pride. He could not recall ever having felt so foolish in his life.

"Ladies," he said, "I have matters to look into before I can form a proper apology. I shall be at the school tomorrow before the first class commences."

Barney walked back uptown silently. A slight breeze caught at his heavy black hair and lifted his goatee. He pulled at the beard savagely. That was one of the first things he was going to do; Miss Julia had always hated it and so off it would come. Second, he would never again make a move without working out an equation on it first. JoAnn Robb was right: he had been concerned about his reputation and the school's. He had strived all his life to be called *Mister*. Jody Robb had said it in a way that had filled him with pain. He had been so busy establishing his bank and planning for his depot hotel that he had not been leading all of his people.

Then he grinned. Nothing ever happened in life without cause. In his head, he began to work out the human factor equation for women. The numbers nineteen and twenty kept getting in his way. He put the problem aside until he could work it out more carefully on paper.

It was a puzzle that would trouble Barney for years. He would die never knowing what the numbers meant. Eighteen years after he was buried beside Julia at Riverside Cemetery, the 19th Amendment, giving women the right to vote, was added to the Constitution. It was 1920.

11

JODY ONCE MORE had lost everything she owned to fire, but besides that found herself the target of more gossip.

Barney felt he had been very badly used by a man he had trusted and fired the desk clerk for taking the bribe from Max Bundy. This caused even more controversy.

More and more of the settlers coming into the territory were from the reconstructed South. It didn't matter if they had been in Denver five years, five months or five days, they all felt they had a right to voice an opinion about a black man firing a white man over the scandalizing affairs of a mulatto woman.

Jody, thinking that out of sight might be out of mind, didn't help her own cause. She moved into the Five Points cottage with Irene Patton. Actually, it was a practical idea for both women. They could share expenses and even share their clothes, because they wore the same size. They were also learning to share something of far greater importance.

"Why have you kept this a secret?" Jody demanded of Irene, a look of bewilderment on her pretty face. "I don't understand—you don't trust me, yet you let me live with you. Why have you been playing the dumb black when your education equals my own?"

Irene looked down at the book Jody had caught her reading, secretly.

"I don't really know," she said sullenly. "I thought this job wouldn't work out, I guess, not for long. And how am I going to catch a husband back in Chicago, if he thinks I know more than he does? I don't want to be a prune-faced schoolteacher. I want a man and children. I want to teach my children all I know, not teach someone else's children."

"But until that man comes along, you are denying these children what you know."

Irene blushed. "I think that man *has* come along," she said softly.

Jody looked at her thoughtfully. "Do you mean Wagon Tom Smithson?"

"Oh, Lord!" Irene gasped. "Is it that obvious?"

"Hardly." Jody chuckled. "But he's the only man who has been coming to this cottage. I love Wagon Tom, but why do you say he's the right man?"

"Because I don't think he would look down on me because of my education. He thinks all children should be taught a trade, as he was. Schooling could be considered a trade, couldn't it?"

"You have just ruined your own argument for keeping it a secret." Jody laughed. "Maybe you'll interest him more if you prove what a good teacher you will be for his children."

Irene rose and went to the clothes press they shared. She dug down at the bottom and brought out a stack of papers.

"I'll need your help with this then," she said.

"What is *this*?" Jody asked, taking the papers from her.

"A secret project since I was fifteen. Something like what you and Mister Goldrick were doing. Bits and pieces of stories my stepfather collected from the slaves who came through the Chicago Underground. That's how Mister Ford knew about me. He and my stepfather worked together."

Jody sat down, the papers in her lap. The cramped scrawl was hard to read and at first she had difficulty concentrating. The names meant nothing to her, but soon she was caught up in the events described.

She wasn't aware that Irene placed a cup of hot coffee by her side. The coffee was cold before she took the first sip, but she wasn't aware of that, either. It was almost dawn when Jody put down the papers and rubbed her cramped neck. Across the table, Irene sat watching, silently and warily. Jody reached over and grasped her hand. There was no need for words.

For the next two months they shared many dawns, but Jody's dream was bigger than Irene's. They would be dealing with young minds belonging to children born during the final days of slavery and after. They would need this background history and more, if they were to take their rightful place in the new West.

Because she needed his help, Jody slowly allowed Owen Goldrick to enter her now almost exclusively black world. By silent agreement, he left outside that world whatever knowledge or gossip he had of the "white" Denver world and how her actions were affecting it. They were two scholars on a scholarly quest. They would finish each night, staggering with weariness but inwardly satisfied.

Owen Goldrick was a genius at obtaining material from impossible sources. Denver was abuzz with the presence of visiting royalty. Posing as a society reporter, Goldrick was less impressed with Lord Dunraven's scheme to establish a hunting preserve in the Colorado mountains than he was with the Earl's beautiful cousin.

Lady Dorothy Gould was an avid reader and had purchased a copy of Meriweather Lewis and William Clark's journals in New York. Owen Goldrick was an avid and successful borrower. To Jody and Irene's journal was added the name York, the explorer's personal servant and trusted companion on their two-year expedition from St. Louis to the Pacific and back. York was the first Negro ever to see the Pacific Ocean from its American shore.

From Army records, Goldrick gained the history of Jacob Dodson and his 840-mile ride in eight days with Captain John Fremont to warn General Stephen W. Kearny of the uprising in California.

But to the delight of the children, Goldrick supplied a real live hero in the classroom.

Jim Beckwourth, the noted mulatto frontiersman, drifted into town to visit his Mexican wife, whom he always addressed as "Lady Beckwourth." To get her name into print he agreed to address the black school children.

A man well into his sixties, Beckwourth wore his hair long to signal the fact that he had been made a Crow chief. He was an excellent storyteller, although he exaggerated his own part in most events. His mountain-men stories left the students wide-eyed and dreaming of adventures of their own. Although he had known almost all of the mountain men for over forty years, he was proud enough of his mixed blood to lean most heavily on the exploits of the black mountain men whose number and deeds Irene hardly had time to write down.

But a new adventure was to overshadow his past exploits.

"He's done *what*?"

Jody had not understood everything Owen Goldrick had just whispered to her. He hated to repeat what he had said out loud in front of her class. He felt responsible enough as it was.

"Jim got into an argument last night with Will Payne, the blacksmith for the Holladay stage line," he said again, trying to keep his voice down. "He killed him."

Jody paled and motioned for Owen to follow her out of the room, but thirteen-year-old Lonnie Peterson was on his feet waving for recognition.

"In a moment, Lonnie," Jody said. "First, I have something to discuss with Mister Goldrick."

"If it's about the mountain man," he said, "we already know."

Jody and Owen looked at each other.

Lonnie Peterson had center stage and was not about to relinquish it. "My paw is the spitoon man at the gambling house," he announced proudly. "He see'd the whole thing and hear'd the whole thing."

"That will be enough, Lonnie," Jody said, but she was drowned out by a chorus of young voices confirming that they knew what had happened, too.

"You mean, you've known all morning?" Jody was amazed. "And none of you said a word?"

But Goldrick understood instantly and was im-

mensely proud of them. They knew, as he did, that it
was the rest of the story that would be most upsetting
to Jody. Now, he decided that it was only right for
them to be the ones to tell her. He saw them look to
Louis Ford, their natural leader, much to Lonnie
Peterson's chagrin.

But Louis hung his head. He had disobeyed his
father once, by not burning the Mulatto Jo books, and
dared not disobey him over this. His eyes pleaded with
Lonnie to step in for him.

For Lonnie, it was a victory over the "rich" kid, and
he was delighted to be the leader, if only for the moment.

"We was told not to tell, Miss Robb. Leastways, not
until the hanging."

The class erupted into protest at such a possibility.
Jody marched back to her desk, sat down and calmly
folded her hands. She waited patiently until every eye
was upon her and every voice stilled. It was a lesson in
classroom discipline she had learned long ago from
Miss Inez.

"Mister Goldrick," she said, "if a bench will fit you,
please be seated. Lonnie, you have something more to
say?"

But the triumph had suddenly soured for the young
man. To break the news was one thing; to go on with
the rest was quite another. He quickly took his seat,
shaking his head.

Owen Goldrick raised a scrawny arm just like one of
her class. In spite of her concern, Jody almost giggled.
"Mister Goldrick?"

He got to his feet slowly, looking about him at the
children. "Pride, according to Mister Webster, is a
reasonable delight in the behavior of others. My delight in your behavior this morning is not reasonable—

it is overwhelming. I take it upon myself to dismiss this class for the rest of the day."

Jody was too surprised to protest. Goldrick now looked at her. "Come," he said. "There are matters that call for our personal attention."

Jody took the arm he offered her and walked from the room. The students stood at her departure, silent and respectful. Then all twenty-two suddenly were thinking the same thing: To arrive home from school at midday would raise too many questions. As one, they sat down and opened their books to study.

Owen Goldrick smiled down at Jody. "That, my dear, testifies to your ability as a teacher."

"Where are we going?" she asked, as he hurried her along.

"*Why* should have been your first question, but I'll not belabor the point. Last night your honor was upheld by a man who is both black and white, has a Mexican wife and has lived a good many years with the Indians. That is a man you do not argue race with. Will Payne was a scoundrel who would argue with a cockroach if that were the only living thing near at hand. It didn't help matters that Beckwourth knew that Payne had evaded military service during the war, service with the South. That's what set off the fireworks—Payne trying to sound like a Rebel when he never was man enough to fight for the cause. One thing led to another and your name was brought up."

"I seem to cause trouble wherever I go," Jody said, feeling miserable.

"Perhaps this was necessary," Owen said.

"How can you say that? A man's life has been taken."

"My dear," he said gently. "A hundred and forty thousand men had their lives taken fighting over the same question. It's not just a question of slavery, but

of human rights. Do you want to be run out of town
on a rail and your school destroyed?"

She was stunned. "Of course not!"

"Will Payne and five of his drinking buddies were
ready to do just that to defy Jim standing up for you
and the school. They didn't take into account that Jim
could take on all six of them at once."

"Where are we going?" she asked again.

"Judge Lovell Tatum is a reasonable man, my dear."

But Denver was not in the mood to be reasonable. It
was suddenly not just a case of Will Payne's death, but
a matter of economics involving his boss. The Holladay
brothers stood to lose a good deal with the coming of
the railroad, and Barney Ford was one of David Mof-
fatt's financial backers. Anything that might discredit
Barney was jumped on. Judge Tatum was caught in
the middle of the power struggle.

"You must understand, Miss Robb," he said, evading
the issue, "that a suspect in a killing is seldom hung
unless the offense has been in connection with horse
stealing. Much as I sympathize with the erroneous impression that Mister Hoog's books have created, as a
public official I must obey the law. Beckwourth must
stay in jail until I place this matter before a jury."

"This is one time," Goldrick said when they were
back out on the street, "that I wish Barney hadn't
fought so hard against statehood. Jury, my Aunt Fan-
nie's behind! Ben Holladay plays poker with that old
goat. So does Bill Byers and Governor Evans. They'll
handpick that jury over a game of five-card stud."

Normally, justice moved very swiftly in the West.
Judge Tatum tactfully waited two days before conven-
ing his court, two days in which Denver could not help
but hear all about the prisoner and his complaints

about being cooped up. He refused to eat and threatened to send for the Crows to burn Denver down.

Jody felt responsible and was horrified to learn that it would automatically be an all-white jury. Five Points was like a ghost town after sunset. Will Payne and his five drinking buddies had failed to do what others felt duty-bound to attempt. To be on the safe side, Marshall Hixson sent for troops from Fort Lyon—

The boy at the door was no more than five and frightened to the point of shivering.

"*Señorita*," he said softly. "My grandmother is most frightened."

Irene Patton frowned, looking down into his small face. "Who are you and who is your grandmother?"

"I am Pedro, grandson of *Señora* Jim Beckwourth."

Jody was on her feet instantly and at the door. "What is the problem?"

"My father wishes for her not to take food to the jail. You talk, maybe?"

"Let me get a shawl."

"Jody!" Irene gasped. "Are you crazy? The Mexicans hate us worse than the whites."

"I've got to do something, anything."

"Then I'm coming with you." Instead of stopping her, Jody handed her a shawl. She didn't know what she could do, but she would feel safer with Irene along.

Maria Beckwourth was a frail, dying woman. Her son Juan Beckwourth was a belligerent, hate-filled man in his twenties.

"We owe him nothing," he said. "I have more fingers on my hands than the number of times I have seen him in life."

Maria spoke softly to him in Spanish. His scowl deepened.

"She says he is still my father. I curse the fact. It has brought me nothing but misery and shame."

"He still needs food," Jody said gently.

"Then you take it to him!" he shouted. "I hope they hang him from the highest tree!"

She slapped his face, the sound as sharp and sudden as a whipcrack. "May God forgive you for saying such a thing. Where is the food?"

He stood looking at her, then he smiled, the cruelest smile she had ever seen.

"It is there in the basket, *señorita,* but it will do you no good. They will permit only my mother to see him, and she is too ill."

Jody looked at the old woman who watched her, her eyes pleading.

"We are of very nearly the same size, *señor.* Give me some of her clothing."

"No!" Irene protested. "You can't do it, Jody."

Jody didn't answer, but stood glaring at Juan.

"Why?" he said, staring at her. "Why do you do this thing?"

"Partly from a guilty conscience, *señor.* But mainly for the children your father came to talk to. They don't have many heroes to look up to. Their faces were full of wonder and awe because of him, and respect."

Juan Beckwourth began to bark sharp commands in Spanish at his son, his cowering wife and his mystified mother.

"I go with you," he told Jody. "They know me and know my mother is ill. You must be old and lean on my arm much."

Jody didn't waste time asking what had changed his mind. She had been rash to say she would go at all; now she wanted it over quickly.

* * *

Juan did the talking, for his mother was known to speak no English. Still, the jailer would do nothing without the approval of Marshall Hixson.

"Give your mother a seat," the guard said. "I'll get the marshall from next door."

Jody sank into a chair next to the desk, trembling so much she looked old and ill without having to pretend. The place frightened her. She cowered deep within the borrowed shawl, never letting her eyes leave the top of the desk. It was littered with wanted posters. The evil countenances the artist had drawn made her shudder.

At first she gave little thought to what she saw lying within the partially opened desk drawer. She frowned thoughtfully. Then her face cleared and a determined line showed at the corners of her mouth. She leaned over, extracted the ring of keys and closed the drawer firmly.

Juan looked at her in alarm.

"What do you plan to do?"

"Hush! I really don't know."

He pressed himself tightly against the wall, clutching the basket of food as though it were the only protection he had against the madness that must follow.

Marshall Paul Hixson sauntered in, gnawing on a toothpick.

"My deputy will help you find quarters for your men, Sergeant Jacobs," he said over his shoulder. "But I don't want them going into the colored area tonight. Harvey, you go along with the sergeant and I'll see to *Señora* Beckwourth."

Jody hadn't taken a single breath since she heard Birdie's name. Now her heart almost stopped. Hixson sat down at the desk and started to reach for the drawer.

Instead, he sat back in his chair. "Juan, I want you to make your mother understand that you can't go in with us, and that she can only talk to him through the bars."

Jody nodded a couple of times as Juan quickly translated into Spanish, then stood up almost too quickly. As she moved to take the basket she had a moment of confusion. She was grasping the keys tightly in one hand and using the other to keep the shawl covering her face. Now, as she took the basket the shawl partially slipped down her head. Juan was quick to pull it back up, but not quick enough.

Birdie took a step toward her and stopped short. He had seen just enough to totally baffle him.

"Was there something more, Sergeant?" the marshall asked.

Birdie opened his mouth, shut it, then opened it again. "Your deputy says he doesn't think he can find housing for *all* us nigger troops."

Hixson slammed the desk with his open hands. "I don't like it, either, Sergeant, seeing this case is what it is and all. You tell that fathead to find beds for all of you and not to come back until he does. I want this damn trial over with before this town blows apart. Come on, *Señora.*"

Jody looked at Juan. There was no way to warn him that she knew the sergeant and she prayed that Birdie wouldn't start asking questions.

She didn't need to shuffle; her legs seemed hardly able to move, she was so frightened. They went down a brick corridor and through a heavy wooden door. Beyond were eight cells, four to a side.

"Company, Beckwourth!" Hixson called. "I'll stay here, *señora.*"

It was the longest walk Jody ever took in her life. The mountain man didn't make it any easier.

"You horn-toothed jackal!" he screamed at the marshall. "You know damn well she's too sick to be in a place like this. What kind of an ass are you, you—"

"Lower your voice and don't look surprised," Jody whispered.

Quickly, Beckwourth glanced about the jail; the other prisoners were paying them no mind.

"What you up to, Miss Robb?" he whispered hoarsely.

"Juan and I brought you some food." She held up the basket.

Beckwourth looked at her. "Juan? Here?" he demanded.

She nodded. "He brought me. Give me your hand!" Quickly she passed him the keys. "I took them from the desk."

He didn't need to look; he could feel what she had passed him. He raised a big hand to his brow and deftly tucked the key ring under his bearskin cap.

"Who would have thought it!" he said in amazement.

"The trial is in the morning," she told him. "It's an all-white jury, naturally, so you probably don't have a prayer. Federal troops have just arrived, too."

Beckwourth shook his head. "I'm sorry, Miss Robb," he said quietly. "I didn't mean to bring you any trouble."

She shook her head. "You wouldn't be here if you hadn't stood up for me. Thank you."

"Thank *you!*" He touched his bearskin hat.

"Where will you go?" she asked.

Beckwourth smiled slowly. "Home. The Crows say I bring them good luck. Maybe they can bring me some this time!"

* * *

Returning quickly to the *barrio,* Jody and Juan parted without comment. That night Jody lay awake anxiously, wondering if Jim Beckwourth had been able to make his escape.

She heard them coming a long way off and knew exactly who it was and what they would be seeking. She was only surprised that Birdie had not come right to her in the first place.

The banging on the door shook the cottage. Jody was out of bed and prepared. She flung the door open even as Irene came sleepily out of her bedroom.

The buffalo soldier gaped at the sight of a white woman in a nightgown. "Well . . . I . . . ma'am, we got orders from the town marshall to search every house in this district."

"What's going on?" Irene demanded, coming to the door.

Jody did not answer; she had not told her about the keys. Behind the soldier stood Birdie staring at her, his face bleak.

"I'll handle this house, soldier," he said and shoved past him. Irene turned to light the Betty lamp, but Jody stood her ground. She had nothing to fear from Sergeant Birdwell Jacobs.

"You," he said, kicking the door shut with his heel, "show up in the damnedest places."

Jody made a face. "I could say the same for you!" She laughed.

"This is no laughing matter! The prisoner has escaped using keys stolen from the marshall's desk!"

Irene collapsed weakly into a chair. "Jody!" she gasped. "You didn't!"

"She must have," Birdie said. "She and Juan Beckwourth were the only ones in the jail all evening."

"Do you have proof of that, Birdie?" Jody asked innocently.

"I have eyes. I saw you for only a second, but I knew it was you."

"Then why didn't you say something at the time?"

"That's beside the point!" he said. "Do you know what you've done? You've committed a crime! You've helped a murder-suspect escape and that's a hanging offense."

"But no one knows I was there," she protested. "They think it was Maria Beckwourth."

"I know you were there," he said grimly. "I am an officer of the law and can't close my eyes to what I know. Besides, it will all come out as soon as Juan Beckwourth tells what he knows."

Irene had sat in her chair looking from one to the other of them, her face flushed and angry. Now she spoke.

"Excuse me, I'm Irene Patton and I take it you are Birdie? Well, you sound to me more like the white side of you than the black side. Get your facts straight first, *nigger*. Jody was with me last night."

"You don't have to lie for me, Irene," Jody protested.

"I'm not telling any lie. I *was* with you, except at the jail. I helped dress you to look like Maria. If you did wrong, then I was a party to it."

"Miss Patton," Birdie said, "I think you have said quite enough."

"You, you Uncle Tom!" Irene's voice was hoarse with fury. "Do you care about what has been going on here? No! The slander, the insults, those vile magazines!"

"I can read, Miss Patton," he said quietly.

"But you're too yellow-dog to do anything about them. Well, Jim Beckwourth did something about it and I'm glad he got away!"

Birdie sighed. "The law will still be the law when he is captured."

Jody said softly now, "They will never capture him, Birdie. He's gone home to the Crows."

"That won't do him any good, Jody. The telegraph is buzzing to every northern fort. The Army will force the Crows to return him."

"Never! They will fight first!" Jody declared, her eyes blazing.

"Is that what you want? An Indian war over one man?"

"You get out of here," Irene shouted, "and stop trying to make her feel guilty."

"That's a feeling she's going to have to learn to live with," Birdie said grimly, "if this whole town blows up over this escape."

He did not report directly back to Marshall Hixson. Instead, he kept his troops patrolling the streets of Five Points and the Mexican *barrio,* his mind aching with confusion.

Lord, he thought, why does she always live on the edge of disaster! And why am I always involved? He'd made an enemy of Irene Patton and made Jody furious with him and held back vital information from Marshall Hixson, all in a matter of hours! There would be hell to pay if Juan talked. It wouldn't take Hixson long to learn that Birdie knew JoAnn Robb. He was only thankful that Hixson was keeping the news of the escape from the white community.

He had looked forward to this assignment. Major Ferguson hadn't let him get within spitting distance of Denver and Jody. But Major Ferguson was back east receiving the Congressional Medal of Honor for his "conspicuous gallantry in action" against the Utes.

He had come into town in the mood for tender

words and possible caresses. He had had time to mull over Barney Ford's advice and found it lacking. He had also had time to mull over Ferris Ferguson's interest in Jody. Only one person could judge if Birdie stood a chance with Jody, and that was Jody herself.

And Jody had sapped his mood like a drought on the plains.

The lights of a saloon caught Birdie's eye. He entered and put his foot up on the brass rail.

"Beer!" he called to the bar-keep.

"Don't serve niggers!"

Casually, Birdie unsnapped the cover of his holster and placed his six-shooter on the shiny surface of the bar.

"I say you serve the sergeant of the guard who's here to keep law and order during the trial tomorrow!"

"Coming right up, sir!" the bar-keep said quickly.

Five beers later, Birdie gave up. In his present mood, he could have drunk a gallon with no effect. He paid for the drinks and walked out, heading back toward Five Points.

He had tried to push the thought out of his mind all evening, but like a viper it kept slithering back. Fear! He had seen the look of fear on the faces of his people at the sight of his soldiers. They were all of the same race, but they were frightened of him. He felt like Attila the Hun.

Jody hadn't been frightened; she had been proud of her accomplishment. She had done something positive and, by law, he would have to turn it into a negative. She, at that moment, belonged more to his people than he did.

It took him a moment to sort out what he felt. Resentment, that was it. He resented being the outsider looking in, while she was now the insider.

He found his way back to the boarding house where he was quartered. He found the lights were on in his room! He went up the stairs two at a time, anticipation mounting with each step. Jody had come to him! He pushed open the door.

"I thought you were going to search all night," Marshall Hixson said, unfolding his lanky frame from a chair. "But it would have been a waste."

"Oh?" Birdie struggled to hide his disappointment at the identity of his visitor.

"Juan talked."

Birdie's heart began to pound again, this time with dread.

"Can't figure him out," Hixson said. "Hated his old man. Made no bones about it. I guess she must have changed his mind."

"She?" Birdie gulped.

"Teacher the blacks got. Pretty little thing and spunky as hell. She even moved into Five Points to spite folks. Can't say as I blame her, what with all the garbage they've been spoutin' about her. Damn fools! Why, I bet she's still a virgin."

Birdie stood silent, his face blank.

"Spunk," Hixson went on, with a chuckle. "Gol darndest spunk I ever heard of. She took Maria Beckwourth's place tonight and stole the keys for Jim. I got that from Juan. Darn if that don't beat all."

"What—" Birdie stopped. "What do you intend to do about it?"

"Do?" Hixson looked surprised. "Not a blessed thing!"

"But the law—"

"Law? Sergeant Jacobs, I *am* the law in this territory! Have you heard me mention the lady's name? Nor will you. I find her actions justifiable under *my* law. Tomorrow, I want those bastards to try a man who is not even in his cell. I want them to try a man who took on six of the worst scum in the territory in defense of a woman's honor. Then let them hang a ghost. Damn, won't that beat all! It's better than anything Malcolm Hoog would dream up for her!"

"And my troops?"

Hixson frowned. "Yes, that's why I've been waiting for you, Sergeant. I want them out of town by dawn."

"But what if—"

"There won't be any ifs," Hixson growled. "This is my town and my territory. If I overreacted calling you, I'm sorry. Tomorrow I'll call for volunteer deputies. If I don't get any, well, that will be a clear-cut message to me." He looked at Birdie thoughtfully. "Have you ever been hungry, Sergeant?"

"No, not like some folks."

"Well, I fought hunger until I was sixteen, all kinds of hunger—food, love, respect. I eat all I want now, but I don't gain an ounce. I got a wife I love, and I get a measure of respect as a lawman. But I wish I had half the guts that young woman showed."

Alone again, Birdie's mood turned somber. JoAnn Robb had bested him again. Would they never meet as equals? As he packed his saddlebags, he came to a decision: he must never see her again.

12

THOUGH THERE had been several light snowfalls in the foothills early in October, the snow had not lasted. Now, as she stood looking out of the schoolroom window the next day, it seemed to Jody that snow must surely come soon. She was praying for snow—deep snow in the mountains between Beckwourth and any pursuers.

Throughout the morning, long lines of steel-gray clouds had been moving over the distant mountains. On the valley floor, there was no wind, no visible sign of it except the clouds.

As Jody stood at the window, Barney Ford's carriage drew up. She saw him pause, studying the sky as he got out. She was tempted to hurry outside to hear the results of the trial, but she stayed where she was.

"Do you think it's going to snow?" she asked when Barney stepped inside. He didn't look at her, but gazed off into the distance somewhere over her head. "Women are meddlesome fools," he announced.

"I only asked about the weather," Jody said.

He looked at her then. "Knowing the way your mind works, I can guess why you're looking for snow. Well, Beckwourth won't need it. He's acquitted—self-defense."

Jody flushed, then laughed. Her cheeks were bright against the gray background of the winter landscape, her eyes shone. Now Jim Beckwourth could return to the Crows without fear.

Barney grinned. "Sure it's going to snow. There's a real storm coming. But, thanks in part to you, it won't be a blood bath too."

"Thanks to me?" she said, eyeing him warily.

"Hixson knows it was you. Told me after the acquittal. It was a brave thing to do, Miss Robb, but possibly not necessary."

"Oh? Why?"

"While Ben Holladay was working on the jury, other people in town were working on the witnesses that jury would have to hear. There was no way the white community could call it anything else but self-defense. But the black community is quietly singing the praises of Mulatto Jo." He smiled at her then.

She blushed. "Oh, no! How did they find out?"

"Juan Beckwourth. He's put you in the same class with the Catholic saints."

Jody groaned. "And Malcolm Hoog will twist it into another lurid novel!"

"That's possible, but too many people know the truth for him to twist it around too much. No matter, you can hold your head up proudly. Down deep, the overall welfare of the community is the most important thing to the majority in this town. They can't hardly help but admire you for your courage and daring." His smile widened. "Imagine, a white woman breaking a black mountain man out of jail."

"Why, Mister Ford! You're beginning to sound just like Malcolm Hoog!" Jody giggled; she was thinking that this would certainly make Birdie change his tune.

Barney pretended to be outraged. "I should hope not, Miss Robb. Now, Miss Julia and I would be most honored if you would move into our guest room"—he paused—"until you find more suitable accommodations."

Jody's smile quickly faded. "I find my accommodations quite suitable, Mister Ford," she said stiffly.

He reddened. "I did sound like a bigot," he admitted. "I am sorry, we just thought—"

"Thank Miss Julia for me, sir, but I'm quite happy sharing this cottage with Irene Patton. She is a remarkable teacher and she has become a very dear friend."

Actually, her answer pleased Barney Ford. From the reports he received from Louis Napoleon and Sarah, he could be very happy with the way Jody was handling the school. She wasn't forcing white ideals and beliefs on the students; on the contrary, she was trying to give them ideals of their own. Living in Five Points would keep her closer to the students and his people.

Still, his equations on her were not entirely to his liking.

"Oh, before I forget," he said, producing a thick envelope from his breast pocket. "This came for you in care of me. The return address suggests that your aunt has finally broken her silence."

Hesitantly, Jody took the envelope. She wasn't sure that she wanted that silence broken. A bell rang and she made her excuses to Barney; she had a class to see after.

The letter from Miss Inez was still unopened and unread when Jody returned to the cottage that evening. Her mind was on an entirely different matter. Birdie.

She raced Irene through dinner and the dishes, which was unusual for her. Then she took an extra long time sponging herself, brushing her hair and dressing again in a print dress instead of putting on her nightgown.

Irene said nothing, but it all meant a man to her and she was pretty sure who that man was. She didn't approve, but not because Jody was white and Birdie black, she just flat-out didn't like the man for Jody. Sergeant Jacobs was, in Irene's opinion, neither black nor white, but a fence-sitter who jumped back and forth to suit his needs.

The expected snow had begun falling that afternoon. It was driving hard against the window panes when Irene finally went to bed, her heart reaching out to Jody, who sat waiting, trying to hide her growing disappointment. Damn the man, Irene thought.

The hours stretched on and the room grew cold. Jody dredged up a million reasons why Birdie hadn't come. At midnight she gave up all hope, blaming the storm. As she banked the fire for the night, she was tempted to add her aunt's still unopened letter to it.

"No," she told herself, "that wouldn't be fair. She at least wrote."

She took the envelope to her room and undressed. It was bitter cold now and she scurried under the covers. By the dim light of the Betty lamp, Jody broke the seal on the envelope and quickly scanned the pages inside. Then she read them again more slowly.

It was like reading a communication from a stranger. Miss Inez was happy with her situation, at least when Maxwell and Clayton Bundy were away from the ranch. Her wish was to patch up her differences with Jody before the holiday season was upon them. She would like very much to have Jody with her at Christmas.

The request stirred many odd memories for Jody. Christmas had always been the best and the worst of seasons for her. She would be one of a half-dozen students at school with no home to return to for the holidays. With that in common, they would include her in their lives, for a few days at least.

Christmas morning she avoided with any excuse she could think of. To soothe the conscience, the neglectful parents would send their daughters basketsfull of brightly wrapped presents to squeal over. Jody could automatically expect two plainly wrapped packages. Miss Inez could be counted on to replenish Jody's supply of undergarments, one size larger than the year before. Hiram Robb, for reasons known only to himself, could be counted upon for a second present, always suitable for a child of six and not a girl in her teens.

Jody had never looked forward to Christmas before and could not look forward to it now. Then, on another odd thought, she wondered idly how the blacks celebrated it. It was something she should consider as a school project.

Extinguishing the Betty lamp, she tried to keep her mind on the school to bring sleep. She did not want to think about Birdie or Miss Inez. But her disappointment over Birdie clung like a burr, and it was some time before sleep came at last.

13

THE SNOW LAY two feet deep when the storm ended. The weather remained cold. Winter, thought Jody, had come to stay; and she walked along the foot-pounded paths with a definite purpose in mind.

She hadn't told Irene where she was going. She had merely announced at breakfast that she was feeling housebound and needed some fresh air. Four days of constant snow had made the cottage seem awfully small for the two of them. Their only visitor had been Louis Ford, delivering food and firewood by sleigh. The snow had made Denver forget about Jim Beckwourth. A portion of Jódy's brain had continued to blame the storm for keeping Birdie away, until Louis Napoleon announced that Marshall Hixson was being given credit for keeping the town calm by sending the troops away. Jody latched onto the news as a new excuse for Birdie. But as soon as the boy had departed, Irene's anger with Birdie exploded.

"That's no man, in my opinion. He should be ashamed, treating you the way he did and then sneaking out of town without a word of apology."

Jody said nothing. She did not want to face the possibility that Birdie might not have wanted to come to see her and apologize. But now that she knew that Birdie would not be coming, she was determined to forget him and occupy her mind with other matters.

She walked quickly. The cold whipped up the color in her cheeks, and she kept kicking the snow loose from the hem of her skirt. She thought how sensible it would be if a woman could wear pants like a man on such a day. The snow was powdery and it glittered when she shook it off. She trod down hard, hearing the snow squeak, putting her weight forward over her knees.

As she walked through the district, greetings were called to her from people she hardly knew. Their acceptance of her warmed and comforted her; and suddenly she realized that Julia Ford was not the person she should be going to see. Julia was too "white" for the information Jody sought. When the next resident greeted her, she swung off the path and plowed through the snow to the ramshackle house.

She recognized the children although none of them were in her class. She struggled to put names to the faces. Carter, that was the family; Carter.

She greeted the children then said to their mother, "It's nice of you to say 'how-do'."

Pearl Carter blinked timidly and put out her hand. "Folks around here call me Widow Carter, Miss. Would you be stepping in?"

Jody nodded and kicked the snow from her feet at the door. She followed Pearl Carter into a one-room multipurpose house. A cook stove, with a faulty chimney, was the only source of heat. The smoke had blackened the rafters. The shack was a miserable, drafty place, but Jody put that out of her mind.

God hadn't granted Pearl Carter a pretty face, but she had a fine, strong body. It was hard to pin an age to her, although the children ranged from six to ten.

"I ain't rightly a widow," she volunteered, as Jody took a seat. "My last man was sold 'fore little Nate was born."

Jody looked at her in amazement. "But have you heard from him since? Don't the children need a father?"

Pearl shrugged. "He were only Nate's pappy, miss. I were a producer from age twelve on. Different pappy for each of 'em."

Jody's jaw dropped. "But how do you manage?"

"Mister Rebus MacCorkel give me money out of his private purse to come here and keep my boys together. He's a nice man, for a Yankee. A gentleman."

"Who is this Mister MacCorkel?"

"He the administrator that come to Lumpkink, Mississippi after the war. He were from Massachusetts. He's a real nice man, miss. He saw to us darkies when the whites left the plantation. He's talkin' about making it like old times."

"How do you mean?"

Pearl looked surprised. "Why, me bein' a producer again for studmen. I be only twenty-two and must have another good dozen children in me."

"But . . . those slave days are over!" Jody protested.

Pearl Carter laughed.

"They be back, that's what Mister MacCorkel says. Once they need field hands again they'll let women like me breed 'em."

My Lord, Jody thought; she's proud of what she was. Aloud she said, "Is that what you want for these four?" She nodded toward the children.

"That's what Providence meant them for."

"Then why send them to school for an education?"

Pearl Carter drew back as if she had been slapped. Her thin face tightened with a look of bitterness; it made her eyes seem even larger.

"Miss Robb," she said quietly. She looked like a child in her ragged dress. "My boys someday be overseers and not studmen like their paws. This learning help 'em do that, 'fore Mister MacCorkel hears about it."

"He's not your owner. You don't have to keep their education a secret from him," Jody said.

Pearl thought a moment. "You sure?"

"Of course I am!" Jody said.

"He say different." Pearl's narrow face was wistful. "Who am right?"

"I think I am," Jody said. "When was the last time you saw this Mister MacCorkel?"

"'Bout a year. I mark a paper and come here."

"Paper? Might I see it?"

Pearl began to shuffle through a shelf of clothing. "I've got it somewhere. Oh, yes, here 'tis. Same, I guess, as the others."

"Others?"

"Two wagonloads from Mississippi. We ain't supposed to act like we know each other, though."

Jody took the paper and read it through quickly. She looked up at Pearl, stunned. "Two thousand dollars!"

A little smile played on the woman's mouth; she couldn't read, but knew the schoolteacher had to be wrong.

"Rebus MacCorkel wrote it out for us. Two hundred dollars. For transportation fees, a hundred dollars; rent, twenty-five; clothing, five; cupboard food, seventy." She rattled off the items, knowing them by heart.

"But there are five of you?"

"I be somewhere different on the paper."

Jody read the paper again, more slowly this time. Her anger rose.

"Look here," she said. "It's rather hard to read his writing. Can I take this home and study it more carefully? I promise not to get you into trouble."

Pearl hesitated, then nodded. "I guess so." She added apologetically, "I never had no chance to learn to read."

Nor, Jody thought grimly, had any of the others, I bet. She could read MacCorkel's writing very well, but wanted the paper as evidence.

Jody hurried away from the house. She spent the rest of the day visiting, but with a dual purpose. By careful questioning, she managed to sort out two dozen other "widow" women with similar pieces of paper. None knew that she had talked with any of the others. She was flushed and breathless when she arrived at Barney Ford's house.

She glared up into Barney's startled face. "I've been uncovering the rebirth of slavery right here in your own backyard. Now I think it's time we talked about the rights of women—black women."

Barney blushed.

"I've gathered up two dozen rather strange contracts today, but to protect the women they must be kept quiet. The figures are inflated, of course, but the meaning is the same. They have sold their children and any future children."

"But . . . but that is against the law!" Barney protested.

"Why?" Jody snapped. "They are only women, after all. They are still slaves to the whims of men who want to use them for whatever purpose is profitable."

Barney turned brick red under his honey-toned skin. He would never get used to this woman, but there were times when he felt she was a blessing in disguise.

November in Denver passed uneventfully enough. The cold continued and the snow lay deep. Quietly, Barney made inquiries of friends in Mississippi about Rebus MacCorkel.

At school the children began work on Jody's secret plans for Christmas. Almost every week an Army patrol passed through Denver. When men heard how many range cattle were being rustled in Colorado and Wyoming, they found it hard to believe, and they wondered where the stolen cattle were being hidden. Occasionally, rail-tie wagons passed through Denver, reminding the town's inhabitants that a railroad would soon link them with Cheyenne.

At the Bundy ranch, the further along winter advanced the more Clayton Bundy expressed misgivings about the leadership of Harvey Longbough. The Army patrols were watching the ranch too carefully. Clay had heard about a man up around Landusky, Montana who intrigued him. In mid-November he sent his brother Maxwell north to size up Harvey Logan.

Major Ferris Ferguson was now divorced but avoided Jody as long as she continued to live with a black woman. Birdie, still jealous of Jody's new standing with the black community, went on every patrol that would keep him away from Denver.

December saw the arrival in Denver of copies of "Mulatto Jo and the Jailbreak." To Malcolm Hoog's credit, the story was masterfully done, but in the East especially, followers of Mulatto Jo's adventures did not see it that way. Used to short sentences and simple words, they did not appreciate Hoog's new-found literary style, and the magazine didn't sell. When the latest Mulatto Jo saga didn't even become a hit in Denver, where the action took place, publisher William Byers saw the future clearly. Malcolm Hoog turned his action pen to new characters, and Mulatto Jo was allowed to fade away forever.

December also saw the arrival in town of Wagon Tom Smithson. The railroad needed a good blacksmith and Wagon Tom was just the man. He brought with him another letter from Miss Inez and a surprise: he was set on marriage. To his delight, Irene Patton quickly agreed, and the date was set for the day after school recessed for the two week holiday.

In the evenings, Wagon Tom would light a great fire in the cottage fireplace and lie down in front of it, drinking applejack; Irene would generally sit down beside him. Jody, sitting in a corner, was working on a rug for their wedding present, using a wooden crochet hook and strips of colorful rags. It was a seven-foot project, for that was the size of Irene's bedroom, which would also be Tom's bedroom soon. Whether Jody would stay on at the cottage after the wedding hadn't been discussed, though she felt already that it was no place for her, around such a loving atmosphere.

She closed her mind to that and thought instead about Miss Inez's latest letter. She liked the news it conveyed: Max Bundy would be gone from the ranch until after Christmas. If she accepted her aunt's invitation to come for the holidays, that would leave the cottage free for Irene and Tom to use for their honeymoon.

And when she returned . . .

Her mind was too full of other matters to think that far ahead. At school, the children were all busy making plaster of Paris casts of their hands to paint and present to their parents for Christmas presents. Popcorn was being strung, and African and Southern traditions recalled and revised to suit a white Christmas. There was too much to do to think about her personal life, but Jody's heart ached more with each passing day.

Then, a week before the school recess, an event took place that kept her from thinking about herself at all. The investigation into Rebus MacCorkel brought the man to Denver on the run. Without a by-your-leave, he moved in with Mattie McHenry, one of the women contracted to him, and began to make plans to move his twelve "widows" and children back to Mississippi.

Barney Ford shook his head over it. "They might as well pack their bags. He can make those papers stand up in court. You'll see."

"See what?" Jody asked.

Barney grunted. "The South is losing its labor force from the cotton fields and the textile mill owners in the North and in Britain are getting scared. Slavery was bad when they were not making a profit off of it. Now they count on men like MacCorkel to legally revive the system."

"And we can do nothing?" Jody couldn't believe it.

"He did pay their way here, give them some money

for support and is willing to pay their way back. I see little we can do."

Jody refused to give up, even though she knew the twelve women were now too terrified to even talk to her. Her only hope lay in Rebus MacCorkel being a reasonable man.

She could tell at once that he was not when she called at Mattie McHenry's. The gangling carpetbagger seated on the McHenry hearth stretched and kicked over a log with his heel. The fire blazed upward, pouring a ruddy light across the nude upper half of MacCorkel's sweating body. Jody didn't even want to think about why he was only half-dressed. Mattie McHenry behaved as if she didn't know her, and the three teen-age McHenry boys treated Rebus like a visiting monarch. It didn't take Jody long to figure out why: the room reeked of tobacco and whiskey. She was sure MacCorkel was letting the boys drink and smoke right along with him.

"That's the trouble, miss. If the Rebs hadn't been whipped so bad, they might still have their darkies on the plantations as paid labor. But the way it is, they are a stubborn lot. They want them back as slaves."

"How are you any different?" Jody demanded.

MacCorkel appraised her thoughtfully. She was standing up to him, and he liked that.

"I offer them homes, jobs and security. Hell, woman, all they know how to do is breed!"

"Because no one has taught them any differently," Jody said.

"Because they are not capable of learning more than just basic things," he countered.

"What you mean is you don't want them learning more than basic things. No reading or writing or thinking for themselves. Keep them stupid for your own profit from them."

Jody held his gaze steadily, and MacCorkel, instead of getting angry, found himself liking it, to his surprise.

"I do have money invested in them, you know."

"No more than other men have invested in horses and cattle."

"It is still an investment that I can't afford to walk away from," he said.

Jody suddenly smiled. "I can understand that." She drew a deep breath. "Would you be willing to sell that investment?"

MacCorkel thought about that a moment, then he said, "Miss, I don't mean to be hard on you, or on your interest in these folk. But you are talking a heap of money for a schoolmarm."

Jody stuck her chin out. "I can at least try."

MacCorkel liked her spirit, though he knew she would fail. His asking price would have to be more than it read on the papers.

When Jody pinned him down, Bill Byers finally admitted that he could not publish her plan in his newspaper because the majority of his readers would be strongly opposed to it.

Jody argued that, if it was reasonable for the *News* to run a campaign to provide Christmas for needy children, why was it not equally reasonable to run a campaign to provide the real meaning of Christmas for these threatened colored families?

This argument angered Byers because he could find no answer to it, but it failed to change his position. He was opposed to the idea and that was that.

"Why, Malcolm Hoog," Jody said sweetly, meeting

him as she left Byers office. "I'm so pleased to run into you."

He was immediately wary. JoAnn Robb was not coy and this approach looked like trouble.

"Miss Robb," he said politely.

"I have been meaning to stop in, but we're so busy at school these days. I want to congratulate you on the jailbreak story."

Now he was really suspicious. "Oh?"

"I was pleased with its accuracy. Juan Beckwourth must have given you a good deal of help."

She had played a double game with his ego and he wasn't sure how to react. Amazingly, it was honestly.

"You must understand the circumstances, Miss Robb. The man's mother was quite ill and he needed money for the doctor. I was more than happy to pay him for his help with the true facts."

"And how much more exciting they made the story! I wouldn't like this to get around, but I allowed one of my better students to read your story to the class."

Hoog beamed with pride. "I am most honored, Miss Robb."

"Well, I must be on about my present project." She started to move away, paused and turned back. "On second thought, Mr. Hoog, perhaps the circumstances surrounding my present project would interest you. It is something your Mulatto Jo would have taken on with relish." She smiled at him sweetly.

Malcolm Hoog was trapped. He had no choice but to stand and listen and learn what she expected from him. He gratefully gave her a bank draft for one hundred dollars before she could talk him out of any more.

"Miss Robb," he said, stopping her as she began

to leave. "Did you ever think that a true account of your life here in the West would make quite interesting reading?"

"You're right, Malcolm," she said over her shoulder. "But who knows what is yet to come?"

He stood looking after her thoughtfully. Mulatto Jo had begun as only a minor character in his mind; she had grown because of reader interest. He had not thought to change her in the last book, but through the eyes of Juan Beckwourth he had begun to see her, or rather her real-life model, quite differently. A publisher in New York had liked his style in the jailbreak story, but not the fact that his heroine was colored. If he could stay away from the colored line, that publisher might be interested in his next work.

He sat down at his desk and stared at the blank foolscap without committing a word to paper.

"Thinking up another blood-chiller?" Byers asked as he was leaving an hour later.

"Not really. I was thinking how interesting Miss Robb's life has been to date."

"Forget her," said Byers. "Cowboys are the romantic thing to think about."

Malcolm agreed, but couldn't get JoAnn Robb out of his mind. Someday, he vowed, he would write her true story.

Malcolm Hoog didn't know it, but he had given Jody a sense of triumph that kept her going in the face of repeated minor defeats. It was Christmas time and contributions were hard to come by. Doggedly, Jody accepted anything offered, a nickel here, a dime there, and gave a heartfelt blessing over a dollar. To her great surprise, she was able to raise over a thousand dollars in the Five Points district.

The white community was another story. Doors were slammed in her face, insults were thrown at her and an odd challenge was presented. "If you can get John Evans to give, I'll match it."

All Jody knew about the man was that he had once been governor of the territory. She went up to Brown's Bluff the next morning to see him. It was the first time she had ever been in this part of Denver; the size of the houses, together with their construction of granite and brick, impressed her.

A bosomy black woman met her at the door and said, "Gubnor ain' seein' nobody," in an impressive voice. Jody could not recall ever seeing this woman in the district and was about to approach her for a contribution when a door opened into the hall and a tall thin man with a patriarchal beard came out.

"What is it, Melanie?"

"Dis here dat woman from dat nigger school askin' fer yah," Melanie said contemptuously.

Jody ignored the tone and stepped forward. "I require only a few moments of your time, sir. I am JoAnn Robb, but I'm not here about the school."

John Evans studied her with interest; she was hardly anything like he would have expected. He was a gentleman to a fault and now he said, "Come in. I can grant you a few moments."

The governor's study had been set up in the northwest room with the back of the desk to the fireplace so he could look through the windows toward the mountains. He indicated a chair for Jody and sat down behind the desk. Jody was quick to explain her mission.

"And how is my old friend Barney Ford helping in this matter?" John Evans asked, surprisingly. "He could afford to stand the whole thing alone."

"I have purposely not approached him, Governor Evans. It seems to me to be a community matter, not something for a single person to shoulder. He does so much for his people as it is."

"His people," Evans said suddenly in a deep voice, "keep us from becoming a state and me from being that state's first senator. I don't think Barney would appreciate your coming to me, Miss Robb." He made a gesture with his hand, as if he were brushing the whole business aside. At the same time, he raised his eyes to Jody's. The eyes were tired and sad and, in an odd way, very shy.

"This, sir, should have nothing to do with past feelings on personal matters. We are discussing twelve women and their thirty-six children. Colorado will never become a state if it is learned that men like Rebus MacCorkel can hold onto colored people here as though they were still slaves. It's a matter of common decency."

The room was silent. Jody didn't realize it but for five years now Barney Ford had felt that John Evans had betrayed him and the colored people. Evans had been badly advised and branded a political hack for declaring his feelings one way in Washington, and another way in Colorado. He still dreamed of becoming a senator. Now he thought that a gesture like this could begin to mend some badly damaged fences.

He quickly pulled over paper and quill and began to write. He handed the note to Jody.

"You will take this to Luther Kountze at Kountze Brothers Bank. I am asking him to be of some help to you, too. However, I do not think it is necessary for Barney to learn of my assistance."

Jody stared at the note. Before she could comment,

Evans escorted her back to the hall and over to Melanie to be escorted out.

John Evans knew that Luther Kountze would inform Barney sooner or later. A feeling of guilt struck him then: he had not acted out of compassion, but to win favor in the eyes of Barney Ford. He was tempted to call the young woman back and tear up the note.

The quick success of Jody's campaign, of which he was very well informed, shook Barney. He had been the leader of his people, the man with the money who had built them a school. Now he felt as if they were purposely avoiding him for some reason, and he was deeply hurt. He almost refused to see Jody when she came to his house that evening. But he was a man to whom directness invariably appealed. Jody wasted no time but read out the names of all the contributors, even if only a few cents had been given, and didn't dwell on how she had obtained five hundred dollars each from John Evans and Luther Kountze. Frankly, the amounts still had her in a state of shock. She had tried to talk Owen Goldrick out of it, but he insisted on contributing what was still lacking to make up the full twenty-four hundred dollars.

"Well," Barney said, miffed. "If you have the money, why come to me?"

Jody smiled grimly. "Mister Ford, you're too intelligent to think that man would bargain with a woman. Money I have been able to get from other people, but you are the only man I know who can make Rebus MacCorkel go through with the deal."

Barney studied her and then glanced at his wife's face. Julia's face was flushed and her eyes wide with emotion. At last Barney smiled. He admired Jody's courage and it had given him a new thought.

"I can do it, of course," he said quietly, "but I might ask you to do me a favor in return."

"Anything," Jody promised.

"I was planning on doing it myself, but I hate to be away from the family at Christmas. Have you any plans?"

"Well"—Jody hesitated—"yes and no. My aunt has invited me to the Bundy ranch for Christmas."

"That should pose no problem. You can go on from there to Cheyenne and catch the train."

"But, Barney!" Julia started to protest.

"Use reason," he said gently. "No one would suspect her of carrying such a large sum of money to Mammy Pleasant in San Francisco, and she can be back before school starts again."

Jody's heart skipped a beat. She did not move or speak. San Francisco! And she would meet Mammy Pleasant and see Carrie again. . . .

14

"WELL, FOR THE LOVE of mercy, JoAnn Robb!"

Jody turned to see her aunt standing on the stairs, and her face was flushed with excitement.

"Child, why didn't you let me know you were coming?"

Jody tried to explain. Events had just piled one on top of the other after Barney had all but made up her mind for her. Her scheme to ransom the widows had nearly fallen apart when Rebus MacCorkel had demanded of Barney two thousand dollars for *each* woman and child. It had taken Marshal Hixson to make Rebus see the folly of such thinking, with the stern threat of jail if he didn't take what was offered and leave the territory. Still, MacCorkel was able to convince Mattie McHenry to return to Mississippi with him.

Then, almost nonstop, Jody had to bring Miss Inez up to date on the marriage of Wagon Tom, the marvel-

ous things *her* students had done for Christmas and
the reason why her visit would be so short.

Miss Inez seemed to understand. Jody was no longer
a child. Maturity sat very well on the young woman
and her aunt felt proud. But she also had stories of her
own to relate and secrets to share.

The ranch had undergone quite a few changes. The
Mexicans and married cowhands were all gone, replaced by bachelor cowboys that Miss Inez hardly ever
saw. The kitchen was now under the command of a
Chinese cook, and with only Clayton's children to
tutor, her days had become quite pleasant.

Unpacking, Jody marveled at the change in the
woman. Banished forever was every sign of plainness.
Her clothing was colorful and stylish. Her brownish-
gray hair curled loosely about a face that seemed to
have a permanent blush. When Lem Bundy's name
came up, her manner was as coy as a girl's. The signs
were all too obvious.

"Has he asked you to marry him?" Jody asked.

Miss Inez actually giggled. "Secretly. Clayton is the
stumbling block. He is dead-set against my becoming
mistress of this ranch."

"And Maxwell?" Jody asked cautiously.

"Frankly, Jody, he is a two-faced pain in the butt.
Sweet to me to gain information about you, and knifing
me in the back to please Clayton. You know, of course,
that he is only interested in you for sexual reasons."

Jody blushed. It was the first time her aunt had ever
raised the subject of sex wth her. For that matter, it
was the first time she had ever called her Jody!

It was like a refreshing spring rain. Jody was able to
express her feelings and fears about Maxwell Bundy
and tell her aunt what he had tried to do to her.

It was the longest talk she had ever had with Miss Inez. Only once did she feel she had to evade an issue.

"No, there is no man in my life."

"Well, just as long as it isn't Maxwell Bundy, I feel better."

Miss Inez had brought about other changes at the ranch besides those in herself. Clay's children were now well-mannered and obviously in awe of her. Lemanuel, in her presence, was like a kitten demanding to be stroked.

Clay hadn't changed. He resented the fact that he had not been told that Jody was coming to the ranch for Christmas. His mind worked in very strange patterns: he was sure that Max had probably talked her into it to help further along the stupid romance between Lem and Miss Inez. He wanted neither woman to marry into his family, but he was cagey and cautious. By every means short of murder he had transformed the ranch cowhands into men who owed their allegiance only to him. Only one of them worked into the plan his mind was now shaping. But one man did.

Rocky White sat before the wood stove in the bunkhouse and stared at Clayton out of drunken eyes. He couldn't believe what the man had just asked of him.

"It's—it's unthinkable," he said, slurring the words. "No decent man would do such—"

"I think," Clay stopped him coldly, "that you're hardly in a position to talk about decency, Throckton Brough-White the Third."

"Oh!" Rocky faltered, but only for a moment. "How did you learn my name, and precisely what are you driving at?"

"Your name was easy enough to find out from my

brother," Clay said. "And I've learned enough from the boys in the bunkhouse to know you are hardly in a position to instruct me in morality."

Rocky's face was white and still, and suddenly sober. "I see," he murmured.

"In fact, I've known for some time. A man who manages cowboys would, you know. I'm only surprised you were able to give your butt and mouth to so many for so long. Those things are seldom kept secret, at least not among cowboys."

"Oh, damn my life anyhow!" Rocky exploded. "Why on earth was I born this way?"

Clay shrugged. "That's hardly my problem. You be at the house in the morning with a couple of horses. I want it to look like you're just going to fetch a Christmas tree."

But looking at him now, Clay thought: He won't have the guts to carry it off! I'd better have an alternate plan ready, just in case.

In two hours, they had covered a mile and a half through the woods. Jody had thought the outing would be fun, but to her disappointment, Rocky kept well ahead so they didn't even have a chance to talk. Just as the sun was beginning to warm the chill morning, they struck a cattle trail that led them into a pasture which sloped toward a small valley. Beside a road stood a small house, a barn attached to it by a woodshed. A curl of inviting smoke rose from the chimney.

Rocky stopped with growing apprehension and stared down at the house. This little-known part of the Bundy ranch should have been empty at this time of the year. A stranger could ruin his plans. Rocky had done many despicable things in his life, but he could not bring himself to leave Jody stranded in the snow.

Just as he turned back to warn her about the plot against her, the attack came. They came out of the trees yelling like savages. The dreadful sound started echoes whirling in the pine trees, seventy feet high. It was a moment of utter confusion.

A whip snaked around Rocky's chest and yanked him from the saddle. Jody didn't have time to react. At once, three lasso loops sang past her ears, instantly tightening about her hips, her waist and her breasts. The three-way tug of war roughly ejected her from the saddle and momentarily suspended her in mid-air. It was impossible to scream. The jolt had taken her breath away and the tight ropes were close to making her black out. Without warning, she was dropped into the snow and dirt. She was tumbled along for several feet until the ropes were pulled taut again, and her body stopped short as though she had run up against a wall. Rocky saw her jerked off the ground again as the air was choked out of her lungs and stomach. When she crumpled like a rag doll, they lowered her slowly, with ironic gentleness, to the ground. The woods grew very still.

Then the men were gathering Jody up and placing her across the lap of one of the riders. Rocky watched them bear the body toward the ranchhouse. Unbelievingly, he realized that they were not going to kill him. He had neither the heart nor the inclination to follow and learn Jody's fate. Slowly, he mounted his horse, then turned and began to ride due west.

He had failed her; he had failed himself as a man. He heard his own voice saying, "Why, you're dead forever more!"

He knew he could never let Lem Bundy know where he had gone. He knew he would never see England again.

* * *

Consciousness came slowly; it was a horrible moment of *déjà vu*. She was bound again head and foot, but this time to the flat bed of a wagon. Her chest, waist and hips were rings of searing pain from rope burns. As her brain cleared, she was at least thankful that she was alive and could breathe again. At least she was alive for the moment.

Logic suggested only one reason for the attack. They were outlaws who had somehow learned about the money she was carrying to Mammy Pleasant from Barney Ford. She didn't want to think about Rocky White; she assumed that he was dead.

But as her head cleared even more, she questioned why she was still alive. That question was followed by another, odd one: she was shivering from the cold . . . what had happened to the heavy woolen riding cape Miss Inez had loaned her? Jody was bound spread-eagle to the wagon, but she could still lift her head.

It shocked and amazed her to find the cloak gone and her dress all in one piece. She dropped her head back on the floor boards. She was shivering again; she closed her eyes and tried to lie still. She could not feel with her hands but could reassure herself in a different fashion. She took several very deep breaths, each time slowly collapsing her lungs. It was baffling to discover in this way her abductors had not spotted the heavily padded brassiere she wore. Her fear of its discovery had been such that she had even worn it to bed the night before.

Its clever construction, she decided, was all that had kept her alive so far. Now she would have to use it to stay alive.

The wagon rolled to a halt. Jody closed her eyes tightly. She heard someone dismount from the driver's seat and yell to someone else to come for the wagon.

She heard the newcomer—it sounded like a black man—question the driver. He didn't answer until he had shuffled alongside the wagon and unhitched a horse from the tailgate.

"Keep her here until you hear from Bundy—those are the orders. I gotta get back to the ranch 'for sundown."

His replacement swore as he mounted the wagon. "Longbough ain' gonna like it."

"Max'll settle any beef he's got."

Jody mistakenly put two separate pieces of information together now as one single fact. All thoughts of robbery vanished as the reason for her capture. It was obviously a malicious manifestation of the godlessness of Maxwell Bundy! All fear left her, leaving only maddening anger.

The driver clucked the horse to a walk up a badly rutted gully. Jody opened her eyes to look straight upward, seeing oddly shaped cliffs against the sky. She lay still, watching the formations close in until the sky was just a narrow ribbon at the top. There was a turning and near total darkness as they traveled for several minutes beneath an overhang that almost touched the opposite cliff. Hidden eyes watched every inch of their progress.

Jody was not aware that she was passing through a devious maze created by eons-old volcanic eruptions. Of the hundreds of *cul-de-sacs* and box canyons in the rugged mountain range there was only one with an entrance to the hidden valley beyond.

Lem Bundy and Miss Inez stared at the tattered and bloody cloak in stunned silence. The cowboys gave the credit to grizzly bears. Miss Inez buried her face

against Bundy's shoulder sleeve and sobbed. Even she
couldn't be sure how many of the tears she shed were
tears of grief and her past treatment of her niece.

Clayton Bundy had planned well. It was half a day
before other –B– cowhands returned to declare that
neither body had been found. Clay would wait a week.
By that time Max should be returning from Montana.
As far as he knew, Clay's order about no women at
the Hole-in-the-Wall had been enforced. Max, he was
sure, would have second thoughts about Miss Robb,
after she had been used for a week by thirty-some different men. He had seen such women who had been
used by the Indians. It turned them crazy. No one
would know that Clay had been responsible, and
wouldn't Miss Inez have to leave the ranch to care for
her weird niece?

Alfreda Landusky let the faded calico dress rise
to her knees as she cautiously climbed into the hay
loft. She was a solidly built girl with a heavy frame
and domineering appearance. By the standards of
the day and age in which she lived, she was already
considered an old maid, although not yet nineteen.

Her coal-black hair, worn long and straight, was
always untidy. Her clothes always looked and smelled
in need of lye and water.

Her stepfather, who owned the best share of the
grazing land in the valley, was overly strict with her,
as he was with his own two daughters. But not even
his restrictions and the harsh ranch life could overcome the fact they were the only young females in
fifty miles. Even marriage had not kept Alfreda's step-
sisters from hankering after every cowboy who was
willing to take them away from it all.

She had set her cap for the new man the minute

she saw him ride into the ranch yard. He was good looking, long-backed and sat his horse well. Round his neck the dusty silk handkerchief, tied loose, told of hard traveling. She watched her stepsisters eye the good high-heeled boots, the firm legs housed in California pants the color of light buckskin, the slender waist with the Colt revolver swinging from the hip, the broad chest and shoulders, and the lean face half-hidden by the shadow of the wide-brimmed hat. She knew she would have to move fast to get this quarry first.

Max Bundy did not want to be friendly with anyone on the ranch. He was there just to blend in, another unknown cowboy. Five miles away was the Logan spread; the Logan brothers had rustled enough cattle to set themselves up in Montana as respectable ranchers. Max was having a hard time convincing Harvey that there would be a lot of easy money for him workin for the Bundy brothers. Harvey keept Max away from the ranch and his brothers, because he didn't want them to know he was even considering such a deal; but he had to admit that honest ranching was a hell of a lot more work than straight rustling.

Max Bundy was coming to the same conclusion. He had never worked so hard in his life. Christmas was two days away and he wanted to get home, with or without Harvey Logan.

That morning he had almost quit on the spot. Everyone else was taking off for a pre-Christmas party at the Logans, and he was left to hay the milk cows. He mentally gave Harvey until noon to contact him and then he was heading south.

Alfreda saw it as her only chance and feigned illness until the ranch was deserted. She was in no hurry. Most would not return until past sundown;

many more not until the next day when the Logan's whiskey gave out, and a few would never come back.

But her slow approach was gaining her only one-syllable answers and grunts from Max. Her last resort, she felt, was the water bucket and an insulting question.

She brought the bucket to where he was pitching hay into the feed stalls and bent to dip a cup into it for him.

"You one of those men who only like it with other men?"

He didn't answer as he drank the water she handed him. It had been nearly a month since he had had a woman and it was near driving him crazy. She arched her back so that her firm breasts pulled her calico dress taut.

"Men ain't got these."

He dropped the tin cup and molded the mounds with each hand. Alfreda knew she had him then and tilted her head expectantly, her lips slightly parted. His hard, thin, weatherbeaten mouth took the kiss and intensified its meaning with his tongue. This surprised and delighted her and she pulled him down into the hay. Her thigh could feel his pleasure begin to rise against her. It was becoming far different from the objects she had secretly watched other cowboys relieve themselves with. He shuddered with erotic frenzy as he fought to release himself.

Without being asked, she raised her dress to her neck and revealed that she was wearing no undergarments. He closed his mind to her face; her body would be Jody's body. He bent his head and began kissing every inch of her naked flesh. She gasped as his tongue invaded her virginity. The sensation made her squirm and roll to the side. He had to move to keep from being pushed away. Because she thought it was expected of her, she immediately filled her mouth with him.

For a second his hardness intensified and then he quickly drew his head back. She had ruined the illusion; this was not what he desired from Jody. But his lust would not be denied.

"Keep at it, honey," he growled. "Keep at it that way." He shoved forward until she was almost choking. His breath was coming in short jabs. "Don't stop. I had an Englishman once with a mouth smaller than yours and he could take me down to the balls."

Alfreda shook her head and pulled away in disgust. She had known it all along: all cowboys were depraved creatures. She started to roll away and rise.

"What the hell?" he roared and pulled her back. He didn't even position himself but pressed down between her thighs. For the first time, then, he was aware of her virginal state. He moved violently, her scream nearly breaking his eardrum. He raised on his arms to escape the sound, but would not stop his devouring lust. Even when he was finished he could not stop. He had waited so long for Jody that he might never stop.

Her piercing scream announced that she had reached her zenith. But his lean body was not allowed a final plunge. With a violent jerk, he was lifted from her and tossed to the ground.

"Max Bundy, you dumb bastard! Landusky ain't but a quarter mile behind me."

Max looked up sheepishly at Harvey Logan. It seemed impossible that the wiry little man could have manhandled his big frame so easily.

"I was only getting a little—"

"Stupid!" Logan cut him off. "Her stepdaddy don't

want anyone getting her ass. Get your horse and get
the hell back to Colorado."

"Not without you!"

"Bullshit! My getting caught here will be trouble
enough for me. Now move!"

Alfreda just lay grinning foolishly.

When they brought Max's horse from the barn they
were shocked to see the white-headed old rancher
and his two sons-in-law quietly riding in.

"Now!" screamed Harvey. They sprang into the
saddle and spurred the horses into a fast retreat. Landusky heard them and directed his sons-in-law to cut
them off. Three guns began to bark in Max and Harvey's direction, pinging into the air as they smashed
and ricocheted off the barn siding.

"You must think I'm pretty damn stupid, Harvey
Logan!" Landusky shouted. "I been watching that
varmint sneak off to meet you for a week. Now what's
your game?"

"I'll get him, Paw. He ain't drawn yet." Dan Williams dug his left spur deep into his horse and headed
to cut them off before they reached the corner of the
ranch house. Landusky screamed for him to stop, but
the wild whinny of the horse and the fast explosions
blazing from his brother-in-law Luke Lumplin's gun
drowned out the warning.

Before Dan Williams could reverse direction, Logan had his shotgun out of the saddle holster. His
stubby finger pulled both barrels. The massive boom
was mixed with the terrified scream of human and
animal death agony. Logan, racing around the corner
of the house, did not see the frightening sight of the
headless horseman as he plunged to earth. The horse
took two staggering steps and buckled from its mor-
tal wounds.

"Dan! Danny!" Alfreda screamed, but would never get an answer.

"He's dead, girl!" Landusky shouted. "Logan killed him. I hope you're happy now, you whoring little bitch. I'll take care of you later. Luke, let's go get the boys and ride those bastards down!"

Max, not waiting for Logan, had headed for the nearest covering grove. Logan, upon finding him, snarled, "You listen to me, jackass, and you listen good. I ain't ever killed a man before now and I'm tempted to make it two. You give me no choice but to go with you now, but I'm boss. You make one false move and I'll ride you all the way to hell!"

Max tried to bluster his way out. "We can't let a posse follow us to my brother's ranch."

Logan spat. "You're even stupider than I thought. We'll make for Hole-in-the-Wall and stay there until Landusky forgets what your face looks like. Jesus, if the men you got are the same, I might as well kill myself right now."

For the first time in his twenty-odd years, Max felt tired. All he wanted to do was go home. There he could forget about everything. But there were some determined to make sure that he never forgot that day. Alfreda Landusky walked by her brother-in-law's body lying in its puddle of blood as though it weren't there: It was no longer a part of her, she was divorced from it, as though the havoc had never been.

As she packed her few belongings in a haversack, she caught herself repeating the first fact she knew: *"Max Bundy, Max Bundy, Max Bundy . . . ."* And then the second: *"Colorado. Colorado, Colorado . . . ."*

A name and a place was all she had to go on. She repeated them over and over as she saddled a

horse and rode out, heading southeast. The words
were like an eternal drip of water magnified: Name
. . . pause; place . . . pause. Alfreda knew, not knowing how she knew, that she carried Max's seed within
her. She would hunt him down and make him honor
that seed.

Les Mullins was not sure what he should do about
the wagon and woman. But there had been only one
woman in town since his arrival—except for those
smuggled in from Laramie. on weekends—and he
thought that was the logical choice.

At first Jody thought it was a man cursing. She
opened her eyes to a strange sight. The woman's hair
was bleached almost white and swirled up on top of
her head like the icing on a cake. Round globs of
orange denoted where her cheek bones were and her
rather small mouth was made almost comically larger
by an excessive application of vermillion lip rouge.
Over it all, but not diminishing it, was a heavy cak-
ing of white powder.

"Cow manure, you old black reprobate, untie her!"

"But, Miss Gabby," he whimpered.

"It's Miss Gabrielle to you, you simple shit. Now
do it! I'll handle that pea-brained Bundy when he
shows his face."

With four quick strokes the man cut the binding
leather thongs, jumped from the wagon and disappeared.

"Come down from there, ducks," Gabrielle Gabon
encouraged, "before too many of these lecherous old
varmints ketch sight of a type of body they ain't seen
since fall." Jody's head swam for a second as she sat
up. She scooted to the end of the wagon and swung
her legs over the tailgate. The woman came to assist

her. It was only then that Jody saw that she was just about as round as she was short. She was decked out in chiffon and feathers of oddly matched hues. It was a dress the likes of which Jody had never seen before—the deep cut revealing the full cleavage and roundness of her breast and the hem line stopping at the knees. From there her pudgy legs were encased in stockings of a purple hue that was startling against the ankle-length red patent leather boots.

"I'm called by most Gabby Gee," she boomed, "mainly because I seldom stop gabbing. I don't need a handle on you, less you care to give me one."

Jody thought she understood the fast-paced prattle. "Most call me Jody."

"Gotcha! Now, let's find you a nest to roost in." She looked up and down the rather crooked street, considering what would be the best of the least. Jody followed her gaze. The dozen misfit buildings constructed of oddly-put-together building materials made the worst of Five Points look invitingly respectable. But the valley itself was quite breathtaking; ringed by snow-capped peaks, the sloping pastureland was snow-free and dotted with thousands of grazing cattle.

"Yep!" Gabby Gee said, taking Jody by the arm and hauling her from the tailgate. "Know your thought, ducks. Thought the same meself—paradise. Well, after some of the railroad saloons I worked from Omaha to Cheyenne, it seemed like it at the time. But a waddy is just as much a drunk and whore-handed servant of the devil as a railroad man."

"Waddy?"

"Rustler."

Jody frowned. What manner of business did Max Bundy have with such people?

She was given a cabin of her own, behind Gabby Gee's saloon. The original occupant hadn't made it back from the last raid. Jody was surprised he had made it to the raid to begin with: the one-room shack was a nest of lice and pack rats. Not asking for any assistance, Gabby Gee stuffed the chimney with rags and built a roaring fire to smoke out the cabin.

"Come, ducks. My place ain't ever seen the likes of a real lady. Might give it some class."

Jody gulped. There was no question in her mind as to what type of "place" Gabrielle Gabon operated. Slowly, reluctantly, she followed the woman out of the cabin and through the back door of the next building.

They entered a room that was commanded by a huge brass bed covered with an elaborate quilted throw and countless china-faced dolls in stunning costumes. The walls were a maze of wooden pegs from which hung gowns of every fabric and color imaginable. There was room for only three other pieces of furniture: a washstand whose bottom shelves were a clutter of perfume bottles and face cream jars and opposite a rocker and a side table, amazingly uncluttered. Upon a lace doily sat a vase of fir and red juniper berries, next to a gilt-edge-framed miniature of an attractive young girl.

"That, ducks, is herself at sixteen. Carried the damn thing all the way from Saint Louie without it gettin' broke. It's stood up better than I have the last ten years."

Jody was flabbergasted. The woman looked at least another ten years older than she claimed to be.

Gabby Gee was no fool. She knew what Jody was thinking. She opened the inner door and motioned for Jody to follow her.

They stepped into a dark and dingy room that was stifling hot from two cook stoves that glowed red. Huge pots bubbled fiercely on each. A tall man with barely enough skin to stretch over his bones was tending them.

"This be our cook, ducks. For obvious reasons we call him Fatty. Ask him what's for supper."

Obediently, Jody asked.

"Slow Elk stew," he mumbled, without turning.

Gabby Gee roared with delight. "That's all he knows how to cook, yearling beef. It's our staple food and sells at the general store for as little as fifty cents a hind quarter."

"General store?"

"Honey, when Jeeter Longbaugh was still alive this was a boom town. It had more law and order than Central City. Our bank probably had more working capital than the Kountze Brothers in Denver, and some of that capital more than likely came from their bank in the first place. Let me show you something." She sailed through another door and Jody was forced to follow.

The room was long and narrow, with a potbellied stove at each end. The windows were so encrusted with dirt that the coal-oil lamps were kept lit constantly. Six wooden tables and benches stood along one wall. Two men, their hats shadowing their faces, sat playing cards. A table away, a hatless old man, filthy and in rags, sat with trembling hands clutching a precious bottle of whiskey he had somehow managed to obtain. Jody stared at him pityingly, but Gabby Gee gave him scarcely a glance. She was gazing with unconcealed pride at the back of the wooden bar.

"Ten feet of silver-backed mirror, ducks. That's

what gives my place real class. My main man behind the bar there is Tim. He's a big one, but gentle as a mouse." She pounded on the bar and turned to face the room as though it were full.

"Alright, you waddy bums, listen up! This here is Jody. Because I can smell out such facts, she's a virgin and is going to stay that way. I'm smoking out the cabin in back for her. The sign says 'no tabs,' but any waddy who thinks he can man a bucket and brush can belly up to the bar now and again when the job is done."

Tim automatically set up three drinks on the bar. Gabby Gee had made an offer that nobody could refuse. Tim, without asking, knew that he would be in charge. Jody was amazed: I'm not being asked why I am here, how long I will be here, or who arranged for me to be here. If she was a prisoner, it was all very strange. But she was thankful for Gabby: no one seemed to talk back to that woman. She volunteered to help with the clean-up. Gabby Gee measured her with sad brown eyes.

"Ain't our way here to ask questions," she said, "but I'm right about you being a virgin, ain't I?"

Jody blushed. "Yes."

"Now look, ducks, we're not strangers any more. Somebody must want you bad."

It came flowing out of Jody, one long, rambling accusation against Max Bundy. Gabby listened intently but made no comment.

"Might be of help," she said instead, "if you carried water to the men." Still, Jody's spirits lifted. Somehow she felt more capable of handling Max with Gabby Gee around.

Bucket after bucket of hot water Jody carried from Fatty's range. The men added lye and salt and washed down the cabin's log walls and split-pine floor. White-wash was then added. The bunk bed was razed and burned and a new one hacked out of rough timber.

First names seemed to be the only ones used. The old man was Dave the Banker, although the assets in his bank were now mighty slim. Sam and Deke were penniless drifters waiting around to get a job from Harvey Longbaugh. The free drinks they were getting for this job were a Godsend.

Night came quickly, dark and cold, to the valley. They continued to whitewash by candlelight. Fatty brought up heaping tin plates of Slow Elk stew and hardtack.

"Made enough for all the boys," he said, by way of excuse for such generous portions. "But they ain't back yet. Brought yours, ma'am, 'cause Miss Gabby is napping."

Jody wasn't sure if the food was exceptionally good or if she was just exceptionally hungry, but she ate every morsel of the potatoes, onion, veal and barley broth.

The valley erupted with gunfire and wild shouts. Jody jumped up so quickly her tin plate crashed to the floor just as the door came banging open.

"They're back!" Gabby shouted gleefully. "Saddle-bags bulging. No one says it's party time 'til Gabby Gee says it's party time. *Party time!*"

The men scooted out; they had free drinks coming.

Jody stood staring. Gabby was lavender from head to toe: a lavender wig, rouge, gown, feather boa, stockings and high-button shoes.

"Come on, ducks."

"But I—" She gulped. "I can't face him. Can't you help me get away?"

"Don't be a fool," Gabby Gee snapped. "The guards

at the canyon will have reported your being here to Jeeter's son. He'd blow the whistle and you'd have twenty of his toughs on your neck in half a minute. Lamb, three of these canyons have exits to the outside, but I'm not even allowed to know where they are. Try to go out the way you came in and you'd have five miles of flat basin to cross. They'd see you sure and haul you right back. Let Bundy come and take you out, that's the only way. For right now, the best for you to do is come along and act your natural sweet self. You can't stay here. You'll catch your death until this whitewash dries."

Nothing could have been a greater ordeal for Jody, but she put her trust in Gabby Gee.

Shrill, excited voices bombarded their ears as they entered the saloon. Gleefully, men were stacking saddlebags on a table in front of Dave the Banker. His eyes were glazed and his hands trembled with anticipation.

Gabby Gee whispered to Jody that the safest spot for her would be Tim's high stool behind the bar. Jody felt as if she were being put into the hands of an old and trusted friend.

Turning, Gabby Gee saw that one man in particular was carefully noting everything there was to note about Jody.

"You," she said, "get that idea out of your head."

"Why?" Harvey Longbough growled. "I do what I damn well please in my town!"

Even though first names were the unwritten code of Hole-in-the-Wall, Longbough's was never used. Perhaps to keep the past alive, he was known only as Jeeter's son.

"She's not one of us. She's a right nice girl, Jeeter's

son. Ain't gonna have you bring that gal trouble. She's a schoolmarm."

"Schoolmarm," he echoed. "Reckon I could use some education."

"From her or the Bundy brothers?"

He made a face then. "You know me, Gabby Gee. I don't like big tits, anyway. If it's more than a mouthful, it's too much."

"Hey," David called. "Where'd ya'all get this money?"

"Telluride, old man. They made it damn easy for us. We rode up just as they were takin' it off a wagon and into the bank. We didn't even have to go inside."

The old man squinted through his wire-rimmed glasses at a bill, backwards and forwards and backwards again, his face puzzled.

"Start stackin' 'em," Longbough said. "We figure it must be over two hundred thousand."

David rose slowly and walked to the back of the bar. He handed Jody three bills he had taken from the table.

"You ever seen anything like these, ma'am?"

She paled; she had thirty similar bills sewn inside her brassiere.

"Yes," she admitted weakly. "They are non-negotiable bank certificates."

"What's non-negotiable mean?" Longbough demanded.

David blanched. It had been twenty years since he had seen the inside of a real bank and liquor had made him forget a good deal.

"It means they have to be signed before they become legal tender," Jody said simply.

"Signed by who?" Longbough demanded.

"By one banker to another banker. Isn't that true, David?" Animation spread slowly over the old man's face and his mouth opened to emit a dry chuckle. "When the bank had gold to write a certificate against. Ain't got an ounce in my bank."

"Worthless?" Longbough gasped. "You saying all this stuff is worthless?"

"As worthless as tits on a bull."

"Jesus, Jenny and Joseph! We're as broke now as when we left yesterday."

Some refused to believe it. "Hell, let's us sign 'em and cash 'em in Denver."

"I'm afraid that wouldn't work," Jody said softly. "You may be thieves but you are not forgers. They would arrest you on the spot."

"Makes sense," Longbough said mildly. He stared at Jody with a look of admiration. He wondered how such a pretty and bright creature like her could have gotten mixed up with an old sourpuss like Clay Bundy.

"Thank you, ma'am," he said. "But what are we going to do with the worthless stuff?"

"Leave that to me!" Gabby Gee came back from the kitchen with Fatty in tow. Each of them carried huge tin bowls in their arms. "Nothing is ever worthless at Hole-in-the-Wall," Gabby said. "It's too damn much trouble getting things in here, so nothing goes to waste. Here, I got bowls of wheat flour and water mixed. Let's wallpaper this old dump with those one hundred and thousand dollar certificates. Drinks are on the house!"

Gloom was turned into gaiety. Harmonica music kept it from becoming work and so did a free-flowing bar. There was dancing and song and more than one head was playfully dunked into the improvised glue pots.

Jody was reminded of nights with the blacks around

the campfire. People with nothing having a good time. These were not desperadoes; they were young men, her age or slightly older, homeless and searching for a place where they could fit. They didn't rustle and rob from the little guy, only the big ranchers and banks. To them it was not stealing but taking their due.

Jody knew that was wrong, but still their cheerful laughter gave her a sense of security. She was treated like one of them and with great respect.

"Ma'am," Jeeter's son said, blushing. "You're a mighty fine lady. Tomorrow, we'll see that you get back to your people."

Jody slept soundly and peacefully. Because the party lasted until near dawn, Hole-in-the-Wall slept like the dead.

Max Bundy was instantly recognized by the guard at the canyon, so he and Logan were allowed to ride unmolested and without any alarm being raised through the narrow passage and the three miles to the valley beyond. . . .

15

It was going to be a cold, gray, cloud-covered day. Max's mood matched it completely. Logan had treated him like an errant child throughout the long, nonstop trip. He was tired, hungry and needed a drink.

There was no need to lock doors in Hole-in-the-Wall, so he took Logan directly into the saloon. The pot-bellied stoves were cold and several cowboys were asleep on the benches and floor.

Logan grunted with disgust. "Some outfit."

To show Logan that he was the voice of authority, Max began to kick at sleeping figures and shout:

"Get up, you lazy bastards! Get up and meet your new boss! Tim, set us up some drinks and then go roll Gabby Gee's fat ass out of bed. Things are going to be different around here."

Tim stood and nearly toppled over on his face. Obediently, he reached for a bottle and glasses. The hand holding the bottle began to shake. Logan was eyeing him with the coldest look Tim had ever encountered.

He recovered himself and went out, closing the door behind him with great care. He stopped for a moment in the kitchen to wake Fatty and whisper to him, then went into Gabby Gee's room.

She was fully dressed and sitting in her rocker. "I saw them coming through the window," she said. Tim nodded as if he tasted the fear in her words. "Then it is the same man."

"I don't think God would be mean enough to put two Harvey Logans on this earth. Say why he's here?"

"Bundy says he's the new boss."

Gabby snorted and rose. For the likes of Harvey Logan she wouldn't even freshen up her face, but went directly to the bar.

Logan saw her in the mirror as she entered but didn't turn.

"Well, well, well. Birds of a feather with a different name. I should have known you would end up with the likes of this crew, Madame Gabon."

"Yeah. I thought I would see how it was to be around real nice people for a change, Harvey. I got tired of tinhorn gamblers low enough to rob railroad-tent saloon owners."

"Watch your mouth, woman. You're looking at the new voice of authority around here, and I don't like whiskey and women around my crew." The words were spit out one at a time.

"Don't push me too far, Harvey. You may have the Bundy boys in your corner, but you don't have me or Jeeter's boys."

"Now, look," Max said then. "Jeeter's dead and his son ain't worth shit."

The outside door came flying open and crashed back

against the wall. Longbough positioned himself in the doorframe, one hand resting lightly on his gun.

"I heard that, Bundy."

At the sound of the booming voice, Logan tightened his grip on his own gun handle. The cards were stacked in his favor right now, but he knew he had to take charge immediately. He eyed Jeeter's son in the mirror.

"Glad you heard. Now hear this. I don't even want you around as a second in command. I need men, not kids who aren't even dry behind the ears."

"Shut up, outlaw!" Longbough could hardly get the words out, his throat was so constricted with rage. "You dirty saddle tramps think you can come here and take over without a fight. Max Bundy doesn't run this town and you ain't going to, either."

Logan barked a short, evil laugh. "You calling me out?"

"Stop it!" Gabby Gee now joined the battle of words. "What we don't need around here is trouble with a stranger around. You get that Miss Jody out of here first, Maxwell Bundy, and then we'll vote on a leader, like we always have before."

Max stood stunned. Logan used his silence to his own advantage.

"It'll be decided right now!" His face was an ugly mask as he jerked out his six-shooter and whirled around. Jeeter's son didn't even have time to draw before the explosion came. The force caught him right at the heart and lifted him high, pushing him six feet back out the open saloon door. The action had been so fast that everyone was momentarily frozen in place.

"That makes two men I've killed." Logan kept his voice low and even. "It'll be easy to make it three or four, if anyone else has a mind to try. Take him away and bring in the look-outs. Knowing the good madame's taste in beds, I'm going to borrow hers for a short nap. I want every man jack of you back in this room in two hours. No whiskey, bar-keep. From now on I say when they can drink and how much they can drink. And Bundy, if you've got a strange cunt in this town, you can just get her packed out of here now, and take this cunt with her."

Max didn't protest; things were happening too fast and his brain was too travel-weary to think.

Nor did Gabby Gee protest as Logan shoved rudely by her. They were thirty while he was only one; they could just make plans while he was sleeping.

"Where is she?" Max demanded.

"She'll keep," Gabby Gee said.

"We'll see about that. She must have come to her senses finally to come all this way looking for me."

"Looking?" Gabby Gee hooted laughter. "She came here trussed up like a heifer ready for branding. She wants to see you about as bad as she'd welcome a rattlesnake in her bed."

"Shut up! You just shut up! Tell me where she is, or I'll kill you, too!" As he started to pull his gun from its holster, Logan stepped through the door and barked, "Put that away, asshole! Tell him where she is!"

Gabby Gee said, reluctantly, "In the cabin behind the saloon."

Max turned to storm off, but Logan caught him by the sleeve.

"On this point, I go along with Madame Gabon, Bundy. You tell this girl to get ready to leave, and that's all."

"But she's practically my wife!" Max's voice was a little shaky.

"Horsefeathers! Your name may be Bundy, but you

ain't no different from these other cocks. No screwing around!"

Max gritted his teeth. No one was about to tell him what to do when it came to JoAnn Robb. He lurched out the front door of the saloon, rounded the corner and spied the cabin. Then he calmed down and started thinking: if Gabby Gee was right, Jody's manner of arrival puzzled him.

He moved slowly to the cabin, trying to sort things out. He hesitated, then knocked on the door. At the first knock, the inside bar was slammed into place.

"Jody, it's me, Max."

She didn't answer.

He forced himself to knock gently.

"Go away!" a choked whisper came through the door. He listened, his ear to the panel. She was right on the other side.

"I've come to take you away."

"Go away," she repeated. "You had your thugs kill Rocky White and bring me here. I'll go nowhere with you."

"What are you saying? I did no such thing."

Her laugh was bitter, and then he heard her sneaking toward the back of the cabin.

It infuriated him. He started around toward the back and spied the woodpile. He grabbed the axe and raced back to the front door. He raised the axe with both hands and smashed it against the door. It was an eight-pound axe and he busted in the split-log panels with a half-dozen blows. He became intoxicated with his destruction of the door. He knocked the logs away one by one and axed at the bar behind them until the bar fell away, brackets and all. Then he opened the door and walked into the warm room.

A fire was burning on the hearth and a kettle was

steaming. He had put nothing but stale water into his stomach in twenty-four hours. The axe dropped out of his hand and he let it lie.

He thought he was standing steady, but he was weaving on his feet. He had forgotten all about Jody even though she cowered by the fireplace, watching him, her eyes round with fright.

"I—I didn't do it," he stammered. "Honest. It must have been Clayton."

"Clayton?" Jody breathed, and then she laughed. "That's a very poor lie."

His chin lifted, but his glazed eyes did not shift from the steaming kettle.

"If I could have a cup of coffee. . . ." He sat down weakly.

Jody was perplexed. One minute a raving madman; the next, hardly able to hold up his own body. If he stayed this way, she could handle him. She poured coffee into a tin cup.

He gulped it down. It scalded him, but the taste was so penetrating he could not stop drinking. Warmth flooded him. He was so tired he could hardly remember where he was.

"Long ride," he said inanely.

Jody took heart. She would ply him with coffee until he went to sleep and then she would have Jeeter's son sneak her away.

Her curiosity had been aroused by the shot and the thought talk might make him even drowsier.

"I heard gunfire."

"Man was killed."

"Who?" she asked softly, and somehow sensed the answer.

"Man named Longbough."

Jody walked to the window and rubbed a circle in the hoarfrost. The look-out men were riding in, but she didn't see them. Nor did she want Max to see the tears that filled her eyes. Man? she thought; he was still a boy—compassionate boy who had not even begun to taste life. Oh, how she was beginning to hate this land where men thought they could play God with each other's lives, each other's property, each other's right to live free.

Free? They were none of them free. They were just like the predators in the woods: the beaver ate the fish, the coyote ate the beaver and the grizzly ate them all.

The next time Jody looked back Max was asleep, his head down on the table. Assured that he would stay this way for some time, she put her mind to her own safety and the possibility of finding someone else to take her away. Because of the early hour, she didn't expect to find Gabby Gee awake, but didn't want to stay in the cabin with Max. As she stepped through the battered door she spied an unfamiliar group of horsemen riding rapidly down a hollow leading from the canyon entrance. More outlaws would reduce her chances of escape. Fear returned gripping her like cold hands, and she fled down the path to the saloon.

Jody bolted at the sight of a strange man in Gabby Gee's bed and, flying into the kitchen, told Fatty what she had seen. Even as Gabby came waddling in from the saloon, the clatter of horses' hoofs seemed to swell from the far end of town.

"Wake up!" Gabby screamed at her bedroom door. "You brought a damn posse on your trail."

Logan stumbled out, filling the door frame. He had a hard time bringing his mind into focus.

"Where's the men?"

Gabby chuckled dryly. "Exactly where you told them to be—all holed up in the saloon like sitting ducks. Great beginning to your leadership."

From the window, Jody caught a glimpse of wild, shaggy horses and ragged, dusty men. Logan saw the same.

"Ain't no posse," he growled, as though that let him off the hook. "A guerrilla band, I'd say. I'll handle them."

Jody found herself suddenly alone in the kitchen. Now she could see that the riders moving down the street were dirty, lean, savage. They wore their hats low over their eyes and kerchiefs covered the lower halves of their faces. Each carried a pistol or rifle at the ready. The presence of this band brought home to Jody her real danger: If Logan could not control them, they would be gone as quickly as they came, leaving behind death and nothing more. They wanted mostly money and arms and had probably heard of the Telluride bank robbery, but they would steal anything. As a woman she would not be safe—nor would Barney's money in her brassiere.

Dull sounds came from the saloon, but Logan was not going out yet to challenge them. If she ran to the cabin, she would be seen, and the battered door would give her no protection. She realized then that she was shivering and almost breathless. Her skin felt tight and cold. Her mouth was dry, and she had a strange desire to keep swallowing.

Waiting and listening increased all her apprehensions. Nothing appeared to be happening. She heard a babble of voices and the shuffling of boots, the slamming of tables onto their sides and then glass breaking.

Fatty moved back into the kitchen to get his rifle. "They all be niggers," he mumbled. "New boss won't parley with niggers. We'll stand 'em off if they open fire."

Jody lost faith in the kitchen as a hiding place. The mention of the "new boss" left no doubt in her mind that this would have to be the killer of Jeeter's son, and that wasn't a very reassuring thought. With simple logic she could not understand why they didn't come out the back of the saloon and circle behind the guerrillas.

Suddeny, explosions of gunfire pierced the stillness. Swiftly, Jody entered the bedroom and went to the window. Neither one was inside the saloon; she believed she would be safer hiding out in one of the unoccupied buildings. The jump from the window would be easy for her.

She decided quickly, jumping down and running in among the bushes. But these did not afford her the cover she needed. She stole from one clump to another, finding too late that she had chosen poorly. The position of the juniper bushes had drawn her closer to the front of the saloon rather than away from it. Just before her were horses: beyond these a group of excited men. With her heart in her throat, Jody crouched down.

A shrill yell, followed by a new barrage of gunfire and departing guerrillas, roused her hopes. She could only assume that the besieged saloon had opened fire first. Several guerrillas appeared to be wounded and were now in flight. The rapid thump of boots stomping through the saloon told her that her idea of coming out the rear had been thought of. Several horses dashed past her, not ten feet away. One rider saw her, for he turned to shout back. This drove Jody into a panic. Hardly knowing what she did, she began to run away from the saloon. Her feet seemed leaden; she felt the same horrible powerlessness that sometimes came over her in a nightmare. Horses with shouting riders streamed past her, but she paid no attention to the words. There was a thunder of hoofs behind her. She turned aside, but the thundering grew nearer. She was being run down.

As Jody shut her eyes and, staggering, was about to fall, apparently right under pounding hoofs, a strong arm circled her waist, tightened and swung her aloft. She felt a heavy blow when the shoulder of the horse struck her, then a wrenching as her arm was dragged up. A sudden, blinding pain drove sight and feeling from her.

But she did not lose consciousness completely. She was being borne rapidly away, and what faculties she had left suggested that it was farther into the valley and not back toward the canyon. Rifle bullets were zinging all about them, and the rider seemed expert at jogging his horse to avoid them.

She was lying across the saddle with her head hanging down. Twisting her head backwards to look, she took heart. The Hole-in-the-Wall bunch had finally taken to horse and were pursuing. Farther back still, the guerrillas were in rapid retreat for the canyon mouth. Once boxed in, this rider would be smart to surrender.

There was a blood-chilling scream from the horse and Jody felt herself flying forward. Man and mortally wounded animal tumbled over her on the ground. A kind of red darkness veiled her eyes; her head swam, and she felt motion and pain only dully. She was lifted from the ground by muscular arms and carried along at a stumbling, jogging gait. She had no strength left to fight the man and attempt escape.

The thought came to her vaguely that she was helping herself more by being a tiring burden in the man's arms. Through eyes that would only barely focus, she could see that they had reached the face of a cliff and he was attempting to climb it. His breath was coming harder; she could feel his arms quivering from the strain of carrying her.

Then she began to curse the pursuers as bullets ricocheted off the rocks nearby. They could kill her as easily as they could kill the guerrilla! She couldn't see his face, but she could feel his emotions through his arms—the tremors of a hunted man about to be trapped. She closed her eyes, sick with what she felt, through him, fearful of the moment when they would both face death.

There was a muttered curse, followed by her unceremonious dumping on a ledge, followed by rapid return fire from her captor's pistol. Then he spoke.

"Must I forever find you in these impossible situations?"

Shock vibrated through Jody, and her eyes flew open. Instantly, she recognized the back of the crouching figure, even though his clothing was hardly military. Then she experienced a strange feeling of regret. It was not pursuit or rescue she thought of then, but sure death. These men would not let a soldier escape alive from their secret hideout.

"Birdie!" she gasped. "Why?"

"Met a man on patrol—who will remain nameless— who told us about your capture and this place."

Jody's hands swept up to her face in surprise. "Then Rocky is alive?"

Birdie's face was tight with suppressed rage. "In my opinion, the man should hang for what he did to you."

He drew in his breath sharply, then he seemed to collapse back into himself and the look in his eyes mellowed. He started to grin.

"For two years we've tried to find this place and a way in. Shocked the hell out of us when we saw them pull back the look-outs. What happened here?"

"I—I'm not sure. I think Max Bundy came in with a new man and he killed the old leader. Why have they stopped firing at us?"

Sergeant Jacobs considered the question, but her words had filled him with excitement. He now had a solid link between the Bundy brothers and the outlaws.

"Either they can't see us, or they are waiting for someone to talk us down." He paused, looking up. "If we could make it to the top, the rest of the patrol is sure to find us."

Jody was stunned. "The others were soldiers, too?"

He chuckled. "Don't let the clothes fool you. We've been carrying them in our saddlebags for months, just for the chance to fool them."

"Your face won't fool Max Bundy," she said anxiously.

As if the thought of Max had conjured him up, his voice echoed up the cliff:

"Jody, it's Max. Tell that man, whoever he is, that we'll let him go if he brings you back down safely."

Birdie grinned. "Good. They haven't figured out who we were yet. Just stay quiet."

For the next three hours, at odd intervals, the call was repeated. The day grew grayer instead of brighter, and a surprising ally was working for Jody and Birdie's benefit without their realizing it.

"Forget it, Bundy," Logan insisted. "He's either killed the cunt or gotten her out of the valley. Either way, you'll never see her again. Besides, we have things to do."

"You've done a pretty piss-poor job so far, Logan." Max glowered at him.

To everyone's surprise, the man took the words calmly. "You're quite right, Max. Ranch life took away my edge. I want the look-outs doubled. I want a full count of our ammunition, stores and money. If one guerrilla band can invade us, others will get the notion and so will the Army patrols. But, because of the timing of it, I think this group just got lucky, following us in." Then he altered his earlier stance. "Tell you what, though. We'll leave a half a dozen men here to take pot-shots at anything that moves on the cliffs."

Snow began to fall a little before Logan's gang rode back to the shantytown. Birdie worried about it more than he worried about the outlaws. The snow would make the climb more dangerous. The air took on a bite and the big silent flakes were hurried along by the first sign of a rising wind.

"We'd best try to climb. The snow will be in their eyes looking up."

It took them some time to find a way up from the ledge, and then they were not sure that they had found the safest one. Even as they crawled up a draw, rifles began sniping at them. The swirling snow was getting into the marksmen's eyes, but still some of the bullets came dangerously close. Jody's skirt weighted around her legs like lead. Often she slipped on the icy rocks and slid back as far as she had come. Birdie would come back and haul her up again. The sharp stones tore at her hands as they crawled upward, winding their way back and forth across the sheer face of the rock.

Midway in the climb, Jody lay full-length against a smooth slope of wet, moss-covered rock and tried to catch her breath. When she looked down she saw lamplight sparkling far below. It couldn't have been more than noon, she reasoned, but the storm was making the valley like night. The thought of getting caught on the cliffs in actual night nerved her to go on.

The next three hours of climbing was a merciful blur. Jody's arms and legs moved mechanically; it was becoming obvious that the storm would accomplish what the riflemen could not.

The wind struck with such force that it nearly tore them away from the rocks. It tore the breath from their mouths and left them gasping. With nothing to protect her but a dress and petticoat the heavy, insidious cold was dangerously numbing to Jody.

Birdie pulled her into a vertical break in the rock that was a little out of the storm. He put his mouth close to her ear and shouted over the wild moaning of the wind. "Jody, I want you to hold on tight here. We can't make it all the way. I've got to find better shelter."

She shook her head stubbornly.

"It will be easier for me to find a place and come back for you," he shouted.

She shouted back. "I don't want to be left alone!"

Birdie saw it was useless. She was near exhaustion and that inner strength in her that he admired so much could no longer be called upon. He knew she couldn't go much further with her long skirt soaked wet, but they had to try.

He reached out and took her hand. He had guided her many times during the climb, but this was somehow different. She felt a tender power come through his fingers that gave her new heart.

For another hour they climbed, bent almost double,

fighting each step, unable to use a free hand or arm to protect their faces from the lashing fury of the snow.

They plunged headlong into an overhang before they realized it. Beneath its roof, the wind was less violent, but the snow clawed at their feet and beat against their bodies.

"These are usually in a series," Birdie shouted. "This way."

The second ledge was smaller, but the third was almost a cave. Its back wall was dry and wind-free; it was all solid rock and bare of anything to use for a fire.

Birdie took one look at Jody and sensed the worst. "Get out of those wet clothes before they freeze on you. We'll secure them to the wall with rocks so the wind can dry them some."

Jody balked. "And what shall I wear in the meantime?"

"The same as me—nothing!"

She looked at him as if he were truly insane. "You're crazy, then we'll really freeze."

He pointed into the fury of snow. The lights in the valley were no longer visible.

"It has to be near freezing out there right now. It's that or have the clothes freeze on your body. Don't worry, I'm more of a gentleman than your horny Max Bundy."

"And what do you mean by that?" she snapped.

He grinned devilishly. He wanted her mad, good and mad so that her blood would pump and flow with the heat. "Seems to me," he said slowly, "he must want pretty bad what he's had before to have you brought to a place like this."

"He claims that was Clayton's doing."

Birdie chuckled. He started to take off his wet clothes. "That's a laugh. Seems to me Clayton's been the one trying to keep Max out of your bed—even the one that got so hot it burned down Barney's hotel."

"You are insufferable!"

He blinked his eyes comically. "No, ma'am, I'se a nigger. Can't ya'all tell by dis 'ere skin a mine?"

"Oh, damn you, go to hell!" she stormed.

He continued his plantation patter. "Lawsy me, ah do believe dis 'ere white gal done cussed her first. Angels of mercy protect us."

Deliberately, he dropped his trousers from the waist, sat on the stone floor and extracted his boots. Beneath his trousers he wore nothing. It was the second time in her life Jody had seen a man naked—one black and one white. It stunned her enough to make her realize that Birdie was right: even if they survived the night their clothing would still be wet in the morning. She turned and went as far back into the cave as possible.

Birdie smiled to himself. She was moving, her blood was pumping and she was thinking rationally again.

He flung his clothing up onto the jagged wall facing and secured them with loose rocks.

"Toss your clothes to me," he said. "Don't worry, it's dark enough so I can't see anything."

Dress, petticoat and undergarments came flying and landed with a sloshing sound. Then came one high-buttoned shoe after another. He was not aware that she was hesitating as he hung her things up with his own clothing.

He sat and waited. Night was coming fast and they were only blurred shadows. Then he looked up, hardly able to see her. He said, startled, "Jody, my darling, you're shaking. This is madness on my part—"

"I'm not cold," she said. "Not in my body. . . . Birdie, I don't know if this . . . this will dry."

"What is it?"

She hesitated. "It's my . . . an undergarment . . . that has some of Barney's money sewn into it that I'm to take to. . . ."

The words trailed off into silence, as she realized suddenly that he had called her "darling." She sat down with a thud and he took the brassiere from her and determined how best to hang it.

"I guess I ain't a good enough nigger for you, but you're a good enough white to do that nigger's errands for him."

It wasn't fair but when the heart is involved, logic goes out the window.

"I'm doing it more for Mammy Pleasant and Carrie Holmes than I am for him, Birdie. They need the money."

"Same thing. Carrie wanted me as a man only when she thought I had a strong interest in you. That's the trouble with the world. People only want what they think someone else is after and they can't have."

"You're wrong," she said. "I think she was in love with you."

"No, *you're* wrong—her egotism is boundless. No doubt," he added indifferently, "she had it all planned to drag me off to San Francisco. The real barrier to her plans, though, was you."

"Me?" Jody said, incredulous, and then suddenly, she understood.

"Naturally, she assumed that I wanted you, and she was right, Jody. But she did not count on Mister Barney Ford and Major Ferguson. They wanted you, too, for different purposes, without me being around."

"But you were around."

"Oh, I confess I made an ass of myself in Denver," he said, with assumed casualness. "But I couldn't risk looking bad again. You had become something of a folk hero among my people and it would have looked like I was just tagging along."

"You tagged me all the way to this place," she pointed out.

"Jody, don't take this wrong, but my men and I would have done the same for any woman in the same circumstances."

"Even to sitting in a cave nude with her?"

She couldn't see him blush. "Damn it, Jody, be reasonable. For months I've fought against my love for you. Sure, blacks have borne children by white men, but that is it. No love, no marriage. All beginning and no ending. We'd have no future."

She rose to her knees, her breasts falling free from her body, and held out her hands to him.

"You want me to humble myself," she said. "I'm not a shameless woman, but I don't care if we are pink, purple, or polka dot—is that what you want me to say? It's true. Only, we do have a future."

"Stop it, Jody! We don't!"

"Why not? We'll go to Liberia where it wouldn't matter. Birdie, please, if you can't marry a white woman, I'll . . . I'll turn black somehow. Or were you lying about your love for me?"

His hand shot out and caught her bare shoulders, the fingers biting into her flesh with bruising force. He pulled her down across his chest. Then he caught himself and his hands loosened. She pressed herself against him and wound her arms around his neck.

"Why did you stop?" she whispered.

"You don't play fair, Jody," he said against her hair. "My God, you don't have to bribe me. I've waited a long time for this, but it is wrong. Jody, you don't understand. Perhaps you will never understand. I want you, but I am the black part of my mother."

"I guess I don't understand that."

"She wanted to kill me. She wanted to kill me at birth. I was taken away from her and suckled by a white wet nurse. She hates whites. That's natural—to hate where you have been most deeply offended. She would hate you, and that I could not stand."

"But she could learn to love, given time."

"But time has run out." He sat up, keeping his arms around her. "I've been saving all these years to bring her here from the south. She was to be here for Christmas before this came up. It's too late for us."

In the ensuing silence, a chilling sound arose, like the shriek of some evil spirit. Jody's hair literally stood on end. It took them several seconds to identify the source, and when they did, Jody's hair stayed on end. A bobcat was perched on the lip of the ledge, growling.

Birdie pulled her closer and whispered, "He's not growling at us. Someone has followed us up."

The blackness, which obliterated sight, sharpened hearing. Along the ledges, several feet away, they heard a shuffle, a scrape, a clatter. The bobcat growled a fierce warning. There was a scurry backwards and silence. The bobcat's growl stopped.

"What are we going to do?"

Jody heard his teeth grate together. "I've no more bullets."

The odd thought in her mind was put into words before she realized it. "Then your mother no longer matters. If we are to die, keep me warm." She nestled close and he wrapped her in his arms.

Both had waited for so long to be together that all else was instantly forgotten. Like children, they touched and fondled and kissed away their inexperience. It was heady wine that stirred their blood. Their bodies grew warmer as their passion increased. The fondling gave each of them time to think and become aware of the virginity of the other. The minutes melted away, and Jody feared he was unsure of his duty and her lack of knowledge kept her silent . . . then she felt the approach of heated flesh . . . then a gossamer touch that sent a quiver up her spine. A pause, then the turgid apex touched in a hesitant fashion. The mind was made up quickly.

With fervor, he plunged deep and could hear her gasping response to the thrilling sensation he was creating.

Here was no pain, as Carrie had made her fear. The tingling sensation built to even greater heights and surged into every nerve. As their passions climbed equally, she sobbed out and rubbed her hands hard against his muscular back. Their combined shudder amazed them and their lips locked together in its glory. Their bodies jerked violently in dual eruption. The jellylike quivering of their insides began to abate. He nestled his head against her cheek and sighed. They were asleep almost before the sigh escaped his lips.

He awoke about an hour before sunrise and shivered. Jody still slept. He rolled into a sitting position and looked down at her. Her golden hair made a soft halo on the stone floor. Her skin was creamy white and soft. Her lips were slightly parted and retained color. He sat studying her face, etching on his mind the curve of the cheek and mouth, the way the hair swept back from the widow's peak.

Cautiously, he rose and felt his clothing. It had dried enough for him to dress. He now felt as if he never should have undressed. It had been like a dream, except for the tinge of guilt. Could they ever again be that close? Here they had been alone in their own world. But the outside world was filled with people who would not understand their love. He sighed and turned, unsure of what his mind was trying to tell him.

The storm had blown itself out; the bobcat was gone. The valley was blanketed by a thick white mantle. No smoke spiraled up from the Hole-in-the-Wall chimneys and there was no evidence that the riflemen had stayed through the night. He decided he had better go and see about the pursuers who had made it this far. The thought of what he might have to do was not pleasant, but if they had gotten the drop on him, it would have been worse.

He made his way back along the ledge slowly, his head pulled deep into his shoulders. It was going to be a horribly cold day. He found two men curled up asleep on the last ledge and began to draw his pistol. He had to disarm them before they discovered that he was out of ammunition.

"Roll over slowly," he commanded softly.

A voice said tentatively, "Good mornin', Sarge."

A soldier turned. He looked as if he had been up most of the night. Birdie felt a surge of contrition.

"So, it was you the bobcat was growling at?"

The soldier grinned sheepishly and rubbed his eyes. "Thought it best not to disturb it or you."

Birdie nodded self-consciously and looked away. "How'd you find us?"

"Followed the echoes of the rifle fire back along the ridge during the storm. Saw you, but didn't want to call out and have them pinpoint you. The mesa is only a hundred more yards up the cliff."

Birdie made a sound that was half snort and half grunt and strode to the lip of the ledge, looking up. In the storm he had been unable to see how close they were to the summit and real safety. Smoke was rising from where the rest of the patrol had camped.

He scowled. "We'd better get on up before the out-laws spot that smoke. I'll get the girl."

The two soldiers grinned at each other and Birdie didn't like what he could see going through their minds. He stalked back to his own ledge and stopped outside the cave.

"Best get up," he called softly. "Your clothes will be dry."

Jody stepped out, already dressed. "I heard voices."

"My men," he said curtly.

She looked at him questioningly. The grim mask was back on his face. The familiar question mark burned in his eyes. And yet, there was something between them now that could not be erased. Not for the first time, Jody felt the powerful quietness his physical presence brought her.

She said gently, "I want to thank you for yesterday . . . and last night."

He turned away without a word. Jody plunged after him, dismayed. The things Birdwell Jacobs did never seemed to coincide with the way he did them. It was as if he were constantly at war with himself—and she ended up being the enemy.

With the help of the other soldiers, the climb was quick and relatively easy. A blanket roll was fashioned into a coat for Jody; coffee was served that was blacker than ink.

From the supply horses, uniforms were distributed and military decorum reestablished. In this way, Birdie thought he could keep the men from thinking what he figured they were thinking. But it was his own guilty conscience that was doing the thinking. He avoided Jody until they were back down on the wind-swept plains; then he could avoid her no longer.

"I'm having Private Lothrop take you on the Cheyenne," he said, with typical curtness. "I've scraped some money together for your rail ticket and some clothes. I've got a list of what man donated what, when you're ready to pay it back."

"I have money in Denver. I'll be back in about ten days."

"I'll have it sent for."

Jody couldn't restrain herself any longer. "Is there some reason why you can't come for it yourself, Birdwell Jacobs?"

Now that she had brought up the subject, he knew he had to speak.

"We each have certain things to do, Jody. You in San Francisco and me to see after my mother. Besides, the longer you stay away the longer that bunch in Hole-in-the-Wall are going to think you are dead or with the guerrillas."

"Are you telling me to stay away longer than ten days?"

"It would help. I would like to catch the Bundys red-handed."

Jody frowned. "Be honest, Birdie. Your real reason is us. Well, after last night, I think you have an obligation to me—whether your mother likes it or not."

Birdie was suddenly silent.

"Haven't you, Birdie?"

"Well . . ." He shook his head wisely. "A lot of women give themself to one man and end up marrying another."

"Well, I'm not a woman like that."

He was growing impatient with her. "I didn't say that you were, only—"

"Only what?"

Immediately, he was cautious. "Only we have a lot of problems to solve before you get back. If I have to

move against the Bundys, I don't want your aunt getting hurt, for one thing. If she can keep her mouth shut
about it, I'll let her know that you're alive."

"That would be nice," she said coolly.

It had been a dim-witted evasion of the main point,
she was well aware. It rankled, but what could she do,
out in the middle of nowhere? It was not in her to
make a scene in front of his men. She saw then that she
had been just as dim-witted: she had made him feel
trapped by mentioning only his obligation to her.
When they parted, she would speak only words of love.

He remained at the head of the column. She rode
along in the main body of soldiers, going over what she
would say to him. She even planned how she could
kiss him quickly and make it look like a whispered
message to the other soldiers.

Clem Lothrop rode up and touched his hat in salute.
He was feeling pretty grand; he had thought for
months that things were bound to come his way. With
that damn fool sergeant out of the way, maybe he
could visit the hot spots in Cheyenne. He had even
heard tell that the Cheyenne Club now had some black
beauties.

"We turn north here, ma'am."

"But I've got to see Sergeant Jacobs."

The main column was breaking off and changing
gait to a gallop.

"He told me to tell you good-bye."

"I—I've things to say to him!"

Seeing her frantic glance after the vanishing patrol,
he laughed. "It will have to wait, ma'am."

"Perhaps I shouldn't go to Cheyenne." Jody hung her
head in misery.

Lothrop said harshly, "You've got to."

"Why?" she said, like a child.

"Because I've got to get you there in time for the afternoon train." Clem thought it might be just as well to talk her a little plain sense. He was new to the outfit and didn't know about her previous association with Birdie. "Besides, the sergeant's a book soldier and don't like to be thanked, especially not by a woman. He ain't the friendly type. He don't want anybody messin' into his life—private or military. A real loner, if you know what I mean."

Jody waved for him to start riding. She didn't want him to see the emotions his words had aroused. *No, she told herself, I won't cry*—that would be foolish. She had no one to blame but herself. He *had* been more of a gentleman than horny Max Bundy. She had said that she was not a shameless woman, but she had acted shamelessly.

It had been a beautiful thing, what had happened between them. She would cling to that and forget that he had said good-bye through someone else.

16

But Jody could not forget. Hundreds of miles of hearing iron clicking on iron rails kept his name alive: *"Bird-eee. Bird-eee. Bird-eee."*

The ferryboat paddle wheels crossing San Francisco Bay sang a familiar refrain: *"No . . . good . . . bye. No . . . good . . . bye."*

She had had no stomach for food during the trip and was pale and drawn by the time she reached San Francisco. The only coat she had been able to purchase in Cheyenne hung on her like a ragpicker's. She didn't care; she just felt a pitiless fatigue.

Her arrival at the gothic mansion overlooking the city presented another shock. The house seemed deserted. The Chinese houseboy made her sit on a porch swing, then nervously disappeared. Two hours passed before he returned. Behind him came a small black woman who stared incredulously at Jody. The young Chinese boy looked scared.

"Who you?" the woman demanded.

"Jody . . . JoAnn Robb."

Mammy Pleasant's look remained puzzled. "Barney say in wire you dead . . . money gone."

They looked at each other. "News travels quickly," Jody said. "Do you think we might go inside and discuss this?"

"No," the woman snapped. "Ain't my house again 'till sundown."

"I . . . I don't understand."

Mammy Pleasant didn't answer and suddenly Jody felt she was being stared at. She turned and saw Carrie at the far end of the wide porch. She was like a drawing out of a magazine—beautifully gowned, the wide-brimmed hat set at a rakish angle on her head, her face expertly painted. Carrie forced herself to smile, but Jody wasn't deceived: she was as frightened as the Chinese boy. Carrie shook her head and put her finger to her lips.

Jody's heart shrank inside her as she watched Carrie's face, wondering what was going on. Suddenly, Carrie's chin came up and she addressed Mammy Pleasant in a quick, high voice.

"Well, here is one ghost I can vouch has skin and bones. Although, Jody, you do look a little like death warmed over."

She crossed the porch and touched her lips lightly to Jody's cheek. "Excuse us if we seem a little strange, but bad news had been our only companion lately. You remember, I told you how the previous owner of this great old house came to collect the last payment and fell from the upstairs porch and died of his injuries? How people started whispering that Mammy pushed him and calling this place 'The House of Mystery?' There was nothing to justify the rumor, but still the court would not allow us to take possession until this evening."

"I'll not sleep another night here," Mammy said darkly. "The new cottage will do me fine."

"Nonsense!" Carrie laughed, but not convincingly enough for Jody. "Here is Jody, safe and sound, and with the—"

"Hush!" the old woman shrieked. "Don't turn good luck bad by mentioning it. Mingh, come." She beckoned to the Chinese boy. "We supper shop."

To Jody's disappointment, Mammy Pleasant was not the loving spirit she had expected. Nor was Carrie Holmes quite the same. For another two hours they sat on the swing, their talk carefully skirting around all the important issues, Carrie went out of her way to avoid any mention of the past and rambled on about San Francisco gossip.

The three women ate a silent meal, with Mammy acting the servant more than Mingh. The money-stuffed brassiere was passed to the old woman after the meal. More to spite Max Bundy than to help Birdie, Jody said,

"For the moment, please don't tell Barney I'm here, or that the money arrived safely."

Mammy cast Carrie a meaningful glance, as if telling her to get to the bottom of this matter. But Carrie was smart enough to realize that she would not get much out of such a travel-weary creature. She showed Jody to a spacious second-floor bedroom and wished her goodnight.

With the burden literally off her chest, Jody collapsed and slept the clock around. She awoke in time to eat a second silent dinner and then joined Carrie on the glider. After the harsh Colorado weather, San Francisco seemed almost balmly. Jody had forgotten that she had spent a spiritless Christmas on the train. The lights of the city, cascading down the hills like a waterfall in the moonlight, relaxed her. Because she and Carrie had shared so much before, the relaxed mood allowed the words to flow.

Mammy had just finished clearing up after dinner. In the evening silence, she heard every word Jody said. When Carrie came in later she saw that Mammy was worried; in fact, she looked almost frightened.

"Where are you going?" Carrie asked.

"To see my old friend in Chinatown." She was holding the bank certificates. Carrie stared at them. "They should go to a proper bank," she said, plainly irritated, but Mammy forgave her that. Carrie had stood up for her against all the rumors and defeats; she couldn't have borne it otherwise.

"Don't want it known I've got the money, chile."

"But it *will* be known the minute they see you enter the House of Soong. Send Mingh to fetch the man here."

To her relief, Mammy agreed. But Carrie's relief was short-lived when Mammy joined her and Jody on the porch to await Mingh's return. As though she had been a party to the original conversation, Mammy took it upon herself to reopen it. She attacked Jody with stinging, pointed remarks, mostly uncomplimentary statements about her dress, her unattractive hair style and how some people never know their proper place— things Carrie would never have believed Mammy Pleasant capable of saying.

Jody was a guest and forced to take it with outward calm, though she was inwardly seething. Then Mammy pounced on her main point of worry:

"Men are fools," she said. "If I had my way you'd be turned out for taking up with a buck. White girls like you ought to be whipped before the town for such doings. Bet your mother wouldn't approve, nor would I blame her. He ain't right, either. Black men all take a sneaking pleasure in it. They always do if the girl's young and white."

The arrival of a coolie-drawn rickshaw kept her from going on, and kept either of the young women from giving her opinion on the matter. An artful change over came Mammy. She rose, smoothed down her dress and went to the steps to greet her guest as though he were royalty. His low bow at the foot of the steps afforded her the same status.

Mammy Pleasant had had a wonderful time her first twenty years in San Francisco. When she learned of the discovery of gold in California, she knew that there would be many opportunities to increase the fifty thousand dollars left her by her dead husband. She was one of the few to arrive in the city with capital and let it work for her.

For a long time everybody was glad to be a friend of Mammy's. The city's leading businessmen ate at her boarding house, and when they needed money for a project, approached Mammy first. She had been a public heroine in those days and generally respected.

But lately nobody paid much attention to Mammy. At first, she had been bewildered by it, disbelieving. She would go down to Fisherman's Wharf, or to some place of business on the hill, and say hello. She would talk about the early days, remind them of how she helped finance this and that and tried to help others—the railroad to bring the gold from the fields down to Sacramento, for instance.

"They let it rust and wouldn't take black money on their new railroad," she would say. Meaning that the "Big Four" of Sacramento didn't want San Francisco people sticking their noses or money into the Central Pacific. But by this time her audience had already turned a deaf ear. She hardly ever got a dime out of them that was owed her.

One man had always felt sorry for her. They were each aliens in their own way. He, too, had suffered during the gold rush days, supplying coolie labor from his homeland. As San Francisco grew and the gold ran out, he converted that labor to cooks, houseboys and gardeners. But, as was the custom, most of the money and profit went back to the House of Soong in China.

But if Mammy Pleasant lost money over the new railroad, the House of Soong profited handsomely from it. Thousands upon thousands of laborers were brought from China, with the House of Soong the major supplier and contractor. But in the old days, when the House of Soong sometimes found itself in financial difficulties, Mammy Pleasant had always quietly helped. That was why now the man had come so quickly.

"Who is that?" Jody said, unable to take her eyes off the tall Chinese who seemed to float up the stairs. He was nothing like the only other Chinaman she had ever seen: the cook at the Bundy ranch, who had adapted himself to western dress. Nor was he anything like Mingh, in his simple cotton coolie trousers and flapping shirt.

This man enhanced his height and burnished-gold skin by wearing an ankle-length loose gown of deep-gold moiré silk. His strange little slipperlike shoes and round cue cap were of the same fabric. Over the gown was a loose coat of chocolate brown with batwing sleeves that nearly touched the ground. Down the front panels of the coat were embroidered dragons of gold thread with jeweled eyes.

His long face was stern-looking, made more so by the jet black mustache that drooped down each side of his thin-lipped mouth. The cue cap covered his entire skull, opened at the top to allow a shimmering black braid to swing casually halfway down his back.

If the embroidered dragons' red eyes were rubies, then his own were onyx and black as midnight. They pierced, rather than looked, and could take in all with a single glance.

"That is Kai Soong," Carrie said. "Frankly, he scares the hell out of me."

"Is he royalty or something?" Jody whispered.

Carrie, observing the whispered conversation taking place at the top of the steps, was slow to answer.

"You might say so," she said at last. "As Old Master Soong, he is respected because the House of Soong is one of the oldest and most powerful tongs in Canton. Through Kai Soong it controls every lesser tong here in California."

"What in the world is a tong?" Jody asked.

"Sort of a family group, but more sinister. They control their people like an anthill. Talk about being slave! Kai Soong rules with a power and ruthlessness that is frightening. No on tries to cheat him more than once, because they are not around for a second chance. At a snap of his fingers, he has his own private army of henchmen do his bidding."

"Is that why he scares you?"

"No," Carrie said slowly. "It's his occult powers. He makes our voodoo seem like a modern science. He's spooky, the way he knows about things that are going to happen before they happen."

Before Jody could comment, Mammy Pleasant and her guest started toward them. The two young women rose respectfully. Kai Soong was overly grand in greeting Carrie, although his deep-set eyes never left Jody. He touched Carrie's hand to his lips, but he only bowed to Jody.

"Welcome, Miss Robb," he said, almost in a whisper, his voice as smooth as velvet, "after a most adventurous journey."

"Thank you," Jody said simply, not knowing how to address him properly. Carrie had only nodded sourly in greeting.

"It is most pleasing to me, as an old friend, that you have brought such good news to Mammy. This time, may wisdom guide her in the application of her money."

"Which means, don't loan it out!" Mammy laughed.

It was amazing to Jody to see the effect the man had on the old woman. Her expression was now gentle and the brown eyes sparkled with mirth.

"Exactly." Kai Soong chuckled. "It will bring miracles for all of you. A beautiful daughter should be granted a beautiful wedding."

Carrie paled, but Mammy hooted with laughter. "Ain't no man in her life, Kai Soong."

He smiled knowingly.

Carrie quickly excused herself and dashed into the house. Jody, feeling she would be in the way of any business discussion, tried to excuse herself, too.

"It has been my pleasure, Miss Robb." This time Kai Soong did take her hand, and held it gently. "You bring luck to this house, perhaps even a new life. May your stay be long and enjoyable."

It wasn't his hand or his words that held her there, but his eyes. They were all-absorbing and penetrating, as though he were reading her soul. But there was more anger than mystery in her: his words led her to believe that Mammy had told him all about her and

Birdie. It was embarrassing to have a stranger imply that a baby might be the result.

"I plan on leaving as soon as possible, sir," she said, taking her hand away.

He pursed his lips, making the tips of the mustache almost touch.

"We do not rule our destiny, Miss Robb. You will leave when fate decrees it." He paused, opened his mouth as if to add something, then closed it, letting his eyes speak for him.

Jody felt their power and quickly looked away. It was almost as if he were ordering her to stay, and it angered her without her knowing why. She nodded a curt good-bye and went through the house to the kitchen. Her mouth was suddenly parched and she longed for a glass of water. She found Carrie sitting very pale, very straight in her chair at the kitchen table. Her hands were on her knees.

"What's the matter?" Jody asked.

Carrie's lower lip quivered. "I told you he scared me."

"What was there to be scared about?"

"All that talk about a wedding."

"What!" Jody almost laughed. "How in the world is that frightening?"

"He knows—don't ask me how, but he knows. He'll put a curse on it."

"Curse? That man? You're crazy." She was exasperated and confused. They were all crazy. "What are you talking about?"

Carrie began to cry. "He thinks I'm white."

"Who? Not Kai Soong?"

"No!" Carrie wailed. "Otis Whiteside. He's a man I've been seeing secretly. He's a ship's captain, works for the lady who owns that big gingerbread house up on the hill. He thinks that because Mammy Pleasant doesn't stay here at night, she's just a servant."

Carrie was appalled at the way Jody stood looking down at her. "And you said it was wrong for me to be with *Birdie?*"

Carrie nodded, totally miserable.

Jody didn't get in another word, because Mammy came stamping into the kitchen. She had her own war to wage and now she laid down the law to Carrie. Kai Soong had all but told her the man's name. Carrie's terror increased. In her heart, she was convinced that she would rather die than be denied her chance to marry Otis.

"I'll not marry a nigger!" she shouted.

Mammy's eyes bulged as if they would burst out of their sockets. Her next words were so spiteful and cruel that they reduced Carrie to further tears. She not only gave Carrie a dressing down, she told Jody what she thought of *her* for wanting a black man. But when she likened both girls to whores, Carrie began to laugh, peals of screaming laughter, drowning out all other sound.

Mammy took one look at her, stepped to the pantry for the water bucket and doused Carrie with its entire contents. She slammed the empty bucket on the floor, swore once, and told Carrie to go to her room and dry off. Then she stormed out of the house and banged herself down on the porch swing.

After Carrie had gone, Jody listened to the swing squeak and sway. She stood where she was, not moving but thinking deeply. She felt like a hypocrite but she thought Mammy Pleasant was quite right. She felt her own situation was quite different, however. She had not made Birdie think she was black.

The house gradually stilled. A long time later, Mammy came back into the kitchen.

Jody forced herself to speak. "Can I get you anything?" Mammy looked at her gravely. "No, thanks." Jody swallowed. "I'm sorry, ma'am."

Mammy's face was not kind; it was not unkind, either. It worried Jody. She would rather have her swear at her the way she had at Carrie.

"Ain't your doing. I may have to move back in here for a while. Don't fret. You can stay till the baby's born."

Jody's eyes widened in disbelief. "Baby? I—I admit I don't know much about such things, but—but it's only been a few days."

Suddenly, Mammy began to chuckle. "Lawdy, what an old fool that makes me. Always did put too much stock into what that chink says. Course you can't tell yet, chile. Might not happen, either. Look at my man and me. We tried 'til we was plumb purple in the face and nothing." Then she sobered. "But that don't change the other thing, do it? What you really think on it, chile?"

Jody couldn't lie. "I think she was wrong, making him think she was white."

"She do that?"

Jody could barely nod.

"She tell you who?"

Jody had trapped herself and didn't know how to get out of it. "Just that he's a ship's captain who works for one of your neighbors."

Mammy's eyes sparkled. "That could be no other than Liberty Wells O'Lee. Fine widow woman who lost her husband to the building of the railroad. Lives mostly in Sacramento. Well, she and I'll settle that man's hash."

"No," Jody said suddenly. "That would be wrong of both of you."

Mammy's face turned unkind again. "And why?"

"Carrie's the one who lied to him. He doesn't know any differently. She should be the one to tell him the truth."

"You're right," said Mammy, watching her. "Which means you know his name. No, I don't want to know, but a favor I do ask."

"What's that?"

"Stay a while. Help me through this mess. I love that chile, missy. I want only what is best for her. This I don't think is best, but she and I would only fight and fuss about it. You get her to be honest with the man. That's all I ask."

"But I have a school and children to get back to," Jody protested.

Mammy grinned. "And your man?"

For a moment, Jody's voice wouldn't work. She wrestled with it, trying to bring out a lie, but it would not come. The burden she couldn't even share with Carrie had to be uttered now, as a dismal truth. Their final words, the non good-bye were recalled in a hoarse tear-choked voice.

"Men!" Mammy snorted, then paused. Her voice was loving and gentle when she went on: "Now it ain't for Carrie and me that I ask you to stay, chile. It's for yourself. Give this time to heal among us. Give that young man time to realize what he might be losing in a proud gal like you. And don't you fret none about Barney and his school. We'll let him know, quietlike, that you are safe—and to keep his black mouth shut."

Jody was tempted. It would give her time to think, to put Birdie and her life in general into perspective.

She knew that Irene could run the school just as well for a week or two. And she was tired. The salty breezes off the bay reminded her of New England and that was relaxing. But . . .

"I have no money or clothes."

"Indeed." Mammy laughed. "When a body risks life and limb to bring Mammy Pleasant thirty thousand dollars, then Mammy Pleasant sees to their needs. And no sass, chile. A bit of that money to get you some clothes ain't gonna seem much. Why, I once gave a man just as much money as you brought me without batting an eye."

"That was John Brown, wasn't it?"

"Good heavens, chile, how on earth you know that?"

"From Carrie, but I've told the story to the children at school."

Mammy blushed. "Sakes alive, chile, you should be teaching them about real heroes, like Barney Ford."

"Barney? A hero?" Jody chuckled.

"Most the same as Crispus Attucks, in my way of thinking."

Jody blinked. "And who was that?"

Mammy looked hurt. "What you teaching those little black boys and girls if you not telling them about the black patriot who died in the Boston Massacre? You ever heard of Peter Salem and Salem Poor? I doubt it. Chile, you am now the student and I am now the teacher. About time somebody heard all that's in this ole nigger's brain."

Jody's first feelings toward Mammy Pleasant had not really been hate, but whatever they had been, they were soon changed to love. For all her financial shrewdness, Mammy Pleasant was barely able to write more than simple English. So that she would not forget them, Jody began to write down the stories the woman related to her. For the next few days, they were almost inseparable.

Carrie had always been a loving creature, but this was rapidly changing to hate for both of the women. She stayed in her room and refused to listen to reason. She swore never to face Otis Whiteside again, for any reason.

Mammy only chuckled. "That chile ain't ever known loneliness or want. Let her stew in her own juices for a while."

The day that Jody had first chosen for her departure day almost came about. Mammy Pleasant was off doing her errands when Mingh came into the sun-filled breakfast room and mumbled the name of the unexpected visitor. At first, Jody felt betrayed. There could be only one reason why this woman was paying an unannounced call at such an early hour. Nor was there time to awake Carrie and have her stand up to her own defense.

"But Mammy is not at home," she said inanely.

"She no ask her," Mingh replied. "She ask you be name, missy."

Jody nodded to him then. In spite of herself, she tingled with excitement, curiosity and dread. From what she had learned from Mammy, this woman had been a friend of President Lincoln's, had entertained and gone shopping with Mary Todd Lincoln in New York City, and was rich and powerful in California. She steeled herself to meet someone as formidable as Miss Inez had been in the old days.

As the caller stepped into the breakfast room, Jody couldn't help but stare. She was one of the most striking creatures Jody had ever seen. She was as slender as a willow branch and far from old; she certainly did not look like a mother of four in her mid-thirties, which Jody knew she was. Yards and yards of teal green crushed velvet, to match her eyes, had been stylishly draped to create her gown, bustle and flowing train, yet leave no doubt about her rounded bosom, slim waist and full hips. An odd cut of velvet and veil sat upon her brown curly hair, like the wings of a bird ready to take flight. Beneath this oddity was a classic-featured face that was open, warm and genuine.

"Forgive my intrusion at such an unsocial hour," Liberty O'Lee said cautiously, unsure of the reception she would receive. "But my business life keeps me on a rather tight schedule."

"Are you sure," Jody said, "that Mingh didn't make a mistake? I can still call Miss Holmes."

Liberty O'Lee, although many nowadays dropped the "O" and just called her Mrs. Lee, hardly ever made a mistake. Before her was exactly what she had expected to find—a flower that had yet to bloom.

"No," she said gently. "You are exactly as my old friend Kai Soong described. You must be Miss JoAnn Robb."

"I am," Jody said, growing increasingly confused.

"Good. Now, don't think me rude, but am I going to be offered a cup of that delicious-smelling coffee? I came over on the dawn ferry and have had nothing but Kai Soong's tea since."

Jody went to the sideboard to pour the coffee while Liberty made herself quite at home at the table.

"I love this view. I almost bought this house once because of it. Kai Soong advised against it. He said it had a bad aura." She laughed. "Mammy Pleasant has proved that to be quite true."

"That's an odd thing to say, Mrs. O'Lee," Jody said, suddenly on the defensive. "A man dies an accidental death and people are quick to regard Mammy as a sorceress. What would you call Kai Soong, whose odd advice you seem to have taken?"

Liberty sat back and regarded Jody with renewed interest. No, she thought, Kai Soong is quite wrong about this one; she is not a simple little creature at all. Her task would not be as easy as Kai Soong had imagined. She instantly changed tactics.

"I would call him a very wise man, Miss Robb. But I meant no disrespect to Mammy Pleasant, I assure you. If I put it badly, I apologize."

Jody felt foolish. "I had no right to speak to you the way I did, knowing all the facts myself."

"I like people who are loyal, Miss Robb. Lord knows, they are few and far between in this world. Are you as loyal to Miss Carrie Holmes?"

Jody frowned and all of her old suspicions returned. "I believe I am."

"Kai Soong thought as much. That's why I came to see you now, when I knew Mammy would be out. The news I have received might distress her. Since it involves an acquaintance of mine, I'm not sure of my own true feeling."

"Don't you mean an employee, Mrs. Lee?"

Liberty stared. "By God, you are an honest woman, Miss Robb. But Captain Whiteside is more than an employee. Because he speaks both the Cantonese and the Hunan dialects, he has been the mainstay of my entire shipping operation to the orient. As such, he is becoming a very rich and influential man, and a very busy one. He is gone from San Francisco for long months at a time. I lived through a similar situation when my husband was building the railroad."

Jody gazed at her solemnly, wondering when she would get to the point.

"Isn't this something you should be discussing with Carrie?"

"That's right," Liberty agreed. "If circumstances were different."

"You mean, because she is a negro and hasn't told him?"

Liberty laughed lightly. "My dear, there is not a soul in San Francisco who does not know that she is Mammy's adopted daughter. She is accepted in all social circles because of her charming self. Does she really feel that she had deceived Otis?"

"I believe she does, and so does Mammy."

"Oh dear, now I see why Kai Soong thought it wise for me to speak to you first. Miss Robb, my fear has nothing to do with Carrie being colored. I just do not want to see Otis hurt her, or Mammy. He is, after all, a sailor through and through."

"Perhaps," Jody said slowly, "you could put it a little more clearly? Frankly, I don't understand."

She *is* innocent and naive, Liberty thought; Kai Soong is right again. And am I going to have to take away some of that innocence the way Kai Soong took away mine years ago? She was surprised at how bitter the thought was.

"All right, straight talk. Otis Whiteside has been a sailor since he was twelve. He's now thirty-two. He's been married twice—an Hawaiian girl, who died bearing him a child, and a New Zealand girl, who was not there when his ship put in again at Aukland. These events happened before he was twenty, Miss Robb. Because of certain Chinese customs—of which I suffered first hand—I have no reason to doubt that he maintains a mistress in China. I suspect that that is what he wants of Miss Holmes—home-port mistress and nothing more. To be blunt, Miss Robb, although

Otis is an excellent seaman, he is not the type of man who courts a young woman just for the pleasure of her company."

Jody was deep scarlet, but after all, she had asked for a clear explanation. "I'm not sure what you want me to do, Mrs. O'Lee."

Liberty hesitated. She had become a rich and powerful woman by heeding the advice of Kai Soong, but for once she doubted him.

"I feel it would be unwise, Miss Robb, to corner Otis with the facts and demand his intentions. Captain Whiteside's ship docks in the morning. He has made a remarkable thirty-two day run from Shanghai. Naturally, I shall honor such an event with a dinner celebration. I shall leave it to you to see that Miss Holmes and Mammy attend—and you, of course. Face to face, in such company, Otis will have to tip his hand one way or the other."

Jody swallowed hard. "It could be a disaster for Carrie."

"Better now than to have her break Mammy's heart by becoming his mistress."

"But how can I get her there, and Mammy, without telling them any of this?"

Liberty smiled sweetly. "When Miss Holmes hears who the guest of honor is, she will be eager to come. As for Mammy, I would like her there to discuss a certain business matter. Now, I must fly. Good day, and thank you, Miss Robb."

Jody saw her to the front door. She stood for a long time wondering why she had been made a party to so much information about Otis Whiteside if she could not pass it on.

Liberty was wondering the same, and again having doubts about Kai Soong. If he expected Miss Robb to talk, he was wrong. On one point she did agree with him: the girl would be a simple but lovely adornment among the guests he wanted invited.

As the carriage rolled down the hill, Liberty thought about the first party she had attended in California. She had been a bride of two months; it was to be a new beginning, almost like a second birth. A multitude of faces flashed before her eye—a thousand scenes, good and bad. At that moment, to be young and innocent again, she would have gladly changed places with JoAnn Robb. Life had been good then. Dan O'Lee had been hers forever more.

She wondered if there was a Dan O'Lee in Miss Robb's life.

17

No ONE, except Kai Soong, took into consideration that the dinner party was to be held on New Year's Eve. Firecrackers and Roman candles greeted the guests to establish a festive mood. The House of Soong provided the food, cooks and serving boys. Liberty provided the setting.

As her guests began to arrive Liberty O'Lee began to detect Kai Soong's wry sense of humor in the event. He had recklessly invited some of the biggest bigots in San Francisco along with a number of prominent men who owed their beginnings to Mammy Pleasant— if not actual cash. There were also a few of Liberty's own financial enemies in the crowd. All attended because they were still pioneer money-grubbers who could not afford to turn down an invitation from Liberty Wells O'Lee.

Jody's problem had been a bit more difficult. Mammy was skeptical to the point of being suspicious.

"He's going to be there, ain't he?"

"Yes, but that has nothing to do with the business she wants to discuss with you."

"Business is discussed in offices, not at parties."

"I wouldn't know about that. But if you want to find out what somebody is really like, a party seems to me a good place."

"What she say 'bout it?" Mammy jerked her head toward Carrie's room.

"I haven't asked her yet."

"Why not?"

"I didn't think it was proper until I had discussed it with you."

Mammy didn't comment. The two women ate another silent meal. Halfway through clearing away the dishes, Mammy stopped.

"She gotta be told. Ain't fair me trying to be a plantation owner and run her life for her."

"I don't see it that way," Jody said slowly, carefully weighing her words. There was much she wanted to say, but she knew it was unwise. "You're a good mother and have your daughter's interest at heart. But there's no law that says you can't meet the man, learn about his background, and then be able to advise her better."

"Chile," Mammy chuckled. "How you get so wise? Ain't nobody have to know I'm looking him over, does they?" Then she sobered. "But, chile, I'se scared."

"That you might like him, even though he's a white man?"

"That don't scare me none. I'se scared 'cause I'se an old woman and ain't ever been to a real party in my life. How's Mammy Pleasant supposed to act?"

Tears glittered in Jody's eyes. "Just like the lady she always is. But I'll share a secret with you: I've never been to a real party, either. I'm scared, too."

Mammy sighed. "Well, *she* won't be. Such doings are her cup of tea. Suppose you'd best be telling her."

Jody thought she had been saving the easiest for last. Carrie listened without comment until Jody mentioned Mammy's inclusion in the invitation.

"What kind of Old South crap is this?" Carrie stormed. "Am I supposed to be escorted by my *mammy*, spelled with a small 'm'?"

Jody didn't raise her voice, but it was full of scorn. "Why, you hateful little creature. After all she has done for you! She was invited on her own, because people respect who she is and what she is. She's not trying to become the mistress of a twice-married man. Is that what that soldier did to you, Carrie? Teach you to run after men who only have one kind of interest in you? If that's the case, think of what that would do to Mammy—and that is spelled with a capital 'M.'"

Suddenly Carrie started shuddering. The shudders brought little percussions of sound out of her throat, a hushed animal whimpering. Then her mouth opened.

"Out! Out of my room! Out of my life, and my personal business!"

Jody backed out of the door. Anger had made her say more than she had planned to, but a truth had been uncovered that made her sick at heart. Carrie had given herself out of pleasure and not love.

Dawn on the day of the party, she came bursting into Jody's room. "Wake up! Wake up! There's a million things to do!"

Jody blinked at her in sleepy confusion.

"Clothes!" Carrie laughed when she had Jody fully awake. "They've given us hardly any time to think about clothes. You will have to help me with Mammy. She has several nice dresses, but never wears them. I will personally pick something from my wardrobe for you."

Throughout the day, Carrie was as playful as a kitten and full of bubbling excitement that was inexhaustible. Jody suspected she was up to something, but held her tongue.

Carrie dressed them both as though she were a costumer for a very important play.

"Mammy, you're breathtaking!" Jody said as the woman joined her in the parlor.

"Ain't I something?" She chuckled, waltzing her small body back and forth. Carrie had spent over an hour hand-curling Mammy's short hair into a million little corkscrew ringlets. The form-fitting black taffeta bodice was set off by ten ivory buttons and a wide white lace dickey collar. At her throat was a magnificent cameo pin. The skirt was a multitude of pleats, with every third panel showing an accordion contrast of white taffeta.

But the real contrast was between the two young women, and it increased Jody's suspicions. Carrie had loaned her a hoop-skirted dress of light yellow crinoline. Yards and yards of ruffling had been gathered into tiers that spiraled down to a hem line that measured eight yards. The bodice was modestly cut to rest on the edge of the shoulders, then sweep down with heavily ruffled sleeves. A six-inch band of gold ribbon was tied about her waist, its tails hanging down as far as the next to last tier. Around her neck was a gold chain and a pendant with yellow diamonds. Carrie had fashioned Jody's hair into long curls that hung on each side of her face, picture-framing it.

She had been most pleased with her appearance, until Carrie came bubbling down the stairs to join them.

She had pulled her dark hair back into a severe bun and pinned it with chopsticks. The dress was of simple cut, with a high mandarin collar and form-fitting sleeves. The beige fraille was plain except for an embroidered sunflower on the left shoulder. A narrow length of deep chocolate lace served as a shawl.

Carrie had tried for simplicity, and the effect was stunning. Without the hair to frame it, her face was revealed in all its natural beauty. The Chinese-style gown enhanced her marvelous figure.

Jody felt suddenly ill-at-ease and horribly over dressed.

"Why?" she whispered to Carrie when Mammy turned to give Mingh instructions.

Carrie grinned. "You'll see. I thought it would be fun to look Negro and Chinese all at the same time."

Jody was worried. "Don't do anything foolish, Carrie."

"Of course not. I intend to let Otis look foolish."

Now Jody did fear what the outcome of that evening would be.

Jody set the buffet plate on the side table and sank down in the velvet-covered Chippendale chair. Her face was flushed and her eyes shining. "Gracious," she said, laughingly. "I've never eaten so many different foods in my life."

Otis Whiteside lowered himself to the ottoman beside her. "It was my pleasure explaining them all to you, Miss Robb."

Jody now wondered why she had feared the evening's events. Otis Whiteside was no barbarian; indeed, she found him to be quite shy and reserved. The big, lumbering Swede with near-white blond hair and muttonchop whiskers hardly seemed the type of man to keep a mistress. Even at thirty-two, his face was still boyish and the light blue eyes full of the desire for adventure.

"Carrie's having such a good time," Jody remarked.

"It tires me out just trying to keep up with her," he admitted. "She certainly loves to talk with everybody at an affair like this."

Jody couldn't help but notice that he sounded hurt. Carrie had been so busy that she had hardly noticed him at all.

"Where is she now?" Jody asked.

"In the salon, talking with Kai Soong."

"That's odd. I thought she was afraid of the man."

Otis shrugged. "Liberty's doing, I would assume. Everyone seems bent on keeping me away from Carrie. Not that I have minded, but it was a little obvious when I was almost commanded to have dinner with you."

"You could have refused."

He dropped his eyes. "I never place myself in the position of looking foolish, Miss Robb. For some reason everyone, except me, has been trying to do that to me tonight."

"Surely not, Captain Whiteside?"

He shrugged his big shoulders. "It isn't the first time I've felt that way. Guess I learned early to sense things like that—not being wanted, I mean. I was twelve when my father took me and my brother Karl to Boston for new boots. I never got those boots."

"Why?"

"Paw had a strong taste for rum and left us outside a tavern while he had a nip. We sat for three hours watching them load and unload ships at the wharf. When Paw came out he was drunk and broke and with three sailors he'd met. I was tall for my age and

they looked me over like a rack of beef. For more
rum money, Paw sold my services to those sailors' ship
for three years."

"But that's terrible!"

"Wasn't wanted," Otis said hoarsely. "Haven't seen
my family since, either."

Jody studied him for a moment as he pulled imaginary lint off the blue serge trousers of his uniform.

"What is it you do want, Captain?"

He looked up at her eagerly. "After twenty years, a
ship of my own. When a captain is also the owner, he
can take his wife with him."

"I see," Jody said slowly. "And you feel there are
people who don't want you to have either."

He nodded.

"I know the feeling, Captain Whiteside. Slowly, I
have been learning to fight for the things I do want,
regardless of what others may think. But there are
certain things in our Victorian society that we all must
abide by, I guess."

He chuckled. "Except for two years, Miss Robb, my
life has been in the Pacific and not the Atlantic. My
view of society is, therefore, more oriental than European."

"Which gives you the unique opportunity of combin-
ing the best of both worlds."

He didn't have an opportunity to comment on that
because Mammy had broken away from a discussion
with Liberty and was coming directly to them. Otis
Whitehead quickly pulled up a chair for her and remained standing, like a schoolboy expecting a stern
lecture. Mammy chattered away at a great rate, and
one thing she said caused Otis to join in:

"Yes, ma'am, we *are* taking more Chinese back than
we are bringing over. Our present ships are designed

mainly for nothing but—well, what we have been carrying."

"Slaves," Mammy supplied gently. "Yellow slaves."

"That's right, Mrs. Pleasant. But they at least get to go home. Since the end of the railroad building here, we've done nothing but take them back and the return cargo has been slim. I think we're going to have a bad year, come summer."

Jody could see the excitement in Mammy's face, but she did not guess its cause. Whatever it was, she was glad of it, because it had replaced the look of disapproval.

"What would you recommend to change that, Captain Whiteside?"

He bent forward, looking at Mammy as if she were the most intelligent person in his world for asking.

"I would forget China for awhile. I would outfit a ship that could safely bring to this port a valuable dry cargo. Sixteen years ago, Commodore Perry opened up Japan, and nothing much has been done with that trade since. What about that, Mrs. Pleasant?"

"Why, I don't know. There's nobody much of that race here to supply with their goods. Not much of a market, Captain."

"No, not in that way. But I'm talking about something the fashionable women of the East will clamor for. Up to this year, it took forever to ship from Japan to New York. The railroad will cut that by two to three months. *Silk* is what I have in mind, ma'am. A ship designed to carry silk without it being damaged by the salt air."

Mammy was looking at him with wide-eyed admiration.

"You one smart thinker. What a ship like that cost?"

Without hesitation, he pulled the ottoman right up to her knees. The facts and figures rolled off his tongue at a rate that was amazing. Gone was any semblance of shyness; he was knowledgeable, forceful and commanding.

At last, Jody saw the man that he really was, the man that Liberty had been trying to protect. But one point left her puzzled: Why wasn't Liberty backing his venture if it seemed so profitable?

"It sounds most interesting," Mammy said. "Might an old woman like me be able to invest in such a thing?"

"Yes," Otis said, a note of awe creeping into his voice.

"Then come see me tomorrow."

Otis gulped, then blushed. "Mrs. Pleasant, I've been at sea for over a month, which is why I have not called on you before. May I also take time tomorrow to discuss another matter that is vitally important to me?"

"As you wish." Mammy grinned. "Come, Jody. It's time for us to gather up Carrie and say our thank yous."

Things, for the moment, were again proper in Mammy's world. The man had treated her most properly in a business sense, and renewed her belief in her own ability to smell out a sound proposition. She had been dubious when the subject had first been raised by Liberty. She had asked the very same question that had run through Jody's mind.

"When you talk with him, Mammy, you will learn something very quickly. He is going to do this thing with or without me. It's not going to do him any good to be backed by the O'Lee money. That would make it too easy and not very fair of me. If you are interested, let's see how interested he is."

"You mean, about Carrie?"

"I must be getting old." Liberty grinned. "Was I that obvious?"

"No more than the whole evening was obvious."

The shameless grin widened. "It's been a little different than I expected. Carrie set the wrong manner of trap. Oh, I admit she made Miss Robb into something quite becoming, but she failed to remember that people don't always act the way we want them to. Otis has hardly made a fool of himself over the charming creature. Now what is Carrie going to do?"

"I should hope nothing," Mammy said sternly. "Proper girls don't chase after men."

Liberty grinned again, but this time only to herself. She never would have had Dan O'Lee if she hadn't done a little bit of chasing.

"Besides," Mammy continued, "if he's a gentleman, it's time for him to speak his mind to the proper person."

And Mammy now felt that Otis Whiteside had handled the matter in the customary manner. She would listen to him, although her mind was far from made up, because he had been courteous to her.

Otis was almost smiling as he said goodnight to them. He did not want to give away the excitement that was mounting in his heart.

Carrie looked puzzled but, to Jody's great relief, much less hostile.

Kai Soong held Jody back for a moment. "A great success, Miss Robb. I predicted you would bring a new life into that household."

"Oh?"

"You were a most beautiful wall standing between forces that could have grown ugly. Someday, when

their marriage has made him the new life in their
family, they will thank you."

"But I have done nothing."

"And do nothing for yourself," he artfully changed
the subject. "Oh, I do not speak about matters of the
heart. As a man steeped in the history of his own
people, may I ask what you intend to do with the notes
you have been taking on the history of Mammy's
people?"

Jody was taken by surprise. She thought only she
and Mammy were aware of her project.

"I—I'll use them when I go back to teaching, sir."

"Goodnight, Miss Robb."

It was a quick dismissal and it baffled her. Why
raise a subject and then flatly drop it? He was, indeed,
a very strange man.

The three women were silent on the short walk
home and as they prepared for bed. Like Cinderella,
Jody hated to part with the gown, but the clock was
literally striking midnight. Carrie came bounding into
the room, her brown eyes bright with happy tears.

"You were magnificent, Jody," she cried. "And what
do you think of him now?"

"Carrie Holmes! What kind of game have you been
playing?"

Carrie stretched out on the bed like a very contented
cat. "I asked first."

"All right. He's a very shy, sensitive man whom you
treated horribly tonight. He isn't at all what I expected."

"I knew you'd help." Carrie smiled. "I'd counted on
your being so beautiful that he would fall madly in
love with you and then I could tear your eyes out.
His too!"

"Charming thought! What changed your mind?"

"Kai Soong, actually. He lectured me on the frail flower that is love." She giggled. "That sounds ridiculous repeated like that, but he was far more poetic."

"I thought he terrified you."

Carrie sobered. "He did tonight, but in a different way. He made me see what I would be losing if I played out my little game. He must have loved very deeply once and been badly hurt. He said I was heading for disaster with my childish behavior. I think that being married to Otis is going to be . . . enchanting. Much better than being the other." She giggled again. "Do you know what Kai Soong said I would have to do to become his mistress?"

Jody shook her head, her cheeks a deep scarlet.

"I don't mean just *that* part, but the hard part—the lonely part of not really belonging and yet being almost a slave. No children, or the fear of them coming accidentally. And always wondering if there was another woman sharing him somewhere else. That scared me."

"Do you think Captain Whiteside is really capable of keeping a mistress?"

Carrie looked up, meeting Jody's eyes. They were developing one of those rare friendships between women where honesty was all important.

"I don't want to know, Jody. His past is no longer important to me. I was trying to be what I thought he wanted me to be because of what I had heard about him. I may have heard wrong, but I don't want to snoop around and find out. If I love him enough, there will be no cause for him to desire a mistress."

After Carrie was gone, Jody thought how simple life would be if her situation with Birdie was only the matter of fighting another woman.

* * *

In the days that followed, she felt that she was being given too much credit for the harmony that prevailed. Then, for a time, she was all but forgotten. Otis was very busy overseeing the reconstruction of a ship he and Mammy had purchased. He had insisted that the work be done immediately. He knew that he had to get his scheme into operation before others found out about it. It was a time for mother and daughter to be alone to discuss wedding plans, and Jody did not intrude.

Her notes grew into full pages and then chapters. Only at the dinner table, when Otis was too busy to join them, would she ask an occasional question of Mammy.

Weekly, carefully worded letters came from Barney or Julia concerning her return. Her carefully worded answers were slim alibis. Before she knew it, she was postponing her return until after the wedding. Around her was happiness; why return to certain unhappiness? It was decided, then, that Captain Whiteside should embark on a maiden voyage prior to the wedding. He would return by the end of March and an April wedding date was set.

Barney's letters now became frantic. The delay seemed preposterous to him. Julia's letters were kinder and more informative: the school was doing quite nicely, although they all missed her and prayed for her speedy return.

It saddened Jody. She thought of them all very often, but somehow she did not miss them. It didn't mean that she didn't love them all, but the realization was growing daily that she just couldn't go back to teaching in Barney's school, or any school. A different world was opening for her, one that she always knew existed but had never been a part of until now.

"Jody, don't be a boob. There are enough people in this town who cannot understand how a Negro woman could put her hands on enough money to buy a ship without you making matters worse. I want you to wear anything that you want from my wardrobe. If these snobbish women are stupid enough to give me wedding showers, then I want them pea green with envy over how we are dressed."

San Francisco thirsted for culture. It saw itself as the New York City of the West. An educated woman was not looked upon as a schoolteacher but as a phenomenon.

The rumor started that Jody was a woman of letters. Augusta Stinton Birch, a leader in the struggle to rid California of the "yellow peril," also chaired the California Literary Society. Her ambition to be more than that overcame her bigotry; Jody was invited to address the Society and present one of her papers.

"They're joking!" Jody said. "Mammy, whatever would I talk about?"

"How about some of those fool questions you ask me every night?" Mammy scowled in mock anger. "Your room's a mess of papers. Must be something on them to read out."

"I couldn't! I just couldn't!"

"Make me no mine. Bunch of ole peahens anyway."

Augusta was unwilling to give up her quest.

"As you should be aware, Mrs. O'Lee, San Francisco must grasp at culture whenever the opportunity arises. Perhaps you could find out why Miss Robb is reluctant to speak to our group?"

Liberty opened her mouth to state why she herself would not want to address such a stuffy, self-centered organization and thought better of it. Another idea came to mind that would make short work of Augusta Stinton Birch.

"Perhaps I could, Mrs. Birch. What honorarium did you offer her?"

Augusta's piggy little eyes blinked in her moon face. "What kind of *what*?"

Liberty chuckled. "When you wish to secure the services of someone like Miss Robb, it is customary to offer them a lecturing fee."

The woman blanched. "But we have only a limited treasury. Whatever could we offer to induce her?"

"That, I should say, would depend on her topic. What is it you wanted her to speak about?"

Augusta flustered. "Her work as a woman of letters, I suppose."

Liberty nearly laughed out loud. It would be so easy to make this pompous creature the laughingstock of San Francisco, but she didn't want Jody hurt in the aftermath.

"Well," she said slowly, as though giving it very serious thought, "if that is the case, a fee of a few hundred dollars would be in order."

Augusta nearly fainted. "Then I'm afraid I must give up the idea altogether. Our membership is too small to raise any such amount."

"More's the pity," Liberty said, ready to put the woman in her place, "because such a woman should be heard by more than just a limited little group."

Rather than take offense, Augusta brightened. "An excellent suggestion, Mrs. O'Lee. Perhaps we could rent the Opera House and sell general admission tickets."

Suddenly, Liberty took a different interest in the matter. She had grown to like the quiet, unassuming young Miss Robb. She was not fully aware of the work Jody so diligently labored at, although Mammy had once said that it was vital to history, and Liberty had assumed she meant black history. But if Jody were to speak, Liberty did not want it to be a failure.

"I think, Mrs. Birch, if you charged a dollar a ticket, I could see my way clear to purchase a hundred. I will also give you a note to my good friend, Kai Soong. You must get him to buy double my amount. That would assure you of the honorarium and all the rest would be profit."

"Oh, my gracious!" Augusta gasped, clutching her breasts. "A profit! That will assure me of the society presidency for next year!"

Liberty had fully expected the woman to balk at the mention of Kai Soong. She was amazed to learn later that the woman who thought all yellow men were the sons of the devil had humbly secured two hundred dollars from him.

And now Mammy changed her tune. "Chile, they offering you three hundred dollars just to do no more than talk. I'd talk from now to next Christmas for that much money."

Jody felt pressured into accepting, but was still unsure about her topic. She lay awake nights quaking with fear.

Daniel Fetterson, publisher of the *Chronicle,* was secured to introduce her. The background information he was able to obtain from her hardly covered a full sentence. To get more, he wired a former employee in Denver.

Malcolm Hoog was in New York and the wire was automatically forwarded to him. The carefully worded answer that Fetterson received back prompted him to write an article for publication the morning of the lecture.

"Celebrity!" Carrie cried, as Jody arrived at the breakfast table. "Listen to this headline: "Literary Society Lecturer Real Life Model for Hoog Novels!"

Jody was mortified. Even though the article never once mentioned 'Mulatto Jo,' she felt as though Malcolm Hoog was once again ruining something for her. Now she was really unsure of her topic. In her opinion, the newspaper article led the reader to believe that she would be relating her true-to-life wild adventures.

Because of the article, she refused to dress as Carrie wanted her to dress. She twisted her hair into a bun and put on a simple gray schoolteacher dress. She would deliver a lecture on the black Estevanico.

The decision did little to calm her. She felt horribly out of place in the Queen Victoria world of the opera house. The interior was almost barbaric in its splendor —the gilt fretwork and bas-relief that covered the walls, the massive chandeliers and the row upon tiered row of red plush seats.

But the seats were rapidly being filled with men in formal tailcoats and ladies in furs, jewels and expensive gowns. The lackluster ticket sales had mushroomed after the appearance of the article. Augusta Stinton Birch, in her box seat, fanned herself importantly, as though she alone had brought about the sold-out house.

As soon as the houselights dimmed, a string quartet played a selection in the orchestra pit. Back stage, after being introduced to Fetterson, Jody nearly panicked when everyone started to leave her to take their seats out front.

"What ails you, girl?" Kai Soong whispered.

"I can't do it! I just *can't!*"

"Of course you can. These are nothing more than students ready to be taught. What you say tonight will become legend in this town."

Suddenly, Daniel Fetterson had her by the arm and was leading her out on the stage. She was thankful when he sat her in a plush chair and took the podium. She tried to concentrate on what he was saying about her, but it was as though he were talking about someone else.

Then, all too suddenly, he was escorting her to the podium and she was staring down at the folder that contained her studiously prepared notes. Her hands shook and she had to lick her lips. Her stomach felt like it was going to shake right up into her mouth. She looked up. The dim auditorium revealed only a sea of indistinguishable faces.

Students to be taught, she thought, and cleared her throat.

"Ladies and Gentlemen, Mr. Fetterson has credited me with accomplishments that seem near impossible for a woman." She paused. She felt eyes upon her and looked up at the first tier of box seats. Mammy, Carrie and Liberty were straining to catch her words at that short distance. Kai Soong sat back, his eyes never leaving her. As if by some oriental magic, his strength seemed to flow into her and take command. She looked out at the audience again and when she spoke this time her voice was stronger and the quavering note of fear began to disappear.

"What he has said is true, but the excitement of it pales when one considers the feats of others in this glorious country of ours. Their adventures make my own seem like a real Malcolm Hoog dime novel—fiction based upon farfetched fact."

A light ripple of polite laughter filtered through the audience. Jody started to open the folder and stopped. There were things on her heart that she now knew were more important to say.

"I am a woman. A woman who, of late, has been granted a rare opportunity to delve into matters that have never become a part of our recorded history—and perhaps never shall be. And why? I don't think the gentlemen present will agree, but if it hadn't been for the serpent in the Garden of Eden, the Bible might never have recorded whose body was molded out of Adam's rib."

Now the laughter came as a released chuckle. They were settling back to listen.

"Twenty-one years ago," she went on, her voice strong and assured now, "somewhere just across the Canadian border, a mysterious meeting took place—a meeting that was to change the course of history, but no where will you find mention of it in the historical records. I could ask you to imagine it, but I can do better than that, for I have been privileged to talk face-to-face with one of the parties at that meeting."

She paused again. The folder remained shut. The audience leaned forward expectantly. She had only her memory to go on, but this kept her eyes glued to the sea of faces below her.

"In a lonely cabin lighted by flickering candles, a thin little Negro woman faced a wild-eyed, gray-bearded man . . ."

The drama and suspence of the early part of the story kept the audience silent and intent until the identity of the Negro woman was subtly revealed. Augusta Birch's fan stopped in midair. She had immediate visions of utter ruination. At any second she expected a stampede up the aisle to the box office and a demand for refunds.

But no one stirred for a solid hour as the exploits of Mammy Pleasant were compared with those of Biddy Mason in Los Angeles, Mary Fields' work with Mother Amadeus, Lolly Davis saving a Jim Bridger wagon train by making her skin white with flour to baffle the Indians and then scaring them away by washing it off.

Jody ended her lecture with a heartfelt tribute. "To-night I have spoken only about these women, but the men of note are legion. They, too, may never see the printed page of history, but these remarkable people of African descent are part and parcel of this place we call the West."

The opera house shook with the applause of a stand-ing ovation. It mattered not to this audience that it had been all black history; it had been warm and human and laced through with delightful anecdotes that had made them roar with laughter. Augusta Birch was in-deed a remarkable program chairman to have brought them such a different and exciting evening. And at such a handsome profit! They could now afford to get more such speakers.

Daniel Fetterson escorted Jody from the stage, his blue eyes electric with excitement.

"My dear Miss Robb, if you write with the same power that you speak, I would be most interested in publishing your work. Have you a lawyer in town who could discuss it with me?"

Jody could barely get out a weak "no." She was still in a state of shock that she had lived through the ordeal.

"Well, is there anyone you would like to have look over the contract after I have it drawn up?"

The name was out of her mouth before she realized it: "Only Kai Soong."

Fetterson chuckled. "I ask for a lawyer and she answers with the shrewdest businessman in San Francisco. Wise, my dear, extremely wise. . . ."

But what had begun as an excuse to keep her occupied now became tedious hard work. Her celebrity status had to give way to the bride, her work curtailed until after the wedding. The parties were all for Carrie and Otis. Then they were gone—a honeymoon trip, combined with business—to Japan.

Mammy began to fret. The big house seemed strange without Carrie and she longed for her little cottage. Spring would soon be lost to her, because of the wedding, and her garden needed her.

And then a loneliness such as she had never before experienced seized Jody. With the manuscript in the hands of Daniel Fetterson, it was like putting a loved one into the grave and having serious doubts about seeing them again in the hereafter.

She knew it was time to leave San Francisco.

18

FOR TWO DAYS back in Denver, Jody savored the heady feeling of what it meant to be the prodigal returned. Carrie's graciously given old wardrobe was new to Denver and made Jody feel like a princess. Kai Soong had advised her not to keep all of her eggs in one basket, so she let Barney's bank have five hundred dollars of the money she had received for her lecture and her book and took the rest to the First National Bank of Denver.

Most of Denver had prospered that past winter. Actually, it still seemed like winter to Jody. She had left San Francisco a mass of flowers and Denver was still brown and gray. Her deposits made, she turned to the problem of what to do with the money.

As much as she loved the children—and as much as Barney wanted her to return—she was just not ready to go back to teaching. Besides, school would be out in another month.

She had a tearful reunion at the Bundy ranch with Miss Inez. It was hard to imagine her as the wife of Lemanuel Bundy, but Jody could see that her aunt was radiantly in love.

Oddly, she could look Clayton Bundy in the eye and see his fear and feel no fear of her own, nor even hatred. She had no real evidence against him, except his avoidance of her, and she accepted that as confirmation of his guilt.

But there was one person on the ranch she could not avoid.

Miss Inez, as everyone continued to call her, kept smiling to herself. She was not like the Bundy men, who hated the sight of a pretty girl carrying a baby inside her. She liked the thought of new life on the ranch, and she had grown especially fond of Alfreda.

"Yes," she told Jody candidly, "it's Maxwell's child. There was a real storm getting him to marry the girl, but why should the child be made to suffer?"

"I was," Jody replied, but to her surprise she felt no bitterness in her tone.

"Nonsense," Miss Inez said. "That's like trying to compare fruits and vegetables."

Jody wasn't quite sure how, but did it really matter any more? She felt as though many years had passed and she was visiting people she hardly knew any longer, Max least of all.

He had taken his hat off and rubbed his grizzled head and stared incredulously at Jody. She had become everything he had hoped for, but now it was too late.

"They made me marry her," he said sullenly, like a little boy.

Jody was torn between pity and disgust. The conviction gradually took hold that she was making life difficult for Clayton, Maxwell and Alfreda. They were terrified of her.

There was no point in dredging up the past; they seemed to be suffering quite enough. That she had been rescued by the Army from a guerrilla band, which was what Jody told everyone, was all that Miss Inez seemed to care about. To keep it that way, Jody cut her visit short.

It was a letter from Carrie, just returned from another voyage to China and Japan, that gave Jody the idea of what to do with her money. But when she approached Barney Ford about it, he was anything but encouraging, calling her plan foolish and ill-advised. Barney's equations wouldn't work out for Jody, though they were amazingly strong for the crop itself.

"Still," he said, "you know nothing about farming and especially this crop from China."

Jody laughed. "And I knew little about teaching and nothing about black history, but I learned something about each."

Barney shrugged. "Our sugar comes from can fields in Louisiana and not from beets."

"Because we have never learned about the sugar beets that they use in China, Barney. And I'm not just thinking about the sugar—the whole plant is put to good use and seems right for the west. The leaves are cooked as greens, or used like hay. The crown serves as food for cattle, sheep or hogs. Even the pulp, after the sugar has been extracted, is used as feed. And the molasses residue is food for animals or humans. All I ask, Barney, is for you to find me six good family men to help me homestead and farm the land."

"That is no problem, Jody, but it will be two or three years before you can start to show a profit."

Jody calculated quite differently. She would buy enough seed to plant forty acres. At the end of the first year she would harvest and sell only the crowns, leaving the beets in the ground for the second year to send out long branches that would produce tiny flowers containing seeds. She would then have enough of her own seeds to triple her acreage and continue the process.

But Jody's ability in the schoolroom did not carry over into the fields or have an influence over nature. She was not a stern overseer and Barney, to Miss Julia's chagrin, had not gone overboard to pick her the six best men he could find.

"Why?" Owen Goldrick demanded, riding out to view her progress in early June, a year after her return from San Francisco, and finding it limited.

"Why what?" she said. "The location? That's quite simple. I'm only three miles south of the new rail terminal in Longmont and very little of the land to the east has been homesteaded."

"Don't play games with me, young lady," he said. "Why do it at all? Horrible waste of talent."

"I'm sorry you see it that way, Owen."

"What other way is there? Your field hands seem to have erected their own quarters quickly enough while your own house is still a shell. You reside in the barn with your plow mules, and they appear to be growing fat and lazy from lack of productive exercise. You forget that I was raised on a farm and would take note of such things."

"This is a different form of farming from what these men are accustomed to, Owen," Jody said defensively.

"Tommyrot! A stern lecture and a black bullwhip would show them how little difference there is in planting potatoes, cotton or sugar beets. *You* are the

novice, not they, and they are taking a hobblin view
of you."

"Hobblin?"

"Lady Hobblin is the source of the phrase. A landed
lady who one day woke to find herself a widow with
a thousand serfs. Despite her rich soil, her crops always seemed to fail, but her serfs didn't suffer. Their
own little garden plots flourished to the point where
they were able to sell the extra vegetables at the
market. Wake up, Lady Hobblin."

Wagon Tom and Irene came next, to stay until
school started again. Jody smelled Owen Goldrick
behind their visit but was grateful for her friend's
concern. The hired hands could get away with little as
long as Wagon Tom was around.

The word gradually went out that Jody was trying
to encourage others to farm and fence in the grazing
lands. This was a matter that Clay Bundy took personal interest in.

Max was at first indifferent. Alfreda was a yoke he
could not remove, could not send away. He stayed
around the ranch all the time, but he would not listen
to Clay. He had nothing to distract him, no woman
but his miserable wife whose presence was an insult to
his manhood—first with her constant sickness, now
with her swollen belly and her great blue eyes. He
had known that he was going to hate the child even
before it was born, and he did. No one could make him
see that the boy was all Bundy. No one had to make
him see that Alfreda was not the best mother in the
world. Free of the child in her womb, she wanted Max
back in her bed. She had started her tongue-lashing in
Miss Inez's presence, but the older woman had not
liked it. Now Alfreda never spoke to Max until Miss
Inez was not around.

"Guess I made a mistake," Clayton admitted cagily to Max one day.

"About what?"

"JoAnn Robb. Hear tell from Miss Inez that she's turned that graze land into quite a farm. Others are doing the same."

"Don't make me no mind, not no more."

Clay was quiet for a moment. "It might, if you're still hankering for her."

Max spit on the ground near his feet. "Little late for that, don't you think?"

"Well, now," Clayton answered slowly. "Might be and might not. Alfreda ain't going to last around here and you know it. Jody might just like ranch life over farm life, if she's made to see how hard farm life can really be."

Now Max was listening. Clayton was conning him, but he was ready to believe anything to rid himself of Alfreda.

At the end of the month a farm, at Erie, north of Jody, was attacked by a small group of invaders—Indians, according to first reports. They burned the farm buildings, took the livestock and set the fields ablaze. But a day later, word reached Jody that the man who had fired the house had been seen to have blue eyes, and when he raised the arm holding the blazing torch, the buckskin shot back to reveal white wrists.

Now the attacks came nightly, getting closer to Jody's farm.

Major Ferris Ferguson, sitting with Wagon Tom and Irene in Jody's kitchen, said, "It was bound to start someday. That they are not Indian raids is obvious. Range war, as I see it. There'll be plenty more attacks like them, now that they've seen how easy it is."

Wagon Tom nodded. "They'll pick off all the little places first. They'll haul down the fences and burn the crops, and the fields are tinder-dry this fall."

"I don't think you have to worry," Ferguson said. "You and your six bucks can protect this place."

"My wife and I have to be getting back to Denver. She's got a school to see after."

"Then all I can suggest is that you take Miss Jody with you for her own protection."

Jody, coming into the room in time to hear him, said angrily, "I will do nothing of the sort! What does the Army intend to do about all of this?"

"What can we do?" Ferguson asked.

Nobody commented; it was true. No one could expect the small Army patrols to stand guard at each and every farm. The front range valley was a hundred and twenty miles long and the raiders had the foothills and mountains to hide in while every move the patrols might make would be plain to see. Besides, the patrols were primarily there to handle the problem of rustling for the cattlemen, and who could say that it wasn't the cattlemen who were trying to scare the farmers out of the territory?

"There's one thing I can do," Major Ferguson said. "I can switch the patrols around and have one of them concentrate on this area."

Jody smiled to herself; she could guess which patrol Ferris Ferguson would not assign to the area.

But Ferguson thought differently. He had behaved, in every way possible, like an officer and a gentleman during his short visit to the farm. He did not approve of what Jody was about, but was smart enough to remain silent. He did not approve of what Birdie had been about in the past several months either, but had been smart enough to remain silent on that subject, too. Now, he thought it high time that each of them learned about the development of the other and bury what ghosts lay between them. Prim and proper Jody, in Ferguson's estimation, had developed into quite a lady. She deserved more than a farm life. Birdie, in his estimation, was becoming less and less effective as a soldier because of the strong influence of another woman. Ferguson thought what he had in mind would be a very wise move indeed, since it couldn't help but open Jody's eyes.

As the autumn days went by, the hands on Jody's farm became increasingly aware that the raiders were gradually closing in. Major Ferguson asked for volunteers to add to the regular patrols. He had been able to find only ten men willing to spend all their time out on patrol. Now, he turned the whole problem over to Sergeant Birdwell Jacobs.

It was an odd little contingent that arrived at the farm. The buckboard was not Army issue: neither was its driver. It lagged a little behind the troopers, but somehow still seemed a part of the whole.

Jody saw the patrol leader ride up the hill to the farm, shifting his eyes from left to right, looking everywhere but in her direction. She said softly to herself, "He knows damn well this is my place. He's afraid to look me in the eye. Now he's going to act surprised."

He did. Birdie beamed all over and said "howdo" to all the black workers and their families, shaking hands and introducing his mother to each of them. But the introduction to Jody was not as warm.

For Laurie Jacobs it was like meeting a stranger. Her son had told her nothing about Jody; therefore she gave her the same dutiful respect she would have shown to any white woman.

"There is plenty of room to quarter your troops in the barn, Sergeant Jacobs," Jody said coolly. "Your mother will be quite welcome to stay at the house."

"No need," he said, a little too tartly. "Mother is quite used to camping out with my troops."

Jody didn't protest; it was obvious to her that Birdie didn't want their past association known. Oddly enough, it didn't bother her. Ever since she had spotted the familiar figure riding up the road things had been different. She had not tingled with excitement or curiosity or dread at the sight of him. She had stood in a kind of void . . . emotionless. She would be the master, and not her heart.

For a week they avoided each other, but it was harder for Jody to avoid Laurie Jacobs. The tall, stout woman was everywhere. For too long she had devoted herself to her son, still finding it hard to believe that they were together again. But the wives of the black workers were a tonic to her spirits; they were home folk. From them she gained a rather strange impression of the mistress of the farm.

"Ain't no white woman that kind to niggers lest she wants somethin' in return. Why ain't she got a husband?" she asked one day.

It was a point they had never considered; it was a point Laurie Jacobs was not given much time to consider that night.

The troop had left an hour before sundown, hoping to catch the invaders in the act somewhere. Just before crawling into bed, Jody thought she heard them return. She listened, puzzled. They had ridden on past the barn to the workers' cabins. Curious, she rose and went across the hall to peer out the windows of the north bedroom. At first, all she could make out was the six cabins and the log barns. Then she saw something so unexpected she could only stand and stare.

A dozen men were forcing the workers out of the cabins. These were not painted Indians; these were men wearing strange white flowing garments, their heads covered by white hooded masks. Another strange thing was the silence. The workers were making no protest whatsoever at having themselves and their families rousted out of bed. Who were these men? What were they about?

Then a slow sickness began to spread through Jody's stomach. A torch was lit and touched to one of the cabins. The flames ran along the bark on the logs, dull red and yellow and tipped with thick smoke. The smoke went up against the trees and rolled into the cloudless night sky. The bark roof caught with a gust of sound, and suddenly the whole cabin seemed to be engulfed by fire. It was unbelievable that anything could burn so fast.

Jody thought suddenly: There is somebody still inside that cabin!

She didn't know how she knew that for a fact, but she did. It haunted her as she raced back to her room and pulled on clothing. Racing down the stairs she paused to take another quick look out the window. The cabin was now an inferno. The farm families were standing together in a knot, surrounded by the hooded men. They did not make any demonstration. They stood perfectly still, watching the cabin burn wtih a dull kind of fascination.

Not daring to think about it any further, Jody went down to the parlor and took down the shot gun from over the fireplace. From a tin box she took a handful

of shells and went out into the night. What she could
do all alone she didn't even stop to consider.

A shadow loomed up out of the darkness.

"What you aimin' on doin', gal?"

Jody looked at Laurie Jacobs as though the woman
asked the dumbest question she had ever heard.

"I aim to try to protect my people and my property.
Lord knows where your son and the troops might be!"

"Do no good," Laurie said darkly. "The devil be on
the side of men like that."

"Do you know who they are?" Jody asked.

"Seen the likes of them in the South after the war.
Ku Klux Klan, they calls theirselves. Ain't wantin' the
blacks to have anythin' but slavery."

"Well, we'll see about that! If you want to help, take
my horse from the stable and try to find Birdie."

"They'd ride me down and kill me 'fore I can get
away."

Jody began to swear. She started to move from tree
to tree, trying to get closer to the cabin compound,
and Laurie followed along. When they had gone far
enough to be within range, they saw the burning cabin
roof fall in. A voice boomed out from behind one of
the hooded masks.

"Let him be a lesson to you all. Unless you want to
burn in your cabins tomorrow night, you all be gone
from here!"

Jody had a crazy impulse to put a shot in the middle
of the whole bunch, but Laurie, who seemed to guess
it, whispered, "Don't shoot, gal. That'd give 'em an
excuse to kill 'em all."

The spokesman shouted again. "Now, all of you lay
down on the ground and cover your heads with your
hands. We ain't leaving 'til you do it."

"I know that voice!" Jady said suddenly.

"Don't talk so loud," Laurie warned her.

"That's the man from Hole-in-the-Wall!"

Jody remembered the voice as if Harvey Logan had spoken to her just the week before. But what he was about here was not cattle-rustling.

She behaved calmly, as if she knew just what she was doing. She motioned to Laurie to walk along with her, but the woman hung back. Jody raised the rifle muzzle.

"Stay where you are or I fire!"

Cursing, the raiders fled in different directions. Her own people made matters worse by running too, not giving her a chance to fire. The raiders didn't worry about making any noise in their hasty departure; they shouted back curses and ugly warnings.

Jody led Laurie at a rapid pace down to the smoldering cabin. Her hands heard her coming and ran like fury, but Jody was in no mood to call them back. Their women and children were too scared to move.

"Cowards!" Jody shouted, then looked at the women. "Why didn't your men use the rifles I gave them?"

She was met by sullen silence. One woman, Mrs. Sharp, was the first to recover her wits. She said the raiders had come up just as everyone was preparing for bed; that at first, like Jody, they had thought it was the soldiers returning. Cabin by cabin, the people were forced out. Art Simms, who had been beaten by Klansmen in Alabama, refused to leave, so the raiders burned his cabin with him in it.

Laurie went to help Betsy Simms, who was a pretty girl and quite young, and told the other women to get their children back to bed. By now, the men, silent and sullen, began sauntering back. They looked terrified.

"Mrs. Jacobs," Jody said, controlling her anger.

"Take Betsy up to my house. You men, get your rifles. Harmon, divide them into groups and stand guard until the Army patrol gets back. If you see someone all decked out in white, shoot first. If anyone needs extra ammunition, come to the house for it."

They looked at her dully. They made her think of wild dogs waiting to fight each other for leadership. They weren't listening to her and it angered her.

She stomped back to the stable and took her mare into the barn to be saddled. She could do nothing more for them, but she could do something about her property. The beet crowns were drying in the fields, waiting to be harvested for feed. She was not about to let the raiders put their torches to them.

She did not use the paths but rode right across the fields, boundary to boundary. She was as alone as though she were the last person on the earth, but she rode on through the night, expecting the raiders to return at any moment.

Not until the sun began to rise did Jody feel free to return. She paused for a moment to get her breath before riding back to the farm.

The sky was like a great silken sheet over all the world, misty in the west, but edged with gold to the east. On a level with Jody's eyes, her farmland rolled and dipped. For hours, the question had been haunting her: Why the Hole-in-the-Wall bunch, and why dressed like Klansmen? That Clayton and Max Bundy might be behind the raids raised even a bigger "why." She had been very careful to avoid them and her aunt this past year. Could she have been mistaken about recognizing Harvey Logan's voice? It was the only evidence she had and it wasn't very solid.

Then there was a familiar sight moving along the

horizon. She knew at once that it was the troopers by the way they rode. For a moment she wanted to ride out to meet them, to be with their leader. But, on second thought, she restrained herself and rode for the farm.

Jody felt her blood rushing through her. The farm was deserted and all the wagons and horses were gone.

She turned to see Birdie's mother watching her from the porch. Her eyes were bright with excitement.

"'Where on earth is everyone, Mrs. Jacobs?"

"Gone. They's scared," Laurie tried to explain.

Jody shook her head. "I can understand their fright, Mrs. Jacobs, but these people have been with me for a year. It's not like them to just leave and take my wagons and horses without asking."

"I told them they could."

"You what!" Jody exploded.

"I told them the Klan would kill 'em if they didn't go."

Jody's lips quivered. "And did you take into consideration what I would do without them?"

Laurie looked at her gravely. "You sound just like a plantation owner. I heard it all through the war: 'Nigger, take care of my land and I'll save you from the damn Yankees!' "

"No," Jody swallowed hard. "You've made a big mistake. It's not the same here."

"Ain't?" Laurie laughed. "I seen how the soldiers are treated. I seen a man burned to death last night. Run, I tell them niggers. Run 'fore they burn you, too."

"Then why didn't you run, too?" Jody shouted.

"I will," Laurie said calmly, "when he comes to fetch me. My boy will take care of me."

"Don't count on it," Jody snapped. "After what you have done, he will have to stay and take care of me."

Laurie looked at her sullenly. "I think not, gal. He ain't got no obligation to you."

Jody could hear the troops riding into the yard behind her. She had a sudden desire to open Laurie Jacobs' eyes to the truth.

"Are you speaking about his white side or his black side or his military side?"

Laurie gasped. "What you talkin' bout?"

Jody eyed her coldly. "When a woman has slept with a man, she learns all of his secrets."

"You shut yore mouth!" Laurie said, watching her. "My boy ain't done that thing yet, I know. You a whore for talkin' like that!"

Jody couldn't help but laugh. "You slept with Colonel Jacobs to produce Birdie, but I'm the whore."

"I was forced to do that thing," Laurie said, her voice rising.

"Well, I wasn't. I did it out of love. I would still be doing it out of love if he had married me."

"Oh God no! Now I know why they after you. They know that you did it with a black!"

"They know nothing of the kind!"

"They do! I could kill you! I could kill you for shamin' my innocent lamb! I hope they burn this house down on your whorin' head!"

"What is all this?" Birdie demanded, striding up to them.

Jody wasn't given a chance to answer. Laurie started right in, making it sound as if the Klansmen had driven off the hands during the raid as slaves, and in the next breath began to attack Jody.

Birdie stood rigid, confused and blushing.

"Well," Laurie demanded, "did you or did you not fornicate with this white hussy?"

Jody began to laugh. "Tell her the whole truth,

Birdie. Tell her it was nothing more than one bastard child lying with 'another bastard child. That seems to be the only thing we have in common."

"Why did you even have to tell her?" he said.

Jody's heart turned to stone. "Sergeant Jacobs," she said icily, "when you have removed your mother from my house I will discuss with you the circumstances of this night's raid and whom I believe to be behind it— without your mother's hysteria getting in the way."

Laurie screamed, "We's leavin', but my son ain't ever returnin'." She grabbed Birdie by the arm and started to drag him out the door.

He hung back. "Jody, I—"

"It is Miss Robb," she said bitingly, "and I'm looking forward to giving my full report on the military handling of this matter to Major Ferguson."

Birdie glared at her. "You brought it all on yourself by bringing our personal lives into it. I warned you how that would affect Mama."

Laurie glowed with triumph. Her boy may have done "that thing," but she still had power over him.

Jody's eyes dulled. Suddenly, she knew it was no use fighting anymore. She would be in the wrong no matter what she said. It had happened before; it was happening again. Men could be the biggest bastards in the world and get away with it. But let a woman go unguarded for a single second and she was a whore and a trollop.

She turned away. There was no sound behind her. She pulled herself up the stairs and to her bedroom door. She was tired, tired of fighting battles that always seemed to go against her. Tears came to her eyes and rolled down her face.

Suddenly, she wanted to sleep . . . forever. If they

came to burn the roof over her head, she would just lie there.

"I'm not mad at you, God, just at some of the people you put on this earth."

19

It was dusk; Jody had slept through most of the day. The stock had not been fed at all that day and now were beginning to make their feelings known. There was no one else to tend to them, and Jody wondered how long she would be able to manage all alone. Though her six hands had not been the best of workers, at least they had done some things.

She wondered if she shouldn't try to find white labor the next time. Two weeks before she had been in Denver on business. Dave Moffat had warned her that the East was starting to slide into a recession and to watch her money closely. At the land office she had seen dozens of drifters and farmers filing claims. If times were getting so hard, she shouldn't have any trouble getting farm labor.

Throwing corn to the chickens, she smelled the smoke before she saw it. She went out into the farm yard and stared in every direction. She could not spot it for a long time, it was such a pale, frail, insubstantial thing against the sky.

But Jody knew what it meant instantly. She was in the saddle and off in moments. She rode to the rise and searched out the source of the smoke. Across the St. Vrain River she could see the fiery line of orange crawling along the northern acres. The whole valley seemed to have gone still. Without thinking that there was very little she could do by herself, she spurred her horse toward the burning beet crowns.

The raiders were swarming all around the fields, setting fire to the rows of sugar beet tops. A couple of men were even going through the hayfield, touching off the cocks.

Even riding at such speed, Jody was able to get the double-barreled shotgun out of its sheath and load it. She was still out of range, but she pulled the trigger for each barrel. The recoil almost knocked her out of the saddle.

A raider looked up at her approach and jabbed into the air with his finger. The other men turned and started running for their horses. Not expecting to get caught, they had not taken the trouble to don their white sheets and hoods.

But among them, in the smoky twilight, Jody did not see Harvey Logan. Still, she kept loading and firing the shotgun, ineffectual though her shots might be. They were good enough to make the raiders ride off and keep riding.

Jody had nothing to fight the flames with but the butt of the gun. She beat at the smoldering clumps until the butt was charred and splintered, and still the fire came on. She didn't even hear the pounding hoofs behind her.

"Get back on your horse and come with me."

Her eyes stung from the smoke and she couldn't see the speaker, but the voice made her seethe with rage.

"Go to hell!"

"Jody, damn it, listen to reason!" Birdie shouted. "If we start a backfire at the river, these flames won't be able to jump across to your other acres."

It was so reasonable that it angered her all the more, having come from him. She followed him without comment, expecting to see the rest of his troops somewhere about.

Birdie gathered up dried beet crowns and twisted them into a taper. He held them close to the hammer of his pistol so that when he fired the spark would ignite them. As though she were one of his soldiers, he barked out orders about what he expected her to do with the taper.

They separated, each going along the curving bank of the river and touching the burning tapers to the dried crowns. When Birdie felt that enough little fires had been ignited, he whistled and motioned for her to ford the river.

Sensing the growing fright in her mare, Jody led the horse across the shallows and turned to look back. The little backfires had joined into a single line of dancing orange flames. Stubbornly, Jody refused to join Birdie, but stood silently watching eighty acres go up in smoke and flame.

They waited, watching the two fires slowly merge. Then they waited some more, praying that flying sparks wouldn't jump the river anyway.

Suddenly, Birdie was laughing. "Why is it I always come upon you when you are a filthy mess?"

She started to spin away but he caught her by the wrist.

"We've got to have this out, Jody."

"Oh? Are you capable of that without your mother here to hold your hand?"

"I deserve that, I know. I should have known that she would get it out of you sooner or later."

"What was there to get? It's ancient history. Now, please let me go. Thank you for helping with the fire."

He let her go, smiling gently. "I can't go away," he said. "I can't run anymore, Jody. It's all my fault. You know I loved you, only we are so different—not just black and white, but in other ways. I never loved anybody before you. Never will again."

Jody pressed her fingers to his mouth.

"Hush, Birdie!" She wept. "Oh, my dear one, please hush, before you say something you will regret."

"I don't want to hush. I've got to tell you about it, Jody. I want to marry you now, despite mother."

Jody didn't want to think about those last words, only bask in the first. She nestled in his arms, shivering. She had waited so long to hear those words from him that it was like a dream.

But his lips were not a dream; they were real upon hers. His arms were real about her. His body was real as it pressed close. Now there was no need for talk. Together, they would not worry about the many problems their union would bring.

Birdie's resignation from the Army was accepted with bitterness by Ferris Ferguson. He was not only losing Birdie but Jody forever. He did not want to see either of them again and asked for a transfer to another part of the country. Out of spite, he held up Birdie's discharge for three months.

It was an odd three months for Jody. Laurie Jacobs moved into one of the log cabins on the farm and had as little to do with Jody as possible. When Birdie was able to come by for a visit, Laurie would try to monopolize his time. Jody understood and thought time would bring the woman around, after her son was married.

Others needed time to digest the startling news. Miss Inez reverted to type and was furious. Max Bundy took the news as a personal insult, and was twice as mean and cruel to Alfreda. Clayton Bundy was delighted; he called off the fake Klan raids and let the real "nigger haters" in Denver know what Jody was up to. He saw her forthcoming marriage as her death warrant.

Barney Ford and Owen Goldrick lectured her in long rambling letters. She didn't answer them.

Wagon Tom and Irene wisely kept their thoughts to themselves.

Jody's barn was a comfortable place to milk in. It was cool and restful. There were no windows, only the chinks in the log walls and the log ceiling overhead. The six cows stood in a row on rough planks. There were no longer any children to drink the milk or women to churn the cream to butter, but the animals still had to be milked. Laurie, her gray-streaked head butting one cow's flank, and Jody, at the next animal, were milking together. They were not trying to make conversation; they were tired from the many farm chores they had to manage each day alone. Birdie had promised to send help, but none had arrived yet.

The barn was quiet with the soft breathing of the cows and the hiss of milk striking its own froth in the pails. Neither woman heard the squeak of the wagon wheels or the man's approach to the barn door.

Laurie's voice rose in a falsetto screech when she spotted him. "Oh, Lord! You tryin' to scare us to death?"

"I's sorry. I's here to see Miz Jody. Don't suppose ya 'members me from de Bundy place?"

Jody didn't quite remember his face.

"I be Amos. Mistah Birdie say I be a better farmer than a cowhand."

"I certainly hope so, because we can sure use some help. Are you alone?" Jody asked.

"Got mah family."

Laurie rose with Jody—she would do some inspecting of her own—and followed them from the barn.

Jody recognized the black woman sitting on the wagon, a baby at her breast. Her eyes met Jody's questioningly, fearful that there might not be work here.

Jody smiled reassuringly. "Hello. Your name is Mary Alice, isn't it?"

"I'm thankin' ya for rememberin', Miz Jody."

"And I'm thanking you for coming."

Laurie hissed, "You don't have to thank the likes of them."

Jody ignored her. "Are there any more of you?"

Amos looked a little shamefaced. "Could be. I were thinkin' of my own family first. How many you be needin'?"

"I had six here before."

Amos beamed. "Ah know where there be three more family men and a couple of singles. All Bundy people 'til Mistah Clayton fired us. We ain't done too good since then."

"Well, let's get you settled and then we can talk about it."

"Just like that?" Laurie said. "You take 'em on just like that, without knowing a thing about them?"

"I know them from the past, Laurie."

Laurie Jacobs snorted and turned away. "A body don't get fired off without good reason. I don't like it."

Nor did Laurie like the others that Amos brought back in the next few days. But she couldn't complain about their industry; they were starved for work and wanted to prove that they were worthy of Jody's trust.

Laurie was a problem by staying in one of the cabins. The single men stayed in the barn until the burned cabin was rebuilt. Jody thought she was being kind by having them build next a new house for Laurie, but all Laurie did was carp and complain about it. She didn't endear herself to any of the new people.

But all of them endeared themselves to Jody in a strange way. Mysteriously, they each arrived with several head of cattle—almost a hundred head when put together in one herd. Rustled? Jody was not about to ask what they might or might not have learned while working for the –B– and Clayton Bundy. The cattle were put to pasture, to graze on the dried beet crowns. Jody almost made a deal for them, but decided to wait until after the wedding so that Birdie could be included in the transaction.

Miss Julia had to browbeat Barney into attending the simple ceremony and the party afterward. He was still dead-set against the marriage, but greatly impressed with Jody's farm and the cattle. Always the businessman, he needed this prime beef for his restaurant and the newly opened Inter-Ocean Hotel.

"Business later," Miss Julia scolded. "This is their day."

The day almost ended in disaster. The minister who rode out from Longmont took one look at the bride and

groom and instantly rode right back. It pleased Laurie
Jacobs no end.

Mary Alice quickly pushed a reluctant Amos forward.

"Nobody done ask before," she announced proudly,
"but my Amos is the Bible-readin' man fur our people."

"He ain't a proper minister," Laurie insisted.

"Never mattered on the plantations," Barney said.
"All they had to do was jump over a broom together
and that was good enough in the eyes of the Lord."

Amos suited Jody and Birdie just fine, but in the
eyes of Laurie Jacobs they were not legally or properly
married. She lay awake the whole night with a horrible thought in her mind: her son was sleeping with
a woman. It sickened her. She was the only love that
Birdie should have in his life.

Jody and Birdie hadn't slept either, but for a different reason. They were like children and they knew it.
They experimented with love and it was vastly rewarding. There had to be no fear of tomorrow. At dawn
Jody sat in the bed hugging her knees with joy. This
man she had married had more to him than she had
suspected. For the first time in his life, Birdie had
really let himself become a sexual being. But at dawn
he was up and ready to go about his chores, and his
new life as a farmer and married man.

For six months Birdie savored the heady experience
of what it meant to be a married man. When he learned
that Jody was pregnant, he behaved as if he were the
first man ever to have brought about such a miracle.
It put Laurie Jacobs into an even blacker mood. She
still refused to acknowledge the marriage and considered that the child would be born out of wedlock.

It was the best of summers and the worst. The grasshoppers came like a massive thundercloud, blotting out the sun and devouring everything in their path. The farmers batted, swatted and burned them by the millions. Laurie gloated, seeing Birdie's discouragement begin to grow. Jody refused to let it get her down.

"Why don't we turn the cattle into the fields and forget the seed crop for this year?" she suggested. "Better the cattle eat the crowns than the grasshoppers."

Laurie snorted. "Why don't you admit that Birdie is no farmer. He's a soldier. Now, it seems to me—"

That was becoming Laurie's customary preamble. Every opportunity she got she brought the Army into the conversation and how much better off Birdie had been then.

Major Ferris Ferguson felt the same. Because Grant was up for reelection the Army didn't want to move any officer anywhere, Ferguson was stuck in the West. He wanted Birdie back to help with the growing Indian problem. The Army now had black officers and that was the carrot Ferguson dangled.

"That would sure make me most proud," Laurie said. "Imagine how the Colonel would feel if he was still alive, son—his boy an officer."

Jody didn't comment. She was learning Laurie's tactics very quickly. That Birdie had a white father was only mentioned when it suited Laurie's aims.

She was born in October with skin like polished pine. They named her Mary Pleasant Jacobs. It was a private matter as far as they were concerned, but some, who did not wish to see Grant reelected, made it a personal matter.

The telegraph operator at the Longmont terminal

rode all the way out to the farm with the message, under the belief that he could turn a handsome profit with the Denver newspapers by revealing the answer he got.

Jody was greatly amused by the wire. It was the first time in years that she had heard from Hiram Robb.

"Birdie, my Uncle Hiram—who would rather not even remember that we are related—is being considered as a running mate for President Grant. He wants me to deny the rumors that I have given birth to a black child. This man is to wire back my reply. Wire him back, sir, that my daughter is no rumor."

The operator did as instructed and didn't make much money on selling the information to the *Rocky Mountain News*, but the news hit Washington like a fireball. Senator Henry Wilson of Massachusetts was named as Grant's running mate and Senator Hiram Robb fumed.

It was their first anniversary; Mary P., as they called her, was two months old. Ferris Ferguson came by, more to boast about his new promotion than to see the child. He was able to stay the night.

In the morning, Birdie was gone with him.

"You what?" Jody screamed.

"I had a very long and serious talk with my son last night," Laurie repeated. "Under the circumstances—"

"What circumstances? He is my husband and Mary P.'s father. His obligation is to us, not to go off playing soldier!"

"You are selfish. You've been trying to harness him like he was a field mule. You've been breaking his spirit, taking away what made him proud to be a man."

Jody glared at her. "Is that his opinion or yours, Laurie?"

"I think I should know my son better than anybody else."

"No, don't give me that. You didn't even have a son until he brought you west. He was the Colonel's boy until the day the Colonel died. Now you're afraid I'm taking him away from you again. Well, let's not even consider my feelings in the matter. Let's just consider the child. I want Birdie here for the sake of his daughter."

Laurie didn't have to put her thought into words. Her face said it all: Birdie had no daughter as far as she was concerned.

Jody was hurt, and furious with Ferris Ferguson. She tried to hide her feelings, but her bed was now a lonely island. Again she was faced with having to make all the decisions alone—at least, she thought that was the case.

Suddenly, the ground was thawing and a robin made a visit to her window sill. In four months there had been only one letter from Birdie and it had been addressed to Laurie. Birdie's disappointment was almost as great as Jody's. He had not received the field promotion that Ferguson had promised, had not even been given his old rank, and was stuck playing nursemaid to the Pawnees on their reservation.

"Well, at least it is a safe assignment," Jody remarked.

Laurie sat frowning to herself. She had only read to Jody those portions of the letter she wished her to hear. She avoided the personal messages to Jody and Mary P. and was not about to let Jody know how bitter and disappointed Birdie really felt.

"You will be writing that Ferguson man," Laurie said. "You will be insisting that my son be given his commission as promised."

"How do you know it was promised, Laurie?"

"I've ears. That's what the man promised Birdie in my own house—officer rank if Birdie would go back into the Army for three years."

Three years! Jody was stunned. She could accept Birdie going back for an Indian campaign but three years! She did write Ferris, but not in the way Laurie asked her to. It was two months before the reply came and it was confusing. A Major Henderson informed her that Lieutenant Colonel Ferris Ferguson had been transferred to California and that they had no Sergeant Birdwell Jacobs on the roster.

Without consulting Laurie, Jody turned to Barney for assistance. He was able to learn very little from the Indian Office of the Department of Interior, as they did not keep a roster of the Army personnel assigned to them. What they were not saying was that the Indian agents and the Army did not get along well together and would not cooperate in a matter such as this.

June brought with it two new problems.

"Worser than last year," Amos said sadly. "Dem hoppers come quicker'n we can kill 'em, Miz Jody."

"Alright. Let's plow up that forty acres south of the river. We have enough seed to replant and maybe the grasshoppers will be gone by the time the beets are through the ground."

"Perhaps ya'all done forgot, but those acres already planted."

"When? In what?"

There was uneasiness in Amos's black eyes now. Miserably, he shook his head.

"Miz Laurie done told us you said tah plant 'em in collard greens, turnips and kale. Cash crop, she say, tah sell tah de niggers in December."

"Cash crop?" Jody cried. "Oh, Amos, every black family in Denver has a garden plot of their own. They don't buy what they can grow for themselves in the summer."

"How were Amos tah know?" he said grimly. "She done say it am her boy's land and we am tah do what she say."

Jody felt sick at heart. "It's alright, Amos. Just warn me from now on when she gives you an order."

Their fights became a daily thing. Jody could do nothing to please Laurie and Laurie tried to rule the farm as though it were hers. The tension became unbearable, but Jody did not weep. The matter now was past the help of tears.

The baby was put in charge of Mary Alice, and Laurie was told only that Jody had some business to take care of in Denver.

20

THE SIOUX BRAVE had been scouting down toward the flats when the horse scented him and snorted. The Indian's first intention had been to sneak up on the campsite to see if he could pick up an easy scalp. He wanted to save up for a new gun; the old flintlock which he had inherited from his father shot badly. For hunting he even had to carry a bow. He had picked up two scalps that month—one a buffalo hunter on the plains, the other a prospector whose scalp had not come off easily and so he was fearful that he would not get the full ten-dollar bounty.

But the horse had obviously detected him and would have put the camper on guard. The Sioux rode off to where he could leave his pony in a cottonwood grove and then slowly worked his way back, as soundless as the dawn's approach. This time the horse did not hear him and he waited to see the camp a little better. As soon as it got lighter he made the surprising discovery that the sleeping figure was a woman. You got ten dollars for any scalp, regardless of sex. This should be an easy ten dollars: the woman was alone.

The Sioux ran down the bank, jumped the stream and stood beside her, fingering his knife. He might rape her—he had never tasted the flesh of a white squaw—or he could hit her on the head and get away quickly. He was still debating when Jody looked up at him and screamed.

He realized that she had not seen him at all, or heard him, either, until that instant. Then he saw that she no longer saw him, she was unconscious. He caught her by the arm and hauled her to her feet and looked at her. He discovered that she had been hurt. Her skirt was ripped open, revealing dried blood on her leg and a piece of bone sticking out of the skin.

He was puzzled. To find such a woman there, alone, and in such condition was strange. It made him uneasy. Had she been left behind by others who would soon return for her? He decided he had best think things over before he killed her, so he dragged her over the ground and put her over the saddle of her horse. He would decide, but not there.

Daylight increased gradually as he led the horse back to his pony. He rode off, changing his course several times so that it would be difficult to track him. Once, a great twittering and fluttering broke out in the trees and he stopped, dead still, and waited. But the birds had not been put to flight by the sound of other horses; they were playing a mating game and making a great racket doing so. The Sioux grunted, relaxed, and kicked his pony forward again.

He was a Brule Sioux and brother-in-law of Spotted Tail. But he had never been successful on the warpath and that winter his wife had died. She had been a favorite of Spotted Tail's, and the chief had accused One With Little Luck of not having been a good provider for his sister. He considered that this woman might be a good present to give to Spotted Tail, but he was not sure.

He decided that she was not an unattractive creature, though the wounded leg might make the gift seem unworthy. Her light, long curly hair interested him. It might bring even more than ten dollars. But if Spotted Tail decided to take her as a bride, bad leg and all, he might just get a new rifle in return. Such decisions he did not like to make on his own.

He found a likely spot, built a fire, set the woman down beside it and waited complacently for her to waken.

Jody was weak from loss of blood. The fall from the horse had been a stupid accident. She had found the earth-lodge dwellings of the Pawnees without difficulty, but the village had been all but deserted. Sky Chief had taken most of his people on their semi-annual buffalo hunt.

The Indian agent William Burgess didn't know the names of the patrol soldiers, but thought one of them came near Birdie's description. He could only give her a general idea of where the Pawnees might be and had no idea when they might meet up with the patrol. But when he learned that she was the wife of the black soldier she sought, he suddenly didn't have any more information to give. He was having enough trouble keeping the black soldiers away from the Pawnee women.

To make sure that she was not there to make trouble, he sent a Pawnee brave to track her. Jody had not been aware of it for two days and when she did become aware of it, it frightened her. She began to ride dangerously to escape her tracker and did not see the tree branch until it was too late. In falling, the horse had kicked her and broken her leg. The Pawnee thought the fall had killed her and went back home to report.

But this Indian sitting in the sunlight before his fire was not the same man, Jody was quite sure. He was even more frightening: his face was striped with white and vermillion paint. Even from a distance, the other man had not appeared to be wearing war paint.

She felt sore and exhausted, but she was alive. She realized that she had been moved. She was lying with her leg up on a rock so the blood would stop flowing. The leg was numb but no longer oozing blood.

Then her mind froze. The little camp was suddenly filled with Indians. Her captor was on his feet instantly, babbling in a language she didn't understand. He seemed to be addressing his remarks to one man in particular.

Spotted Tail was a squat, slightly bowlegged man who did not quite come to his brother-in-law's shoulder. He pointed to Jody's horse and laughed.

"You are well named, One With Little Luck. You give me this skinny woman for my squaw and expect a rifle in return. What is wrong with rifle strapped to her pony?"

One With Little Luck felt very foolish; the thought had never crossed his mind.

"I take her back for you," he said quickly, to hide his embarrassment.

"No! Pawnee are hunting our land. She must go with us!"

"But her leg is bad."

"And it is bad luck to give a damaged gift. It might be best to shoot her."

Spotted Tail stooped down and poked Jody's leg with his forefinger, staring at her. He knew that such an injury must give great pain, but she had not flinched or cried out. He poked again. Finally, she understood.

"It must be numb," she said.

He shook his head, not understanding.

Jody pinched her arm and said "Ouch!" Then she pinched her leg. "Numb!"

He repeated it, then he said to two braves, "The leg is like dead. The bone must go back inside. You pull on her heel, and you hold her firm about the waist. I watch."

He smiled, and some of the paint cracked on his cheeks. He described with his hands what the braves were going to do. Jody nodded. His eyes roved back and forth from the wound to her face. Now there was pain, great pain, but she gritted her teeth and fought to keep from fainting. Spotted Tail smiled broadly and thought: This one has great courage. I have no desire for a white woman, but I like her courage. I let her live until we take care of the Pawnee thieves.

He directed that branches be cut to make a splint for the leg. He tore up one of her petticoats and personally tied the branches to each side of her leg. Now he must be the only one to touch her until he decided her fate. One with such courage might bring him great luck that day against his worst enemy.

The Pawnee were weak women in his eyes. They had given in easily to the whites and ceded them land that the Sioux felt was theirs. They had worked for the white man, fighting the Sioux who tried to keep the iron rails from being laid across their land. It was time for the Pawnee to pay for all their past mistakes—one hundred and fifty years' worth.

Jody had a horrible sense of *déjà vu* upon reaching the rise. The valley was a mass of mounted Indians, with more riding in at every moment. They were all painted for war, and the sights and sounds of the raid on the Ute agency school flashed through her mind. She wasn't sure what tribe this was, but instinct made her pray that Birdie's patrol wouldn't come riding along.

The valley was filled with hundreds, perhaps a thousand, warriors. Those on the fringes let out a fierce cry when a war party came riding in with a white captive. His hands were tied to the pommel of his saddle and somewhere along the way he had lost his hat. He kept his darkly handsome face black, without fear.

Spotted Tail seemed greatly pleased with the report he received and sent the captive back to ride alongside Jody. The young man eyed her with open suspicion.

"Ma'am," he said, nodding his head. "How'd you all find yourself in this predicament?"

He had such a heavy southern drawl that Jody couldn't help but smile. "I might ask you the same. I'm Mrs. Birdwell Jacobs. I fell from my horse and broke my leg. That chief had his braves set it for me."

The man pursed his lips. "William Wickersham, at your service, ma'am, although I can't be of much service at the moment. You all are right lucky. That Indian is Spotted Tail, one of the most blood-thirsty Brule Sioux of all. I'm amazed he didn't just kill you and take your scalp."

"What a pleasant thought, sir. How do you account for your still being alive then?"

If he hadn't been tied, Wickersham would have

scratched his head on that. "Only thing I figure, ma'am, is the men that captured me have seen me with Steve Estes, the agent for the Brules. Surprised them that I was with the Pawnees, I guess."

"With the Pawnees? Was there an Army patrol with them? I'm looking for my husband," Jody explained.

"Has been, off and on, over the past month. Wish they had been with us today. We've been hearing reports about Sioux being around, but didn't see any until today. Sky Chief had a number of his men up on the plains, killing and skinning buffalo, when about a hundred of these devils came charging. Sky Chief was killed and scalped along with a couple dozen of his braves. My friend Platte and I were getting the women and children and the pack horses into a ravine. We were supposed to keep anything like this from happening."

"Women and children?"

"Yes, ma'am. They do the drying and packing while the men are off hunting—about a hundred women and fifty children."

"And how many men?"

"About two hundred and fifty."

"And these are so many! Surely they don't mean to attack them again."

Bill Wickersham couldn't look her straight in the eye. "Well, ma'am, Platte and I went out to parley with them and put a stop to it, but they fired at us and forced us o move back. Then they captured me and took my revolver. But what was that you were saying about your husband?"

"I have reason to believe that he is with that military patrol."

"I don't see how that is possible, ma'am. They're all niggers, even their officer."

Jody started to explain, but just then Spotted Tail began moving his warriors out of the valley. Guards came and rode with Jody and Wickersham and kept them from talking.

The Sioux and Pawnees had continued to fight after Wickersham's capture. The Pawnees had organized a defense line and come out of the ravine. They had been battling the Sioux for about an hour now. Suddenly, they saw the advance elements of Spotted Tail's seven hundred. In panic, they fled back into the ravine. With frantic haste they began to pull the robes and buffalo meat off their horses and endeavored to mount their women and children. Spotted Tail split his force into threes and attacked.

"Oh, God, no!" Jody screamed. But her cry was lost in the rifle fire. Before the words were even out of her mouth, thirty-nine women, ten children and a number of braves were shot down while trying to mount their horses.

The Pawnees fled in terror down the ravine to the Republican River and then down the valley to the east. The Sioux guards forced Jody and Wickersham to ride along in the wake of the chase. A rear guard stayed behind to plunder.

Wickersham was silent. He didn't have to guess the eventual fate of himself and the woman. Why they were still alive was a mystery.

The bugle call cut through the Sioux war cries like a knife. On the horizon was a line of fifty blue-uniformed cavalrymen, riding hard. Spotted Tail cursed his scouts. He had no wish to clash with the military. He signaled his force to split again, this time riding off in eight directions.

It utterly confused the young black lieutenant. It was his first battle experience and he began to give conflicting orders. The patrol sergeant was just as green and repeated the commands. The bugler just honestly gave up on which order to signal next.

The best trained soldier in the patrol was no longer a sound-thinking one. Ferris Ferguson had exacted a horrible price to gain personal revenge against Birdie and Jody. That Birdie could obtain a field commission had been a ruse and a myth, but the papers Birdie signed did commit him to three more years of military service. Ferris had destroyed Birdie's file before turning the command over to 23-year-old Hanson Davis. Ferris had smelled Hanson's fear of command and had painted the "buffalo soldiers" as real desperadoes, with Birdie the worst of the lot. Every time Birdie tried to find out about his commission or stepped out of line, Hanson busted him down a rank and ridiculed him. Birdie was too ashamed to let Jody know about his horrible blunder and so had written to his mother. He was crushed when he did not hear from either woman.

Twice he decided to desert; twice he was caught, the first time by the military and the second time by the Pawnee Scouts. Lieutenant Hanson Davis, knowing nothing about Birdie's background, wanted to make an example of him. Those men who had served with Birdie before kept their mouths shut; they wanted to see the "proud nigger" brought down a peg or two. The Pawnee Scouts were given free reign to do as they wished. They beat and whipped and tortured Birdie as if he had been a Sioux captive.

Thereafter, he was a very docile soldier, to the delight of Hanson Davis. No one was aware that the Pawnees had broken a blood vessel in Birdie's brain, and that Birdwell Jacobs had ceased to be Birdwell Jacobs. He followed orders as they were given, because that had been his training since he had first stood at the Colonel's knee.

Out of all the conflicting bugle commands now, he heard only one. He spurred his horse down into the valley and back up the ravine, his revolver drawn and ready to fire.

Up on the crest, Jody saw him. Even at that distance she could not mistake him. The Indian guards had been just as confused and had ridden off without Jody and Wickersham. Now she urged her horse to the lip of the ravine and shouted:

"Birdie! Birdie! It's me, Jody! Up here!"

It was the noise that distracted Birdie and not the actual sound of his name. He reined his horse and looked up. Just then, a badly wounded Pawnee brave rolled over onto his back. His scalp was gone and the blood nearly blinded him, but somehow he was holding on to the last shred of life. The horse and rider above him were just a red blur, but it had to be a Sioux. The Pawnee used his last minute of life to raise his rifle and fire.

Jody's scream echoed and reechoed down into the ravine and far down the valley. She scrambled from her horse and collapsed in a heap on the edge of the ravine.

Her mind reeled. It wasn't just the still form of her husband that she saw, it was a stomach-turning vista of man's inhumanity to man, regardless of race or color. Savage brutality was everywhere. Dead Pawnee women and children were lying among the dead horses. The Sioux rear guard had stripped, scalped and mutilated the bodies. They had gathered lodge poles and piled bodies on the poles and burned the dead and dying Pawnees.

Jody saw and yet she did not see. She sat as though she were one of the dead.

A black soldier came to cut William Wickersham's bonds.

"Who was that soldier who died down there?" Wickersham asked.

"Somebody once, nobody now. Birdie Jacobs by name."

"Birdwell Jacobs?"

"Same. Ya'all know him, su'h?"

Wickersham shook his head slightly. "No, but I think I know someone who did."

"Gentlemen!" Barney Ford roared, and paused. He had been given two minutes to speak before the Senate Statehood Commission. "Am I addressing the senators who formulate Indian policy without ever having seen an Indian? Are you, therefore, the same senators who formulated black policy without ever having seen a Negro man or woman? You ask me to give you help in the forming of the state of Colorado? I ask you first for a full investigation of the battle of Massacre Canyon."

"Each Indian agency blames the other and together they blame the military. The military seems to want to blame Birdwell Jacobs. What horrible infamy is this that a dead man is to be made the scapegoat? *I do not buy it!* You think because he is black you can rest your sins upon his grave? The Colorado Territory can't be bought that cheaply as a new state."

"Sir," Senator Hiram Robb interrupted. "The incident of which you speak did not even take place within the borders of what will be Colorado. I find your remarks out of order."

Barney smiled grimly. "I thought you would, sir." He opened his mouth to go on, then quickly closed it. He let why he thought so drift away into silence.

The Commission chairman was suddenly confused. He looked from Barney to Senator Robb and then at his gavel.

"Do you have anything further to say, Mister Ford?"

Barney hesitated and Hiram Robb grew increasingly nervous. Was he to be continually embarrassed because his bastard niece had married a black man?

"Mister Chairman," he intoned quickly, "I move that this matter be referred to the State Committee on Indian Affairs for investigation."

The motion was quickly seconded and passed, and the meeting was adjourned.

Hiram Robb breathed a sigh of relief. He had friends who could bottle up the investigation for months, even years.

Barney Ford smiled to himself. His equations were quite right still on the prospects of Colorado becoming a state. He would let the good senator stall it as long as he wished, because Barney knew that the country had to face up to another of his equations first.

21

THE DIME SAVINGS BANK in Denver was solid, but not the rest of the country. The panic hit in September. Within days several of the major Eastern banks had failed, wiping out millions. The panic quickly spread west. Hardest hit were the bankers, manufacturers and farmers.

Jody was caught in the crunch. Except for the money she had placed in Barney's bank, she was wiped out. She hardly knew it or cared. She sat hour after hour, day after day in the parlor rocker, and it might as well have been the edge of the ravine for her.

Bill Wickersham had brought her home and gained enough information from Amos to go on and report to Barney Ford. He had also made arrangements to bring Birdie home.

Laurie also sat in the parlor, staring at the unopened pine coffin, holding tight rein on the wild grief that tore at her. As long as she didn't look inside, then the coffin couldn't possibly hold her son. She had heard so much from this man Wickersham, but would not believe a word of it.

Jody had heard too, and hadn't heard.

The moment came when Laurie finally turned and looked at Jody, and saw with surprise that she was not the only one grieving.

"Why," she whispered, "you did love my boy, didn't you?"

"And I killed him."

"No, chile, don't be sayin' that." Laurie began to cry. "That man told me what he found out about what they did to my . . . *our* man. Ah'm the one that killed him. Ah'm such a stupid old plantation nigger slave. Got myself a bit too high and mighty. Made me feel right proud when he were in uniform and the others looked up to him. Reminded me of the Colonel, he did. Don't know why, weren't allowed to associate much with the Colonel after Birdie was born. It was all one big dream on my part, then and after comin' west. Ah began to see him as another Colonel, just as important as his daddy had been. My ambition killed him, chile."

"Don't blame yourself," Jody whispered. "I was the one who took him away from the army in the first place and put him on the farm."

"Yes," Laurie sighed. "But he came. He wed. He left his seed. We now gotta say good-bye."

"When?"

"Dat for you to say, chile. You am his wife."

There were no words Jody could find to answer that, so she held out her arms. Laurie came to her, whimpering like a lost soul. Each had lost so very, very much within that casket. Birdie could not return for either of them. They had each stolen a part of him away from the other and now both were losers.

"What now?"

"The good Lord will be tellin' us, chile, ah hopes."

The Lord didn't seem to be on anyone's side—except Barney Ford's. Irene, after two miscarriages, was about ready to give Wagon Tom his first child and asked to be let out of her school contract. The pawn shops on Wazee street filled to overflowing with the dreams of people who could no longer afford them. Derelicts roamed from bar to bar on Larimer Street in search of escape from a world suddenly gone sour.

"While you are all sitting around on your backsides doing nothing," Barney told a group of Denver businessmen, "I intend to do something for my people. Last time they helped me build a school for nothing. This time I'll put them to work building the finest structure this side of Saint Louie."

But Barney had to watch his pennies, too. The three-story Colorado Free School rose rapidly, but it was made of wood. The mills made Barney an offer on lumber that he couldn't afford to turn down.

Owen Goldrick had the perfect answer to the question of a replacement for Irene Smithson. Barney thought otherwise. He had worked out an equation on a certain individual and stubbornly insisted on putting it to the test.

"Now, don't ya'all be worrin', Miz Jody," Amos said. "We done put away enough of Miz Laurie's field goods, got plenty of firewood an' can let the cattle graze. We do jest fine 'til next spring."

For Amos, spring seemed a long way off. For Jody, it would come much too soon and with no seed capital to start over.

"That's the size of it, Barney. My farmers can make it through the winter, but I have Laurie and them and little Mary P. to think about come spring. I need a winter job and a cottage to rent."

Jody looked over at Laurie and smiled. "We've already talked that over, Barney."

Laurie preened with importance. "We is of an independent mind, Mistah Ford. Borrowers ain't independent people, as my daughter-in-law and I see it."

Barney also saw something else: Jody needed the work for more than just the money. She was thin and pale and haggard. She needed something to get her mind off Birdie's death.

"Well, there is little I can do except send you over to see the man I hired to run the new free school. I've given him free rein on the selection of teacher."

It looked more like one of the Brown's Bluff mansions than a school. It was gleaming white, with an abundance of windows, and trimmed with flaming red gingerbread. The third floor had been divided into small apartments for the teachers and dormitories for the live-in students. There were far too many schoolrooms, in Jody's opinion, but then Barney was looking to the future. Oddly, Jody questioned a part of that future. While waiting to be interviewed she had observed three teachers preparing their classrooms for the opening day of school. All three were white.

William Wickersham crossed the foyer and saw her in one of the vacant classrooms. He was not aware why she was there. He stopped in the doorway to watch her . . . she looked so lovely! He still could not believe that she had been married to a black man. It was something that was beyond his comprehension. Even as a youth in Moultrie, he had never desired a black woman, perhaps because the opportunity had never really presented itself. He and his brothers had

been tutored privately at home and then sent to
England for eight years of schooling. Still, he had
been undecided about what path to follow in life
upon returning home at eighteen. It was easy for his
brothers; they would follow right along in the foot-
steps of their father, Dr. David Wickersham.

Fate and the Civil War directed all of their steps.
Even after twelve years, he still could not believe
the toll the Wickersham family had paid for a style
of life that really wasn't their own. They had never
owned slaves but had black servants—a cook, a maid
and a butler. Even now he was not sure what his father
had paid them; these were matters he was never troubled with. The family was wealthy enough that it was
never troubled by money worries.

Young William Wickersham had tingled with excitement, curiosity and dread at the thought of war. But
as the war progressed it etched some terrible scenes
upon his memory. In the first eighteen months of conflict he lost two brothers, another early in 1864. Late
that year his own leg was shattered by a cannon ball.
His limp would remind him forever of that fateful day.
It was a day of miracles and a day of horrible night-
mares.

The miracle was that Dr. Wickersham was the sur-
geon at the nearest field hospital and saved his son's
leg. But the man was hardly his father any longer.
After thousands of such operations, David Wickersham
was a drunk—a mean, savage drunk. He drank to get
the smell of blood out of his nostrils and to put himself
to sleep without seeing maimed and mangled young
bodies.

But as successful as he had been with his son's leg,
he was not so successful with his next patient. Without

chloroform the young man went crazy as Dr. Wicker-sham attempted to amputate his leg. Too quickly to be stopped, he grabbed an instrument away from Wickersham and plunged it into the doctor's heart. Lying on a recovery table, William had seen it all.

For the next three years he saw that nightmare mirrored in his mother's face as she withered away into nothingness. For the next five years he tried to escape it all—buffalo hunter, Indian agent, trapper, wanderer —anything that didn't require his brain cells to function.

He limped into the schoolroom, and when he was close by, Jody saw him at last. Joy and sorrow mingled in her bright eyes.

"Mr. Wickersham," she said. "What are you doing here?"

"Doing?" he said testily. "I reckon I ask myself that question often enough. And what, might I ask, Mrs. Jacobs, are you doing here?"

"Oh, no! Now I know why Barney didn't give me a name. I assume, Mr. Wickersham, that you are the new head of the school."

"It would appear so, although I still question my sanity in accepting the position. I am well taught, but I have never taught anyone in return. However, I gather Mister Ford was more interested in my natural ability at organization and administration."

Jody had been studying him intently. This was hardly the same man she had shared captivity with. His dark curly hair had been neatly cut and the shaggy mustache was no more. Buckskins had made him look squat and fat when he was actually quite tall and thin. The black eyes seemed always on the alert and cautious, and were out of place in a face that was darkly handsome and gentle. He didn't sound like the same man either; gone was the lazy Southern accent, replaced by a well-educated one.

"Then you are to be complimented. This school is a far cry from the old one."

"The old one? I was under the impression that you have only the one child, Mrs. Jacobs."

"That's true, Mr. Wickersham, but, you see, I was one of the first teachers in that old school." She paused, then went on quickly before she lost her nerve. "And I'm here to apply for a teaching position again."

"Were you Miss JoAnn Robb?" he inquired gravely, as he took a seat at the teacher's desk.

"I was."

He was taken by surprise, but he was thinking: Wouldn't this be a bad time to bring back one of the old teachers? Of course he knew she was amply qualified—far more than the three he had already hired. But would she be a challenge to his authority? Could she teach the subjects that he was going to demand of the students?

"There are going to be many changes," he said cautiously.

"I am very adaptable," she said, suddenly fierce. "And I already know most of the children."

He was startled, when he looked at her again, to see tears in her eyes.

"I suppose we can give it a try. The pay is a hundred a month and we supply living accommodations." He stopped suddenly. "I just thought about your child."

"My mother-in-law will be able to take care of her while I am teaching during the day."

Wickersham hesitated. "Well, I, will she be living with you?"

"I don't see why not."

Wickersham blushed. "Well, you see . . . she is black and the other teachers are—"

The look on Jody's face dried up his words.

"Bigots, Mr. Wickersham. They would have to be bigots. Are they going to be color-blind in the classroom?"

"I'm sorry. It's just that—oh, well, let's give it a try. Come, I'll introduce you to the rest of the faculty."

Faculty! Administration! Curriculum! Spit and polish and discipline!

No wonder Jody, now classified as Upper Level teacher of English and History, felt ill-at-ease. She was not very well accepted by the other teachers, who were stern and spinsterish. They taught more with the end of a ruler than with their brains. They shared the unspoken thought that they were wasting their time by trying to teach blacks.

Jody tried to teach as she had always taught.

"We are here to educate, not coddle, Mrs. Jacobs!"

"It is American History, Mrs. Jacobs, not black history!"

"I spend many long hours at night, Mrs. Jacobs, making up those lesson plans. Why can't you keep your classes up to them?"

Hardly a day went by that William Wickersham didn't find one excuse or another to jump on her, deride her work, or call her down for straying from his lesson course.

It delighted the other teachers and gave them much to giggle over in their own apartments at night.

"Peahens," Laurie would say.

"It's all right. We only have to put up with it a few months and then we can go back to the farm. I'm just sorry they treat you the way that they do."

"They only hurtin' themselves, chile. They be jealous dat you got yourself someone to cook and clean for you. Their place am a disgrace."

"Laurie!" Jody gasped. "You haven't been going into their rooms have you? I don't want to give them any reason to complain to Mister Wickersham."

Laurie looked hurt that Jody would even think such a thing. "Don't need to go in. Can smell their dirt and see the roaches crawlin' through to our kitchen."

It was a health point that Jody thought should be raised with Bill Wickersham. He chose to take it wrong and accused Jody of trying to get extra work for Laurie as a maid. Jody fumed all that day, but Laurie only laughed when Jody told her.

"Ain't a bad idea," she said, loud enough so her voice would carry through the thin walls. "But I ain't goin' tah do it for no nigger wages."

That night the rooms and kitchen shared by the other teachers were quietly and sanitarily cleaned.

Barney Ford made only one exception to his rule of not running the school on the stories brought home by his children. That same night when Bill Wickersham visited him in his Dime Savings Bank office Barney asked him suddenly,

"What happened to all the black history these children were being taught?"

"We have no one qualified to teach it."

"Oh? I was able to get hold of a few copies of this little book from San Francisco. Seems to me you might recognize the name of the author."

For all his vanity, Bill Wickersham knew when to keep his mouth shut. He would handle it in his own way. The books were given to the other teachers to read and they promptly forgot them.

"You look tired chile."

"Dead," Jody said. "Laurie, I don't understand it! Drill, drill, drill. It's not my idea of teaching. What's horrible is that he knows better."

"Yes, and it's worse than that."

"What's worse, Laurie?" Jody asked. "You know something that I don't?"

"I think so, chile. Look, honey, you got yourself some powerful black ideas and he's got himself some powerful white ideas. But he's still a man and you're still a woman."

Jody studied her mother-in-law. It never ceased to amaze her how Laurie could sound like a "plantation mammy" one minute and speak without a speck of accent the next.

"What are you driving at?"

"That man keeps after you because he's just too damned scared to admit that he's fallen in love with you."

"There's sense in that," Jody said thoughtfully. "Still—"

"I know, chile. You've given him no reason to think of you that way."

"Of course not! All we do is fight and argue."

"Because he knows you're right and he's wrong. Don't fight back for awhile. See how quick that takes the wind out of his sails."

"But I don't want him to fall in love with me."

Laurie smiled to herself. To her way of thinking it just wasn't right and proper for so young and pretty a widow, white or black, not to think about getting married again.

Besides, she and Bill Wickersham shared a secret. During the day, Laurie would sneak into his quarters and tidy them up a bit, even leaving the leftovers from their table every now and then. Her favors would be rewarded just as mysteriously. Laurie would suddenly find the wood box filled or a sack of groceries outside the door.

Alfreda had stayed. She had, through guile, gotten herself pregnant by Max again. But it had seemed a pretty desperate ploy to them both; they didn't share anything in common. Max now blamed Clayton. Clayton had said he could force Alfreda to leave the ranch and Jody to leave her farm. Alfreda hadn't but Jody had, and Max was right where he had always been. But the Bundy ranch was not quite the same. No one could afford to buy beef, so very few cattle were being shipped or sold. It wasn't even profitable to rustle them. There was almost no money left that Lemanuel was willing to lay out for hired help. Everyone was let go and most of them drifted up to Hole-in-the-Wall to wait for spring. Things just had to get better.

Things weren't much better in Hole-in-the-Wall. There wasn't much use trying to rob a bank when there was no money in it.

But at the end of January, Bill Wickersham had a stroke of good luck and Clayton Bundy a stroke of bad luck.

Clay came back from Denver, his thin face grey with misery. Max took one look at him and swore.

"Damn it, don't tell me you didn't sell them cattle! I gotta have that money for the doc so she don't have this kid."

"Shut up!" Clay hissed. "That damn nigger bought the cattle. Cheap bastard would only pay five cents a pound of the hoof. But that ain't the worst of it. Public school burned down and they're gonna put the whites and blacks together."

"They can't do that."

"They already done it, you stupid bastard. We can't find work for our cowhands, but Mister Barney Ford sure seems to find work for every black nigger coon in Denver. And that pussy you kept chasin' is right back there teaching again."

"Jehosaphat!" Max exploded. "Didn't you go and talk to our friends about any of this?"

"Talk?" Clay growled. "Damn your hide for being such a stupid fool! They're scared shitless. They've disbanded and got no leader. How in hellfire do you expect them to do anything?"

"Then I'll be their leader!"

Clayton stepped back. He began to laugh, the laughter rising until it was a horrible cackle. "You do that, little brother, you just go and do the impossible."

Hatred doesn't require much leadership; certainly not intelligent leadership. Hatred does require money to prime its pump and buy a few free drinks—and Max knew instinctively where to go for sympathy and money.

He arrived just as school was letting out. He had purposely made himself look as disheveled and forlorn as possible. At first, Jody didn't want to see him at all, but she was thankful at least that Laurie wouldn't be in on the conversation. She now shared everything with Laurie, even everything that had happened in the past. Laurie knew all about Maxwell Bundy.

Max should have been an actor. The bleak story he told about conditions at the ranch, about Alfreda's pregnancy, was all quite true, if slightly exaggerated. But his lies were the most powerful argument of all.

"A penny a pound is all they want to offer on the cattle, and what with Miss Inez being so poorly—"

"My aunt is sick?"

"She don't want you knowing, Jody. She don't even know that I'm here—that would just about kill her. You know what a proud woman she is."

Jody sat down again behind her desk and stared moodily into space. It was a fact that the Bundys had caused her a great many problems, but it was also a fact that Miss Inez had been her guardian for eighteen of her years.

It also seemed like fate that she had deposited only half of her monthly check the day before, planning to use the rest for a down payment on spring seed.

She was embarrassed that it was all that she could afford. To Maxwell Bundy it looked like a million dollars.

Five dollars went for pillow slips, cardboard and sheets. Another five was expended on many schooners of beer, accompanied by many hours of talk. No one could prove otherwise, so Max continued to lie. He painted a vivid picture of his recent imaginary trip through the South and how the blacks were taking over everything, just like they were doing in Denver. He claimed to have papers naming him the Grand Wizard of the Invisible Empire of the South, but no one ever saw them. When men don't have a dime in their pockets and get free schooners of beer in their hands, they will believe anything. But for once Max did play it smart. No man was allowed to learn the names of more than two other members to whom they would pass information. They were just so many anonymous white peaked hoods to one another, but brothers in their shared hatred.

Because it started as little more than petty harrass-ment, it was ignored as little more than a bothersome fly that would vanish when the season changed.

* * *

Jody started to decline the offer, but then the humor of the situation struck her. Bill Wickersham needed her help. Ever since they had been forced to take in the white students, Wickersham had tried to make himself more agreeable.

"I do have to think about the farm," Jody pointed out.

"You have hired men who can think about the farm. Who is there to think about the students? We are so far behind that we have to run into a summer session. The other teachers won't stay—I doubt they will come back next year. I can't handle all of the classes alone."

"All right." Jody smiled. "For a little while. But I don't want to teach next year either, if the farm is profitable."

"Then I hope it fails."

"You really don't mean that," Jody said gently. "You are just worried and tired."

Bill sat very still, looking at her. "I am worried," he said sadly. "I am scared to death of losing you, Jody. I'm afraid I've fallen hopelessly in love with you."

Jody stared at him incredulously. Except for Laurie's constant kidding, she had seen no sign that he even knew she existed, other than as a teacher.

"Now really, Mister Wickersham, you don't have to softsoap me. I said I would stay. And, according to your own faculty rules, you had best go back to calling me Mrs. Jacobs."

"Damn my stupid, arrogant faculty rules!" he said. "Damn my hatred for the black students. I try not to hate. I try not to think that they were the underlying cause of what wiped out my whole family. Why can't I just accept them as people?"

"You seem to accept Laurie that way."

"I accept the kind little things that Laurie does for me, and that makes me a hypocrite. Without saying it out loud, I've let her do these things for me just as if she were a servant not to be seen or heard from."

"Just like the gentleman who fills the wood box," Jody said gently.

He reddened. "That's different."

"Is it? It is an act of kindness, no more or less than what Laurie does."

"Please," he whispered. "I'm so confused lately. Please tell me how you came to marry a black man."

Jody inhaled sharply. It was really none of his damned business. Then she knew that she wasn't being fair; it wasn't something to be ashamed of or hidden away.

"Because I loved him," she said simply.

"Do you think that you will ever love that way again?"

I don't see how, Jody thought. There was still a terrible hurt in her heart whenever she thought of Birdie. She was a prisoner in a cold and lonely bed that had a ghost for a constant companion. Or had her love been stronger from the start than Birdie's had ever been? She wondered.

Suddenly, without thinking, she said, "I hope so," and fled from the room. . . .

22

THE TROUBLESOME FLY was now much more than a nuisance. Denver was growing increasingly troubled over Klan activities.

They disappeared as quickly as they struck. At first it was only crosses left burning as a warning in front yards. One night, Henry Bellows was badly beaten up. Henry, who was fast becoming the number one drunk of the Five Points District, couldn't really say what had happened. The whites said that he probably just fell down: the blacks thought differently.

But then an incident occurred that no one could ignore. In mid-July, a farm family from Henderson were on their way into Denver to sell their produce. It was still well before dawn, but the white sheets and hoods were unmistakable. The man was flogged, his horse shot, and his son and daughter forced to fornicate for the Klansmen's enjoyment.

The faceless attacks continued. With no counter-attacks, with no one even trying to deter them, Max Bundy's vanity got in the way of his judgment. He began to boast that he was the Grand Wizard.

The news was passed from man to man. The whisper traveled around town like the flitting of an owl through the dark.

"I know it's a big favor," Barney said, "but it's the only clue that we have. We have got to find out if this is just more of Bundy's craziness or if he really is behind it all."

Jody looked doubtful. "I'm not sure how I could find out. I haven't seen him since early spring."

Owen Goldrick cleared his throat. "That's odd. He's been staying in the hotel where I live all summer. He's even told me that he carries messages back and forth between you and your aunt."

Jody was silent. She had not heard from Miss Inez at all, nor had she heard from Max about paying back the money she had given him.

"If that's the case, Owen, then suppose you tell Maxwell that I have a message for Aunt Inez. . . ."

Max came, full of more lies and ready excuses, but he quickly repayed what he owed her. He was handsomely and expensively dressed, she noted.

"Everything fell right back into place this spring. The ranch is doing real well."

Dear God, she thought; I am nothing but a fool in his eyes. Doesn't he realize that I am well aware of the price of beef and the state of the economy?

"I'm glad. I wish I could say the same about my farm."

"It would do a lot better, Jody, if you hired real farmers and cowboys and not a bunch of people who are probably stealing you blind."

It was the perfect opening, but she ignored it.

"And how is Aunt Inez?"

"Fit as a fiddle! She and Lem are away in Chicago for a month."

"How nice for them."

This time no sad story about Miss Inez's health, nor any mention of Alfreda. But where had his sudden wealth come from? Jody could venture a good guess.

"I notice there is a lot in the paper lately about Harvey Logan. What a fanciful name they have given his gang—the Wild Bunch. I'm sure that when they capture whoever robbed those banks in Kansas they'll find it wasn't Logan after all."

Max frowned. "Why do you say that?"

"I have very good ears, Max. He was the leader of that Klan group who raided my farm and killed one of my farmers."

"Then why haven't you reported him?"

Jody laughed; she hoped it sounded convincing. "What proof is just a voice, Max? But when they unmask him I'll know for sure." She smiled. "After all, we both know that he is a cold-blooded murderer."

"The Klan hasn't committed any murders."

"What about on my farm?"

"That must have been a fake bunch, Jody."

"Behind those masks, who can say who is fake and who is real?"

Max was silent for a long moment, frowning. She had struck right at the heart of his vanity. "That's a good point."

Although it had not been prearranged, William Wickersham could not have picked a better time to walk into Jody's classroom.

"Oh. I'm terribly sorry. I didn't know you were busy."

"No, come in, Bill. I would like you to meet Maxwell

Bundy. Max, this is William Wickersham. Max is . . . well, my aunt's brother-in-law. I'm not sure what that makes us."

"Mister Bundy, my pleasure." Wickersham was all smiles. "In my native South, my dear, that would make you kissin' cousins."

"Forget the cousin part," Max said, warming to Wickersham's Old South manner immediately. "I've been trying to kiss this beauty for years."

"I fully admire your taste, su'h," Wickersham said, laying on the accent. "Ah'm of the same frame of mind. Now, Miss Jody, I don't mean to be makin' you blush."

Jody put on a stern face. "Shame on both of you. Are you forgetting I am a proper widow woman?"

Both men frowned and looked at each other. He knows, Max thought. He knows she was married to a nigger and doesn't like it any more than I do.

"Excuse my asking, sir," he said quickly, "but I couldn't help but notice your limp. War wound?"

"An outward manifestation of the conflict, Mister Bundy. Within my heart are five black-bordered Confederate flags for my family."

"My condolences, sir," Max said, adopting Wickersham's Southern gentleman manners. "That is a heavy price to pay for the freedom of the slaves. I'm surprised that you can teach them."

"Surprised? Mister Bundy, I would teach apes to survive the times that General Grant has brought upon the country. *Apes,* sir, and there is little difference."

Max saw the storm clouds building in Jody's face and knew that they had gone too far in front of her.

"Perhaps, sir, you know the Steak and Ale? I'd be honored to have you accompany me there for a bit of supper and more conversation."

"Good idea," Wickersham said, and then his face fell. "But I have some school matters to discuss with Mrs. Jacobs first. Perhaps later?"

"Your pleasure, sir. Your pleasure."

"Shall we say in an hour then?"

"Fine. Good-bye now, Jody!"

Max sailed out. He smelled a convert, an intelligent, war-veteran convert. A man who could really stir the Klan into action.

Jody and Bill remained silent until they heard him riding off. Then Jody began to giggle and Bill laughed.

"I think, my dear, I have become a much better agent for finding out what Barney Ford wants to know."

"How did you know who that was? You've never met Max before."

He blushed scarlet. "I saw him come in and—"

"And you ran to Laurie to find out?" she finished.

He looked sheepish, like a little boy caught swiping cookies.

"Laurie told me what Barney wanted. I don't think it's right of him to ask such a thing of you," he said quickly, seeing her smile.

"Then you plan to accept his dinner invitation?"

He laughed then. "My dear, on our salary, any free meal offered should be a free meal accepted."

"Be careful, Bill. Max may seem simple, but he can be very complex."

"And I am a very complex man who at times can be very simple. But I already owe a great deal to Mister Maxwell Bundy. Do you realize that for the first time you broke down and called me Bill? That makes me love you all the more."

Jody had to turn away suddenly to hide the tears filling her eyes. "No, Bill, I can't let you go through with this—not if you are doing it just to prove your love for me. I haven't tried to force my ideas on you and won't now. Please, I think I've learned enough, so carry on from here."

He didn't answer and when she turned, he was gone. She raced to the window and saw him walking toward town. Watching him go, she said a short and simple prayer. "Go with him, God. Give him the strength that he will need against Max Bundy."

It was Max who needed strength against Bill Wickersham. The man could outdrink him, outtalk him and fill his head with fantastic dreams. And still Bill had said very little. He had dropped the treacly Southern charm for the man-to-man approach and had repeated every half-baked statement made by every overboastful Confederate soldier from 1861 to 1865: boasts that should have been burned away by cannon fire, but would live as long as men knew how to lie. But there was one point that troubled Max about the man.

"You think much about Jody?" Max's tone was vaguely suggestive.

"No more than I think about any woman."

"She's got a black kid, you know."

"I know."

Max said bitterly, "Damn the black stud for sticking her."

"I don't like the blacks myself," said Bill. "It's what makes me wonder about her. You ever had a black gal?"

"No!" said Max quickly.

"Me neither. I spit on the white man who would lower himself to such a sinful thing. He should be flogged, just like they been flogging some of these

I would personally flog any white man I
...lain with a negress."

...k and stared: he was getting very drunk.
...nything about my past?" he asked sud-

..."We've only just met."

...oment more, his head swimming.

"...n drunk."

...started to say goodnight. Max

g...

...t to the important stuff."

...dly. "No, we didn't, Mr. Bundy.

Ma...the Invisible Empire of the South

are...in public places."

H..., leaving Max baffled. Barely able

to fo...down the street and up the stairs

to hi...e was a little scared. Was this man

a rea...e Klan? It sure as hell sounded

like it.

Then two other thoughts came into Max's mind.
Jody could ruin him in the eyes of this man and with
the Klan. Jody knew he had screwed a negress. Then
came the oddest thought of all. Wickersham's words
kept echoing in his brain. "It's what makes me wonder
about her . . . It's what makes me wonder about
her. . . ."

Maxwell sat up on his bed, a cold sweat breaking
out on his forehead.

He gasped. "He's wondering about her because he's
wondering about me. That's no good. I gotta do something and quick!"

Quick is not always smart. Jody's farmers had
worked hard. Amos cursed himself now for not having

persuaded Jody to let him put practically all the ploughed land into wheat. They couldn't afford more sugar beet seeds from China and had settled for corn. Now wheat prices were soaring in the east.

The corn was all gathered, the husks braided and the silo filled. But, considered in terms of six families and their livestock, it looked like a lean supply. Still, Amos held out hope for the winter wheat that would be ready for harvest in a day or two.

That hope was dashed. No one could say how it started, but the brush fires spurred by the November winds consumed like an angry grizzly bear, taking with them the wheat, the corn silo and three of the log cabins.

"What we gonna do, Miz' Jody?"

She wasn't crying, but her eyes looked tragic.

"What we have done before, Amos. Make do through the winter and try again in the spring. Do we have enough?"

"Don't need as much. Three families done left. Say it's easier bein' slaves in de south than in de West."

"And you, Amos?"

"My belly ain't empty, Miz' Jody."

But Jody's belly was full of gall.

"I can't prove it, Bill, but those fires had to be set deliberately. Every time I get mixed up with Maxwell Bundy, I come out on the short end of the stick."

"Is there a reason for it?"

"It is going to sound like pure vanity on my part, but I've refused to marry that man more times than I care to remember."

"Even after Birdwell Jacobs?"

Jody frowned. "That's funny. I can't really recall him showing the same interest in me since then. Of course, he is married now."

Bill didn't comment. He had met Max three more times since their first drunken dinner and a wife had never been mentioned, while Jody had come into the conversation many times. Now Bill worried about what he might have said that was wrong. He sensed that something troubled Max in his presence, but he didn't think it was Jody. Then why the attack on her property?

A knock on the door kept him from thinking about the subject any longer. It was Barney Ford.

"We saw your light. May we come in?"

"We" turned out to be an *ad hoc* committee. Jody, already there, was invited to stay. She was the only woman in a gathering that included a former governor, the mayor, the sheriff, three bankers and some of the leading merchants in town.

"If anyone should ask," Barney said with a grin, "this is the first meeting of the new school board." Then he sobered. "And they are concerned whether there will ever be a second meeting. We have heard about your farm, Jody, and I am sorry."

"Heard?" She was astonished. "But I've only just heard in the last hour myself."

"Then they are growing even stronger than I feared. For the past hour they have been parading around downtown in their sheets exposing your double standard. They proclaim that you are a slave owner in the country and a teacher of black supremacy in the city."

"Who will believe such lies?" Jody said softly.

Bill swung around to look at her. "Those who wear the sheets, that's who. Their targets have been small and without a cause. Jody, he means to make you the cause and ruin you."

"Who's this 'he'?" the sheriff demanded.

"We have everything but hard evidence that Maxwell Bundy is behind the whole Klan operation."

The sheriff frowned. "My hands are tied without solid evidence. John, you said you and Barney had an idea about that."

John Evans looked at Barney and then squarely at Bill.

"Son, the only way we can get solid evidence is to have someone inside the Klan."

Bill's eyes shone. He had had the same idea. "It's possible, Governor Evans. Maxwell Bundy has been getting closer and closer to inviting me in."

Jody's head jerked up. "You mean, you would be a spy?"

Bill looked at her, his black eyes hard. "I've done dirtier things," he said.

Jody turned to him, anger mottling her cheeks. "When have you ever—"

"Everything about war is dirty," he said calmly. "This is just an extension of the last war. If we let it go on, if we sit back and do nothing, then they are automatically the victors. Today, they are just going against the blacks. Tomorrow, they may start going against those whites who support the blacks. The day after that they will start going after anyone who doesn't think the way they think they ought to think."

"Well said," Barney applauded.

Bu Jody was standing before Bill, her hands gripping his wrists.

"No," she said. "I won't have it, Bill. They will kill you if they find out."

Bill looked away from her toward the dark classrooms beyond.

"What good is this," he said, "if we have to teach in

fear? And there is the real irony. Max Bundy won't suspect me because he thinks I'm teaching apes."

Max stood looking at Bill Wickersham. Then he took out a cigar and lit it, his lips curling in to a cruel smile.

"Damn good plan, Bill. What a way to celebrate the ten-year anniversary of the end of the war. It's so good, I'm going to let you lead the raid. Get your horse ready and I'll spread the word for ten men to meet you down at Cherry Creek. You can get there and back by morning. No one will be expecting a raid on a night when it's almost twenty below zero."

Bill Wickersham left Max's room, an uneasy feeling growing in the pit of his stomach. For nearly three months, things had gone almost too smoothly. By putting together bits and pieces, he had been able to determine that Max had recruited nearly a hundred Klan members, but never let the same men ride together too often. That was a puzzle to Bill until he started keeping a record of all the reported raids and realized that Max had to have another group that he used from time to time for special jobs. Then, by accident, Bill stumbled onto the truth.

Clayton and Maxwell Bundy were using the Klan as a cover for their old agent operation. All through the summer and fall, the Bundy cowhands had been rustling cattle and driving them east to Dodge City and Abilene. The money was then used to purchase rifles and thousands of rounds of ammunition. These were shipped by rail to Cheyenne, where Clayton and some of his hands would collect them and cart them. Donning their masks and sheets, they traded the guns to the Cheyenne and the Sioux, convincing them that they were all brothers trying to rid the Indian land of the "buffalo soldiers." This was where the Bundy's new wealth was springing from.

But it was taking more time than Bill had thought it would to, gather the hard evidence that the sheriff required. On some raids, he had been able to warn the sheriff so a posse could arrive in time to abort the raid. But Max had kept him off the really important raids, until that night.

Bill hesitated before climbing into the saddle. He was tempted to do what he had done before—ride back to the school and tell Jody to warn the Sheriff. But the uneasy feeling in his stomach told him that this was a test of some sort. If Max Bundy suspected him of being a spy, then he would have to settle that issue quickly. He settled into the saddle and pulled his coat collar up around his ears. The wind made the night seem far colder than the twenty below. He turned his horse's head in the direction of Cherry Creek.

"He went toward the creek," Max said, turning from the window.

Clayton stepped from the closet. "Don't mean a damn thing. I still don't trust that slick-talkin' bastard."

Max chuckled. "Well, tonight will tell. We'll smoke him out in more ways than one."

"You better be right about this, Max. Things like this don't make us any money, you know."

"It will in the long run, Clay. That's why I only wanted to use you and three of the boys from the ranch. It will set this town on its ear and prove to the Sioux that we aren't lying about the strength of the Klan."

"Screw the Klan. I just want the Sioux to buy those rifles we swiped from Fort Lyon."

"Trust me, Clay. Just trust me."

Clay never had before and questioned his judgment in doing so now.

Jody shivered inside her shawl. Never had she been so cold. The wind brought the icy air right inside as though there were no walls. To try to keep the living quarters a little warm, she had the potbellied stoves in each classroom going full blast. This was fast consuming the fuel supply that Bill and the older boys had hauled in. The stoves glowed a rosy-red, but two feet away there was no heat. There would be little sleep that night.

Damn, Jody thought. Why does Bill have to be away on a stupid Klan raid?

She was aware that she was cursing his involvement more and more. It was putting more of the school burden on her shoulders, and the two new teachers they had hired as replacements, one black, one white, were next to worthless.

A knock on the front door at the far end of the hall startled her. The clock in the foyer said almost nine, but she could hear someone fiddling timidly with the knob. "Come in," she called.

The door opened and closed quickly. A thin little voice said hesitantly, "I'se got a message."

"Then bring it to me."

The boy approached timidly. She peered at him, trying to see his face, but he wore his coat all the way over his hatless head.

"Who are you?" Jody demanded.

"Rolf Jarrett, ma'am." His voice was soft, breathless. "Has ya'all a Miss Laurie here?"

"Yes, what do you want of her?"

"Dis man tell me ta come to de school 'n tell Miss Laurie dat Irene and de baby am right poorly."

"Oh, bother! What a night for them to need her help!"

The boy was shaking so badly he hardly had the strength to stand.

"You'd better go into that classroom and warm yourself by the fire while I go get her."

As the coat came down off his head, Jody looked at him again. "I don't believe I've ever seen you in school, have I?"

"We all jest got in town, ma'am. Sent by Pap Singleton from Kansas. Storm made us pull into town or freeze."

"Funny that Wagon Tom didn't send someone who would have known the way and gotten here faster. Well, I'll get Laurie."

The boy was still huddled by the stove when Jody came back downstairs with Laurie. It was hard to tell the youngster's age, but now that he was no longer huddled over with the cold she could see that he was tall and he looked strong. Jody suddenly had an idea.

"Rolf, would you like to earn a quarter?"

He nodded. He had, amazingly already, earned one quarter for bringing the message to the school. It was unbelievable that he would be able to earn a second quarter in the same evening. That was more money than his whole family had earned in a month.

"Fine." Jody smiled at him. "I'm running out of firewood and coal. It's stored in a large shed behind the school. Tell Miss Laurie where your wagon is and she'll stop on her way and tell your family where you are."

Laurie listened to the boy's directions, puzzled that the wagon was a good little way from Wagon Tom and Irene's cottage, but she would deliver this message because he was going to help Jody while she was gone.

After seeing Laurie off, Jody instructed Rolf on how to stoke the stoves and went upstairs to check on the living quarters. Normally, they would have had only ten live-in students at the school, but between the Klan raids and the cold weather, families had saddled them with twenty-eight to care for. The real burden fell on Laurie; Barney was paying her extra to feed the horde. Nor could Bill persuade the other teachers to help.

"Oh, blazes! You've nearly let the fire go out in here!"

The look on Helen Demooth's face was bitter. "It's Iris's turn to fetch the wood. I've carried up my last load."

"Iris is supposed to be looking after the girls," Jody pointed out.

"Well, she isn't," Helen pouted. "She's already in bed."

Jody marched across the room and pushed back the curtain that hid the bunk bed section of the room. A bundle, tightly wrapped in a quilt, lay on the upper bunk.

"Iris Delaney, get down from there! I want those little girls seen to *at once!* Helen—firewood! And there will be no sleeping tonight!"

Jody slammed from the room and across the hall to her own quarters. Here it was pleasantly warm. Laurie had kept the fire up before leaving. Jody took a potholder to open the stove door and add more coal. She adjusted the damper and dusted her hands.

Next to the stove, Laurie had pulled up Mary P.'s bed. The child was sleeping, warm and snug. Jody sighed.

"You are a blessed angel, my darling. The only one who is not giving me any trouble."

As though her words had asked for further trouble, a ruckus broke out down the hall. She flew in that direction, praying it would not wake Mary P.

The boys' dorm was Bill's department. He had only to look stern and bedtime was a quiet, peaceful affair.

Jody barged in on a snowstorm of goose feathers and caught a flying pillow right in the pit of her stomach.

"Enough!" she shouted. "Who is responsible for this?"

Eighteen little bodies went scampering for bunk bed, trundle bed or bedroll. The room had been designed to sleep no more than six; at the moment there wasn't a spare inch of floor space to walk upon.

"All right." Jody glowered at them. "I'm going downstairs to fetch Mister Wickersham. By the time he walks back through this door, I expect to see this room immaculate and eighteen pairs of eyes closed tight."

She closed the door and leaned wearily against it. She knew what was coming; they were not easily fooled.

The giggle gave the ring leader away. "Ain't heard his horse come back, so she can't be fetchin' him."

She flung the door open so quickly that they all gasped.

"But I can be fetching his bullwhip, Harold Jackson. I now hold *you* responsible for what happens in this room."

She closed the door and walked away. How could she stay angry with any of them? They were only children and had been cooped up inside the school for three days.

She looked in on the ten little girls; they were all asleep and Jody sighed. There was still no sign of Iris

Delaney, but as long as things were peaceful, she would let it ride for the moment.

She went, instead, into Bill's old quarters. He was now sleeping down in his office so that this area could be used for a kitchen. The kettle sang merrily on the range, and Jody began preparing herself a pot of tea. That would warm her inside before she checked the frigid downstairs again.

The range was connected to the main chimney that came right up through the center of the building. Right now, it was smoking badly where the stovepipe went into the fieldstone. Jody closed the damper down a bit, mentally calculating: eight potbellied stoves, plus two ranges, were feeding smoke into the chimney and it probably couldn't handle such a heavy load.

She sat at the little kitchen work table, waiting for the tea to steep, and was not aware of the figure that crept stealthily by the door and down the hall.

Iris Delaney was damned if she was going to stay up the whole night looking after a bunch of sleeping little girls. With a blanket wrapped around her nightgown, she pulled down the ladder-hatch to the attic and silently climbed up into her private hiding place— away from work and responsibility.

Rolf Jarrett was overwhelmed. The man who had given him the quarter for delivering the message had just given him another quarter.

"I'll take care of it, boy. You get on back home before you freeze."

Max Bundy thought he was dealing with just another nigger boy whose mind could be diverted from everything but the money he was making.

Rolf was elated, but he paused at the edge of the

schoolyard to look back. The man was motioning to someone in the shadow of the fuel shed. Four figures in white sheets and hoods emerged and entered the school. Then the man put on a sheet and hood and followed them in.

Rolf shrugged, hunched his shoulders and started to walk away. He had never seen a Klansman before and didn't know what it meant, but in his fourteen years he was getting used to white folks being a little peculiar. He didn't know the date for Halloween, but thought this must be it.

A quarter mile down the street he stopped suddenly. He had received two quarters and been offered a third. If he was smart, which he thought he was, he would march right back and collect that third one from the lady.

Having been at the school, Max Bundy knew the layout of the ground floor. The central staircase was open to the unused second floor and was then enclosed up to the living quarters. No one had considered another, outside stairway necessary.

The men moved quickly. Hot coals were removed from the five ground floor stoves and the stoves were crammed with dry, easily ignitable firewood. The dampers were then opened wide.

Two scuttles of live coals were carried up to the door leading to the third-story stairway, dumped and fanned into flame. More coals were scattered down the central stairway and also fanned into flame.

Clay Bundy began to worry a little bit about the scheme. "Hell, Max, how they gonna get out?"

"It'll only take a second for them to smell that smoke, Clay. She'll have those nigger kids down in the yard in nothing flat, through the fire and all. Hell, it'll take a good hour for those stairs to burn through." He laughed, adding, "I told you this would smoke Bill Wickersham out."

"I still don't see how."

Max's grin was pure evil. "Why, that a man could burn down his own school for the cause is going to upset me so I'm going to denounce him *and* the Klan. Hell, we don't need the Klan anymore!"

Clay was still dubious, but his main concern now was to get away, and fast.

Rolf darted back behind the trunk of a tree. He didn't want the man knowing that he had come back. He waited until the horsemen in sheets rode away and then he waited some more. He shivered; the rosy glow from the windows was warm and inviting. He carefully crossed the schoolyard and opened the front door.

Jody put down her teacup and went to jiggle the damper on the stove. The smoke was getting worse. She took a wooden spoon and tapped gently up and down the stovepipe, to knock the soot loose in case it had become clogged. The soot dropped down on the fire and made the stove smoke even more. Jody quickly went to check on the stove in her rooms and in the girl's dorm; they were also beginning to smoke badly.

Cold as it was outside, she would just have to dampen down the ground floor stoves; they were just overloading the chimney and not really giving that much warmth.

She ran down the enclosed stairway and pulled the door to her. A lung-searing blast of heat and smoke knocked her back. Coughing and gasping, she picked herself up from the step and tried to peer beyond the flames.

My God! The whole ground floor must be on fire!

She had the presence of mind to close the door while she gathered her wits. A million problems sprang into her mind as she ran back up the stairs.

"Helen, we have—" She stopped. The room was dark and cold, but lamplight from the hall revealed a shape in the bottom bunk bed. Jody cautioned herself to keep calm. She walked over and gently shook the woman.

"Helen," she whispered. "Wake up! We have a fire. I want you to go quietly into the boys' dorm and wake them up. Make a game of it, but they have got to start tying all their sheets together. We have got to lower them to the second-floor balcony and then down to the street."

The young teacher sat up staring and blinking; she was not sure if she was awake or dreaming.

Jody tried to smile, to reassure her. "We must act quickly and sanely."

Helen Demooth knew then that she was awake and in great trouble. Her moon face screwed up in protest and she wailed: "We're going to be killed!"

Without hesitation, Jody slapped her face. "Shut up and do as I say!"

It was said calmly, but had the force of a summer thunderclap. Before the girl could react, Jody was out of the room and on her way to warn Iris Delaney.

The teacher was not in the girl's dorm. Jody didn't have time to question why. She clapped her hands loudly three times.

"Girls! Attention! Please wake up! This is a fire drill. Please rise quickly and begin taking the sheets from your beds and bedrolls. I will be back in a moment to tell you what to do with them."

Next, she entered the boys' dorm. Helen was still not there and Jody had to repeat the instructions she had given the girls. She was afraid to leave either group alone now and charged back to the teachers' room. Helen was standing in the center of the room calmly brushing her long golden hair.

"I need you," Jody shouted, "and where the hell is Iris?"

"I haven't the slightest idea," Helen said coldly. "She often disappears."

The woman was not going to be any help, Jody realized now, except for the simplest of requests.

"Helen," she said quietly. "I am getting the children organized. Go to my room and bundle up Mary P. Bring her here and put her on the bunk. It will be easier to lower the children from this room and the kitchen. And if you see Iris please tell her to come and help."

Jody was racing off again. It was easy to instruct the boys in the proper knots to secure the sheets together; it took a lot longer with the girls.

God, how she prayed for Bill and Laurie to come back at that moment! But it wasn't to be. The help Jody had she couldn't count on, and the help she got had not been counted on at all. . . .

Rolf Jarrett stood for only a second, staring at the flames that were consuming the stairway. It was unbelievable; the stairs had been alright when the lady went up to fetch—

The lady! The lady with his quarter was somewhere above. Rolf didn't even stop to think; he charged right up through the flames, the stairs cracking under

his weight. Maxwell had been horribly off in his estimation; because of the cheap pine Barney had been
able to purchase for its construction, the stairwell was
lasting only minutes, not an hour.

The smoke confused Rolf. The second-floor doors
were all closed and he could not tell which one led to
the next floor. Then one of them came flying open. A
round-faced woman with long golden hair took one
look at him and let out a terrified scream. He screamed
back to calm her, but she raced by him and started
down the main stairs.

With a tremendous roar they began to buckle and
collapse. Rolf was forever after uncertain if it was the
woman or the building that emitted the death scream.
The sound sent him bounding up the closed stairway
he had been seeking.

He came charging out on the third floor and nearly
collided with Jody.

"The stoves!" she screamed. "What did you do—
overload the stoves?"

Rolf blinked and answered, truthfully, "The man
said he would take care of them."

The words, at that moment, meant nothing to Jody.
She was just thankful for help.

"In that room," she commanded like a field general,
"is a teacher with a group of boys. Bring them to that
room over there, with their sheets. I will go for the
girls."

Rolf didn't find any teacher with the boys, and never
once thought that this might have been the woman
he had seen. His family had always considered Rolf a
little slow. But at that moment his mind was lightning
fast.

"Fm countin' eighteen of ya and ah wanta see da
same number of sheets and da same number of hands

clasped together. Here, boy, take mine. I'm leadin' yah from dis here room, across dat dere hall an' den de real fun begin."

Jody was not having as much luck. Panic was beginning to set in with the younger girls; their knots were tied wrong and the smoke was beginning to make them cough and gag.

Everything after that seemed like a slow-moving nightmare. . . .

Bill Wickersham had waited nearly two hours at Cherry Creek alone. It was, he reflected, wryly, prudent of the other Klansmen to elect to stay by their hearths on such a night. He was frozen through to the bone. He kept his head buried down on his chest and gave the horse free rein to get him home.

They were almost there when Bill heard a rumble that brought his head up. He saw a tongue of flame a hundred feet high, roaring up from the main chimney of the school. Before he reached the schoolyard, burning soot was falling back down on the roof of the building and igniting the shingles. He jumped from the horse and started running blindly forward, his mind unable to grasp fully what he was seeing.

There was an explosion, then another. The kerosene lamps had become overheated and all of the windows on the ground floor had been blown out. Bill was looking for any sign of the children when Wagon Tom came up, panting, followed by Laurie and a group of townspeople who had seen the smoke.

They didn't even have time to speak before a scream drew their eyes upward. The smoke had awakened Iris Delaney. It was now so thick in the attic that all she had been able to see was the outline of the dormer window. She had beaten it open frantically and crawled out on the roof. In her panic, she was not careful of her footing. All those below could do was stand and watch her tumble down the roof peak and off into space.

"I'll see to her," Wagon Tom said quietly.

"No," Bill said hoarsely. "Laurie—you. The rest to the back of the school. I hear the children."

More people were arriving at the scene and trying to form a bucket brigade. But it was hopeless.

Rolf and Jody had gotten about half of the children down to the second-floor balcony by the time Bill Wickersham and the others came around the building. The found a ladder, but it wasn't long enough to reach so Bill had to shimmy the rest of the way up on the corner drainpipe.

"Get all the way up to the top rung," he shouted down at Wagon Tom. Even before the tall black man was there, Bill had taken a child by the arms and dangled her over the balcony railing. Wagon Tom was just barely able to grasp her by the legs.

"Let her go!" he shouted.

The girl let out a horrible scream as she started to fall forward, but Wagon Tom was braced and ready to catch her. He swung her out and down so that the man on the ladder just below him could take her and lower her to the ground.

One after another they repeated the awkward process until someone came up with some lengths of rope.

"Tie it securely to something in the room," Bill shouted up to Jody, then heaved the rope.

She and Rolf barely had it tied to the leg of a bunk-bed when Bill came scrambling up.

"You boys keep using the sheets," he ordered. "Some of you take this rope and go in and start using the window in the next room. Jody, put a girl on my back and I'll take one up front. Now, hold on tight, girls."

Down he went, the two little girls crying into his ears, nearly breaking his eardrums. As soon as they were snatched from him, he was back up again. Fear crawled agonizingly along his nerves. The heat was becoming such that he questioned whether they would be able to get all the children down safely in time. Tears stung his eyes, and the inside of his throat was raw.

"Give me two more and why aren't the boys using the other rope yet?"

"I'll go see," Rolf volunteered.

Bill didn't know who the boy was but looked after him gratefully. Jody wordlessly lifted another child to Bill's back while he lifted one into his arms. Then he was out the window and gone again.

Rolf stood in the hall a moment, amazed. It was so smoke-filled that it was like being in a heavy fog. He groped along the wall with his fingers, feeling for the next doorway. He found it, but the door was closed. It was also very hot to the touch. Light shone from underneath the door and he didn't have to be told what manner of light it was. Fire was eating up through the floor of that room.

He inched his way back to the balcony. "Dey musta gone de other way," he told Jody. "I'll find 'em."

Jody didn't look around. She was too busy trying to coax a seven-year-old boy into climbing down using the knotted sheets.

"Find Miss Demooth too, Rolf. Tell her to bring my baby from the bunk in the next room."

There was no woman in the next room and a horrible suspicion began to grow in Rolf's mind. Was the woman Miss Jody was looking for the one who had rushed by him on the stairs? He felt all over both bunks. There was no baby, either.

The smoke at that end of the hall was becoming near impossible. The flames had consumed all of the inner stairwell and were now eating through the hall walls. Rolf was about to give up and go back when he heard a sound from one of the rooms.

The nine boys in the room were near panic. They could not get the rope to knot the way the sheets had.

"Gimme dat," Rolf said. His hands hurriedly secured the rope to the leg of a bed. Then he noticed what was on that bed: Mary P.'s eyes were bright and staring up at him.

"I get ya in a moment, honey." He chuckled, relieved that he had found Jody's baby.

But a new fear was drowning that relief. The floor was getting so hot it was burning right through the soles of his shoes. The nine boys were now so badly frightened that they didn't even feel the heat on their bare feet.

"Now, get dat rope over ta de window and start gettin' down. I take de baby and be right back ta help."

He lifted the baby from the bed and wrapped a blanket about her. She didn't whimper or cry and he dashed into the hall before she might start crying and give the boys a new reason for panic.

Flames shot across the hall in front of him and then receded. He was suddenly horribly afraid. He hugged the child close and swallowed hard. The floor beneath him moved like the waves of an invisible sea.

Then it happened. Behind him the whole floor of the room he had just left gave way with a furious crack and then a rending roar. If the nine young voices cried out in their fall, Rolf was not aware; the sound was muted by the crackling inferno.

His mind now totally dazed, he managed to make it

back to the room. Jody was busy getting the last two children to climb down to the balcony. Rolf rushed forward to give Mary P. to Bill Wickersham. He opened his mouth to report on the fate of the others, but for the life of him he could not speak.

Bill however understood. He took the child and hurried back down the rope. By the time he reached the balcony a knot of ice was forming in his belly and cold sweat had broken out on his forehead. He felt the child in his arms and still felt nothing.

He lowered the blanket-wrapped bundle to Wagon Tom with extreme care.

"Give it to Laurie," he whispered, his voice breaking. "Tell her not to say a word about it yet."

Tears sprang into the big man's eyes. "How many more?" he was able to get out.

"Just three," Bill croaked. "Just three. . . ."

23

THAT SAME NIGHT a U.S. grand jury was formed to investigate the fire. Barney Ford was named to sit on it, the first of his race to serve on such a body in Colorado. It was a bittersweet assignment for Barney. It had cost twelve lives to bring people to their senses.

The jury worked around the clock for three days with Rolf Jarrett as the star witness. His testimony persuaded others to speak, and allowed the grand jury to hand down strong, well-founded indictments.

But justice was thwarted. Clayton and Maxwell Bundy, along with every cowhand at the Bundy ranch, were swallowed up by the oblivion that was Hole-in-the-Wall. Lemanuel and Miss Inez were shocked when 947 Winchester rifles were found on the Bundy ranch and confiscated. Their shame was such that, shortly after, the Bundy ranch was sold.

It was a year before Jody learned that Lemanuel and Miss Inez had taken Alfreda with them to resettle

quietly in Montana. The way she learned it was quite
strange. An intruder got into the Montana ranch house
one night and Alfreda, frightened, killed the man. It
wasn't until the lamps were lighted that they discovered that Alfreda had killed her own husband. Max
Bundy could no longer be a threat to Jody.

Clayton Bundy? The stories varied. Some said, years
later, that he died in Argentina with Butch Cassidy.
Some said he reformed and lived to ninety-two as a
Mormon in Utah. Some said . . . but who really cared?
His name, along with his brother's, had been on everyone's lips on the day of the indictment. But the next
day no one wanted to mention their names at all.

Denver was sharing a common grief. All over town
services were held for the twelve who had died. They
were private, family affairs. But there was one the
community felt it should share in.

Jody paid no attention to the words the minister said
over her daughter's little white casket. Her head ached
and her mind worked slowly, painfully, her grief-
stricken thoughts groping through the age-old question
of why.

At first, she was not even aware that the block
around the church had been roped off and that hundreds of people stood silently waiting. It was a sea of
black and white faces there to pay homage to a child
they had never known.

Once Mary Pleasant Jacobs was placed in the ornate
hearse, Bill Wickersham took Jody by the arm.

"Let's walk," he said quietly.

Jody nodded. She didn't care; her dulled brain could
command anything of her limbs without her really
caring.

It was four miles to the Riverside Cemetery. Mary

Pleasant Jacobs was the only one who got to ride; everyone else walked.

Before the hearse was spread a strange carpeting for it to roll upon and for the hundreds of feet to trample. Men stepped forward, not caring if their faces were seen now, to put down white hooded masks and sheets.

This was Colorado! The twelve deaths had nearly cost its people their dignity! They could openly admit their shame because they were a breed apart. They had nearly buckled under to bigotry and prejudice, but now they were free. They were Colorado men and women for Colorado!

"And you must do what they are doing," Bill said softly as they walked along.

"Do?" Jody asked blankly.

"They are asking for forgiveness."

"They killed my child!"

"They didn't, Jody. You can't go on thinking that way. I love you now more than I ever have before. I want you as my wife. I want us to have children to take Mary P.'s place."

Jody shook her head. "There's no use in it."

"Stop being so damn tragic," he said. "Think of others for a change. I have no family. You have no real family. Laurie is about to bury her only grandchild. It's the only one she ever will have unless we give her more. That's right! Us! She's the only grandparent our children will ever have. Oh, they won't be of her blood, but who gives a damn? I love that woman just as much as I love you, and let's think of her for a change. She feels guilty because they conned her into leaving you alone. It's eating her up inside. Hell, I've buried my whole family. You've only buried a husband and a child. But I'm alive, you're alive, and

Laurie is alive. And walking behind you now are hundreds of people who are alive. If you are dead, then let's put you right down in the cold ground with Mary P. and the others!"

It took time, just about as much time as it took to build the solid-brick Mary Pleasant Jacobs Elementary School. Just about as much time as it took for William Wickersham to be named the State Superintendent of Schools. Just about as much time as it took the new seed in Jody's womb to show that it would soon be a child.

A man-child, Laurie was convinced, because of Jody's size. But neither size nor decorum could keep Jody away from Cheeseman Park on the afternoon of August 1, 1876.

Many had been asked to speak that day, but Jody had come to hear only one man. He had fought long and hard to keep the territory from becoming a state until his people could be a part of the whole. For once, Barney Ford used the words of others to make his message ring loud and clear:

"We hold these truths to be self-evident, that all men are created equal, that they are endowed by their Creator with certain unalienable Rights, that among these are Life, Liberty and the pursuit of happiness . . ."

One hundred years since its founding: the Union now had a centennial state.

A state with pride. A state with a heritage.

FIFTEENTH IN
THE MAKING OF AMERICA
SERIES

THE
HOMESTEADERS

Nebraska territory in the late 1800s was a harsh, rugged land where survival depended on how well a man could handle a gun, how long he could work without dropping, and often how fast he—or she—could run when the enemy was at his heels. To this God-forsaken land came hundreds of drifting souls, seeking a place to make their homes and fulfill their dreams of prosperity and freedom.

Among these pioneers was Joseph Barrow, a dedicated and determined man, and his beautiful step-sister, Jessie, whose blazing spirit ignited in him passions that he had never known before. Together they faced the most awesome challenge of their young lives, as they set up as homesteaders in the wild country where women were almost unheard of—and a kindly gesture from a neighbor even rarer.

SIXTEENTH IN
THE MAKING OF AMERICA
SERIES

THE FRONTIER HEALERS

In the chaos that followed the Civil War, a turbulent tide of men and women surged across the Mississippi to escape the unspeakable horrors of a broken and humiliated South. Some chose to cast their lot in the sprawling, raucous mining town of Virginia City. Among them was the beautiful half-breed, Yvonne Beaunais, and her daughter, Tangeree. Yvonne's burning ambition was to provide her daughter with the education that would open up the tantalizing new world of medicine that had been denied her.

Together they administered their healing herbal remedies to the sick and dying. Together they defied the threats of Matthew Lassiter, who ran Virginia City like a fiefdom. And together, they fought against heavy odds to improve the quality of living in a brutal frontier town—and sought their own private fulfillment in love and life.